How We Mortals

BL

THE GODS

MÁIRÍN MC SWEENEY

ARABY

First published June 16, 2022

How We Mortals Blame The Gods is a work of fiction. All incidents and dialogue, and all characters with the exception of some well-known historical or public figures, are products of the author's imagination. Where real-life historical or public figures appear, the situations, incidents and dialogues concerning those persons are fictional and are not intended to change the imagined nature of the work. In all other respects, any resemblance to persons living or dead is entirely coincidental.

To request permissions, contact the publisher at arabypublishing@gmail.com

Paperback: 978-1-7396-4620-2
Ebook: 978-1-7396-4621-9

A CIP record for this book is available from the British Library.

Developmental Edit by Henrietta Rose-Innes & Susan Cahill
Copy Edit by Vincent Czyz
Cover art by John Nolan (john@nolanart.com)
Cover design & formatting by Donna Cunningham of BeauxArts.Design
Photographs by Daniela Harmsen

Araby Publishing
Co. Dublin.
Ireland

arabypublishing.com

For my mother, Maura and my father Ted.
Your endless support has pulled me through the worst and
pushed me towards the best. Thank you!

"Ah how shameless—the way these mortals blame the gods. From us alone, they say, come all their miseries, yes, but they themselves, with their own reckless ways, compound their pains beyond their proper share."

—Homer

The Odyssey 32–34, Book 1, Zeus

Contents

Cast of Characters & Soundtrack

In order to make your reading of my well-populated novel clearer, I have decided to list all 74 of the characters (p 305) in the order in which they appear. My excuse for taxing your character limitations is that in order to shadow Joyce's *Ulysses,* which contained 84 characters, I need a world just as complete.

Dublin is a city of music, and just like Joyce, I felt it could only come properly alive by framing the story in the sounds of the city. Therefore, I decided to embed a soundtrack into my novel (p 309).

Chapter 1

OMAR

- Calypso -

8:00 AM

BADUM, BADUM, BADUM. Mr. Omar Wilde was always surprised by the sound of his heartbeat. It reminded him of a friend knocking at the door to bring him unwelcome news. He preferred not to know.

He'd nearly caught her this time, propped up in her bed, whispering to the computer screen. It sent his heart racing to imagine *him*, whoever he was. She had been restless this morning, distracted. He found it hard to talk to her these days, to understand what she was thinking. Her touch was faint, as though she were a shadow-woman moving through a world he could not access. He had suspected for a long time that her thoughts lay elsewhere, had migrated to another's bed. She loved to mess with those emails — like a proper invalid, tapping away at that laptop of hers. As soon as he walked in, a panicked look crossed her face, and she minimised the window. Better off not knowing. Still, a man has his pride.

"Looks like something important."

"It's nothing, Omi, a note from Matt Phelan. The concert this evening. You coming?"

"I'm traipsing around the Bloomsday performances doing reviews today. It's over about nine, so I should make it."

"Mm, grand then." She glanced at the screen.

"Flora?"

"Yeah?"

"You look nice today." He fumbled with the cap in his hand.

"Thanks." She kept staring at the screen. "Can you boil the kettle before you leave? Don't want to have to get out of bed twice."

Omar sighed. "Right, luv. See you later."

She didn't even look up to watch him leave.

Passing through the kitchen, he turned on the kettle and glanced at himself in the mirror in the corridor. Looked older than his thirty-eight years. Mother's dark liquid eyes. Short, voluminous, peppered hair. Skin the colour of the desert. He stood out in a country of melanin-starved Celts. Sometimes he thought this was a good thing, like when Flora called him her handsome Moor. But that had stopped years ago. A great smothering silence had grown between them. Now they breathed the illusion of life into ceremonies constructed from stilted habits. He glanced at the black-rimmed glasses that lay on the hall table beside him. He didn't really need them, but they afforded him a layer of protection, a subtle barrier against those of a curious nature. Today he could do without them.

Closing the door behind him, he hopped in the car and headed towards New Street South. Rush-hour traffic at its worst. If only he hadn't got her the bloody laptop. Taken his place, it had. Losing the baby, that had changed things. Had never been right since then. How long ago now? Eleven years, yes, fifteen years married. Eleven years, imagine. Ruairí—she'd wanted an Irish name. To signify newness, beginning again. Never quite got his tongue around it. Would've been doing the Holy Communion if she got her way. What did he know of the Pillars of Islam, apart from a few chunks of the Qur'an his mother forced him to learn? Still, one never forgets.

He looked out the side window. Camden Street was awash with people moving at speed through the chaos of the early morning. A group of Spanish students chattered as they pushed their way past the Asian market. Two older women were adorning their stall with the day's fruit. One of the students – slim, dark, and covered in piercings – slipped her hand into a box of litchis. With lightning speed, the small, high-boned shop woman standing behind her grabbed the offending hand, screaming profanities in her native tongue. The girl came to life, flinging the little woman's arm from side to side to escape her angry grasp. Two sharp languages collided. "*Puta madre, dejame! Dejame, ostia*!" the girl shrieked.

Traffic flowed forward. Omar pressed the gas, glancing back quickly. He saw the girl's friends yank her away from her tormentor. Triumphant, their group raced past him, taking a right down Grantham Street. A female Garda was tripping her way through the crowd on the other side of the street. She picked her way through the traffic to the hysterical Asian woman, with a "here we go again" look plastered across her face. Omar chuckled and bit into his foil-wrapped sandwich. Red light again.

His mobile erupted in the seat beside him.

"Wilde?" Willy Farrell, his boss, could burst an eardrum with a single emphatic syllable.

"Yeah, hang on a minute, Willy. Got a mouthful of sausage."

"Wilde, where are you?"

"On Camden Street, traffic is hell this morning."

"Listen, I need a story for the "Inside People" section of Friday's *Indo*. Helen's called in with laryngitis or some bloody contagious thing, so you're it! What can you do for me?"

Omar swallowed the last mouthful.

"Shit, Boss, I'm on the Bloomsday Centenary reviews all day. Don't know if I have time."

"Well, make time. It's an emergency. Give me a call back in thirty minutes with an idea.

And Wilde ...?"

"Yeah?"

"Be at the office – lunchtime. We'll renegotiate your contract, ok?"

"Right, Willy, right, that'd be great. Call you back in a while."

"Good man."

Omar cursed. What was he going to do now? This man would drive him mad. Right, think, think. He glanced out the window as he passed a halal shop. An older, bearded man sat with an agitated-looking youngster on the step of the shop. The young man gesticulated, his jeans falling around the crack of his arse. He waved his finger in the bearded man's face. *Some things are the same in all cultures.* Omar flashed back to Egypt with his parents. They had visited twice. He must have been 11 or 12 the last time. His father had hated it, the stifling heat and the lack of a decent drink. It had been the source of many arguments between his parents.

Manoeuvring right into Grantham Street, Omar searched for a space. The footpath looked good enough, so he mounted it in front of a swish red-brick townhouse. He turned to grab his notepad and realised he'd forgotten his dictaphone. Bollox, not again. Get it after. He ran back into the flow of people on Camden Street. The same two men were at it in front of the halal shop. As he approached, a teenage boy exited the shop and tried to break it up.

"Would you both stop it? Everyone is looking."

The young man glared at the teenager. "Stay out of it, Khaled!"

"Your brother is seeing some ... God knows who she is!" said the older man.

"I can date who I want. Go back to the desert and give me some peace."

"Cheeky scut!" The older man sighed. "Is it so hard to date a woman of your own culture?"

Omar stood to one side staring at the travel brochures in the agency window next door.

"It's you who makes it harder for me."

The old man shrugged. "Hanan, you will be the death of me."

"Anyway, Sarah and I aren't serious. It's a bit of fun."

The older man shook his shoulders in a gesture of resignation. "We'll see."

"That sounds like a threat. Khaled, are you hearing this?" Hanan turned to the teenager seated on the vegetable boxes by the window.

"Dad's right."

"Jesus, I'm surrounded by zealots. You're nineteen for God's sake. Go out and have some fun like everyone else your age."

"Fun is for those wasters I went to school with." The boy jumped to his feet. "They're a pack of knackers who get sloshed on cider and smoke doobies on the corner of St. Stephen's Green. No thanks!"

"Oh, for God's sake."

"You need to respect your tradition more. Anyway, those Irish girls are all slags."

Omar inched his way closer, waiting for a chance to interrupt.

"You're Irish, too, you eejit. You were born here! What is wrong with everyone in this family? We're not in Lebanon anymore, thank God! I've never been there. You've never been there. What the fuck is wrong with you?"

"Mind your language, boy," interrupted the older man.

"Aaaaggghhhh. No wonder everyone is suspicious of us in this country!" Hanan swept past Omar in a cloud of anger.

Omar took his chance to interrupt. "Sounds like things are a little heated."

The older man cast an eye over Omar. "Can I help you?"

"Omar Wilde. I work for the *Irish Independent*. I'm working on a story about being Muslim in Ireland. I wondered if you might have a few minutes to chat with me."

The old man stroked his beard, his brown eyes sizing up Omar. "Well, I don't know. What is this article being used for?"

"Trust me, Sir, I'm a Muslim, or at least I was born a Muslim, in Egypt actually, so I will be sympathetic. It's for a section of the newspaper that looks at different people's lives in Ireland. I'm not out for a big exposé or anything. Want to show how ordinary people are getting by in this country, that's all."

The man hesitated and looked at Omar. "Ok then, I guess. Come on in. I'm Mohammed." He gestured to the suspicious-looking teenager. "And Khaled."

Omar reached for his notebook. "Do you mind? Makes it easier to get things exactly right."

"Course."

He nodded his head and sat on a wooden stool behind the cash register. Omar pulled another stool beside him and began to write.

"June 16, 2004, Interview 1. - Islam in Ireland."

CHAPTER 2

KINCH & OMAR

- Telemachus -

8:00 AM

KIERAN JAMES LYNCH opened his eyes. Light flooded in, thudding, tremorous. The body beside him shifted slightly.

They had slept there after a hard night out, for lack of a better option. Empty beer bottles littered the floor of the men's toilet. The stench of piss and puke stuffed his nostrils. In the dream from which he'd just awakened, his mother had come to him. Pale, naked, translucent. Hovered above him like a dying moon. The last of the moonlight reached out to give him a message he couldn't quite understand. When he could summon the energy, he dragged himself to the doorway. Howth Head lay like a dark slumbering beast, the sky around its head burgeoning and explosive.

A strip of black cloud deposited its load on the other side of the bay. *Thank God I'm on this side … Northsiders get all the bad luck.* A cigarette pack lay by his side, begging to be opened. He flicked a match alight, pulled on the short, white stick, and pushed the air from his lips with a light groan of pleasure.

Through the small, broken window of the toilet, Kinch could see a crowd gather outside the entrance to Joyce's tower.

"How the hell did Joyce stick living in that?" he said, kicking his immobile friend.

Gerry groaned, opening a bloodshot eye.

Kinch chucked the box of cigarettes at his slumbering friend. "Come on you poxy Corkman."

A barely audible groan.

"Leave me be, Kinch, you bastard!"

His friends had been calling him that ever since he got the part as Stephen Dedalus in the *Ulysses* performances. The bauldy Kinch: Stephen's blade-edged alter ego in *that* novel that no one ever bothered reading. Not that, with a name like Kieran Lynch, he hadn't sought it out all the same. Joyce's creation felt like a suit he was born to wear.

"Fifteen minutes." Kinch grabbed his backpack and ran into the cubicle behind.

The Corkman winced, pulled the black curls from his eyes, and tied them behind his head.

"Have a jump in the Forty Foot Ger, that'll cure your head quick enough!" Fragments of himself looked back from the broken, grimy mirror. *O, madam, my old heart is crack'd, it's crack'd!* With the sole of his newly polished shoes, Kinch crushed the remnants of a dying cigarette. Thin, stained fingers stroked the end of his goatee, swept upwards through the dirty-blond crop. Every inch proclaimed his status as tortured, penniless actor – pallid, crumpled, yet passable. *Not bad for a hard night's drinking.*

Where had he found the pinstriped waistcoat? One of those old geezers' shops on Talbot Street. Looked the business all the same. He stuffed the nose rag in his top pocket and glanced across the bay. The morning ferry crossed the horizon towards Dun Laoghaire. A finger of light pushed it gently across the bay, out of reach of the sodden, grey clouds. Kinch placed the black Latin Quarter hat on his head and stepped out into the crisp June air. Stripped to his boxers, his wrecked-looking friend raced past him and leapt into the dark cold of Dublin Bay. His head exploded back out of the water.

"Almighty God! Aggghhhhh!"

The crowd moved to the shore wall to see what all the commotion was about.

"No worries, ladies and gentlemen, just a hypothermic, drowning Corkonian. An everyday sight around the Forty Foot these days."

"Boy, it's like melted snow in here."

Kinch made the sign of the cross over the shivering body in the water beneath him. "Gotta go – don't die on me, you mad bastard." He picked up his potted ashplant – a tiny sprig growing from seeds he'd planted weeks before – and climbed the ramp towards the tower entrance. The crowd squeezed their way through the door of the granite tower.

An ageing woman pointed a plump finger and screamed, "Look, someone dressed up. Must be from the book!"

His body stiffened and the ghost of Dedalus stepped inside. "Stephen at your service, madam."

"Kinch ahoy!" called a gravelled voice from deep inside the tower.

"I'm coming," Stephen said, turning.

"Jaysus, Lawlor, you'll bring us all down with you." The Gift Grub crew were taking the piss out of some government tribunal or other. The Taoiseach, "Bertie", was in a dither about Lawlor's shenanigans.

Omar belly-laughed, wondering at how the country could continue to prosper with the endless corruption – tribunals sucking at the bones of a government no one took seriously. *Thank God I'm not a politician. Need to have an ego of steel.* The interview with the boys and their father had gone well, but there was something about the younger boy, the way he stared: cold, unyielding.

Omar turned into Heytesbury Street, observing an unfamiliar clicking sound in the engine of his car. A car more than ten years old in this country was considered a piece of junk, no matter its condition. This worked to Omar's advantage because his scrupulous nature meant he kept things long after the shelf life dictated otherwise. He mounted the curb beside the red-brick townhouse, 7 Long Lane. Eight years ago, he bought it before the price of property went through the roof. If they were out there looking for a house now, he would've been living in a shack.

Wondering whether she'd still be in bed, he passed through the doorway, its wood newly painted red. He easily heard her voice from the hall below.

"Babe, I'll be here, I promise ... What? ... No, no he's out all day ... some shite about Bloomsday ... Oh, sorry, I didn't mean that ... You know I do ... yes ... yes." Omar's stomach lurched. He hesitated, wondering whether he should let her go on incriminating herself, but what was the point? Making a fuss about it wouldn't make any difference. He rattled the front door to give her a signal.

"Flora, I had to come home. Left my dictaphone behind like the bloody eejit I am." He entered the bedroom and pretended not to notice her on the phone. He moved quickly to the dresser to pick up his things. His eyes traced her in the mirror as she pressed, he assumed, the red button and put the phone carefully on the bed beside her.

"You've got a head like a sieve. That's the second time you've done that in two weeks." She looked flustered, the dark auburn waves of her hair tossed and wild around the edge of her green silk nightie. Omar turned to face her, exhaled lightly, and picked up his dictaphone.

"I know I'm a fool, a real fool. Can't seem to get my head around anything nowadays. Must be the stuffy atmosphere."

"Stuffy. Are you mad? I know it's warm for Ireland, but stuffy is not a concept that this country has ever experienced. Try Kraków in summer."

"Yeah well, I'd better go, luv. Farrell is putting me under pressure today." He moved towards the doorway, avoiding her eyes.

"Omi?"

"Yeah?"

"Good luck today." She threw him a look mixed with affection and sorrow, a look of regret and recognition. They both knew that it was beyond voicing, beyond rejection – a mutual void of acceptance.

CHAPTER 3

FLORA

8:15 AM

SHE HEARD THE DOOR CLOSE behind him. *Poor Omi. He deserves better*, she thought. *I wish it were different. I really do!* Her head burned from a mixture of anger and guilt; a potent concoction drummed into her through years of Catholic school. That and an angry grandmother who wrestled daily with her God. *The oceans of prayers I send Him and he lets our country be raped over and over,* her grandmother would rant while nonetheless marching off to Mass every day.

What could Flora do anymore? After she lost the baby, she decided that if there was a God he was a right bastard, so she didn't want to know about Him anymore. All the same, there were certain things she missed about Poland: the smell of baking dough from the corner bakery in downtown Kraków, the easy smiles of the people as they chatted on the market stalls, the crawling pace of life as people moved like chess pieces towards an uncertain future.

She remembered a certain similarity in the eyes of the Irish when she arrived sixteen years before. Now things were different. Much had been swept away in the whirlwind of prosperity. Not that she didn't like the buzz of success. It was everywhere, that roaring Celtic Tiger. Bars oozing with energy and crowds of people chatting animatedly at the corner cafés. She felt herself evaporating in the whirl of excitement. She knew why. In the corner of her memory. What good were memories to her now? Stale memorials. His image shot through her brain: a little bundle of possibility. Just gone.

It's his birthday next week. Would have been eleven. Omar will forget. Well, she couldn't blame him. Better to forget. She hated when he got that look in his eyes, that sad acceptance of how things were. Why couldn't he be stronger, better able to stand up to her, to surprise her, but that was never his style. Who could blame her that she had to find that elsewhere?

Her phone flashed the time. *Half past nine, better get a move on, need to see him today. Dying for it I am! God my hormones are racing.* She moved into the bathroom and began to run a hot bath – her greatest pleasure no matter what mood she found herself in. The nightie fell to the ground, and she stared at herself in the mirror. Nothing much had changed in the previous twenty years. She cupped her round breasts, sucked in her stomach, and squeezed the skin underneath her buttocks. None of the dreaded orange peel. *Not bad, but for how long?*

The water of the bath rose slowly. She sat on the edge of the bath, poured lavender oil into the rising water, followed her form in the mirror as it reshaped itself through different movements. At the age of thirty-eight, she could seduce a twenty-two-year-old and hold his attention above all the soft-skinned beauties that surrounded him. This continued to surprise her. Her power lay on the fringes of acceptability – somewhere in the darkest shadows of a mother's love, unfulfilled and craving deliverance. She climbed into the bath and sank into the hot water. It surrounded her, entered her. It felt like him, warm and comforting. She would hold his youthful limbs, long and muscular, to her breast as he slept, quietly dreaming in the after space of exorcised passions: would rue the possibility of what she could have been but never was.

If Ruairí had lived, she may never have felt this screaming desire to possess such a young man, but it was what it was, and she couldn't deny it. He needed her for the same reasons – to bring his dead mother to life through her – and she marvelled at the lust that could drive them through their search for dead love. Omar suspected, and that made her feel sick with guilt, but he could never be that to her, never bring back that which she had lost. What's more, his touch reminded her of Ruairí. She couldn't bear him inside her, grunting his sadness through her body like a distant phantom of the man she had once loved. He did his best to try to make her happy, but they had lost something long ago. Replaced by a groaning apathy, a comfortable habit that neither of them was willing to dig themselves out of.

Taking a palmful of shampoo, she worked it through the tangles of her dark hair, scooped the bubbles in her cupped hand, and caressed her body with the sweet-smelling liquid. She slid her right hand over the cup of her breast, the tips of her fingers circled her protruding nipples. Her left hand played with her belly button, slipped its way slowly towards the soft, pink folds of her vulva. She tickled herself gently, a slow tingle that built through the bubbles of the water. Allowing her legs to fall open, she thought of him, shifted her form in the liquid. The water splashed onto the floor, and she exhaled in a long, slow groan of release. Her arms fell over the sides of the bath. She slid her mouth below the waterline and floated.

The phone rang on the chair beside her. A name flashed on the small screen: *Bláithín. I have a lesson with her this afternoon. Not answering that now.* She left the phone on the chair and climbed out of the bath. The ten o'clock news came on the radio in the background.

"Pope asks for pardon on torture and burnings during the Inquisition."

Five Hundred years later, no less! Better late than never I suppose. Granny will be pleased!

The stray hairs around her eyebrows were getting harder to shift. Why in God's name was it that as women advanced in years they were in a never-ending battle with the matted sprouts of hair that threatened to cover every spare inch of bare skin? Men, of course, spent their time trying to stitch the hair back in. It was one big celestial piss-take at the expense of humankind.

"Portugal plays Russia in the European Championship tonight ..."

Well, that's Omar out for the night. Good news.

The razor slipping up the line of her inner thigh, she took care to shave the hair around the edge of her vagina.

"Non-nationals nervous of referendum results ..."

No kidding!

She repeated this movement on the other side and pondered the recent national referendum. The Irish had been very welcoming when she'd landed in the country with her violin in hand and not much else. If Matt Phelan hadn't spotted her playing in the Kraków Philharmonic Orchestra, God knows where she'd be right now.

She exited the bath slowly and glanced at herself in the mirror. The pink glow to her skin made her look younger. There was a softness to her belly that hadn't been there before Ruairí. Now she cherished it as a memory of the brief life feeding inside her. She placed the razor into her black day bag, moved into the bedroom, and opened the bottom drawer of the wooden cupboard. Reaching into the back of the drawer, she pulled out a lacy, black bra with matching briefs. They were wrapped carefully in a crumpled square of white paper that had *Happy Anniversary* scripted on it in silver writing.

Time to get some use out of this.

A tag was still attached to the bra, and she sheared it off with her teeth. A woman came on the radio from the Refugee Council giving out yards about how the Irish had been taken in all over the world for centuries, and now that it was their turn, they dug in their heels, refusing nationality to non-national babies born in Ireland.

It's a worry.

She didn't have much to begrudge, but what if Ruairí had lived? How would she have felt if her baby had been rejected by the place of his birth? It didn't seem fair. She didn't know all the facts, but it just didn't feel right. It reminded her of the Purgatory that Father Kopinsky spoke of endlessly in Mass when she was a young girl. It horrified her that un-baptized babies were sent to float in an ether of nothingness, belonging to nowhere, receiving love from no one. Dogma of any kind frightened her. What lay behind the *Yes* votes of the four out of five people who crossed her paths daily? Their smiles and nods of acceptance now seemed uncertain. Not that she felt it personally, but she worried for others around her. The world was becoming a fragile place, bursting at the seams and barely able to contain the humanity within.

She slipped carefully into the briefs and leaned forward to fit her ample breasts into the cups. With a widening smile, she reached for the indigo-blue sweatshirt dress that lay on the back of the chair. It fit over her shoulders with ease, and she watched as the thin material clung to the soft curves of her body. She looked in the mirror at the face of a woman who could deceive so many people. It was a strong face – high cheekbones, full, red lips – but behind her green eyes, she could see a cold glint. Flora supposed everyone developed a hard layer in the end.

She glanced out the window at the small garden she'd nurtured with determined care. The sun had dried the earth around her azalea bed. It was hard to keep up at this time of the year. The summers were getting warmer, thank God. She slid her feet into a pair of low-heeled sandals and slung a satchel of brown leather over her shoulder. Light streamed through the doorway into the small living room. It caressed the edge of her shoulder and she smiled, knowing he would be with her soon.

CHAPTER 4

KINCH

- Telemachus -

8:15 AM

"HEY JOHN, NEARLY FORGOT my paycheck, mate. Should be under the desk with my name on it." Kinch nodded at the thin, moustached man who sat behind the desk at the entrance to Joyce's Tower. The man picked at his teeth with the top of his pen and nodded at the crowd as they exited.

"Sure thing, hang on a minute." He emptied the contents of the drawer onto the desk: scrawled-on post-its, several Bic pens, a half-eaten Mars bar, and a deodorant stick. "Nope, doesn't seem to be. Are you sure?" His resemblance to James Joyce combined studied effort and genetic fortune.

"Feck, it's the third time I asked Mr. Lacey for the cheque, and he keeps putting me off, the bastard." Kinch banged his right hand on the oak desk.

"Sorry."

"It's not your fault, but does the bollox not realise I'm a starving actor? Does he think I get this bony arse from an abundance of riches?"

"Ah, you know what they're like, Kinch. It's all about the bottom line nowadays."

Kinch picked up the ashplant. "Yep, well better get on with it. Still have a trillion more performances to pack into this day. At least I got fed during that one. Bloody plant will drive me mental."

"Watch out for the holly bush, friend. Full of pricks." John winked.

Kinch had no idea what he was on about, but he smiled and followed the last of the crowd out the door into the sunlight.

A shivering Gerry was perched on the seat of his battered Honda 50.

"Good man yourself, ready and waiting."

"I'm bloody freezing, boy." Gerry wrapped his arms around himself and shivered wildly.

"Well, that's what you get for listening to me, mate," replied Kinch. "Should know better. Anyway, let's hit the road. Want to meet up with Bláithín before I have to rush to Sandymount Strand."

"How're we goin to both fit on the bike with that plant like?" asked the Corkman.

"That's where the actor's bony arse comes in handy. Plenty of space," Kinch replied.

"Ok, but where is she? Because I have to go busking in town. Need some spondoolics."

"I'm meeting her for a coffee in Bewley's on Grafton Street. I have to tell her something she won't like." Kinch threw his leg over the Honda and clutched his plant as though it were a prized pet.

"Wha? Can't hear you!" said the helmeted Corkman.

"Nothin. Grafton Street, GRAFTON STREET! OK?" he shouted into the back of the helmet. Gerry stuck his thumb in the air and took off.

They whizzed through the streets of Dun Laoghaire. A horde of people busily exercised the length of the West pier.

What was it Joyce had called it again? Oh yeah, a disappointed bridge. A large lump of rock projecting out into the sea. No destination, incomplete. How oddly appropriate that seemed to his undetermined path through life.

The morning ferry had just arrived from Holyhead and a steady flow of yellow number plates were weaving their way out of the port.

The British invasion three times daily, like an endlessly repeating loop of history. At least we can send them back with empty pockets. Reparation of a kind.

They hit over a speedbump, and a fist of dry earth from the plant catapulted itself all over Kinch's black suit.

Great! A mucky Dedalus. Well, I suppose he never washed.

Gerry began singing "The Rocky Road to Dublin" with a guttural, Corkonian curl. Kinch joined in as they negotiated a series of speedbumps through the Blackrock suburbs.

Can't believe a Corkman knows "The Rocky Road" word for word. You'd think it would be against his religion."

They stopped suddenly at the hospital lights.

"Cead Mile Fáilte," Kinch sang at an unsuspecting woman who, given her attire and looks, was Romanian.

With a look of suspicion, she pushed a *Big Issue* magazine in his face. He scrambled with his free hand to dig two euros from his pocket. The woman coaxed his efforts with a look of urgency. The lights changed and Gerry took off at speed, the desperate woman chasing in vain.

"Jesus, Gerry, I was trying to buy a magazine," Kinch screamed through the rushing air.

"What, boy, what? Can't hear a thing through this helmet."

Kinch didn't even bother replying. He continued to clutch the plant in his right hand. *Well, at least I tried.*

He could feel the phone buzz in his pocket. It was probably her, the woman who drove him to obsession. Nowadays he couldn't drag his thoughts away from her for more than five minutes. So unfair to Bláithín. He knew it was time to come clean, but Jaysus, he was no hero, and who was he to argue with years of tried and tested male cowardice! So, he'd break it off – only fair. She'd be none the wiser (only fair to him).

Gerry stopped the bike by the Fusilier's Arch, and Kinch hopped off.

"Thanks a million, man. Good luck with the busking. Where will you be? Maybe I can catch up with you later." He flicked his blond hair out of his eyes.

"Sure like, how bout The Barge? 12:30 PM Great for lunch by the canal." The traffic flooded past, and Gerry pushed his way back into the flow.

Kinch gave him the thumbs up and crossed the road to fight his way through the throngs of shoppers weaving their way up Grafton Street. A crowd had gathered around a tall, lanky comedian with glasses and a protruding nose. He strutted gamely through the crowd, a small microphone strapped to his ear, eyeballing potential victims.

It's McSavage doing his terrifying the masses thing again.

"There's England, like a great stalking beast, bent over the small, cowering figure of Ireland," declared the lanky comedian as he proceeded to grab the imaginary figure of Ireland and hump her with dirty enthusiasm.

Kinch nearly choked on the club orange he was drinking. The slightly uncomfortable crowd rippled with laughter. He weaved through the bodies and imagined the masses to be a giant snake slithering through the curving street. The serpent moved silently through the tall buildings, its great dappled scales shining in the sunlight.

Bláithín's father, Minister O'Leary, passed him at speed. "Listen, Denis, the feckers are out to get me again. That cunt in the tribunal is doing a right stitch-up job. Just need to call the bloody wife to calm her down, and I'll see you in ten." Minister O'Leary continued bashing his way through the crowd like a blinded bull.

Kinch narrowed his eyes in contempt. *Cunt is right. St. Patrick didn't manage to banish all the snakes from Irish shores.* Bláithín's father had never liked him – thought he was a right waster because he wasn't out there raking in the millions like the rest of them. *At least he'll be happy I'm out of the way.*

The usual clutch of people stood under the clock outside Bewleys, waiting for their boyfriend or their psychiatrist or God knows who else. He looked up at the old Victorian clock.

Ten AM. Shit don't have much time.

The large glass door shone in the sunlight as he passed through it and into the dark back room. His eyes moved around the space, over the wooden tables, past the wine-velvet seating and unlit fireplace. She was sitting under one of the larger stained-glass windows at the back, staring at a piece of paper. Dressed in a sky-blue bodice, a flowing navy skirt, and high-heeled, lace-up boots, she looked every inch Molly Bloom. Her deep black hair fell in unruly strands from the flowered clasp on the top of her head.

Damn! There she is! Got to do it.

She scanned the room, spotting Kinch as he lifted his hand to catch her attention. The pixie-like face lit with a smile. He didn't smile back. A current of confusion darted through his body, and he moved towards her slowly.

"Hey, how's the crack?" He placed the ashplant on the seat beside him.

"Oh, all right, a bit sick of the smell of kidney. Puke."

"Can imagine." He pulled a cigarette from the pack in his pocket and knocked it on the edge of the table. "Did the house scene go ok?"

"Didn't have much to do in this one really. It's the soliloquy that's terrifying me. I've practiced it a million times and I'm still shitless," she replied. "I must be mad to have taken it on."

"You'll be great. You were made to play Molly."

"Are you planning to light that or just abuse it?"

"Very funny. Listen, Bláithín. I ..."

She pointed at the plant. "What the fuck are you doing with that?"

"It's the ashplant. You know ... he carries it around with him ... in the book."

She scrunched up her face in disbelief. "Wha? You're joking right?"

Kinch looked at her smiling face. *God, this is going to be more difficult than I thought.* "What do you mean? Listen Bláith ..."

"You're actually serious. Jesus, you can be such an eejit. An ashplant's a walking-stick, babes, not a bloody plant. Least I think so. You haven't even read the bloody thing, have you?" she asked.

"Shite, yeah, of course I have. I'm sure you're wrong, but for feck's sake it's impossible to figure out what's happening half the time. Are you telling me I'm wearing half this bloody thing for no reason?" He pointed to the stains on his suit.

Bláithín clutched the sides of the table, choking on her egg with laughter. "God, you're gas, babes." She stroked him affectionately on the cheek, and he felt his skin harden under her touch.

A group of eager tourists had gathered at the table beside them, pointing and whispering. Kinch played with his cigarette box, cursing the smoking ban that denied him the immediate stress relief of a good old-fashioned rush of nicotine.

"Hey babe, it's like being a couple of film stars." She leaned over the table and took his hand. He pulled it away and began to play with the egg on her plate.

She sat backwards slowly. "What's the matter? You're acting a bit funny."

"Listen, I know it isn't a good time for this, Bláithín, but, well, I just can't help it. How do you even say this without sounding like a tosser?"

"Say what?"

"Well, how about I think I need some space, or maybe we should take a break, or perhaps the overused, I just don't think we're right for each other. Jesus, I'm sorry, I just don't know how to do this."

The tea travelled up her nose and she began to choke. "Wha? I don't understand, but I thought we were getting on great."

"I know we're good friends and all, but Jesus, I'm bored Bláithín. I just need a bit more," he whispered.

"A bit more?" Her voice rose. "Would that be a bit more affection or a bit more sex or a bit more money or a bit more love? Because, you know, I gave it all away to you if you haven't noticed. Let me check ..." She emptied the contents of her pockets on the table with a bang. "Any extra love lying around? Nope, all given away to Kieran bloody James Lynch by the looks of things!"

"Christ Bláith, get a grip," he whispered, gesturing for her to sit down. "The whole place is staring at us."

"Great, they probably think it's the lost chapter of *Ulysses*, eejits." She waved her arms around her body in a gathering gesture. "Yep, the lost chapter, folks, performed for you for free today, and in the title role of lying, scheming bastard is the great Kieran Lynch!"

Kinch took his jacket from the back of the chair. "Christ, I've had enough. Can you see why I'm leaving you now, you feckin' lunatic?"

"Is that part of it? Is that part of the book?" questioned an excited group of young Americans sitting near the fireplace.

"Yes indeed, 'The Phaeacian Games,' the 'All's Fair in Love and War' scene," Bláithín replied at the top of her voice.

Kinch picked up his hat and started to move for the door.

"Kinch, you bastard, you forgot something!"

The plant hurtled in his direction. He ducked and it hit the empty fireplace behind him. The Americans scattered wildly. Bláithín rubbed her hands, picked up her shawl, and stalked out the front door.

The guy at the cash register stared at Kinch with a "You can shaggin clean that up" look on his face.

Get out of here fast.

Kinch's phone was ringing on the table beside him, and he could see that it was her again. He couldn't wait to tell her that he was free, hers alone, but this wasn't the moment. He let it ring out, picked up his things, and ran.

CHAPTER 5

BLÁITHÍN

9:30 AM

SHE HADN'T BEEN EXPECTING that. His moods shifted a lot these days. It was to be expected with the anniversary of his mother's death. Anyone could understand that. Bláithín had done her best to soothe the deadening pain of such an unresolved ending. After all, she'd encouraged him to go and see a shrink, and that had helped a lot. She lit a badly needed cigarette and sat by the edge of the Molly Malone statue to soak up whatever relief it could give her.

Could do with something stronger. Gotta find Gerry. Might sort me out.

A young man in torn jeans and a tie-dye t-shirt sat in front of her, drawing a portrait in coloured chalk on the path. Two or three people lingered around him. He worked diligently from the portrait of a handsome, middle-aged woman that lay beside him, capturing the haunted shadows that oozed from her dark-green eyes. Bláithín sat down at the Molly Malone statue. "Afro Celt Sound System" played on the stereo beside him. She admired the talent that could imitate another's creation to such perfection. It was the type of craft that lay in the shadows of recognition because it wasn't born from "original" thought.

Such bullshit, she thought. *We're all the spawn of another's moment.* She threw a euro into the near empty hat.

A woman who reminded her of Kinch's mother passed by. She'd been an ordinary but kind woman. Her excessively religious nature had freaked Bláithín out, but she didn't quite understand why Kinch had to be so cruel in the end, refusing to pray by his mother's bed. Even Bláithín would have given in to that one. She had been a religious child, reciting her prayers every night like the best of them, but when she woke up and looked at the state of the world, she decided that God didn't deserve her attention. Nonetheless, she still found herself knocking out an "Angel of God" prayer when she really needed it. Just in case.

That last day was hell, his mother's gasping breaths as she begged him, his composure stony. He could never forgive himself for the stress it caused her in the end. Bláithín had done her best to console him.

Bláithín didn't deserve this, to be cast aside just when he was getting his feet back on the ground. It was cruel, when she had done so much. She had held him as he sobbed through the whole sorry mess for God's sake, put aside her own priorities just to pull him through it all. It just wasn't fair. The tears began to drip down her pale and freckled face. She pulled clumps of her raven hair around her like a protective shield.

Shit, everyone's watching. Why does he always have to make me lose it in public?

The old straw shopping basket she'd found in the second-hand shop on Liffey Street was beginning to bug her. *How the hell did they carry something this big around with them all the time?*

Still, she was in character, and she had to look the part. Her head was pounding.

Must have been the joints from last night. Feck it, I really need a line.

The artist turned to look at her. "You look a little worse for wear. Everything ok?"

"It's nothing."

"Well, if you're sure?"

"Thanks." She wiped her eyes with her sleeve and forced a weak smile.

"I like your painting. I don't know how you can copy that so perfectly."

"Years of practice, sure, anyone could do it," he replied. "Just requires a sharp eye and lots of bleedin patience."

"I doubt that." She liked his smile. Soft, comforting. "Who's the woman in the painting? She reminds me of someone."

"It's Lady Lavery or, depending on who you talk to, Caitlín Ni Houlihán. Have you heard of her?"

"I think so. Was it something to do with our old currency or something?" She struggled to drag a lost scrap of history from her scrambled brain.

"Spot on. The original painting for our old banknotes, done by her husband, John Lavery, who just happened to be the most famous portrait artist of the time. Picked it up off the Net ... cracks me up that no one even remembers it now. Short memories around here."

Heavy Dublin accent, she thought to herself, *but cute in a down and dirty kind of way.*

"No kidding? Who was she?" She couldn't give a shite really, but a chat would cheer her up.

"Hazel Lavery. A real beauty. And a really wild one – had loads of lovers. My kind of woman."

"A bit feisty, was she?" Bláithín said cheekily.

"Like I said, my kind of woman." He smiled, stood up, and moved awkwardly towards her.

"What's with the old dress? Gettin into the mood with the day that's in it?"

"They're actually paying me to wander around like Molly Bloom. The bodice is killing me though."

"I'd be happy to take over. Do you think I could pull it off? Could do with a few extra bob." He sucked in his stomach and strutted around.

Bláithín laughed. "Impressive."

"Now you're smiling. Much better." He winked. "You know, whoever the bastard is you deserve better."

Bláithín was surprised at this sudden leap in confidentiality. "I don't know what you mean."

"A beautiful girl like yourself with raw-red eyes at 10:00 AM has either just been jilted or is coming down off a wicked high." His tone was soft and consoling even if his words cut straight to the heart of the matter.

"Is that a question?"

"Only if you want it to be."

That smile again. Familiar somehow. "Ok then. The first part – spot on. The second – I wish."

He nodded. "I see. I know the feeling. I got my own heart smashed to pieces a couple of months ago. She ran off with my bastard of a brother, no less."

"Ouch."

"I even live with the fecker and have to see the two of them together."

"Double ouch."

He scribbled on his hand awkwardly with the chalk. "At least you know there's an eejit in this square foot of space who's worse off than you."

"Maybe."

"For sure." He hesitated and continued. "You're gorgeous."

He seemed to really mean it. Kind eyes. "Thanks. Even if I feel like a train wreck right now."

"It'll pass." He moved closer and lowered his voice. "Am I wrong in thinking that you like a bit of the white stuff to help you through?"

She shuffled nervously, a little afraid of this sudden shift. The urge to numb away the sadness was there, but she didn't know this guy – nice as he seemed, he could be dodgy as fuck. Still, it was what she really needed.

Fuck it, fuck it, I can't.

"Really, I wouldn't mind ... only it's a bit early. Feel like shit, but ... no thanks anyway," she replied.

"Well, if you change your mind, here's my number." He handed her a self-made business card. "Inspiration Portraits – that's me business, normally like." The gold print on the card spelled out an address in Ballymun.

"You never know. Nice meeting you. By the way I'm Bláithín." She stuck out her hand for the customary shake.

"Yeah, Paul."

"Right, Paul." She nodded at his drawing. "You're very talented you know."

He blushed. "Thanks. I do me best. Where I come from, this doesn't change much, I'm afraid."

"Keep at it. You've got the heart for it." She smiled warmly.

"Thanks, gorgeous Bláithín, or should I say, Molly?"

She lifted her skirts and waved them around. "Yes, to say yes."

He laughed and winked as she walked away, heading down Nassau Street.

Maybe later. Maybe I'll call for some stuff. I need it, and he seems decent enough. Very Northsider, but still. I'm such a bloody snob, just like the rest of them. Nice guys haven't a hope. Life sucks.

She walked away, and her phone beeped a message. Her mother was trying to get a hold of her again to perform at her father's function that evening. She'd had it up to here trying to explain to the woman that she wasn't a performing seal for her father's politician cronies. Their understanding of *Ulysses* probably went no further than attempted buyouts of the aforementioned B&I ferry boat to Holyhead or a double yankee on the Gold Cup horse of the same name. She'd learned her lesson when she found herself auctioned off at one of those glitzy fundraising events in The Burlington Hotel. She ended up having to go on a date with a balding, pot-bellied associate of her father's, a man from Mayo whose idea of charm was to bring her to Bordello's Strip club, ply her with copious amounts of Moet & Chandon, and encourage her to lap-dance with an unfortunate Lithuanian stripper. No bloody thanks! Anyway, it was mortifying having anything to do with her dad these days. All the tribunal stuff he was caught up in made her blood run cold. She didn't know what to believe.

She walked along Nassau Street to the National Gallery and stepped into the road to cross towards the Lincoln's Inn. An arm grabbed the neck of her jacket and pulled her back just as a double-decker bus whizzed past the end of her feet. She fell in a heap of legs and arms on the path in front of the gallery.

"Jesus, that was close!" muttered the dark-skinned young man.

"Hanan, what the fuck just happened?" Her sharp blue eyes were alive with fright.

"God girl, are you suicidal today or what?"

"I ... I don't know ... sorry?"

"That bus was coming straight for you!" He lifted them both off the ground.

"Sorry, I'm a mess at the moment."

"Just as well. You can be spotted a mile off in that get-up. Sexy ... oooohhhh!!" He glanced at her from head to toe with a look that made her ears glow and her body tingle.

"Yeah, well, I feel like a train wreck. Kinch just dumped me. Did you know this was coming? Be honest!"

"Jesus, no. He never let on a thing. I swear!"

She eyed him suspiciously. He looked genuinely surprised, but she knew how close he and Kinch were. The male brotherhood was impenetrable when it came to protecting lies.

"Mmmm. Well, your pal has fucked me up royally – today! When I have to look my best in front of the whole of Dublin. Bastard!"

"I'm really sorry Bláith. Bloody eejit!" He blushed and she smiled inside. She knew he had a soft spot for her, but he just wasn't her type. Nothing she could do about that.

"I'm just nipping over to the Coffee Dock. Come on over. It'll get your mind off things."

"Ok. A caffeine injection might do me some good."

They fought their way through the flow of students exiting the glass doors of the Trinity College Arts Building. The wall was plastered with a mishmash of posters for visiting bands, affirmative action groups, student organisations, and visiting lecturers. One poster caught her eye: Low, the American Mormon rock group, was playing in Christ Church Cathedral that night. Kinch loved them. He'd promised to bring her as an early birthday present.

So much for that now. She was pissed off because she really wanted to see them, but he'd be there, and she'd probably beat the shit out of him if she saw him again today. *Bollox.* The tears began to swell behind her eyes.

"Ok?" Hanan touched her elbow gently.

She knew the one sure answer to shut up a questioning man. "Just woman's stuff, you know."

"Right, right," he replied. "There's Sarah with her crew ... Hey hun!" he shouted over the buzz of students.

"Crap, you never said she would be here."

"She likes you Bláith, I swear."

"Rather sit on a bed of nettles naked."

"For God's sake, she didn't mean it."

"Which part? The 'frustrated heifer' or the 'horse-faced hippy'?"

Sarah sat, perfectly groomed as always, in the middle of the group, holding court. Perfectly tight jeans wrapped around her perfectly slim figure like a skin, blond hair ramrod straight and glowing in the sunlight. Her eyes were a type of blue that glowed scarily, like they'd been touched up by a Vogue cover artist. Bláithín couldn't understand for a second what Hanan saw in her apart from "the obvious."

Beside Sarah sat Will, every inch the rugby boy. He usually dressed in striped Polo shirts and paraded around campus with some preening blond attached to his arm. His current flavour of the month, Portia, sat on his right, blathering on about some inane party she'd been to the night before. Still, he wasn't so bad. He'd once helped Bláithín to change the tyre on her bicycle when she was a little worse for wear and incapable of clear thinking. She tried to fight against her anti-rugby attitude, but just the sight of large groups of beer-swilling polo-shirt wearers made her want to puke.

Hanan sighed. "Jesus, you women are impossible but ok."

"Listen, I'll see you later ... maybe at the concert, ok?"

"Later, then."

She glanced back at Sarah, who was giving her the evils. Bláithín turned on her heels but couldn't escape the sinking feeling of darkness that fell over her like a heavy menstrual cloud.

CHAPTER 6

KINCH

- Nestor -

9:30 AM

AS SOON AS HE STEPPED into the ebb and flow of the crowd, his body slumped heavily, and he felt slightly faint.

What the fuck just happened? Need to find Gerry, bollox, need a drink.

He turned onto Wicklow Street. A band was playing the usual indie-rock fare in the corner of Tower Records. The drumbeat thudded through his brain like lead through glass.

Jesus, they're shite.

"Don't leave the day job!" he shouted through the door to a puzzled-looking group of teenagers, thrashing wildly at the back of the shop.

Gerry was not in his usual spot in front of the International Bar.

Damn, where's the bugger when I need him? He lit another badly needed cigarette and scanned the street. Across the road the sign above the Butler's Café caught his eye: *Philip Lacey, Art Promotions.*

Might as well see if the tight bastard has my money. This day is shaping up badly enough as it is. Sucking on his cigarette, he climbed the steep stairs. *Promoter of the Arts my arse. All he gives a damn about are his appearances on the* Late Late Show.

The peroxide blonde behind the desk was putting the finishing touches to her scarlet nail polish.

"Yes, hi, would Mr. Lacey be around by any chance?" he asked.

"Wha? Yeah, sorry just give me a second," finishing off her last two digits carefully.

"Tough job."

"Wha? No not really. Just a minute, the phone's ringing." She dipped her head in a disturbingly unattractive manner, placed the loudly ringing cordless between the base of her palms, and pressed the answer button with her nose. "Mr. Philip Lacey's office. How can I help you?" She strangulated the vowels in an effort to impress.

I'm not the only thing the mean bastard is scrimping on around here.

She dismissed the person on the line and manoeuvred the phone back into the cradle with her head.

"Impressive talent," he offered with a sly smile.

"Tanks, yeah. I've bin workin on me phone voice."

"Very nice. Clearly you were made for this job."

She batted her eyelids furiously and adjusted her top downwards. "Gee tanks, ehm, sorry wha is your name again?"

"Stephen, Stephen Dedalus," he replied.

"Right ... Steve. I'll just get Mr. Lacey for you."

Kinch smiled.

Lacey sat in a black leather swivel chair, his feet resting on the small locker by his desk.

"Ah, Kinch, how the hell are you, my lad? Looking good in all that black, I must say." The nasal tones of his faux-British accent grated on Kinch's nerves. "Very much the part. Yes indeed."

Kinch smiled. *It's far from Oxford you were raised, you posh bollox.*

"Glad you approve, Mr. Lacey. And about that ..."

"Sit down, sit down, lad, for God's sake. You're going to spend enough of this day on your feet." Lacey guided him forcefully into hard wooden chair and grabbed the hat off his head.

"Quite a hat. Love the old style, don't you? So much more civilised. Don't know what the youngsters are wearing nowadays. My nephew goes around with holes deliberately put into his trousers, and he wears the blasted things around the rim of his behind. All those outside influences from across the Atlantic and God knows where else, don't you think?"

"Well, I don't really know, but ..."

"Yes, yes, I'm sure you agree. The country is invaded for God's sake. Hard to tell who's who nowadays."

"At least we invited the invaders in this time," interjected Kinch, determined to interrupt the monologue.

"Poppycock, no mind of our own anymore, lad, I'm telling you."

"Indeed, you are. Ehm, Mr. Lacey, you wouldn't have that cheque for me, would you?" he asked gently. *Foot and mouth disease is what you have all right, mate.*

"Of course, my boy, I'm happy to hand out money where money is due." He walked to the filing cabinet and pulled an envelope from the top drawer. "Once you've worked for it, you've earned it. Not like the wasters begging in the streets and stuffing up our dole queues."

"But the country is at near full employment, Mr. Lacey! And anyway, the bloody Irish are too fussy to do menial labour now."

"Maybe so, but not for long. Look at Germany for God's sake. Rightly stuffed after dropping that wall. Does nobody any good to weaken borders. Destroys cultures." His over-fed cheeks blew up like a baboon on heat. "Don't tell me you're not terrified by the state of the South Circular Road with all those Arabs up to God knows what! New York first. Who knows when the rest of us are going to get smashed into when we least expect it." He handed the envelope to Kinch. "Prevention, nine-tenths of the law and all that. We'll deserve it otherwise, I tell you. Turning a blind eye never did anyone any good."

"Christ wouldn't agree," Kinch said.

He raised the glasses off the bridge of his nose and stared. "I never took you for a believer, lad."

"I believe in what's out there on that street, the dark and light of it all."

"Ah, the ease of vagueness. Need more than that, my boy, need structure to hold it all together."

Eejit! Bloody eejit! "You've been around longer than I have, Mr Lacey. No doubt you know better." He stepped backwards, turning to face the door.

"How's that girlfriend of yours? Acting her part today as well, fair dues?"

Bollox, will I never get out of here? "She's not my girlfriend anymore, and she doesn't like me very much right now, but she'll be fine."

"Sorry to hear that, my friend. A fine lass. Mutual, I hope?"

"Not exactly. I'm sorry, I need to get to the strand, Mr. Lacey." He grabbed the door handle with determination.

"Don't mind those women, lad. They are the downfall of us all." Lacey bent to pick up a newspaper from the desk.

"I nearly forgot – you still do a bit of writing for the *Irish Independent*, don't you?" He waved the paper in Kinch's face.

"From time to time, why?"

"You wouldn't drop this letter in for me lad, would you? It's to the editor. Mustn't keep my thoughts to myself, I feel. Better to get out there and voice them. Might do some good you know."

Kinch pushed the letter into a pocket. "I'll try, but today is busy."

"That'll do, my boy. Got to fight together to preserve this culture. Take out the sword and give it a whirl," he said, mock jousting with the air.

For Ulster will fight And Ulster will be right. "Go raibh maith agat agus go mbeidh brón agus ocras i do theach féin," Kinch said boldly.

"Got the first part, lad, but what was that second bit? Rusty at the Gaelic."

"God, Mary, and Jesus be with you," Kinch replied.

"Fine thought, fine thought indeed, my lad. Good morning to you." He moved back to his chair.

"Good morning, Mr. Lacey." Kinch tipped his hat downwards and left the building at speed, much to the dismay of the preening blonde at the door.

CHAPTER 7

OMAR

- The Lotus Eaters -

9:30 AM

OMAR DECIDED THAT it was too nice a day to be fighting traffic in his car. He reached into the passenger seat for his bag and slung it over his back. The lock on the driver's door had been dodgy since the last time he'd dropped Flora off at Matt Phelan's.

That jumped up cuckolder! Thinks he's God's gift and so does Flora. No justice.

He struggled with the door, giving it an extra bang with his hip. *I gotta get that lock fixed.*

He pulled out a sheet of paper from a jacket pocket and headed towards the city centre. The sound of St. Patrick's bells drifted over the hum of the traffic, and he walked steadily towards them. A double-decker bus pulled up at the stop, one hundred yards ahead. He eyed the young woman who stepped onto the path in front of him. She was wearing a pale-blue summer dress cut just below the thigh. He could see the line of her thong; the light material curved around the fullness of her buttocks. His eyes dipped around the edge of her hips. Her dress swung above her long, tanned legs like a hypnotic pendulum.

I hate the summer, it's like torture.

The girl disappeared into a Spar shop, and he sighed with sad relief.

The queue in the sub-post office on Kevin Street Upper wasn't too bad. It was Pension Day and two aul dears were nattering away in front of him about the awful heat and the state of the young ones nowadays dressed like hoors in their tiny miniskirts, and what about the new smoking ban, which meant having to be out on the streets like a homeless person to enjoy a fag anymore. Immediately in front of him was a heavily pregnant young woman.

"When are you due, luv?" asked the old lady. She tapped the young woman's stomach knowingly.

"Yesterday, but dey say you usually go two weeks over wid de first one, so here I am. Fit to burst, I am."

"Do you know if it's a boy or a girl, luv?"

"Raader not know. Me fella, Nelson – he's from Nigeria – he wants to know, but I keep tellin him, dere's no fun in dat sure."

"No fun at all. Sure, we couldn't know in our day, and it did us no harm apart from a few little, fat boys goin around in pink, frilly babygrows." The old lady erupted into a high cackle of laughter. "Nigeria is it. You're goin to be havin one of those gorgeous creamy babies then, you lucky thing."

"Yep, at least I won't have to worry about me child bein burnt to a crisp like me mammy had to. Could end up with a Samantha Mumba or Phil Lynnot if I'm lucky."

"Better Samantha than Phil, luv – poor lad – but I'm sure your baby will be a stunner."

"Next!" called the lady from behind the bulletproof cubicle. The pregnant girl moved forward. The aul dears continued nattering.

Omar noticed a poster on the wall advertising a trip to Granada in Spain. His parents had been there on their honeymoon, while his mother was on one of her concert tours in Europe. He remembered her talking about the markets of the Albaicín, an ocean of competing aromas: the sticky smell of Arabian spices and the pungent odour of smeared dog shit. Apparently, it was a place where the smells of the Orient blended with the incense of the Catholic Rite – a confused concoction of religious origins and cultural identity, a bit like himself.

I must go there. Place of my conception.

The two pensioners still gossiped in the queue ahead of him. The pregnant girl moved away to lick her stamps.

A middle-aged woman with dyed honey-coloured curls stared out blankly from the bulletproof cubicle. "What can I do for you ladies?"

The aul wans dug a wad of postcards out of their pockets, and Omar knew he would be in for a long wait. Outside the door, he spotted a guy dressed in black. He couldn't see his face, but there was something about the way he moved that looked suspicious. The man pulled something over his head. Then another one appeared. He had something in his hand ... a long knife. Omar's stomach lurched, and he froze to the spot. He could see now – they were wearing balaclavas. The door opened suddenly. Before the others had even noticed, the smaller man had slipped the bolt upwards and locked them all inside.

The taller of the two moved towards Omar, a butcher's knife in his grasp. "Get the fuck down. On the fucking floor. NOW!"

One of the older women began to wail.

A small stocky man pushed his way through and forced everyone onto the floor. "Shut the fuck up, lady!" It was a young voice. Couldn't have been more than eighteen.

"You. Open the fuckin safe!" The lanky man towered above Omar, his bloodshot eyes bulging through the slit of his balaclava like joke-shop eyeballs.

Omar felt an odd calm wash over his initial panic. "I don't work here, mate."

"Open the fucking safe, you shite." The youth pushed Omar to the back of the room and plastered his face up to the bulletproof glass counter. The postal worker had barricaded herself inside and was reaching for the phone.

"Don't fucking touch that, bitch, or he gets it."

Omar felt the knife shove against his throat until it nipped the underside of his chin. "I don't work here ... I don't work here." He repeated this like a mantra, in calm, steady tones. *High as a kite. Gotta calm him down. Jesus! Thank God it's not a gun. Wish that woman on the floor would just shut up.*

"Open the fucking door, bitch!"

The woman inside was motionless. She stared at the balaclavad youth with a look of disbelief. He smelt of ginger spice and lemon soap, had a guttural Dublin accent. Omar realised that he would soon be the casualty of this pathetic attempt at daylight robbery if he didn't join his assailant in waking the woman from her stupor.

"Open the door, for God's sake. I have a knife to my throat." The startled woman moved to the door and turned the lock. Omar felt the grip loosen from around his neck, and he was pushed to the ground violently.

"You! Don't fucking move!" screamed the other black-clad youth. He danced around the room on his short legs like a bantamweight.

The woman opened the door. The lanky youth scrambled into the room, forced her to open the safe and empty the contents into a large sack. Omar placed his hand on the shoulder of the old woman who lay beside him. She was shaking with fear.

He whispered into her ear, "It'll be all right."

She smiled at him weakly, and he held her hand to calm her down.

"Jaysus, man, hurry up! We need to get the fuck out of here."

Omar stared at the shoes of the agitated thief. The small feet continued to shuffle – white Gola Runners with blue stripes that had seen better days.

"Right, man, let's get the fuck out of here," said the other. "Keep the fuck down, everyone, or we'll slit yous."

Omar picked himself up off the sobbing woman and checked that she was ok. He watched the two men unlock the door and exit at speed.

He helped the old lady off the floor. "Are you all right, Ma'am?"

"Ok, love. Feeling a little shaken but in one piece. The little bastards. If I could get my hands on them, I'd wring their necks!" Her grey perm shook vigorously.

Omar looked around the room. The other pensioner and the pregnant girl were picking themselves up off the ground. Omar recognised the old man: the newspaper seller who sat on the corner of Exchequer Street and St. Andrews Street. Omar had never spoken to him, but he was one of those characters you couldn't help but notice.

"Are you both ok?" The newspaper seller appeared to be breathing laboriously.

"Just need a minute, son. The heart isn't the best. I think that knocked the stuffing out of me." His chiselled face looked unnaturally red as he leant his slight frame against the door of the cubicle.

"Should I call a doctor? It's no bother." Omar guided the frail man to a plastic chair in the corner of the small room.

"No, son, I'm grand. Just need a minute to recover. Little bastards got the better of me."

The grey-haired lady looked concerned. "I think you should let him call, Mick. Sure, what harm is there?"

"No, no. I don't like all that fussin, Kitty. Sure, look ... amn't I grand already?" He picked himself up off the chair and forced a smile.

"Well, if you're sure," said Omar.

"Couldn't be surer, son," replied Mick. "Was on my way to Paddy Powers to put a bet on the Queen Mary Stakes. After that bit of drama, I reckon luck has to turn my way."

"Maybe you're right. Might put a bet on myself. If you're all right, I have to run and catch a few of the *Ulysses* performances."

"What's that, son? *Ulysses*?" He glanced at the listings. "By God, I heard he's a good horse and with the day that's in it, sure why not?"

"Well, I didn't really mean ..."

"Buy you a pint, son, if he comes good. Goodbye ladies. It's bin an excitin mornin."

Omar excused himself and raced for a taxi.

Chapter 8

FLORA

10:00 AM

When she had spare time on her hands, Flora often found herself drifting towards the National Gallery. She ate her sandwich on the canal bank, made her way down Baggott Street and right into Merrion Street past the Dáil. There was some commotion outside the stone arch of government buildings. A group of people held placards – "No to American fighter planes landing in Shannon!" – and chanted "Stop Bush visit!" for the RTE television cameras.

Flora had been asked to perform, supporting Christy Moore at the "When Bush come to Shove" concert, organised by the Irish anti-war movement for the following Saturday night. Even though she was no fan of the current American president, she'd turned it down. She felt somewhat guilty, but she had a serious aversion to politics and anything that was remotely linked. Growing up in communist Poland had taught her to steer clear of ideologies, no matter where they came from. When she was a young music student in Kraków, everyone had been in a flap about the fall of communism and pushing Lech Walesa into power. To be honest, she'd been too busy trying to figure out how to get away to "be involved," but she knew there was a place for such enthusiastic people. She just wasn't one of them.

The sun drifted in and out of focus behind a floating sea of white. Every time it broke through, a warm blush washed over her skin. She climbed the steps of the large stone edifice. A message reminder beeped in her pocket. Bláithín's name flashed at her from the screen of her mobile.

"Flora, sorry will be a little late for the lesson. Kinch just broke up with me. Need to talk. Feel like shit. See you at 12:00 PM ..."

Blast, don't need this drama. Need to be careful.

She entered the long central corridor of the gallery with its high ceilings, arched doorframe, and soothing light. A slow-breathing calm descended upon her. She loved it here. The solace of creativity was something she could never get enough of. Her own creative nature lay on the darker side of this force – the need to exorcise pain and unfulfilled passion. She would pound a heartbeat into the strings of her violin until her demons disappeared into the air like phantoms on the edge of daylight. Here she felt something that was the opposite of that dark energy. The colour and form of the paintings moved through her, a sweet opiate, a delicate embrace.

It was a rare opportunity to surround herself with stillness. She loved churches for the same reason despite the association with her Catholic past. Slowly, she moved through the rooms. Her eyes scanned the paintings: the fall of a young girl's arm in the sunlight, the blood-red dawn of a battlefield, the dark tears of a crying child. She felt her emotions speed and blur through wave after wave of colour. She knew where she was going. Always to the same spot – a large canvas tucked away in the corner of the new Millennium Wing of the Gallery. Taking the empty seat, she sat down in front of Sir John Lavery's "The Artist's Studio." She had stared at this painting many times and couldn't shake it off. It drew her in, and she couldn't exactly explain why.

A classily dressed woman sat bolt upright at its centre, her perfectly groomed hair contained within a violet Clara Bow hat, curls escaping delicately around the rim. It was a strikingly beautiful face – high cheekbones, dimpled chin, languorous eyes. Flora felt the seduction of this woman's gaze. She wanted to capture her confidence and make it her own. A little girl sat beside the woman, looking like a porcelain doll. There was no hint of a mother's affection in the space that lay between them. The child seemed no more than a delicate possession.

Flora was fascinated. She felt admiration for this woman despite her obvious lack of maternal instinct. That same instinct cast a depressing shadow over Flora's life. She coveted this woman's cold confidence, the impenetrable yet beautiful shell that rendered her impervious to pain. No doubt it was a lonely way to live, but at least it prevented the dull pain of unfulfillment. Beside them lay a fine-boned dog, its face oddly shadowing that of its owner.

The artist, painting, could be seen in a mirror at the back of the elegant room. She knew that this was the man's own family and marvelled at the passionate detachment with which he could portray the distances that lay between them. The admiration and fascination he had for the woman at the centre of his life was palpable. It was also obvious that he struggled to contain her beauty in a space that he could control. She suddenly felt sorry for Omar – sorry for his inability to shape her energy into something he could handle. Washed with sadness, she turned to leave.

"The Laverys," commented a man seated by the edge of the doorway, a guard to judge by his security uniform. "Beautiful woman, wasn't she?"

"Yes, indeed. I love this painting." Eager not to be dragged into an unnecessary conversation, she moved towards the opposite doorway.

The guard was determined to continue. "They say she tried to fling herself into Michael Collins's grave at the funeral – she was his lover, you know."

"Really?" The fact that Hazel Lavery had been the Irish Revolutionary leader's lover did not surprise her – fit the bill. Interested though she was, she was not in the mood for conversation. "Sorry, I've got to run." The Irish had a way of striking up a conversation in the most unlikely of places. Although largely an attractive trait, there were times when she wished for silence, and this was not a concept that sat easily in the minds of this chatty nation.

He nodded his head. "Well enjoy, love."

She headed back through the original Gallery and descended the winding stairs into the Shaw room. At the end of the high-ceilinged space, a teenager sat transfixed by a large canvas. It struck her that he was a boy of an age that typically wouldn't be caught dead hanging out in a gallery.

The painting that so fascinated the young man a battle scene. Bodies lay strewn around the edge of a burning building. At the centre stood two majestic figures: a woman and a man. Flora wasn't sure what they were doing. She glanced at the explanation on the left-hand side of the painting. "The Marriage of Strongbow and Aoife" by Daniel Maclise. Now it was obvious. *A wedding in the middle of a battle, how odd.*

The boy continued to stare at the painting. A schoolbook sat beside him on the bench. The name Khaled Hussein was scrawled across the cover. She moved to the bench and sat beside the boy, who barely registered her presence.

"Powerful painting."

Silence. His eyes glanced sideways with a look of discomfort.

"You like this a lot. Do you mind me asking why?" She realised she was committing the offense that she had been so eager to escape two minutes before, but there was something about this boy that intrigued her. He looked at her with unsmiling eyes.

"It makes me angry."

"Why is that?"

"Strongbow. He just invaded Ireland with his powerful army, murdered everyone, and married the daughter of a traitorous Irish King. He claimed something that wasn't his and destroyed an ancient culture with arrogance and evil. It's like what's happening to my culture. Being wiped out by that bastard Bush." His voice suggested controlled anger. His eyes were cold and impenetrable.

"What do you mean by your culture? You sound Irish to me."

"Islam. I live here. I'm a Muslim and that makes me a citizen of the world of Islam, a member of the ummah. That's more important to me." He lapsed into silence.

Flora thought carefully about what she should say next. "To be honest, I don't know much about it although my husband was born a Muslim. But were you born here?"

He nodded.

"So your parents moved here from?"

"Lebanon."

"I see. A lot of trouble there. Have you ever visited?"

"No. I want to go there very badly. I just don't belong here. It's not my place."

"Well, I'm not from here either. Polish, actually. Do you know anything about Poland?" She didn't expect a positive reply.

"The pope is Polish, right?"

"Yes, that's right, comes from Wadowice, not far from Kraków where

I grew up."

He turned to look at her properly, his dark eyes cold, unsmiling. "Are you Catholic?"

"I was born a Catholic, but I don't believe in any religion really. Too much warring comes from all that."

"Sometimes the war is necessary."

There was something in his voice that scared her. Not that she thought this boy could do her any harm, but maybe he wished he could. "What do you mean?"

He picked up his backpack to leave. "I think I had better go."

"Sorry, I hope it wasn't something I said. I ... I just would like to understand these things better."

"There's nothing to understand. Sometimes the gap's too wide, lady. I need to go."

Before she had a chance to say goodbye, he disappeared down the corridor at speed. *What a strange kid.* She was left with a heavy feeling of disquiet, a fractured uneasiness.

Her mobile flashed the time: 11:40 AM. *Better get back for Bláithín. Wish I could put it off. No choice, I suppose.*

The heavens opened as she exited towards Merrion Square. A wave of umbrellas flooded past her. She cursed the fact that she'd forgotten her "just in case" umbrella again. As she raced across the road, she spotted the boy going in the side gate of Merrion Square Park. A cold breeze invaded her body. *Should try and understand Omar a bit better, understand his world.* She pulled her scarf over her head and made a vow to herself to try a little harder, just a little harder.

Chapter 9

KINCH

- Proteus -

10:00 AM

UNAVOIDABLE MOODY BASTARD, that Julian Guinness. Kinch, cap on head, nodded at the stern-looking man waiting for him on the Sydney Parade station platform.

The small, bespectacled man winced. "Do you call this on-time?" His thin face glowed with anger.

"Don't get your knickers in a twist, Julian."

"Your attitude leaves a lot to be desired, young man,"

The Dart shed its motley load of tourists. The two men joined them in walking towards the strand.

The small, balding man fidgeted with his boater hat and mumbled quietly.

Can't believe he's a Guinness. Our national brew in the genes of a fool.

They turned onto Strand Road. The crowds were gathering by the Tower wall.

A day of towers. Wonder where my flower is? Bonking some other bloke who has more to offer no doubt. Usurper. Hope that's not true. Hmmm, wonder? Been awfully friendly with Gerry these days. Jesus, not possible. Don't even think it. Wouldn't do that. A friend, right? Agggghhhh! Must take up meditation. Silence the little man. Driving me mad. Unavoidable moody thoughts. Unavoidable queues of memory. The sound of her singing, the sight of her naked on the pisspot. The trickle of sound between her slender thighs. I could have sucked it out of her. Sweat ran down his pale skin in large beads.

"Right Kinch, the throngs await us," Julian said.

He approached the crowd. A black woman with exquisite, dark eyes stood at the back and fiddled with her programme.

"Ineluctable modality of the visible."

Julian was off, breaking into narration as they passed the people and stepped down onto the crunching shale of the beach. Kinch silently followed, in character.

"Signatures of all things I am here to read – seaspawn and seawrack, the nearing tide, that rusty boot ..."

Kinch looked down at his feet. *Hope I don't scuff the hell out of these new shoes. Not exactly designed for a seaside walk.* The crowd followed blandly. He closed his eyes. *Wonder who that woman is? Striking, yeah, beautiful. Black beauty. Strong black thighs wrapped around me. Now that would be something. Wonder how she moans?*

"Ineluctable modality of the audible."

Like a deep low whisper, a saxophone's mounting breath, God, it's hard to walk in the dark. Don't trip. Make a fool of yourself. This lot, shuffling worshippers of the word. And the word was made man. Transubstantiation of the mind. Cannibalistic hordes devouring the thoughts of another. Have to define that which is indefinable. Bet they couldn't put pen to paper if they had to ...

His foot slopped through the remains of a jellyfish, splattering the ends of his neatly tailored trousers. *That's a tenner onto the laundry bill right there. Their problem, not mine. God, that felt like stepping into a dead brain. Slursghhhsss. Suppose it was.*

"Am I walking into eternity along Sandymount Strand?"

No, just into the North Wall if I don't open my eyes soon. Damn, be a bitch to be blind. Feel your way, man. Careful, careful.

"Open your eyes now."

I will and thank God for that. Whoah, the light. Floods in like a breath while drowning. Without it, darkness. Too late then. Like that poor bugger fell off the Cliffs of Moher. Must have felt like flying then THWACK, the lights go out. Not a bad way to go, I suppose. The roar of the waves sucking you into the dark. Scared of the edges myself. Too tempting to try. Can see it all now, Bláithín wailing up a storm – "But why, WHY? He seemed so happy." — Would never come up with the truth. "Just to see what it felt like." Still, I like tripping around here too much for that lark.

The crowd followed at a distance, Julian filling Kinch's silence with words.

"The dog's bark ran towards him."

Here he comes. Hope he knows what he's doing. Afraid of the buggers since O" Malley's dog – practically savaged me! Good boy, good boy – no … not the trouser leg: shit! Whose bloody dog is this anyway? Probably Lacey's – clueless, like him. Grin and bear it. The Cockle pickers, a long time since I saw that. Ghosts from the past. No one could be bothered anymore. The smell of my childhood. Mother used to love them, or was it periwinkles? The blinking eye…small souls of the sea. God, they could scream for something so small! A pot of death – found that hard to take. She heard nothing. Odd that. Just craved the taste of salt. Loved to suck it out of their tiny, limp bodies. The smell of memory: that's what it is! Hmmm! Alone now.

"His lips lipped and mouthed fleshless lip of air: mouth to her womb."

Now there's a thought. Me inside her, growing. Safe. Rest of our lives trying to get back in. Explains it really, the endless search for pussy, especially hers, my Polish flower. You're like her. Aren't you? Mother. How strange we humans are. Mother coveter – Mother fucker. Hah, that's what I am. A slave to the void. Oh well, brings me pleasure all the same, filling the gap! God, I wish she would touch me now. Later, I'll see her later. He's out for the day so no danger. Time for the letter. Might as well take out Lacey's. Give it a bash. Sure, it's a pile of dung! Foot and mouth disease is what the man has, that's for sure. Need to scratch myself down there. Blast, they're all watching. Rub against the rock. Aaahhhh, better now.

"Touch me. Soft eyes. Soft soft soft hand. I am lonely here."

I wonder, am I? – without mother. That's where it begins – with her - safe. Closer to where it ends now. Closer to her anyway. Lie down, down on the sea-washed rocks. It will seep away into the sand, the sadness. Think of something else. Ah Yes! Imagine my flower, caressing your thighs, moving her gentle skin around the hump and flow of it all, the hard grasp and pull. Oh God, they're watching. Stop, stop! Those thoughts are moving up into the cold air. Quick, jump up, move briskly, oh shit! Think of him, that bastard, Reidy. That'll bring it back to earth. Good, good, that's it, keep moving. Oh slowly now – slowly, slow … oooooooo.

"In long lassoes from the cock lake, the water flowed full."

You've got to be kidding me – now I have to whip it out for all to see! Jaysus, there's method acting and then there's bloody mortification. Hope I drank enough. Remember, turn your back to them. No need for the shock factor. Probably think I'm fakin. No bloody fear after a river of tea. Right, that's it. Aaaahhhh!!

"In cups of rocks it slops: flop, slop, slap ..."

Slip, slup, slep, indeed it does. There go the trousers again. Needed that all the same. Jesus, I hope that gorgeous black woman couldn't see. Mightn't measure up. The Irish may be the blacks of Europe, but not sure we'd compare. Wonder why she's here. Must be tough. God, I can't believe they're following me around like sheep! Guinness is still droning on. I could do with one – a pint o plain, yer only man, ha. Here we go, the final act of indignity: stick the finger right up there. It's not every day you get to pick your nose on cue. A good wipe now, bloody thing still dangling. The edge of the rock. My God, this is mad. Jimmy boy, you have a lot to answer for. Anyway, that's it. Out of here.

CHAPTER 10

OMAR

- Hades -

11:00 AM

OMAR SAT IN THE LAST CARRIAGE with two other journalists, Dick Cowen and Mark Jameson. Monsignor Reidy sat beside them in flowing vestments. As the carriage tripped its way slowly past Dermot O'Hurley Avenue, he spotted that lad, Kinch, dressed up in the Dedalus garb. *Meant to interview him later, must give him a buzz.*

The Monsignor shifted nervously in his seat and sank backwards out of the light. Jameson leant out the window with his camera.

"Dedalus ... gotta catch that," he muttered, snap, snap, snap. "Should be a good one."

"Wasn't that lad's mother your housekeeper, Monsignor?" Cowen tapped the notepad in his lap.

"Mary, yes ... grand woman, lovely woman, God Rest her."

Omar noticed an odd nervousness in the demeanour of this otherwise ebullient man. *The pope's footman. Looks like Shakespeare. Odd that.*

Cowen leant forward. "Saw your letter in the paper today, Monsignor. Glad to see you're supporting the big man on this Limbo thing."

"Well, son, if we can't admit when we're wrong, what hope is there, eh?" Reidy adjusted the flow of his cassock.

"What's that?" asked Omar.

"Haven't you heard Wilde? The pope's abolished Limbo, the place where unbaptised babies were damned to float into eternity." Cowen smiled mischievously. "I guess eternity is finite after all. What a bloody relief!"

"Nasty business, that Limbo. Scared the hell out of me as a child. Never seemed right now, did it?" said Jameson.

The Monsignor looked irritated. "What's done is done. We can forget about all that now. Get on with the dirty business of living."

Jameson pointed his camera towards the window and spoke out of the corner of his mouth. "Good man, that John Paul. A bit slow off the mark sometimes but gets there in the end, I suppose."

Omar strained to see what he was shooting. A group of children were jumping off the walls of the bridge into the river. *The Dodder's looking a little murky these days. Kids must be mad. Catch something dodgy from that they will.*

"Yes, but he hasn't exactly apologised for all that child abuse business in Ferns. Sure, they all protected that bastard. Monsignor, you must admit that." Cowen wasn't going to let him off the hook.

"We did what was right in the end, Dick. That's all that counts. Even the pope himself could do with some forgiveness." The edge of his voice had curdled into something uncomfortable.

Omar felt he should dissolve the building tension. "Sure, that's all past us now, Cowen. No point in harbouring grudges."

Cowen's eyes narrowed. "Wilde, aren't you a Mecca man? Hardly in the position to comment."

Omar felt himself stiffen.

Cowen winked broadly at Reidy. "Sure, myself and the Monsignor here have an understanding. He knows I like to stretch his limits."

The Monsignor smiled back. "You're a terrible man Dick."

They laughed, forming a circle of understanding in which Omar was clearly unwelcome. He had always felt awkward around Cowen. In the office, the spiky man had made it clear that he didn't like Omar. He had a sneaking suspicion that if his name had been Seán or Oisín, Cowen would have treated him with substantially more respect.

"Never been to Mecca in my life, Dick." Omar forced a smile.

Jameson, ever the peacemaker, tried to change the subject. "So, Monsignor, you've been demoted to a lowly priest, I see."

Nice Fella Jameson, no harm in him.

"Indeed, indeed. Does it suit me, the old garb?" He stroked the length of his long, white cassock. "I'm not much of an actor. Thank God Joyce didn't give the priest any lines. I just need to look the part, and that I can do."

Cowen spoke up. "You've got to hand it to the man. He has us all running around acting the Mick one hundred years after he put pen to paper. Quite a legacy from a man who spent half his life in another country bitching about how awful this one was."

Omar sat on the edge of the conversation. His three companions continued to natter intimately. The carriage continued to trip its way slowly over the Grand Canal Bridge. The horses' hooves pounded the tarmac: clip, clop, clackity-clack. *Syncopated symphony. Soothing. Like her practising in the parlour. She'll be practising later. Better keep away.*

He could see the old gasworks building in the distance. A flurry of cranes littered the blue sky. Omar imagined the city to be a growing insect trapped inside its cocoon, its limbs stretching and changing shape daily. He had a horrible feeling this evolving creature might drown in its own juices before it had a chance to blossom into something beautiful.

"There's Matt Phelan, richest man in Dublin." Jameson pointed at the tall, well-built figure. He sauntered along the footpath as though he owned the world.

"Is it? Ah yes." The Monsignor tipped his cap towards the man, who responded in kind. "Talented man. That show of his, *Celtic Waters*, put this country on the map, it did. Impressive stuff."

Omar squirmed. Everyone thought that Flora had a thing with Phelan. He wasn't sure himself. Either way, *the man's an arrogant prick. Do I really want to know?*

"Wasn't your wife in that show, Wilde? Quite a player she is." Cowen arched his eyebrow and tapped his pen vigorously.

"Ehm, yes, travelled all over with it. It was great. She's travelling next month, to Belfast, with the Three Tenors."

"Indeed," said Cowen, a glint in his eye.

Omar nodded one too many times and turned towards the window. *Nosy buggers. No one knows, no one really knows.* He thought of her, the look of concentration as she plucked the strings with her index finger, the sweep of her bow. *Two strings to it but no more than two, surely?*

As they passed the walls near Trinity, he noticed the hoardings, overflowing with upcoming events. A man was plastering a poster for *Low,* playing in Christ Church Cathedral that evening. The cortege turned into D'Olier Street and picked up speed as it approached the bridge. Omar eyed the billboard men lined up across the bridge: *THE TRAVELLER.*

Haven't read that one yet. Must have a look. Can't see their faces. Like ghosts amongst us.

"There's the Nigerians, making a few extra bob on the side. Clever lot, that lot." Cowen was clearly looking for a response.

Jameson squinted at the window. "Look Arab to me. At least some of them."

"We have two Nigerian priests in the Pro Cathedral – Father Ogunbusola and Father Njoo. Good men," responded Reidy. "Don't know what we'd do without them these days."

"Low on the native enlistments, are we, Monsignor? No one left to convert."

"No, Dick, there's always someone." Reidy's smile lifted the corner of his thin mouth.

"Parnell Street is looking like downtown Lagos these days, so I'm sure you must be cleaning up there."

"The African people are devout people. Good, simple, God-fearing people. We've lost our simplicity in the middle of all this madness – not necessarily a good thing, Dick, even for a cynic like yourself." Reidy clutched his cap as the carriage hit a bump.

Omar felt it was time to enter the conversation. "Can I ask you, Dick? Have you ever written anything positive about our immigrants? I saw that article you wrote about the ritual sacrificing of animals by an African family in Finglas. It's just hatemongering. It doesn't help with the overall picture."

"Listen, Wilde, stick with the arts features." Cowen leant forward and waved his pencil in Omar's face. "Real news is about exposing all aspects of society, even the nasty ones – and that was nasty, man."

"Gentlemen, gentlemen, enough of that. Let's agree to differ." The Monsignor raised his voice.

Omar wished he could hop out of the carriage and leave the bad air behind him. They turned left, past the Ambassador. The shutter of Jameson's camera clicked rapidly. He snapped a shot of a group, dressed in Victorian mourning garb. They doffed their hats at the passing carriages.

"They really get into it, some of these literary heads. Looks great but I have to admit, I've never read *Ulysses*. What about you guys?" asked Jameson.

"Me neither," added Cowen. "You two?" He nodded at Omar and the Monsignor.

"No, afraid not," replied Omar.

They all turned towards the Monsignor.

He smiled. "I'll leave it up to you fellas to decide whether a Monsignor has read the most scandalous Irish book of all time!"

"You have, haven't you? Need to know the enemy, after all," replied Cowen.

The Monsignor narrowed his eyes. "As a matter of interest, how many of you good men have read the Bible cover to cover?"

Cowen laughed. Jameson looked at Omar blankly.

"Well, you can't expect the Arab to have read it, surely." Cowen gestured towards Omar.

"Actually, I have. Maybe not cover to cover but enough to know what it's all about. And you, Cowen, I suppose you're an expert on the Qur'an?" Omar wasn't going to let him get away with any more of his snide comments. Cowen stopped tapping his pen, sat back in his seat, and grunted without saying anything.

"Touché." Jameson threw Omar a look of acknowledgement.

The carriage stopped suddenly. They were right outside the Black Church on the Western Way. A real funeral was jamming up the street. Three Gardaí on horseback attempted to unravel the intertwining of the two funeral corteges, one fake and one real.

Jameson jumped up to the window. "It's the real thing blocking the way. Isn't that mad?" Omar peered out at the shiny black hearse. He could see a young woman walk slowly behind the hearse. She was dressed in black and clutched the hand of a little boy. A tall man with a shaved head wrapped his long arm around her. She stared blankly at the tiny white coffin. It sat uneasily in the wide back space of the hearse. Omar felt a wave of nausea wash through him. *Newborn, so tiny.* He recognised this scene. *Ruairí.* The name repeated in his brain like a sickening mantra.

The Monsignor made the sign of the cross and mumbled a prayer of some kind. Cowen sat quietly in the corner. Jameson's camera shutter sounded like a demented hummingbird moth. Their horse-drawn carriage made its way slowly through the crowd.

"Shame when a child goes before the parent. Against the order of things," commented the Monsignor.

How would he know?

"Indeed." Jameson glanced at Omar.

"Thank God the poor little thing wasn't born last week," Cowen muttered out of the corner of his mouth, "or it would be floating around in Limbo as we speak. Probably unmarried, those two."

All three turned to look at Cowen without saying a word.

"What? I'm simply speaking the God's-honest truth," he continued defensively.

"There's a time for humour, and a time for respect, and you are sorely in need of a lesson in the latter, Dick," said the Monsignor.

Cowen sank back into his seat and began to scribble on his notepad like an idle schoolboy.

Everyone lapsed into silence.

The carriage passed a hairdresser's shop called Rita's, packed with mid-morning perm washes. Next door, at the Allegro chipper, a gang of young boys wrestled playfully. A postman emptied the morning mail into a large brown sack.

They continued down Phibsborough Road towards Dalymount Park. Two large, muscular men rolled metal barrels full of porter from the Guinness lorry to the door of McGowan's. The grey-haired barman stood outside the door – sleeves rolled above his elbows. He directed the day's feed of porter through the door, a cigarette dangling from his mouth.

Jameson jumped up to the window to point his camera at a commotion on the Cross Guns Bridge. Several Garda cars had cordoned off an area along the canal. A body bag lay on the edge of the bank. A crowd of people lined the bridge, staring at the water below.

"The Grim Reaper is having a busy day today," said Cowen. "Bet it's a jumper."

"Sure, it's hardly high enough for that," said Jameson. "More common to jump in front of the Dart these days if you want to do yourself in."

"Gruesome thoughts, boys. Never a good thing to take your own life. Best not to talk about it," said the Monsignor, looking in the other direction.

"By the way, Monsignor, do they still go straight to hell, or has the pope done away with that too?" Cowen winked at Jameson.

"Very funny, Dick. Sins are sins. That'll never change, and I'd say you've got a fair few notched up, so watch that smart talk," said Reidy, with a quick smile.

Omar stared at the nails on his hand. *Could do with a clean. Wish they'd give it a rest.*

"It's a cowardly thing all the same," said Cowen.

Omar stared at him coldly. *What would you know about courage? Sometimes it's too much, that's all.* His father's face flashed through his brain. *He didn't mean it. Leaving me that way. His eyes, sunken and empty, heartbroken and drowning. What do you know of that?*

"It's just a sad thing, Cowen." Jameson shot Omar a look of sympathy. "We all have our own private hells to live with. It's just harder for some than others."

He knows. Kind man. All over the newspapers after all. My mother's absconding. My father's descent. Not that Cowen would notice. Cold Fish.

"We shouldn't speak ill of the dead, one way or the other," said the Monsignor.

Omar sank deep into thought. The sound of his mother's voice singing "The Irish Lullaby" floated through his mind. They passed under the shade of the trees on Prospect Road. The old Victorian sash windows revealed faces: smiling, creviced, curious, indifferent. Dublin's eyes peered out as the carriage moved slowly through the leafy street.

The others continued to chatter.

Omar dreamed. His thoughts flew above the roofs of the fine Victorian houses. Like a bird caught on a drift of air, he dipped and dived through the alleys and lanes, past women at washing lines, children in playgrounds, packed offices. Swirled through the scent of the sea, followed the line of the river as it widened, past the Docklands, the Point Theatre, over the queue of people who poured onto the Ulysses ferry, and out into the breadth of the bay. Dublin Bay, wide and bright and wild.

Chapter 11

KINCH

11:00 PM

THE FUNERAL CORTEGE PASSED and turned left into Bridge Street. Kinch eyed his watch. *Right on cue.* The Gardaí had barricaded off the route. A line of horse-drawn Victorian carriages trotted past solemnly. The black of the carriages gleamed like rain-soaked coal. Although he admired the austere beauty of such a display, Kinch felt a shiver run down his spine. It was as though Death himself were coming to visit the people of Dublin – to populate the empty casket with a city's people. They lined the roadway, excited tourists popping off cameras, while curious locals looked on. He thought of his mother, lying quietly in her grave, deep in the bowels of the earth. A claustrophobic dread invaded his senses.

Where is your God now as you rot in the bowels of the earth? She came to him in a dream the night before, begging him to believe, her ghastly figure floating in the fogs of Purgatory. He woke soaked in the sweat of guilt. *Why was your belief not enough, mother? Why did you need mine? I cannot give what I don't have.*

The horse hooves clipped past. A group of foreign students waved at the lead carriage as though it were a royal parade.

A small, plump girl in front of him jumped around with excitement. "Hey guys, isn't that cart just too much!" Her smile stretched across her face unnaturally, elongated by the train-track braces that filled her mouth like some weird inquisitional torture instrument.

Thank God I come from a nation where wonky teeth are a sign of character and a life well-lived.

The last carriage passed by. He recognised its occupants instantly.

There's the Moor. Nice bloke. Don't have anything against him. Just has no balls, poor bugger. Oh my God, HE's there too! I feel sick inside, all holier than thou in that floaty garb of his. Must be doing the priest's part. How ironic!

"Hey, dude, can I have a photo with you? You look so hot in your costume." The girl with the train tracks grabbed his arm. He winced as the group of giggling college girls crowded around him.

"Fromage," said the girl.

He extricated himself and wished them well, not meaning a word of it. When they'd gone, he stuck on his headphones. He knew it was a bit odd to see Stephen Dedalus wandering around like that, but he had them as well hidden under his hat as he could manage, and he needed a soundtrack to his life, to guide him through his moods. U2's "11 O" Clock Tick Tock" blasted into his brain. *Perfect.*

The crowds collected behind the funeral cortege, and he followed them down Pearse Street. They turned into D'Olier Street and headed for the bridge. Ahead of the cortege, he could see a row of sandwich men standing on O'Connell Bridge in perfect formation. Each wore a placard with a single letter; together they spelled out THE TRAVELLER.

Kinch had applied for a job with this funky new travel publication but got no reply. Now he fantasised about being sent to some far-flung destination and actually being paid for it. He was keeping an eye on the cheapest Ryanair flights and hoped he could come up with something original.

The sandwich men stretched across half the bridge. They looked foreign. *Probably paid a pittance.* Behind them the sun caught the point of the Spire, and light shot in all directions into the sky.

He passed the enormous stone statue of Daniel O'Connell. The "Great Liberator" towered above him, covered in a sea of bird shit. He felt oddly depressed as he turned into Abbey Street to get away from the crowd. Just ahead of him were the *Independent* offices.

Bit early for the cheque.

He retraced his steps and made his way to the front of the luminous Anne Summers shop. Littered with multi-coloured dildos, flavoured condoms, and lingerie that left nothing to the imagination, it contributed perfectly to the trashy cheap and cheerful development of Ireland's number one boulevard. It wasn't long ago that the mere mention of the word "dildo" would've sent the population skulking into a corner with shame. *Got over that one quickly. Howya Missus. It's far from that crotchless bodysuit you were raised.*

He nodded at a middle-aged woman with greying roots. She was trying to chat with him, so he paused his iPod.

"I'm lookin for somethin to keep the hubby happy, luv. It's his sixtieth. What do you reckon?" She held up the aforesaid item with a dirty grin.

"Yeah, I'm sure he'll love it." *But maybe not with you inside it!*

"Better than Viagra any day, wha?" She cackled loudly and poked Kinch in the ribs.

"God yeah, any day."

Her eyes widened suggestively. "Get you goin would it, young fella?"

Jaysus! If my girlfriend was in it, yeah, definitely.

"Lucky girl, to have a fine young man comin in here to buy her somethin hot an sexy."

Feelin my leg, oh bollox.

"My aul fella's still got it in him, though. Don't think cos we've one foot in the grave that we're not still mad at it, let me tell ya. Still, everyone needs a little spicin up, don't they, luv?"

"Sure, yeah. Sorry, in a rush, gotta go." He sped to the back of the shop behind the X-rated items. *Christ, the aul ones are gone mad nowadays.*

He peeked around a vibrator stand and could see that the woman was cashing up her purchase. A dazzling array of male members hung in front of him. *Holy shit, look at the size of that one.* He was definitely "above average," but still felt inadequate faced with this choice.

"Not switching to the other side on me are you, man? We're a dying breed, us heteros."

"Hanan! Jesus, you frightened me. What the fuck are you doing in this salubrious establishment?" He'd liked Hanan from the first minute he'd met him at Sarah's party four months before. He was an easy-going guy, no bullshit about him.

"It's Sarah's birthday next week, so I thought I might surprise her with a hot little number. Bit of a pressie to myself, I suppose." He held up a red silk bra and thong with matching suspenders. There were little black roses edging the top of the bra and panties.

"That should do the trick. Up to the same thing myself." A wave of panic hit him like a cold shower when he realised how this would be misinterpreted.

"But I thought you broke up with her this morning. In a right state she was. I saw her about an hour ago. Second thoughts or what?"

"No, I mean, yeah, that's right. We broke up, but I thought I would get her something to make her feel a bit better." *Shit, scrambling, bound to smell it.*

"Bit weird. She might get the wrong idea. Sexy lingerie doesn't usually mean "I'm breaking up with you."

"Yeah, I suppose you're right. I'm no good at this breaking up stuff." *Cringe, I look like an eejit!*

"Think I should give you a few lessons? Although, come to think of it, I'm usually on the receiving end." He slapped Kinch on the back amicably. "Listen, fancy a quick scoop?"

Shit, that was a close one. Gotta watch what I say. She'd kill me. "Yeah sure, why not? Still have thirty minutes to kill before I head in to get my cheque in the *Indo*. Like everyone else, they owe me a month's worth."

"Bit strapped myself, but always a bob or two for a pint, you know."

"Priorities, Hanan, priorities. I know."

"Let's head round to The Flowing Tide for one."

A sea of people floated up and down O'Connell Street.

Hanan sighed heavily. "Christ, they're never going to be finished with those bloody road-works. I don't know what this street looks like without a building site."

"It's called regeneration, I believe. More like mass destruction and wanking bollox to me."

They laughed as they turned into Abbey Street and walked towards the National Theatre.

"Ever been to the Abbey, Hanan?"

"Yeah, went to see *Othello* last year. My Dad loves that play because Othello's an Arab. It's fecking stupid. He latches onto anything which promotes 'our' culture. Normally gives me a pain up my hole, but I have to say it was brilliant, man."

"I wouldn't have taken you for a Shakespeare lover."

"Hey, us Arabs are good for more than blowing up buildings you know."

Kinch laughed nervously. "I was thinking of the fact that you don't often see an economist with a copy of Shakespeare in their clutches."

"Right." Hanan gave him the sceptical eye and walked ahead into The Flowing Tide. "To be honest, I'm a bit worried about my little brother, Khaled." He gestured to the balding barman. "Two pints please."

"Why so, man?"

"I've caught him reading all kinds of subversive shit on the Net. About Al Qaeda and Bin Laden. It's not that I don't think he should be curious, but he's such a zealot about the whole thing." Hanan creased his brow and lowered his voice. "I wouldn't say this to just anyone, man. I trust you. It's hard for a Muslim to even mention this kind of stuff without being stuck in the fecking stereotypical box that everyone loves to see us in. I fecking hate it!"

"It must be really shit. Jesus Christ, it's not so long ago that there were signs up in pubs across the water saying 'No Blacks, No Irish, No Dogs.' Memory's short, man. You guys have taken over the hotspot – much to the delight of the boys up North."

"Yeah, it's a double whammy for me cos I'm Irish as well. Can't fuckin win!"

"Yer pints lads." The portly barman delivered the pints while making the sign of the cross over them with great aplomb. "Hope they're creamy enough for ye now, lads. Enjoy."

Kinch was always amused by the reverence that surrounded the pouring of a pint of Guinness. It was a rite of passage for the uninitiated into the secret labyrinth of the Irish mind. The fact that it did not "travel well" was a proud confirmation of the importance of its origins.

"About your brother, he's probably just going through a lot of adolescent angst and all that shite. Maybe you should have a chat with him," Kinch suggested.

"I've tried, honest. He just tells me to fuck off back to my Irish friends. Stupid fecker thinks he's living in the depths of Lebanon." He looked frustrated, anxious, seeking answers.

"Do you want me to suss him out? I think he likes me since I let him share that joint last week."

"You did fecking what?"

"Hey, I saved your ass. You were sucking face big-time with Sarah in your room, blasting music. I was just chilling out in the living room thanking God I couldn't hear a thing. It woke him up. It was all I could think of to stop him going in and seeing you *in flagrante.*"

"Feck, really? Sorry. I mean, thanks. I think. Anyway, yeah, yeah. Listen, can you come round later? I can tell him you're interested in hearing that weird electronic music he's been fucking around with."

Kinch grimaced. "You're jokin. I'd rather shite nails than listen to that stuff."

"Ah go on. He knows you're into music, so he might swallow it."

"Jesus. All right then. Not sure about today but if there's any time I'll text you, ok?"

"Great, yeah great."

They lapsed into a comfortable silence, sipping their pints slowly.

CHAPTER 12

BLÁITHÍN

12:00 PM

BLÁITHÍN ARRIVED AT LONG LANE as the midday bells chimed from St. Patrick's Cathedral. She tied her black bicycle to a lamppost and took her violin case out of the wicker basket. As she walked through the iron gate into the tiny front garden, the door opened. Flora stood, illuminated by the sunlight. There was something different about her today – her lustrous hair, the dress clinging to her rump like the skin of a fruit, the red of her lipstick – a distinct uncontainable beauty. *Hope I look half as good as she does at her age.*

"Hi Bláith, are you ok?" Flora looked concerned. "You're looking great in that gear."

"I feel like shit. Can you believe that he dumped me? Today of all days."

Flora closed the door behind them and ushered Bláithín into the living room. It was full of life's bric-a-brac arranged comfortably around a wrought-iron fireplace. Cosy.

"I know, it's not fair, but did you have any sense that it was coming?"

"Honestly, no. I said something I probably shouldn't have."

"How do you mean?"

Bláithín shrugged her shoulders. "We were out on Howth Head at the weekend. You know how it is ... so beautiful and romantic with the gulls soaring and the cliffs. I kind of got carried away ... told him I love him." The tears began to build behind her eyes. "I couldn't help it. I know, I'm an eejit!"

"I see." Flora put her arms around Bláithín's shoulders. "Men are such cowards."

Bláithín let the emotion flow through her. Hoped this experienced woman would comfort her in a way that her own mother was incapable of doing.

Flora glanced at the photo of a sleeping newborn framed in silver on her bookshelf. "When I lost the child, Omar just disappeared inside himself. Shut tighter than a Baltic Sea barnacle. It's their way."

Bláithín started. "You lost a child?"

Flora continued to gaze at the photograph and nodded silently.

Bláithín's voice dropped to a whisper. "Who's that? It's not ...?"

Flora reached for a box of tissues on the coffee table beside her. "We took it in the hour after he was born. He was gone but still there – somehow."

A chill ran through Bláithín. "I see."

"He's always here." She touched her chest. "So, you get on with it."

"I can't imagine."

Flora offered Bláithín the tissues. "Omar just pretends. I pretend along with him. It gets us through the day."

Bláithín took a step towards Flora. "I feel so stupid for burdening you with my troubles."

"It's ok." Flora stepped away and forced the edge of a smile.

Bláithín sat on the red couch beside the fireplace. "We don't have to talk about it. It seems ..."

Flora sat on the couch beside her and continued as though nothing had changed. "Maybe you're better off without him. He was never reliable – was he?"

Bláithín nodded. She felt something had changed. A small indiscernible flicker, a ghostly note. "I don't know. I know he's a little lost, but I guess that's part of the reason I like him so much."

"Lost little boys are dangerous. You never know what they're thinking or what they're up to." Flora looked towards the photograph.

Bláithín detected something in Flora's voice. "What do you mean? Do you know something I don't?" A piece of stray knowledge perhaps? A clue to a fact that eluded her?

"Of course not, no. I just mean that Kinch is always a little distant. Isn't he? You can't be sure, that's all." Flora got up from the couch and walked around the corner into the kitchen. "Can I make you a tea, hun? Make you feel a little better."

"Mmmm. Yes, please."

She looked around the room, while Flora pottered about in the kitchen. Many of Flora's paintings hung on the walls. Female forms in sketches and outlines, fragmented creatures that moved like glistening shadows under the skin of the ocean. Flora's violin sat beside a music stand in the corner. Bláithín felt safe here. The old walls were like whispering ghosts, and for some reason, that comforted her. Now it contained Flora; her bright, feminine force was everywhere. There was no hint of Omar in this space. It was almost as if she lived alone.

"Sugar and milk?" The soft voice drifted around the corner.

"Just milk, thanks."

"I recognise the woman in the reproduction you have hanging behind your violin stand. Who is she again?" Bláithín struggled to place the face.

"It's Lady Lavery."

"Right, that's it. There was a guy painting her on the footpath by the Molly Malone statue today. Never noticed you had her on your wall before."

"I just put it up this week." Flora came out from the kitchen and placed two mugs of tea on the wooden coffee table.

"Really. Coincidence that. I like her face."

"Me too. There's something in her eyes I recognise." Flora poured some milk into the mugs of tea. "Can't quite put my finger on it."

Bláithín moved closer to the painting. "She looks like you."

"Do you think so? Funny, I never saw that." Flora sipped the tea, glanced at herself in the mirror, and then at the painting. "Maybe so."

Bláithín fiddled with a copy of *Marie Claire* that was sitting on the table in front of her. "Maybe I should read my horoscope to see what disaster's coming next."

"I don't believe in all that rubbish. No one can predict what's coming next. Just have to do the best we can right now."

"Jesus, that's optimistic," said Bláithín. "I suppose there's no point in asking if you think I can get him back then?"

Flora smiled. "I don't mean to be so negative. Maybe ... I think it's best to be cool about it all. Stand back ... don't crowd him out. You never know.

Men hate to be pressured."

Bláithín knew that Flora was no fool when it came to men. She could see how their eyes followed her everywhere she went. "I'm not so good at playing the game, unfortunately."

"Who is?" replied Flora. "Have you spoken to your mother about it?"

"You know what she's like. She'll be delighted ... hated him in the first place ... thought he was a waster because he wasn't some big investment banker or techy millionaire whom she could brag about."

"Is she really that bad?" asked Flora, sipping her tea.

"Trust me. My friends call her Godzilla for a reason."

Flora looked at her watch, put her cup on the table, and moved towards the corner of the room.

"Maybe we should start the lesson, hun? I'm afraid I'm a bit pressed for time today." She picked up her violin case, unzipped it, and placed the shining instrument on her shoulder.

"Yeah, ok. I'll probably suck, I'm in such crap form." Bláithín reached for her violin.

"Just put your emotion into the playing. It can work wonders. Trust me."

Bláithín moved to hug Flora. "You're a good listener and a good friend."

The violin dropped to Flora's side as she offered a limp-armed hug. "Let's get started."

Bláithín thought she sensed irritation in her voice. *I must be imagining it. Don't know what I feel anymore.* She picked up her instrument and placed it gently in the crook of her neck. Flora adjusted the music sheet on the stand in front of her.

"The Lark Ascending" by Vaughan Williams. Are you ready?"

"Ready."

The bow moved slowly along the length of the strings; her delicate wrist formed a soft, fluid shape in the air. The wisp of sound seeped into the room like a sleeping child's breath. Flora closed her eyes, and Bláithín stared at the page with a look of intense concentration. A wave of calm washed over her. *I will find him again – he will love me.* She wove her thoughts into the strings of her instrument and allowed the music to soothe away her worry.

CHAPTER 13

OMAR / KINCH

- Aeolus -

12:00 PM

"WELL NOW, AS FAKE FUNERALS GO, I'd say that went well. What do you boys reckon?" Monsignor Reidy lifted his cassock and stepped out of the taxi in front of the *Independent* offices.

"Even better than the real thing, Monsignor." Jameson held the door open for Cowen and Omar. "Come on, Cowen, get your arse in gear."

"I will follow," sang Cowen, stepping out of the car and falling about laughing with Jameson much to the bewilderment of the Monsignor and the embarrassment of Omar.

"Right, lads. When ye've finished yer messing, I'm off to the bauld editor to talk about a piece I submitted this week." Reidy turned and disappeared up the stairs.

"Is it our jobs you're after, Monsignor?" shouted Cowen up the stairs while taking out a fag and lighting it. "Rather have mine than his, I tell you. We journalists may rank just above lawyers on the lying-bastard's scale, but priests, they're in a league of their own."

Jameson handed him a light. "Reidy's not a bad sort, Dick."

"If you like your rats clean and in coat-tails, I suppose not." Cowen took a long drag.

Omar had had quite enough of this conversation and turned to go his own way.

Jameson grabbed him by the arm. "Hold on a minute. There's a good chap. Just need a small favour."

"Yes?" Omar cocked a weary eyebrow.

"I'm up to my eyes today with the Bloomsday special. You mind just dropping this film at the camera shop on Bachelor's Walk, and collecting it after?"

"All right then, Mark. But you owe me one." Omar was sick of being a gofer for all and sundry, but he liked Jameson.

Jameson chucked him his camera. The two boys went inside. Omar raced across O'Connell Street, turning right beside the river.

Pockets of people scurried from the surrounding office buildings, desperate to get their one hour of release from the drone of daily activity. Short-skirted women with ironed hair and men in blue ties and pink shirts chattered madly, hyped up on coffee and adrenaline. He could feel the sweat mat his hair to the side of his head.

Mad heat. No wonder they're out in droves.

He looked across the bridge. Several sandwich men had broken away and were having lunch at the end of the boardwalk. R sat lazily on the edge, seemingly uninterested in the conversation. E listened intently while V gesticulated wildly, clearly dominating the conversation. To his right stood another man wearing E. He poured out tea from a flask. Omar could just make out A and L, who nodded vigorously when V got excited. He wished he could know who these men were, where they came from, how their lives had been reduced to a single letter. Instead, he picked up the camera and began to snap. He zoomed in on their faces. Snap, snap. There was something about this little group: They didn't smile, staring out at the passing parade with detached fascination as though watching a 3D film they could never be a part of. The shutter stopped suddenly, and the roll began to unwind. *Could have something there.*

After Hanan had left, Kinch looked around the walls of The Flowing Tide. The National Theatre's nearest pub was like a museum. Posters and photographs of the famous dead covered the walls: Michael Mac Liammoir, Cyril Cusack, Siobhán McKenna. He wondered whether he could ever reach these walls, earn his place in the collective memory of a people, exist after the last breath had been sucked from his lungs. That was the point, after all – all this artistic endeavour – achieve the impossible. Live on. But what did he know of these people really? Images on paper and celluloid. Voices falling from a cracked recording. These small fragments and shadows created an impression, a distorted reality, a reconstituted "memory." He wondered when he'd stop remembering his mother; when she too would blur into shadow.

He sipped the froth from the bottom of his pint glass and looked at his watch.

Shite, better text Gerry. Can't meet him at The Barge.

He punched out a message on his mobile, pulled on his jacket and hat, and walked out onto the street. As he approached the door of the *Irish Independent*, his phone beeped in his pocket. The message was from Gerry: "In trouble. Can't explain. Need your help. At Pearse Street Garda Station. Can you come please?"

Damn, what's that about? He hit the call button, but it was busy. *Better text.* "Hi, mate, everything ok? Heading into the *Indo* offices. I'll try to call again when I'm out."

He couldn't imagine how even Gerry had ended up in a police station in the space of a couple of hours. *Hope he's ok.*

Abbey Street was a mess. The new Luas tram tracks were being laid at last although Kinch remained sceptical about whether it would make a blind bit of difference in the city that had raised traffic hell to a fine art.

Kinch spotted Hanan's weird brother, Khaled, on the corner of O'Connell Street, talking with a sandwich man wearing a V. Coincidence that. Has that "world is ending" look on his face. What does he want chewing that poor bloke's ear off? V for vexed I'd say.

Pressed for time, he speeded to the *Independent* offices. The day's paper sat in a pile just inside the door. He grabbed a copy.

Government fighting again. What's new? Bloody tribunals never end. What's this? The Columbia Three were freed … Gerry will be happy. He climbed the long stairs to the busy office. *Into the belly of the beast.*

The main office was a buzz of activity. Bertie Macken, the deputy editor, busily tapped on his laptop. His white hair sat wildly above his thin, friendly face.

"Ah, Lynch. Good man. Was worried you wouldn't show."

Newspapermen, insisting on the surname at all times. Muscular barrier to emotion. Guess it helps them to 'lynch' an acquaintance if the story requires it.

"I'll always show up for a few extra bob, Bertie, no fear," replied Kinch.

"Listen, I'm off for a few weeks. Just wanted to give you the schedule for those upcoming theatre and film reviews. You'll be ok for those I assume?" Bertie shuffled through the mound of papers on his desk.

"Grand, no bother. Where you off to?"

"The wife's brother has a place on the Algarve. I'll be hanging out with all the tax-dodgers. Maybe get a few free pints off them." He laughed and continued to push paper around his desk. "Jaysus, I can never find anything when I want it." A pale, red-haired woman sped through the office and dropped a package onto Bertie's already overflowing desk.

"It's the piece about the Bloomsday breakfast. President was there and all. Gay Byrne was shite at the acting," she said laughing.

"Are we talking Gay or Gabriel?" asked Kinch with a pained expression.

"Gay, I'm afraid. I know, I know. What the fuck is the world coming to?"

She sat down at her desk nearby and ripped open a stack of envelopes. A rip ran the length of her brown tights into the back of a filthy white runner. *Lois Lane you're not.*

The large office buzzed with ringing phones, heads in corners tapped madly at laptops, shouted questions from one side of the room to the other.

"Kate, are we running with the illegal migrant piece?"

"Yeah, bottom, left-hand corner."

A sub-editor dashed over to Bertie's desk. "Here's the first-page layout for tomorrow."

"Good man, I'll look it over." Bertie eyed the headlines. "Check it out...'Minister O'Leary nabbed in 50,000-euro bribe for Stillorgan land deal'. Ha ... I always knew he was a dodgy fecker." Bertie hesitated and looked up at Kinch. "Don't you know that pretty daughter of his? What's her name – Roisín?"

Kinch shuffled nervously. "Bláithín."

"Isn't she playing Molly Bloom at some do in the Shelbourne later?" said the deputy editor.

"Yes."

Bertie smirked. "I never saw you so lost for words, Lynch."

"Nothing more to say." Kinch smirked back.

"Fair enough. How're you getting on with all the commotion?" asked Bertie.

"A bit wrecked," Kinch said. "Off to the National Library next. Feel like a minor celeb though. Probably as close as I'll ever get."

"Ah, here's the bloody thing!" Bertie grabbed a piece of paper from under a half-open sandwich in the corner. "Sorry about that." A piece of lettuce had stuck to the corner of the paper, and he wiped it away.

Kinch picked up the schedule with the tips of his fingers and placed it carefully into the black satchel he was carrying.

"Jaysus, you're some knacker, Macken."

"It takes one to know one, Lynch." He winked. "Head over to Eileen in accounts and she'll sort you out, good man." He turned back to his laptop and began to type furiously.

Kinch turned to leave when he remembered the brown envelope in his bag.

"Shite nearly forgot. Bertie, I have a letter from that windbag, Lacey, moaning on about the state of Ireland or some rubbish. Can I leave that with you?" Kinch placed the envelope on top of the pile beside the laptop.

The wiry man continued typing. "Not bloody Lacey again! Well, we're running out of toilet paper. I'm sure I can put it to good use. Good luck today, Lynch."

As he turned to leave, the door at the street side of the main room opened. A mumble of familiar voices emerged.

"Do you hear that Flaherty's at it again? Planning some big extravaganza called ... wait for it ... *Celtic Tiger*. Can you bloody believe it?" Mark Jameson's nostrils flared wildly.

"Well, I enjoyed *Celtic Waters* all the same," interrupted the Monsignor.

Jesus, it's him again. What the fuck? Twice in one day after a life of avoidance. Need to get the hell out of here before he sees me. Bloody cheque. Kinch stepped sideways, into the accountant's office, and hid himself behind the door.

A round-faced woman, with spectacles balanced on the end of her flat nose, eyed him curiously. "Hiding from the law again, are we Kieran?"

"No, sorry, just don't want to cross paths with them," he whispered, pointing to the group assembled outside the deputy editor's office.

"Very mysterious. What've you been up to now?"

"Nothing, Eileen, too complicated to explain. Listen, do you have that cheque for me so I can get the fuck out of here?"

"Sit your arse down there, lad. I have to go upstairs to get the chequebook. God you're a mad one." And she was out the door, throwing her eyes to heaven.

Kinch sat behind the coat rack. The gossiping group didn't spot him through the open glass door, and he cocked an ear to their conversation.

"Was given the knees-up by Phelan. The fool is actually going to help finance the bloody thing," said Cowen in disbelief.

"Fair fucks to the man. He made a bloody fortune on the other one, sure, why wouldn't he?" Farrell turned to the Monsignor for agreement.

"Quite so."

"Right lads. How's this for a description? He gave me a copy of the proposal. '*Celtic Tiger* is a green-tinted hymn to Ireland, with pastoral panoramas and bucolic scenes of winsome lasses,'...Mad!" Jameson clutched his sides with laughter. "Can you bloody believe it?"

Cowen cocked an amused eyebrow. "Only colic lasses left around here."

"Wait for it, there's more ... 'St. Patrick is represented by a group of monks who alternatively pray and dance about while banishing a nest of snake-women from Ireland'." Cowen and Jameson were creased double with the laughing.

"Wha? We should be so lucky!" said Cowen.

"It sounds a tad over the top, doesn't it, lads?" said the Monsignor.

"Over and above and out the other side. I think Flaherty has finally lost it," said Farrell.

Kinch played with his hat in his lap.

"Wait, the best is yet to come. 'He high-kicks his way through British Colonisation, the Famine (now that's tasteful!), and the Easter Rising'."

"Tiocfaidh ár La. Adams and the boys will love it," said Farrell.

Cowen jigged around the room, high-kicking madly, and knocked a tray of papers onto the floor. "Can't you see Pearse dancing his way out of the GPO, proclamation in hand?" Eileen passed through the office and cursed vociferously about the mess that she, no doubt, would have to clean up.

"As we said, banish those snake-women," whispered Cowen.

They all laughed in unison.

Eileen slipped back into her office and handed Kinch the cheque for two hundred and fifty euros. "Here you go, Kieran. Don't put it all on one horse."

"Thanks, Eileen. Might have a spin on Ascot today sure. Any suggestions?"

"I actually heard Jameson talking about Magnier's horse, Damson or something ... yes, Damson."

Kinch eyed the back door for a quick exit. "Mmmm never heard of it. Thinking of backing that other filly, Ulysses, the day that's in it and all."

"Well, sure you'd be mad not to."

Kinch glanced back at the group in the office.

Cowen moved to light a cigarette.

"Outside, Dick. No unlawful activity in this office." Farrell edged the protesting journalist towards the door.

Cowen headed outside muttering under his breath.

Kinch grabbed his hat. *Shite, Cowen will see me now. Never mind.*

"See you, Eileen." He sped down the stairs, tripped on the bottom step, and fell on his hat.

"Mr. Lynch, you're in a bit of a rush." Cowen flicked a match off the side of the wall.

"Yeah, Dick, a lot to do today, man."

"Is that right? Not trying to avoid anyone, are you?"

A double-decker bus passed by spitting fumes and noise into the air. Kinch strained to hear.

"Don't know what you mean. Listen, do you have a fag there? I could do with one." Kinch cocked a head towards the stairway, making sure he could hear whether anyone was coming.

"Yeah, sure." Cowen tapped the side of the box, and a cigarette popped out.

"Thanks, man."

"No problem." Cowen turned and disappeared up the stairs.

Kinch picked up the old Trilby and punched it back into shape. *Thank*

God these were made to last. Right, out of here. Gotta call Gerry!

The Oval Pub was packed for lunch. Omar saw the Monsignor and Cowen disappear inside.

An unlikely pair. The Pious Papist and the Cocky Kerryman. Off for a scoop. Could do with one myself.

A truck was parked outside the main entrance to the *Independent.* Two burly, tattooed men effortlessly threw boxes into the back while two others raced up and down the stairs, depositing the afternoon edition load on the path beside them. A skin-headed man bashed into Omar on the stairway.

"Sorry, head. In a bit of a rush."

The old wooden stairway rattled underneath the man's heavy boots.

Rush, run, rattle, never ends. Omar entered the office. The editor and deputy editor, bent over the day's broadsheet, were deep in conversation.

"President Putin attends the meeting of the Shanghai Cooperation Organisation (SCO) on anti-terrorism efforts." Bertie pointed at the headline. "Russia and anti-terrorism, Bush will be pleased ... We should stick that headline above this one."

Willy Farrell looked over his shoulder. ""Continuation of the National Emergency with Respect to the Risk of Nuclear Proliferation Created by the accumulation of weapon-usable fissile material in the territory of the Russian Federation"." Farrell laughed. "Are you trying to stir up trouble, Macken? I thought the Global Giants were getting on these days."

"Once a cannibal, always a cannibal, boss."

Farrell grinned. "Fair enough. Stir that pot."

The editor continued perusing the daily headlines. "Did ye hear that one lads? Muslims applying for citizenship are being told they can have only one wife. Poor bastards! How will they ever survive?"

"I'm still trying to get rid of mine." Bertie Macken lifted his head from the laptop. "Maybe we can make a collection. Spare wives to be handed over to the National Muslim Congress by Irish charitable organisation."

"Shower of misogynist wankers," Kate piped up from the far corner of the room.

"Is that us or them, Kate?" asked Farrell.

"Definitely you lot!" She stood up, sucked her thumb, and flicked it in the direction of the three laughing men.

"Hear that, Omar? You're only allowed one wife now. Will Flora be enough for you?"

Bertie cocked an eye at the other two.

"She'd be enough for me." Farrell spoke out of the corner of his mouth.

Omar decided not to take the bait. "Listen, Will, can I have a word about that piece I was supposed to give you?"

"What piece?" asked Farrell. "Bertie, we just heard the Columbia Three are being put on trial for training the Farc. Need to get that on the front page for the late edition. Tim'll drop it over to you in an hour." Farrell turned to go back inside his office.

"Willy, the feature piece you asked me for this morning. I have an idea but ..."

"Damn it, Wilde, what are you talking about? I gave that piece to Cowen. Never heard back from you, man. Gotta be quick off the mark. Kate, make sure to drop the Ascot results on my desk as soon as they come in. Any tips anyone?"

"Magnier's horse is hot for the main race," replied Kate. "Do you want me to a put a few quid on for you, boss, when I'm over in Power's?"

"What do you mean you gave it to Cowen?" interrupted Omar.

"Stick on twenty quid for me, Kate."

"Are you listening to me?" said Omar.

The editor moved to shut the door.

"Jesus, Wilde, give it a rest. I'm up to my eyes. I don't have time for this. Just get those reviews over to Bertie by the end of the day."

"But what about my contract? You said ..."

"I say lots of things, Wilde. Another time." He shut the door in Omar's face.

Omar could feel the humiliation creep up the back of his neck. *Bastard! I'm running to stand still in this place. Why do I bother?* He looked around the office, and everyone seemed engrossed in their tasks, perhaps a little too engrossed. He crawled back to his desk and sat down despondently.

Eileen stopped at his desk. "A small surprise for you, Omar."

He stared at the printed cheque, his eyes devouring the numbers. "Two hundred euros. What's that for Eileen?"

"A present from the Revenue. Actually, I've been taking too much tax off you. Forgot your tax-free allowance. But sure, you can have a ball now. Enjoy." A gap-toothed smile spread across her freckled features. This small woman's pleasant nature dissolved the sharp bite of his colleagues like aspirin in an overworked brain.

Kate raised her hand over the top of her computer. "Fancy a flutter with that, Omar? You might as well."

Omar stared at the small piece of luck that had landed on his desk. "What's the name of Magnier's horse?" He flipped the cheque over in his right hand.

"Damson." Kate bit on the edge of her pen.

A plum horse for a plum sum. Omar crossed the room. "Here. The lot on Damson." He signed the back of the cheque and handed it to Kate.

"Whoah! Good man, Wilde. Now that's a proper bet. More balls than the big man himself." She nodded in the editor's direction.

Omar felt a wave of satisfaction pour through him. He returned to his desk somewhat appeased. His stomach grumbled beneath his striped shirt. *The time? Davy Byrnes time. Right – lunch.*

CHAPTER 14

BLÁITHÍN

1:00 PM

ALL SHE COULD THINK OF after leaving Flora's house was finding Kinch and convincing him that he was wrong. They had something – she knew it. She'd texted him a million times, but he wasn't responding. He'd be at the National Library around 2:00 PM, but she wanted to speak to him before then. She'd tried to ring Gerry, but he wasn't answering either. It seemed like the whole world wanted to blank her out. As she got closer to St. Patrick's Cathedral, the bells chimed 1:00 PM. She had to hitch up her ample skirt so it wouldn't get caught in the bicycle chain.

Hope I'm not flashing the world.

The violin case was strapped to the rack at the back of her bike, and she prayed that some crazy bus driver wouldn't send it hurtling into outer space. Kevin Street was a mess of traffic as usual, and she wove her way through the cars and buses. She could feel the sweat drip down the back of her neck. *I'm definitely overdressed for this lark today. Damn!*

Camden Street lights turned red. She spotted Hanan on the other side of the street, sitting outside his halal shop with his younger brother. What was his name? Kaleb or Kalid or something? The lights turned green. *Always been curious about what they sell. Maybe he's seen Kinch.*

Turning right she just avoided being creamed by a taxi eager to plough its way through the intersection. Hanan was deep in conversation with his not-too-happy-looking brother as she pulled up outside the shop.

"How goes it?" she asked cheerfully.

Hanan jumped to his feet. "Bláith, heading home?"

"Not exactly, I was just wondering if you've seen Kinch around."

"Actually, I just had a drink with him in The Flowing Tide. Left about thirty minutes ago."

"You know where he was going?"

"Said something about heading into the *Irish Independent* for a cheque or something."

"I'm leaving," said the brother, throwing her a look of disdain.

Hanan grabbed his brother's arm. "You're going nowhere, Khaled. We're not finished yet."

"Make me," said the young man with a look of defiance.

Hanan pushed his brother onto the seat beside him. "Don't push me. Just sit down and don't move."

Bláithín suddenly felt uncomfortable. "Listen, don't worry about it. I need to head out anyway."

Hanan softened his voice and smiled at her in the same way he'd smiled at her that morning, in the way that made her feel uncomfortable but happy at the same time.

"Listen, Bláith. I know you two had some problems, but I'm pretty sure he's realising what a fool he is. I told him he was mad, and I think he might have a little surprise for you ... I told you nothing."

She could feel her heart pound through her eardrums. "Really? Are you sure?"

"Just a hunch." Khaled stared at her as if he were ingesting a box of nails she had just fed him.

"Listen, thanks, Hanan." She leant over her bike to hug him. He held on for just a fraction longer than she'd expected.

"I told him I think you're gorgeous," he said, stumbling over his words.

She could see Khaled put his fingers in his mouth behind Hanan's back. She shot him an "I've seen you look" and he grinned back at her.

"Right then, see you later, Hanan. Thanks."

"No prob."

She angled her bike across the road and headed off into the traffic. *That brother of his gives me the creeps. Must check to see if Gerry is at his usual corner.*

She passed a group of eager Bloomites. They waved madly. "Molly, Molly, flash us a bit of that fine thigh of yours." A pot-bellied older man in a pinstriped suit and boater made groping signs with his sausage-like hands.

Jesus, sloshed on a breakfast of kidney and champagne, no doubt.

"Blazes Boylan has nothing on this." He grabbed his crotch with enthusiasm.

Bláithín winced. A well-dressed woman hit the man with a well-made handbag.

"Really, Owen, you're mortifying me."

A group of equally well-oiled men fell around the place laughing.

Bláithín shouted back. "You should be so lucky, mate." She flew past him and right into Exchequer Street. The newspaper seller, Mick, stood on the corner, chatting animatedly with the barman of the Exchequer Pub. No sign of Gerry though.

"Hi, sorry, Mick, isn't it?"

He stroked the end of his moustache, "Yeah, love, and you would be?"

"Just a friend of Gerry's ... the Corkman who's always busking across the street. You haven't seen him, have you?"

"No, love, no. He's gone AWOL, but if I do, who shall I say dropped by to our little corner of the world?"

"Bláithín, if that's ok?"

"No bother."

She looked down at the headlines plastered across the front of Mick's stand: "O'Leary Took 50,000 Euro in Bribe for Stillorgan Land Deal."

Jesus, Dad. What the fuck have you been up to now?

She pointed at the pile of *Evening Heralds* sitting beside the old man's arm. "Could I have one of those please?"

"No problem. That O'Leary fella's a right chancer, isn't he?"

She could feel the blood rise to her nostrils.

"Robbin us all blind he is, sittin in that big mansion of his out in Dalkey."

"Yeah, yeah. Listen, thanks." She walked away from the older man in a daze. She balanced her bicycle in one hand, the front page of the newspaper in the other.

> Bernard O'Leary, Fianna Fáil Minister for Justice and ex-Minister for Finance, is embroiled in scandal once again. A reliable source claims to have been present at the house of Fresh Air tycoon,

> Michael Power, on October 22nd last year, when Minister O'Leary accepted a 50,000 euro "donation" from the prominent businessman. O'Leary has been closely linked to the controversial purchase of land at the old Bórd Gais site on the Stillorgan Dual Carriageway. The beleaguered minister, on his way to the High Court to seek a judicial review of the Mahon Tribunal's entitlement to examine him on statements made in the Dáil, refused to comment, except to say that he had a solid alibi, his daughter's birthday dinner at their family home in Dalkey ...

Bláithín could feel her legs buckle underneath her. *Has he not caused me enough trouble already, Jesus?* The ringtone burst from her phone. Her mother's name flashed at her like a beacon. *Fuck, fuck, better answer it.*

"Mum."

"Bláithín, I've been trying to get a hold of you all morning. Did you not see my missed calls?" The tone of her mother's voice affected her moods as dramatically as a hormonal surge. She dreaded those first few seconds when she would answer the phone, not knowing whether her day was about to turn away from her. Predictably, her mother's stress vibrated through her eardrum like a migraine.

"I'm up to my eyes, Mum. You know I've loads of performances today."

"Have you seen the papers?"

Thanks for asking me how they went! "Just this second. What the fuck is he up to now?"

"Don't curse and don't talk about your father like that."

"For God's sake, Mum. Give it a rest. How the fuck can you continue standing up for him?" She was sick of it. Sick of the lies, sick of the heartache, sick of having to be loyal to a man who barely acknowledged her existence.

"This is not the time for one of your tantrums, Bláithín. We need you home right now," said her mother.

"What? Are you mad? I have to get ready for my performance tonight. Anyway, part of the deal is that I wander around Dublin in this turn-of-the-century gear so that the tourists are kept happy."

"To hell with the tourists, Bláithín! This is your family and we need you NOW!" Her mother's voice exploded through the earpiece. Bláithín dropped her bicycle with fright, her violin case spilling onto the road. A Mercedes headed in her direction at speed and she scrambled to pick it up.

"Bláithín?" Her mother's voice continued to reverberate from the mobile.

Mick ran to help her pick up her bicycle.

"Are you all right?" He stood the bicycle against the wall behind her.

She held onto her violin for dear life. "Yeah, thanks."

"Bláithín!!!" She put the mobile to her ear.

"Mum. Jesus! I nearly fell in front of a car. No need to rip my ears off."

"Are you all right?" It sounded like an afterthought, an inconvenient interruption to the flow of necessary conversation.

"And if I wasn't?" She liked to bait her mother. It had become a game that the two of them had perfected in her adult years.

"Oh, for God's sake, save the dramatics for your performance."

"Mum, you have such a way with words."

"All right, what do I have to do to persuade you to come home now?" She could hear the strain in her mother's voice as she attempted to soften her approach. "I'll drop you back in this evening, I promise."

Though Bláithín wanted to step out of the crazy loop of her parents' lives, she was always sucked back in. A sense of duty always seemed to override her common sense in the end.

"Ok."

"Take a taxi. We'll pay for it." Her mother's relief was palpable. "See you soon."

"And thank you too, mother," muttered Bláithín as the phone beeped back at her.

The taxi pulled up beside her house on Coliemore Road, and she was besieged by a crowd of reporters.

"Ms. O'Leary, can you corroborate your father's story?" A young female reporter shoved a dictaphone in her face.

"Bláithín, what do you think of your father's activities?" A TV3 microphone nearly clocked her on the chin.

"No comment." She shoved her way through the jostling group. What she hated most was that it made her feel like she had done something wrong, like she was responsible for her father's behaviour.

Nigel Murray, her father's henchman, stood inside the electronic gates. They clicked open and she slipped through, leaving him to fend off the invading reporters. Her mother appeared at the doorway, dressed immaculately in a cream, linen trouser suit and mauve, silk scarf. *Jesus, even in a crisis she looks like Hillary Clinton.* Her black labrador, Buffy, pushed its way out the door, bounded down the steps, and leapt on Bláithín, showering her with saliva-laden licks.

"Hey, Buff, you beauty. Down girl, yes, yes." Most of her adolescence had been spent with Buffy curled up at the end of her bed, and she sometimes thought that the only one in the house who truly cared about her was this affectionate creature. She managed to extricate herself from the enthusiastic attention and climbed the steps towards her mother.

"You didn't say anything to those vultures out there, did you, darling?" asked her mother, ushering her into the bright, spacious hallway.

"Just told them that I was working my second job, lap-dancing in Lapello's on the night of October 22nd. I didn't screw up, did I?"

Her mother squinted her well-plucked eyebrows and pursed her lips. "Really, you don't have to be such a smart-arse all the time."

Bláithín turned left through the large oak doorway into a brightly lit reception room. "Where is he?"

"I'm here." She turned around. His shirt was open at the neck. The sky-blue tie was yanked open and hung around him like a medal. His white hair, normally groomed and immaculate, flew around his head wildly.

"You look a little worse for wear, Dad." She wanted to delay the process of "getting into it." That never ended the way any of them wanted it to.

"You look lovely, Bláith." The worst of it was that she loved her father. For all his weakness of character, impulsive meanderings, and downright corrupt behaviour, she could still see the man he once was. The father who'd spun her bedtime stories so fabulous that her little friends would beg to stay over to hear them, brought her fishing every Sunday in summer on Lough Dan, and called her his "piseóg áilinn" whenever he was around to kiss her goodnight. But now he stood before her, defiant as ever in the face of accusation, totally unable to see his own faults. This was even though, at one point or other, the front page of every newspaper had run a story about him being one of the most corrupt politicians the country had ever seen.

"They're after me again, love. I really need your help this time." His voice was soft and vulnerable, a voice she knew from her childhood when he'd said things he really meant.

"Maybe they have good reason, Dad."

"Do you have to always take their side, Bláithín? Did it ever occur to you that I might be innocent?"

"Not often." She knew she could be cruel, and she didn't like it, but she was past niceness.

"Well, I am love, but it's his word against mine, and I need you to back me up on this one."

"But you know damn well that you left my birthday dinner at 9:00 PM that evening, Dad. It had barely got going. I wasn't so impressed, remember?"

"What I remember is I went upstairs for a lie-down, Bláithín."

"Memory is a very fluid concept around this house. I remember you hopping in your Merc with Nigel and disappearing for the night."

"Jesus, Fionnúala, will you help me with her? She's impossible." Bernard O'Leary sank into the brown leather armchair, sighing heavily.

"Don't bother, Mum. I remember what I saw." *I won't be pulled into this, I won't.* "Why didn't you get Gráinne or Rachel to back you up? They love to blow your trumpet. You know how I feel about these things." She could hear her voice jump an octave, the blood rushing through her veins like caffeine.

Her father stared at her intensely. "The twins are already on my side, but I need you as well."

"Dad, they'd say anything to keep you happy. All they're thinking of are their precious trust funds. One year to go and then we'll see the loyal daughters act go out the window." Her mother jumped to her feet and moved towards her like a rabid animal.

"Bláithín, you are going to stop this "I'm a rebel" thing and listen to me. It's actually very simple. The night in question was your birthday party. Your father went to Nigel's house to discuss the case of that Senegalese boy who was being deported. He has no one except Nigel to back him up, and he's not exactly Mr. Popular where those vulturous bastards are concerned."

"Language, mother."

Fionnúala O'Leary glared at her daughter. "Bláithín. If you don't help your father, he will lose his job. Do you know what that means? Forty years of hard work for this country down the drain, not to mind no Dáil pension. For God's sake, can't you put your high ideals on hold for once for the sake of this family?" Her mother shook with anger, and it looked as though her perfectly bobbed haircut was about to fall off her head.

"Dad, I just need to know, and please be honest with me, if I ever meant anything to you ... Did you do it? Did you take that money as a bribe? Did you help Power purchase that land? Yes or No." She looked him straight in the eye.

He held her gaze. "No Bláith, I didn't." The two of them stood transfixed in a moment of appraisal - appraisal of the truth, if any, that lay between them. It was no longer tangible to her. The word of her father had become a shifting mist, an ungraspable wisp of air. She struggled to contain it and shape it into a truth she could understand. He rubbed the end of his nose with his finger. She had noticed this habit of his over the years and knew what it meant.

"I don't believe you." Her father slumped in his chair, defeated. "That bag of foul hot air is well ripped open for the world to see now Dad." She felt her heart rip in two for this man who she loved so much, but she could no longer fight her own beliefs.

Her mother grabbed her shoulder and smacked her across the face like an errant child. "Get out of this house. Get out now before I throw you out."

Shocked, she picked up her satchel and moved towards the door.

"And if you think you're getting a penny more from that fund of yours, forget it! You're on your own. Out, get out!" She looked towards her father, and he looked away.

She walked slowly down the front steps and fought the urge to cry. *What now? Shit, the bloody journalists!*

They waited for her like greedy seagulls, clumped around the doorway. *Just say nothing.*

"Ms. O'Leary. You're looking a little upset. Had a fight with your father?" A young wiry reporter stuck a microphone in her face. *Shit, a camera.*

"No comment." She pushed her way through the crowd and walked at speed towards the Dart station. Several reporters tried to follow. "No comment. Leave me alone!" They backed off and she began to run, her skirts billowing around her calves. The tears flowed, and she struggled for breath. She ran faster than she ever remembered running, away from the whole sorry mess of her life.

CHAPTER 15

FLORA

1:00 PM

FLORA ARRIVED AT THE DUBLIN Adult Education Centre on Mountjoy Square just in time for her lunchtime lesson. The centre gave English-language courses for non-nationals. Flora had persuaded them to let her use a room to teach the violin to asylum-seekers desperate for something to do while they waited for their work applications to go through. She knew only too well the struggle to fit into a new and different space and offered her services for free.

Sandra Comfort Sampson, a Nigerian woman, had been coming to the centre for lessons from Flora since she'd arrived in Ireland with two young daughters four months before. She sat by the doorway to their practice room, her normally bright eyes staring dully at a spot on the wall in front of her. Beside her stood Father Ogunbosola, a priest from Sandra's country. He'd befriended her when she attended his services in St. Mary's Pro Cathedral. Although Flora was wary of priests, a by-product of her stifling upbringing in Poland, she found Father Ogunbosola to be kind and modest in his beliefs.

Sandra's two little girls sat beside her, making rude noises. Always up to some mischief, they irritated Flora at the best of times. If she ever missed having children, being around these two was enough to make her feel better. The little girl, Efe, saw Flora coming and stuck out her tongue behind her mother's back. Flora took a deep breath. She tapped the dazed woman on the shoulder.

"Hi, Sandra. Are you ok today? You don't look great."

"Oh, hi. No, I'm not. Can we go inside?"

"Of course, how are you guys?" Flora turned to the little girls and forced a smile.

Efe picked up her little sister's hand, pulled her finger and farted. They exploded into laughter.

"Efe, apologise to Mrs. Wilde this instant," said her mother.

The little girl scrunched up her pretty features in a gurn. "Soooorrry."

"Efe. Sit down with your sister and keep your mouth shut!" Sandra turned to Flora, her eyes offering an apology. "Really, I'm sorry. I don't know what to do with her sometimes."

Flora had some ideas about what she would do with her, but she kept them to herself. "No worries. Sure, all children are the same."

Sandra looked like she'd been crying, her eyes puffy and red.

Flora ushered them into the tiny room where they normally practiced.

The priest followed with the girls behind him. Flora could see them in the mirror making devil signs in shadow on the wall above the priest's head. She smiled despite herself and shut the door behind them.

"What's wrong, Sandra?"

The woman placed her head in her hands and started to sob, her shoulders heaving with the stress. Flora put her arms tentatively around her and glanced at Father Ogunbosola.

"I'm afraid Sandra has a big problem, and we're wondering if you can help."

The two girls, for once, sat down quietly, holding hands, and looked nervously at their mother.

"What happened?"

The details of Sandra's story had come out over coffee several months before. A shy woman, she took her time to trust people, to know that they were someone she could allow into the delicate spiral of need that had become her life.

"They're deporting us in a couple of days. No more appeals. I ... don't know what to do anymore." Her hazel eyes fell back inside her head, heavy with fear and grief.

"Oh no. They can't." Flora looked over at the girls, who were staring nervously, clearly unsure of how to react to their mother's distress.

"I know ... they don't care."

"But they have to."

"Caring is an impediment to progress in this world, I'm afraid." The priest looked grim.

Flora felt a wave of pity creep through her body. Sandra had told her that she'd fled from Nigeria with her girls because her traditionalist parents-in-law were insisting that they be circumcised. They believed that she and her husband, Michael, had become immoral imitators of a degenerate Western culture. They were planning to snatch the children to have the barbaric custom carried out on them. Sandra's plan was that she and the girls would seek refugee status in Ireland. Michael would follow later.

"But surely this is her basic human right, to protect her children?"

Father Ogunbosola replied. "Apparently, it has something to do with the definition of an asylum seeker. They're afraid that if women are seen as a "particular social group," the country would be at risk of an influx of women claiming asylum on the grounds of gender-based forms of persecution, which are, of course, extensive. Anyway, I'm not sure they believe her story."

"I see."

The priest continued. "I'm afraid logic, not compassion, is the rule of thumb for this modern world of ours."

Flora was not stupid. Being an immigrant herself, she understood that this small country could not absorb every poor unfortunate. But this woman was not just an abstract precedent. She was sitting in front of her, a real woman with a real problem. Flora decided to help her.

"I can't let them send the girls back," Sandra insisted. "I can't."

There was a tone in her voice that filled Flora with dread.

"Mummy, where will they send us back to?" asked the older of the two girls, clutching the hand of her little sister tightly.

"Nigeria, Orisa, where we came from in the first place," replied Sandra. "I'll explain later."

"But I want to see Daddy. Why can't we go?" The petite six-year-old shook off her sister's hand defiantly.

"We just can't, Efe. Bad things will happen." Sandra turned to the children and held their hands in hers. "Let me just talk to Mrs. Wilde for a minute. We'll talk later, I promise." The little girls looked at Flora with curiosity and nudged closer to the quiet priest who placed a tight, protective arm around them.

"It's all right, girls. God will look after you all. I promise," said the priest in a soft voice.

Flora smiled lamely at the priest. She was sure that God was way too busy elsewhere to notice the plight of this little family. "But what can you do?"

Sandra stared at Flora silently, clearly unsure of how much she was at liberty to reveal.

"What? Sandra. You can trust me."

"Can I?"

"Of course. I would do anything I could in your situation." Flora knew what it was to lose a child. She knew that it felt like dying, like a long, slow, suffocating death that one could never escape.

Sandra continued. "I'm going to run. I'm going to hide with the children. Father's going to help me."

Flora nodded mutely. "I see."

"I can't tell you anymore, but I just need one favour and I have no one else to turn to," Sandra whispered.

"She needs you to put them all up in your house for one night – tonight," interrupted the priest. "I'm going to make some alternative arrangements, but I need until tomorrow."

"You, the music ... it's helped somehow, Flora. That's why I thought of you. I know you have a kind heart, and you know the hurt of losing a child. You know how that tears you apart."

Flora reached out and hugged this woman whose life was teetering on the brink of disaster. She found herself thanking God that she didn't have to live like this, that her pain had found a space where she could manage it.

"Ok, sure. I need to talk to Omar, but that will be fine. Don't worry."

I hope this isn't a mistake. Omar shouldn't mind. Bleeding heart that he is.

"Thank you so much." Sandra began to cry again openly, and Flora continued to hug her.

The children sat quietly, their faces a picture of confusion and worry.

"What time do you want to come over?" Flora wondered when she would have the chance to warn Omar.

"I have to bring the children to the doctor on Ormond Quay this afternoon, and go back to the house to pack our things, so I was thinking around six?"

"Six. That's perfect. I have to head out at 7:30. I'm playing at the *Ulysses* Centenary recital in the National Concert Hall tonight. Is it ok if I leave you guys something to eat? You can just watch the telly for the evening. I should be back around 10:30."

Gives us two hours. Better than nothing.

"Thanks so much." Sandra looked at her watch. "We've got forty-five minutes left. Do you mind if we play?" Sandra picked up her violin.

"Are you sure you're up to it, and with the children here?" asked Flora.

"I need to. I need to feel something other than fear." She looked at her children. "They're used to me practicing. Girls, you'll be quiet for mummy while I practice with Mrs. Wilde, won't you? You don't mind, Father?"

He nodded quietly. "Will be a pleasure to hear what you've been learning Sandra," replied the priest.

"Hang on one second." Flora ran to the cupboard in the corner. She pulled out two pieces of paper and a box of crayons and handed it to the children.

"They use this room to teach English to families. Lots of stuff lying around." Not quite sure what to do with the crayons, the girls immediately began to draw on each other's faces. But at least it kept them quiet.

"Say 'Thank you,' Efe, Orisa."

They stuck on their fake smiles. "Thaaaanks."

"Now, Sandra, what would you like to play?" asked Flora.

"'Salut d'amour'. I've been working on it." Sandra placed her bow against the strings.

Flora sat down opposite and nodded her head silently. This time she would watch and listen.

Sandra creased her brow as she struck the opening chords. The bow flew back and forth through the air, cut the silence with three sharp, violent blows, then softened into a sublime breath of sound.

Flora thought about Ruairí and what she would have done to protect him. *Anything, absolutely anything. When it comes to a child there are no limits.* But she knew Sandra was fighting an uphill battle. This was a small country and if the powers that be wanted to get her, they would find her. It all depended on who you knew in a country of four million people, and Sandra knew no one. Even if these girls were not exactly angels, she couldn't bear the thought of them being subjected to such horrors. *Get the word out. Contact the media. What else?*

Sandra continued to play.

Wait a minute. Bláithín. Bláithín is Bernard O'Leary's daughter. Of course. Could I? No harm in trying.

Sandra tripped over a note and stopped playing.

"That's good, Sandra. You've been working hard. I just need you to close your eyes and feel the modulation of the phrases. Feel how they dip and swirl – how they move with your emotion. Well, you know what I mean," Flora said awkwardly.

"Right, ok. I'll start again." Sandra closed her eyes, and her bow flew like a weapon.

Flora began to tap out a message with her phone on silent. "Bláithín, I need your help. My friend is about to be deported. Horrible story. Can I call? Could you possibly talk to your Dad? Two little girls" lives are at stake. Call me in an hour. I will fill you in. Luv Flora XX."

"That's good, Sandra, very good." She decided she wouldn't say anything until she knew whether it could make any difference. What would be the point?

Chapter 16

KINCH

1:00 PM

A GROUP OF SWEATY MEN were working on the Luas tram lines, which were due to open at Connolly Station in four months. *Probably take four more years, the rate these lads work. Still, should be fun ding-donging it across the city. Like old times.*

Having left the *Independent* offices, Kinch had an hour before the performances to check what was up with Gerry.

A large, hairy man poured water over himself, babbling in a language that Kinch thought he could recognise.

Poles. Building the city for us, they are.

Crossing over to O'Connell Bridge, he spotted The Traveller men chewing on some sandwiches. V seemed very exercised about something. Kinch had a close look at him as he passed over the bridge.

They don't look so happy. Must be sweltering.

E had wandered off, looking disgusted with the situation. The other four sat to the side like bold children in the face of a reprimanding teacher. Kinch read the letters from right to left as he passed ... L ... A ... E ... R.

It's like a game of human scrabble.

A moved to the other side of E and picked up a hammer, which he waved at V while screaming in an Arabic-sounding language.

Kinch chuckled to himself. *Must go down well with the ladies. "So, what do you do for a living?" ... "Well, I'm a letter." Feck – who knows? – maybe better than saying "I'm an actor".* He crossed over into Westmoreland Street. Herds of people shoved past him, nattering wildly. The lunchtime crowd poured into Bewley's Café.

Feeling a little peckish. A quick sanger will do.

He stood in the queue for the takeaway sandwiches. There was a poster on the wall for the Joyce recitals in the concert hall that night. *That's my lady. Wouldn't mind seeing her outside the bedroom. Not possible.* He reached for his mobile and tapped out a text "Need to see you desperately!! 4:00 PM ok? Got a surprise for you ..."

"Excuse me, sir, what would you like?" asked the Latina-looking girl behind the counter.

"Ham and coleslaw on a brown roll please?"

She shuffled away, slapping mounds of butter onto the roll.

There go the arteries.

Her hair was chopped into the side of her head, a long tail travelling down the back of her neck. *Mullet girl.* A multitude of earrings populated her small ears – a tiny stud in her nose providing the finishing touches to a look that Kinch found seriously unattractive.

Pretty girl underneath all that mess. No accounting for taste.

"Anything else, sir?" she asked lazily.

"That's grand."

She stuck out her hand. "Three euro fifty." Kinch could barely see her through the mounds of sticky buns and creamy eclairs.

He took the brown paper bag, ripped it open, and stuffed the end of the sandwich in his mouth.

Mmmm. Needed that!

Continuing to chew on the sandwich he crossed the wide street, zigzagging his way through speeding double-decker buses.

Jesus, it's a death-trap around here.

The coleslaw dripped down the front of his face. He chewed quickly, attempting to get as much of the sandwich into him as possible before he reached the Garda station. A large glob of mayonnaise attached itself to the pocket of his jacket.

Bollox, beginning to look like a homeless man.

War of the Worlds was playing in the Screen Cinema.

Wells is turning in his grave. Give that one a skip.

Two Bean Gardaí sat on the steps of Pearse Street Garda Station, basking in the sun now that it had decided to stick around for a while.

Kinch stopped to finish his sandwich.

Don't know why I feel so guilty every time I go into a Garda station.

He scrunched up the paper bag and lobbed it towards a bin at the corner of the room. It teetered on the edge and fell to the floor. The glass screen at the reception area was pulled shut. He rang the silver bell and waited. A tall Garda pulled aside the screen.

"Yep?" He bent his large frame over to peer out at Kinch.

"Hi, I'm just looking for a friend of mine, Gerry Deasy. He sent me a message saying he was here."

"Indeed. Hang on a minute." The towering Garda moved into the adjoining room. Kinch could see him talk to a small woman and point in his direction. She nodded and came out to talk to him.

"Hi, do you mind me asking who you are?" Her country accent tripped off her tongue like a song.

"Kieran Lynch. I'm a friend of Gerry Deasy's. He asked me to come here. Is he in trouble?"

Kinch felt increasingly uncomfortable. *What the hell has Gerry been up to now?*

"You could say that all right, Mr. Lynch. He's been arrested for robbing a post office on Kevin Street Upper this morning. Do you mind me asking where you were this morning at approximately ten o"clock?" She stared at him intently.

A wave of panic passing through his body. "You don't think I had anything to do with this, do you?" He felt his leg begin to twitch.

"Just answer the question and I'll be sure you hadn't."

She reminded him of Sister De Victoire from first class. Used to scare the shite out of him with her foot-long bamboo.

"Well?" she reiterated.

"Ehm, let's see, ten o"clock. I think I was in Bewley's with my girlfriend ... ex-girlfriend ... I think." *Was it that or Lacey's? Not sure.*

"Is she ex or not? You don't seem sure." She eyed him suspiciously.

"Yes, yes, ex ... we broke up this morning, actually."

"Really, well let's hope for your sake she doesn't hold that against you. Might need her to corroborate your story."

A sweat bead hung on the end of his nose. "Do I look like I'm going to be robbing a post office dressed up as Stephen Dedalus, Gard?"

She jotted something onto the notepad in front of her. "Dressed up as who?"

"You know, Bloomsday. One of Joyce's main characters. Loads of wankers stuffing up the streets in boaters and pinstripes. Surely you must have noticed."

"Are you being smart with me?" She gave him that De Victoire look.

"No, Guard. Just trying to explain why I'm dressed this way."

"I don't give a flying fuck if you go-round with a pair of Mickey Mouse boxers on your head, just don't get smart with me, lad. I've enough shite to be dealing with around here." She waved the pen in his face.

Frustrated old biddy. A good shag would sort you out. "Of course, Guard. Listen, can I speak to Gerry? Is he here?"

"Yes, he's here. You can see him with me in the room. Come through the door over to your left." She walked away and into the adjoining room.

Christ Gerry, what the fuck?

The door opened in front of him.

"This way." He followed her small stocky frame. They turned left into a corridor with several locked rooms. She rummaged for the keys in her pocket and opened the heavy metal door. Gerry sat in the corner of a dark cell. A small, barred window leaked light into the room from above his head. The walls were covered in graffiti. He sat in the corner on a wooden bench, bent over with a heavy look in his dark eyes.

"Kinch, thanks for coming, man."

The Garda stepped in behind him and shut the door.

"Jesus, Gerry, what the hell is going on?" Kinch was very aware of the woman standing silently in the corner.

"It's a mistake, like. That's all. Mistaken identity. I keep telling her. It wasn't me." His eyes pleaded to be believed.

"But how did you end up in here then?" Kinch looked to the woman to help fill the gaps. She said nothing.

"They picked me up in Digges Street Upper in front of the council flats. I swear I was only passing through, and I keep telling her I was in the wrong place at the wrong time." He pointed to the stone-faced Garda. "The real guys were dumping their gear behind the flats as I passed by. I asked the langer for a smoke and got caught in the middle. The cops came swarming in like rats. Now they think I was with them! It's savage, boy."

Kinch turned to the Garda. "The others must say he wasn't one of them. Don't they?"

She smiled without speaking.

"The langers are fingering me as their accomplice. Sick joke. Kick a Corkman day."

"What? This is mad!" Kinch sat down beside his friend and put his arm around his shoulders.

"How come you were found with eight grams of coke stuffed down your boot then? Cork snow was it?" said the Garda.

Kinch looked at Gerry and arched his eyebrows in a question. Gerry shifted uncomfortably looking away towards the wall.

"Gerry? Is there something you want to tell me, man?" Kinch scrambled through his brain to make sense of it all. Was it possible that his friend was lying? He would have trusted Gerry with his own life, but suddenly he felt unsure.

"Gerry?"

"Not here, like, yer wan's a right stella boy."

The woman in the corner raised her eyes to heaven.

"Listen, can you get me a lawyer? I'm not saying another word until I get a lawyer, like? Can you do that for me?"

"Yeah, ok, man. I'll have to think about it. I don't know anyone off the top of my head, but I'll look into it."

"Soon Kinch, please. I'm all over the shop."

Kinch nodded.

"Right, let's break this little party up then, boys." The mousey-haired Garda shuffled Kinch towards the door.

"Hang in there, man. I'll get back to you later." Kinch had no idea what he was going to do, but he gave his friend a reassuring smile nonetheless.

"Thanks, boy. Thanks a lot." Kinch nodded at his friend and followed the small woman from the room. He watched as she locked the heavy door behind her.

She pointed, indicating Kinch should head down the corridor. "He's guilty as sin. Don't let that sincere friendship act fool you."

"I'll be the judge of that, thanks."

The truth was he wanted to believe Gerry, but he had to admit he'd been acting strangely lately, getting lots of mysterious calls that he'd never explain, looking tired way too often. Kinch had been suspicious that he was taking drugs again, but Gerry hid it well. He knew what Kinch would do if he found out he was back on the blow. Kinch had been through enough, dragging him through rehab six months before. It bugged Kinch that it was what everyone expected anyway, being an ex-addict and all that. He persuaded his friend to prove them wrong.

Bollox, Gerry, I trusted you.

The Garda opened the door to the reception room.

"See you later then."

"Yeah. Bye." The scrunched-up piece of paper he'd fired at the bin was still on the floor. *Bollox, bollox, bollox! I don't need this.* He kicked it with full force. It flew out the front door and down the steps. Kinch followed it and stood at the bottom wondering what to do next. He looked at his watch. *Twenty minutes to "the National Library" scene. This is a mess.*

As he crossed the road towards Trinity College, he took out his mobile. He scrolled through the numbers in his address book looking for inspiration. He stopped at Bláithín's name. She would be massively pissed off with him, but she loved Gerry, and her dad was so connected maybe she could get him to help or at least give a name. He sighed heavily and pressed call. The tone rang four times.

"Kinch?"

"Yeah, hi, how are you?"

"What do you think?" Her voice sounded broken, like she had been crying.

"I'm sorry Bláith." He began to think this was a bad idea.

"It's not just you. I'm at the Dart station. I've just left my dad's house – I had to fend off a million bloody reporters. Have you heard? He's involved in another bloody scandal."

"I heard. Never a dull moment with that man," replied Kinch.

"We had a fight."

"Really, sorry. I'm afraid I'm not going to help. I've something heavy to tell you." He felt guilty that he had to drag her into his problems, considering everything.

"Oh Jesus, no. What now?"

"Gerry's in jail. They think he robbed a post office this morning. He swears he didn't do it. I want to believe him."

"No way. Was it in Kevin Street Upper? I passed by just after."

"Yeah, that's the one. Listen I need to find him a lawyer, obviously not an expensive one. Any ideas?" Kinch walked at speed up Dawson Street.

"Christ, Kinch, I don't know. Well, there's John ... John Fenton. He's a family friend. Helped Dad out a lot, but he fell off the wagon recently, so I know he's a bit desperate for work."

"Can you just ask him, Bláith? I'll owe you."

"Be careful saying something like that." He heard the hope in her voice, and it made him feel like he was a right bastard.

"Being careful was never my strong suit." He had to try not to cross the line.

"Kinch, can we meet up and talk everything over, please? I've calmed down now, and, well, I just think we need to talk things over." Her voice was soft and pleading.

I'm sorry, so sorry. He turned left into Molesworth Street and headed towards the Dáil. "Today is crazy, hun, especially now. Can we sort Gerry out and talk about things later in the week? I promise I will." He felt guilty because he knew that nothing would change, but he needed her now.

"Ok. I'll get back to you about John. I'll have a word with him."

"Thanks, Bláith. You're the best." He hung up the phone. The predictable crowd was gathering outside the National Library. He ran over the lines in his head.

What was the first one again? The first was always the worst. Oh yes. "Monsieur de la Palisse was alive fifteen minutes before his death."

He stepped through the great wooden door of the National Library, descending into the character as he passed through.

CHAPTER 17

OMAR

~ Lestrygonians ~

1:30 PM

BUTLER'S COFFEE CHOCOLATES – smooth, sweet elixir of the gods. Mmmmm. Sticky sweet pleasures.

Omar watched a young blonde scoop large lumps of chocolaty ice cream into a cup and smother them with a treacly-looking sauce. The machine swirled and whirled the sauce into a creamy delight. An eager child danced around her mother in anticipation. The child grabbed the cup, devoured the contents, and deposited half of the sticky sweetness down the front of her blue summer frock.

Slip, slop, slurp it up. Love in a cup.

He moved past the door of the café, wishing he had time to indulge himself, but he was already late for the traditional Davy Byrne's lunch. He hoped to grab Mr. Bloom downing his glass of burgundy and have a quick word with him for the paper.

His stomach groaned like a distant sea swell. Vinegar-laden wisps of air assaulted his nostrils, wafting from the various eating establishments that lined O'Connell Street.

Fast food hell.

Families, young teenagers, and bunches of students fell out from the doors of Burger King and Mc Donalds.

Lips oozing burger juices, mayonnaise, ketchup dripping over chins. Savages chomp chomping on dead animals like it's their last meal. Puts me off. Could nearly be a vegetarian at the sight of that.

At the bridge, the sandwich men were beginning to reassemble. The small group he'd seen earlier was still clumped at the end of the bridge. Two of the men were bent over the bridge, breaking off pieces of bread and throwing them into the murky Liffey. The seagulls swirled like demented tadpoles above their heads. They ducked and dived, attempting to grab the falling bread before it hit the water.

Liffey sauce, now that would test the guts.

V, E, A, and L sat solemnly, waiting for the others to approach them.

Veal, now that's a meat for the heartless. Pack them up like rats in a sewer, stewing in their own filth, unable to breathe. Must taste the misery in the meat.

A large Guinness lorry passed by.

Miss the smell of the hops all the same. The meaty sweetness that oozed up the river with the wind, the smell of old Dublin, rats gorging in vats of treacly stout. All cleaned up now. Not the same. Still, tastes good – thank God!

He stood at the end of the bridge, waiting at the lights to cross into Westmoreland Street. People raced across the street, wove their way through the rushing traffic, buses missing them by inches.

Jaywalking nation. It's a wonder we're not all wiped out by now.

Omar held firm to his spot on the kerb, watched for the light to change while the crowds pushed by him. They eyed him suspiciously as if to say "Who do you think you are, toeing the line? Trying to show us up are you mate?"

"Omar, is that you?"

He took his eye off the light and turned. "Mrs. Keane. How are ya? Haven't seen you in ages."

His father's friend had the same pleasantly smiling face, although she had let her hair go grey and this seemed to emphasise the lines of age etched into her fine features.

She gathered him into a tight hug. "Ah, it's great to see you, Omar."

"You too. You look great." He meant it in a way. *Graceful ageing. Never a bad thing.*

"My God, Omar it's been years. You've become a stranger to us."

"I know. Sorry about that. Life runs away with you, I suppose." He knew why he'd distanced himself from this woman and the family he'd grown up beside. It was too painful to be reminded of his father – to be reminded of how he had left him alone, and the way he'd done it. That gradual descent into hell after his mother had left them. He'd never understood how she could just disappear into another life, never contact. Although, from what he could remember, she was never around in the first place, always off on some concert tour leaving his father to look after him. The humiliation was too much for the poor man to take. The papers lapping up every detail of her affair with Roberto Salieri. Omar did everything he could to forget.

"Ah, I know the way it is." She looked at him with a look that seemed to say, "I know why. I want to forget too."

"How's Flora?" She veered them away from the uncomfortable space of memory that had silently passed between them.

"She's great, thanks. Doing very well with the music. Off to Belfast with The Three Tenors next week."

"Isn't that brilliant? No children yet or anything I should know about?" She poked him amicably in the ribs.

He smiled weakly. "No."

"Ah sure, there's time yet," replied Mrs. Keane. "Speaking of which, our Annie is in Holles Street as we speak. The poor thing has been at it nearly three days, God save us. I've been in there with her but just taking a break because I'm exhausted. I'm so worried about her, but the doctors say it often happens with the first."

"Annie, God the poor thing. That sounds like torture."

Annie Keane, you beauty. Deep hazel eyes. Long ago – love it was.

"Omar, you should go and visit her when it's all over. She'd love that." Her moist blue eyes smiled at him warmly.

"I don't know. I haven't seen Annie since, well ..." He thought for a second "Since the funeral." He tried not to think of that now. Twenty years ago. How he'd found his father floating in a bath of his own blood, his wrists gushing into the water. That was all he could see now – the awful sight of him, leaving this life. He never understood how his father could leave his son like that. All they had was each other. Had he simply not loved Omar enough? He would never know.

"Has it been that long? My God. Well, more reason you should go and visit Annie. She talks about you frequently, you know. You two were like peas in a pod growing up, the cutest pair of young ones around. Your father ..." She hesitated. "Your father and I used to imagine ourselves growing old, being looked after by the pair of you lovebirds. Strange eh, how things work out?" Her voice became weak and wistful.

"Who is she married to? He mightn't fancy an old boyfriend turning up."

"Well, that's just it. She's not, I'm afraid. Got pregnant by some lad she'd only been seeing a wee while. Ran off and married someone else as soon as there was another offer. Stupid little fecker. I'd murder him if I got my hands on him." Her small head shook furiously.

"How awful. I see. Well then, maybe, I'll drop in to see her."

"Do Omar, do. She'd love it. She'll need cheerin up after this ordeal." The small, handsome woman took him in her arms again and held him close to her.

"It's so good to see you, Omar. I miss you and I miss him too, you know. He's alive in our dreams, love, isn't he?"

Omar felt a wave of nausea wash over him. "Yes, Mrs. Keane. I suppose so."

"Breda, love, Breda. For God's sake, we're all adults now."

"Right, Breda." The green man began to flash, and Omar felt the need to cross.

"Sorry, Mrs. ... Breda, have to head, but I'll drop in later, I promise." He meant it too. To see Annie again. That would be something.

"Bye, love. See you then."

He waved at her as he crossed into Westmoreland Street.

Annie Keane, pigtails and freckles. Sherbet dripped across your pert little chin. You pulled me into you, showed me what's what, taught me how to love you. Then I saw her – Flora – and I forgot you, pushed you into the space where memories are locked up.

He passed the nick-nack shop on the corner leading to Temple Bar. It was packed with tourists purchasing leprechaun hats, lucky shamrocks, and lumps of Aran bog.

They'd buy anything wrapped up in a pretty package nowadays. Mad.

He glanced right towards Temple Bar. A crowd gathered in the distance. Coloured objects floated high above him, drums beat wild energy into the warm air. Curiosity got the better of him, and he diverted to take a look. A young man covered in piercings was walking in his direction.

"Sorry, just wondering. What's going on over there?" Omar asked.

"It's that Macnas crowd from Galway, dressed up as Celtic Cannibalistic Giants or some lark. All looks the same to me, mate." The young man smiled broadly. Omar could see the gleam of a tongue ring as he spoke.

"Thanks."

The man nodded and plodded off in the direction of The Palace Bar.

Must be funny, tasting metal all the time. Everything tinged with cold steel. They say the women love it – down there – like an ice-cube throbbing through their warmth.

Omar inched his way towards the crowd to take a look. The hypnotic rhythm of the drums expanded as he moved towards the parade. Above the heads of the crowd floated exotically colourful creatures – gargoyle heads, grotesque creations of purple clay, green-velvet skin, bulging, burning eyes that danced frantically above the delighted crowd. They clutched giant, ornate spears and dipped and dived around the edges of the people, occasionally grabbing an unsuspecting child and dumping them in the large clay cauldron at the centre of the parade. A one-eyed monster swept up a tubby child who was happily demolishing a large ice cream. He screamed and dropped the ice cream on the foot of a none-too-impressed Asian woman. The giant whirled him in the air and placed him carefully in the large pot. *Na Fir Bolg. Bet that little plump one tastes good.*

A small woman grabbed her camera to snap her precious boy in action. "It's all right, honey, I'm here. You're fine. Smile, Smile." Snap, snap. "They'll take you out in a sec. You look soooooo cute. Cheese."

A man dressed in long, dark robes walked slowly in front of the assembled crowd, reading above the swell of the drums. "I have been assured, by a very knowing American of my acquaintance in London, that a young, healthy child, well-nursed, is at a year old a most delicious, nourishing, and wholesome food, whether stewed, roasted, baked, or boiled. And I make no doubt that it will equally serve in a fricassee or ragout."

Omar laughed. *Good ol Jonathan Swift. A sick but entertaining man.*

The crowd roared with approval.

Right, enough of that. Gotta get to Davy's.

Omar turned right onto Westmoreland Street and passed under the stone pillars of the Bank of Ireland. He gazed across the road at the ageing stone façade of Trinity College. Gossiping students gushed through the grand stone arch. A small clutch held placards and screamed loudly in unison. "No to American military planes landing in Shannon!" The other students pushed past, more concerned about getting to Nude for a bite of lunch.

Some things never change. Meet them in ten years, suited and tied, downing a brandy in The Bailey. Need them all the same, the protesters, the dissenting voice.

The Molly Malone statue shone in the sun.

Ample bosoms. A beautiful thing. Remember how it tasted after Ruairi, sweet suckling milk dripping over the edge of my tongue. Strange to me now.

A group of tourists watched a young man drawing on the ground. Omar nearly bumped into the businessman in front of him, who jumped suddenly when a blob of white landed on his shoulder and dribbled down his well-tailored jacket.

"Cunting birds, mother focker. It's focking Armani for Christ's sake." He whipped out a handkerchief and dabbed frantically at the pungent goo.

Omar looked upwards at the circle of pigeons above his head. *Bullseye lads. Stupendous accuracy and sharply observed choice of target. Bravo.* Omar chuckled to himself as he passed the cursing man.

Grafton Street was thronged as usual, and he battled his way against the sea of rushing people. A band of Eastern Europeans belted out a lively round of traditional polkas. Two little girls danced, arms locked together before a lively accordion player.

Great stuff, not unlike our own diddley-I.

Brown Thomas windows looked like the inside of a Vaudeville costume tent, dripping in satin, silk, beading, and baubles. *Pretty to look at, impossible to buy. Wish I could buy Flora one of those.*

The last window was done up like a Victorian concert hall. Mannequins dressed in red velvet and opulent beading sat in rows, clutching ornate fans. A bow-tied mannequin held a conductor's baton. A violinist sitting beside him was dressed in sky-blue silk and creamy lace.

Omar remembered his first meeting with Flora. In the National Concert Hall, a memorial concert for his mother. She'd died that year in a car crash somewhere in America. Not that he felt much. She'd been gone so long. He'd mourned her loss a long time before her public had to. Nonetheless, he'd sat, dickied up in a monkey suit, mutely reverent, as a series of celebrities sang their way through his mother's repertoire. "To honour the lifetime achievement of Zaria Sha'rawi, the Egyptian Songbird."

As they drifted through the soundtrack to his life, he sat wallowing in the misery of his parents' story until he saw Flora deep inside the core of the orchestra, this woman with burning eyes. She played with the type of abandon with which his mother sang — eyes shut, oblivious to anything outside the beauty of the sound. Flora's dark-green eyes and sumptuous curves complemented her passionate bow-work perfectly; her whole body moulding the shape of a wild beast as she beat life into the strings of her violin. Omar couldn't keep his eyes off her. He knew that she was all that he could love from that point onwards. That's why it hurt so much now, the blankness of her stare. She looked through him, not at him.

Mother, Flora, both lost to me.

He dragged himself away from the window and turned left into Duke Street. He could see a mad crowd piling out of Davy Byrne's onto the side of the street. The usual assemblage of lawyers, merchant bankers, would-be telecom entrepreneurs, and other young wannabes packed The Bailey, opposite Davey's.

Give me the Joyceans any day.

A young woman exited The Bailey ahead of him. She was perfectly groomed, not a hair out of place, and legs the length of the Champs Élysée.

Probably a model. Bit too skinny, but nonetheless, mmmm.

A slick-looking man in a tailored shirt, his arm linked in hers, walked beside her. A red Hermès bag hung off her left shoulder.

Out of nowhere, a bicycle flew past Omar. The tracksuit-clad rider ripped the bag from the shoulder of the young woman. She screamed. Her escort ran after the cyclist, who disappeared towards South Anne Street.

Jaysus. That was quick work.

Omar decided he couldn't contribute to the situation and edged his way through the gossiping Bloomsday revellers outside Byrne's. They watched the mini-drama with fascination.

Who can blame him, poor bastard? The only tracksuit this lot know is the one their personal trainer monogrammed in gold thread.

He scanned the inner sanctum of Davey's for a sighting of Bloom at his lunch. *Nowhere to be seen.* A barman collected the towers of glasses piled high on tables.

"Sorry, just wondering is the guy playing Bloom around?"

"Take a look at the clock mate. Left five minutes ago. Stuffed his face royally, he did."

Omar looked at the clock above the bar. *2:05 PM. Damn!* He looked around the bar and there wasn't a space to be had.

"Sorry, I couldn't get a cheese sandwich to go?"

The barman angled an overladen tray back towards the bar. "And a glass of burgundy in a tumbler, no doubt."

"Actually, no, I don't drink, but a ginger ale will do."

"Don't drink, is it? Ah, I understand, overdid it in your youth?" The barman shot him a look of sympathy.

"No, I never drank actually." *Here we go, the look of horror – an Irishman who doesn't drink. Should be shot on sight. Why bother explaining?*

The barman shook his head ruefully. "Right." He eyed another customer with a "Can you believe this character look?" Omar was well used to it. *Yes, life without an alcohol-soaked liver is a possibility. Worse than murder around here.*

The burly, moustached barman deposited the tray, lifted the counter, and shouted Omar's order to the kitchen.

Omar found a spare inch to lean against the wooden counter. He observed the swell of people, many of them dressed in turn-of-the century costume. *Like time travel, it is.* A pot-bellied man sat opposite chewing the ear off an unfortunate victim.

"I'm telling you, Damson's the one. Put the lot on that one. I have a friend who knows the trainer, and he says it's a sure thing. A sure thing." He shook his head with a wink, dribbling some Guinness on his beard as he drank.

"Is that right? I'll keep that in mind, sir. Mighty good of you." The drawling Yank smiled, sipping neatly on a malt whiskey.

"Fine day for the festivities, thank God," piped up a ruddy-faced man standing beside Omar at the bar.

"Indeed, lovely day. A bit hot if anything," Omar watched the sweat drip down the man's thick neck.

"Could I stand you a quick whiskey while you're waiting?"

"That's very kind of you, but I don't ... actually, I just can't drink right now, but thanks."

"Ah, right, I understand," replied the man with a conspiratorial wink. "The antibiotics, is it? Summer sickness is the worst. I know all about that."

I don't think there's a single person in this country who understands. Never mind.

The barman slapped the sandwich down in front of Omar. "For the man who never drank."

The man beside Omar looked at him out of the corner of his eye. "Is that right? I thought ..." He caught the barman's eye and lapsed into silence.

The two shared a puzzled look.

Omar scrambled in his pocket and dug out a clump of fivers. He put one of the notes into the barman's outstretched hand.

"Go raibh maith agat." The barman raced to the till and placed the change on the counter in front of Omar. Omar wrapped up his sandwich in a napkin and left.

He took a large bite, the sun's glare blinding him temporarily as he walked down Duke Street. With his other hand, he rummaged in his leather satchel for his sunglasses.

Must have left them behind. Hang on ... my keys?

He sat down on the side of the path in front of The Duke pub and emptied the contents of his satchel on the side of the street.

Blast, no keys. Left them hanging inside the door. Can't go back. God knows what she's up to. Don't need any more surprises. Where's the schedule?

He picked up a piece of paper and had a good look.

Let's see ... 2:00 PM Bloom & Dedalus in the National Library. Right by here. I'll have a quick look.

He placed his things back inside the satchel, stood up, and headed towards Dawson Street. A man with dark glasses and a guide dog sat at the corner café reading the newspaper.

Wha? Didn't know they made newspapers in Braille nowadays. Bloody odd. Hang on a minute, know him. That actor fella, John Cronin. Jaysus, hard to know who's who today.

He crossed into Molesworth Street, heading towards government buildings. He passed the Passport Offices and spotted Matt Phelan heading in the same direction on the other side of the road.

Blast, it's him. Swaggering arsehole, pinhole, and boater, of course. Head down. Mightn't see me. Feel sick.

Omar slowed his pace and watched as the tall well-dressed man headed for the steps of the National Library.

That's it. Not going in there now. Can't look him in the eye. What does she see in him?

He turned left into Kildare Street and passed the entrance to the National Library.

CHAPTER 18

BLÁITHÍN

2:30 PM

THE TRAIN FLEW PAST Dun Laoghaire pier. Bláithín hung up the phone and stared out the window. A cluster of little sails bobbed in the sunlight, like Chinese lanterns in a distant parade. A shy wind blew the tiny vessels across the grey-blue light of the sea. She could see the *Ulysses* ferry heading out for its midday run to Holyhead. It moved slowly from behind the Poolbeg Towers and out into the stretch of the bay. Her head was pounding, and she popped two aspirin to give her some relief.

A wagonload of Italian students got on at Blackrock Station. Though she normally loved the pitches and undulations of Italian, today it cut through her like cold ice. The train pulled off again slowly. The tide was disappearing into the horizon.

Better call John Fenton.

She still had his name in her phone. He'd got her out of deep shit when her friends sent her that CD case full of cannabis from Spain. She nearly had a heart attack when customs at Dublin airport called to say they had a package they wanted to open in front of her. John managed to get her out of that mess without breathing a word to her parents. He was a decent fella – that had meant a lot.

The Italians were hurling a bag from seat to seat with roaring enthusiasm. She poked the number into her phone and cupped her ear to block out the noise.

"Hello, John Fenton's office ..."

"Hi, this is Bláithín O'Leary. I wonder would John be available, please?"

"One second and I'll see."

She wasn't sure whether it was the same woman whom she had dealt with last year. They all sounded the same to her – spoke like they had gum stuck to the top of their palettes. Probably did. It was a miracle he could still afford a secretary, considering work wasn't exactly flowing his direction.

"Bláithín."

"Hi John. Listen, I'm sorry to disturb you, but I just need an opinion about a friend of mine." The signal from the phone bumped around. She kept one eye on the Italians, while the bag flew back and forth over her head like a football.

"It's hard to hear you," he replied.

"One second, I'm on the train. It's passing Sydney Parade. Always improves after that."

John, she knew, had a soft spot for her.

"I can hear you now. What was that Bláith?"

He'd taken her to a lawyer's fundraising ball once, dressed up to the nines. After a few too many whiskeys, he'd tried to kiss her. It was awkward, and she'd put him off as nicely as she could. Not a word had been said since then.

"John, it's about my friend Gerry. I think you met him once with Kinch."

"Yes, I remember. Looks like a cross between a heavy-metal Satanist, and a drug dealer."

John was a snob but a funny one, a typical Dublin Four boy whose idea of casual dressing was a pair of well-ironed slacks and the latest Lacoste shirt.

"He's in trouble. Been arrested. They think he was in some post-office heist that he claims he was nowhere near."

"Oh he does, does he? Wasn't he in rehab the same time as you?" he asked bluntly.

"Yes, John, he was, but that doesn't make him a thief, and I'm sure he hasn't touched it in months – I'm sure of it." Even as she said the words, she knew she was on dodgy ground. An ex-drug addict could never be sure, no matter how hard they tried. She knew all about that.

"Uh huh." John didn't believe her, but she didn't care, she'd fight as if she did. Someone had to.

"Anyway, he hasn't got any cash. He's in big shit and he's my friend. Can you do me a big favour and look at his case for me. I'd owe you forever."

An over-fed Italian boy ran frantically between two boys dressed in Roma t-shirts. Bláithín ducked out of the way as the bag whizzed past her head once more.

The matter-of-fact lawyer in John took over: "Where is he?"

"Pearse Street Garda Station. Kinch knows everything. I can text you his number."

"Are you still seeing that waster?" he asked

"No, we just broke up, well ... I don't know, we might get back together." She doubted herself as she spoke.

"Really? You're too good for him, you know."

"No one's too good for anyone else. There's just people who match or don't." She knew this was aimed at him and that he wouldn't like it, but she couldn't help it.

He hesitated. "All right then, give me both their numbers. I'm busy for the next while, but I'll get back to you."

The train pulled into Lansdowne Road, and the signal began to break up.

"Thanks a million, John ... are you there ...? John ...?"

A piercing, low beep echoed in her ear. *Thank God for that. Text him the numbers.*

The floating bag hit her smack on the back of the head, and she dropped the phone from fright.

"Jesus. Feck!" She turned on the students who sat scrambled back to their seats.

"Sono spiacente," muttered the plump boy, picking up the bag and scuttling back to his seat.

The Roma wearers were creased up with laughter at the other side of the corridor, and Bláithín let rip. "Would you ever just leave the poor fecker alone! Give us all a bit of peace for God's sake."

The boys stopped laughing and sat down, nudging each other in the ribs. She could feel the tears begin to well behind her eyes again, pressing against her eyeballs, waiting to be triggered by something random – like a floating bag. She picked up the phone and texted the business cards to John.

Two fat tears slid down her cheeks.

Feck, feck! I want something to make me feel better. Anything.

She thought of that guy she had met in the morning. *What was his name again? Paul something. Hang on. Card here somewhere.*

Her bag was stuffed with all sorts of unnecessary things, and she rifled through it until she dug out the card. Rubbing her finger around the edge, she hesitated, knowing where it would bring her. She looked out the window as the train pulled slowly past the perfectly cut grass of the National Rugby Stadium. Everything was grey and foggy, bathed in a deadening light.

I just need to see again, to lift myself up a bit. She rang the number.

"Hello." It was him, she was sure.

"Ehm, hi, this is Bláithín, the girl from this morning from beside the Molly Malone statue."

"Ah, hi, how's it goin? Feeling a little better then?" He sounded surprised.

"Yeah, I guess so. I was wondering, your offer from earlier. The snow ... Just need to feel something ... well, you know," she said, guilt drowning her tongue as she spoke.

"I know exactly. Come on over then. I'll actually be at my home address." He hesitated. "The Ballymun Flats. I'll be here for the afternoon. Do you know how to get here?" he asked doubtfully.

There wasn't a person in Dublin who didn't at least know roughly where the flats were. The tallest buildings on the Dublin skyline, they'd been built as a cutting-edge social experiment in housing in the sixties but had descended into drug-infested squalor.

"No, but I'll just hop in a taxi from town ... are you sure?" She felt foolish to be heaping her miseries on a stranger.

"Does the pope pray?" he replied cheerfully. "Would love to see you again."

"Right, I'll be there inside the hour."

The train pulled towards Grand Canal Dock.

Might as well hang on until Pearse Station. More likely to get a taxi. Bit of a risk, but I've had it with this day. Feck it.

She stuck on the headphones of her ipod and tuned into Today FM. Bell X1's "Beautiful Madness" drowned out the noise of the carriage. She gazed out at the Docklands. A multitude of cranes edged the skyline like a herd of giraffes moving slowly through a great industrial jungle. The sun shimmered in dappled waves across the surface of the Dock water, the train travelling slowly through the galaxy of glass and metal that made up the hundreds of new apartment buildings on the waterside.

Five hundred thousand euros for a glassy shoebox. What a bargain! Rather live in a caravan. The travellers have it right nowadays.

The train began to slow as it entered the red-brick façade of Pearse Station. A crowd piled by the door, each person desperate to be the first to join the surge of people that moved at speed down the corridors of the grand old station. Bláithín joined them.

She emerged onto the street under the railway bridge on Westland Row and hesitated.

Feck, I know nothing about this guy. I must be mad. Maybe just a drink instead.

Her phone beeped to signal a message.

Message from Flora. What's that about? No more. I'll read it later. I can't take anymore. Why does everyone want so much from me today? Aaaaggggbhh.

At that moment a taxi crossed the lights at Pearse Street and moved towards her. She stuck her hand in the air, and it pulled up beside her. She lowered the sound just enough.

"Ballymun Flats, please."

The driver looked at her curiously. "Ok."

She hunched into the corner of the taxi, exhausted. Her body was drained from a mixture of relief and disappointment: relief that she'd soon be able to feel something other than sadness, disappointment that she was too weak not to need that.

Paul Noonan sang into her ear about stumbling in the darkness. She understood.

Chapter 19

FLORA

2:30 PM

SHARDS OF SUNLIGHT BOUNCED OFF the path on Mountjoy Square. Flora reached for her purple sunglasses and walked towards O'Connell Street. She loved the colour purple. It was unpopular, rarely in fashion, but striking – her own style. People commented on it. She liked that. In the second-hand shops of Temple Bar and George's Street Arcade, she lived out her fantasies of being other women: the women she read about in the pile of old magazines she kept under her bed. At home, she liked to sit by the window and pour over the images from these pages, imagine these people as they had been in life, drifting off the pages to wander through her house as though they had never left this world.

An old man whizzed by on a bicycle, shirt sleeves rolled up above his elbows, his basket full of vegetables. He gave her a nod as she crossed Gardiner Street. She liked the way the Irish could look each other in the eye and say hi without even knowing each other. This had surprised her when she first came to the country. Nonetheless, it wasn't so common these days.

She glanced at her reflection in a shop window. The wine-coloured sweatshirt dress clung to her body, fell just above the knee, and formed a perfect arc around her breast-line. She felt chic with a hint of danger: a subtle provocateur. Egyptian-style sandals wound around her long legs, punctuated the simplicity of the dress with a stamp of funk. Her lipstick was a shade redder than usual – a suggestion, an invitation she knew would be acted upon. Her dark hair was half piled on her head, stray curls falling gently around her oval face; a hint of eyeliner traced her dark-green eyes.

Hope he's up for it. His strong mouth. Need it against my skin.

Lady Windermere's Fan, by Oscar Wilde, was showing in The Gate Theatre. She had glanced at that once because Omar left it lying around the house. God knows why anyone would ever read a play. Omar's habits baffled her sometimes. Loved to boast about his Wildean heritage. Some distant, ten-times removed cousin of his father's, apparently. Mills and Boon was more her thing. At least he brought some of those home from the book market from time to time. Men were always handsome, women passionate, and the end happy. She liked that. Omar was always trying to read something complicated like that book they were all banging on about today. She had a look at it. It confused her – left her wondering what the hell the writer was on about. Omar said it was like a great, impenetrable symphony. You could have fooled her.

The little green man began to beep frantically, and she crossed the road into Parnell Street. It was like being transported temporarily to a Nairobi side-street – mothers carrying babies wrapped in colourful African prints, hip-hop music oozing from local cafés, a hairdresser advertising wonderful weaves. She loved dipping through these mini-worlds that had grown up in the tiny corners of Dublin. It made her feel less foreign, less alone with her differences.

Tomasz was outside Zagloba, the Polish pub, having a fag with a couple of mates from the building sites. He spotted her as she crossed the street and waved with a smile. He was the only family she had in this country – the son of her favourite aunt, Anna Kalata. She'd grown up beside him in Kraków. Aunt Anna's apartment had been one floor up from Flora's mother. Families stuck together. Flora hadn't been close to her mother, who was a conservative communist, a member of the old guard unable to cope with the changes brought on by Walesa and the move to democracy. Flora had learned to keep her mouth shut while secretly plotting her escape from this claustrophobic world.

The one way in which they'd communicated was through music. Maria had been a keen pianist and was delighted when her young daughter took up the violin, eventually playing with the Kraków Philharmonic Orchestra. The enormous pride her mother took in the work of Chopin and Gorecki, fellow Poles, led to many trips to the Filharmonia Concert Hall. Her mother had imagined a life for Flora full of recognition and success, like that of the great Polish violin virtuosa Ida Haendal. But Flora had other plans.

Since Flora had left Poland, they hardly ever spoke now – her mother immediately passed the phone to her weary father, Andrezej. Affable and passive, he acted as a Cold War interpreter between the two women in his life, trying his best to pass on essential information, such as deaths, births, and marriages, without getting dragged into the screaming rows.

Her brain shifted into Polish thoughts, Polish words, the Polish space she so rarely accessed these days. When she reverted to her own language, she felt like she'd shed a layer of skin; she felt lighter, unburdened by the space of understanding that lay between her and a language she was now confident in but could never breathe without effort.

"Looking lovely as ever, my dearest cousin." Tomasz spoke in Polish.

She felt like a child when he enveloped her in his large, muscular arms.

"Thanks, cousin. I just happened to be nearby, and I knew you'd probably be here for lunch, being a creature of habit and all that." She nodded to the unfamiliar faces behind her.

"Flora, this is Antoni, my pal I told you about from Gdansk, and Piotr. They work with me."

The younger, blond man smiled at her, his dark eyes shifting from side to side, unable to fix her in his sights.

"H - h - hello," said the man, his fair skin rising in colour.

Pretty but shy. Needs a soft woman to wrap around him, give him some confidence.

Flora extended her hand.

The older of the two had the ruddy complexion and hard-edged features of a man who'd grown up in the countryside. He looked up from his whiskey, acknowledged her presence with a nod. "Hot day, we've been sweating gallons in that warehouse. It's like an oven." He spoke with a thick, rural accent. After taking a slug from his glass, he continued reading the *Gazeta*, Ireland's Polish weekly newspaper.

Tomasz moved inside to get her a gin and tonic.

She sat beside the two men and attempted to start a conversation.

"Anything interesting in the paper today?"

"The usual ... lots of talk of job creation, emigrating young people, summer concerts. Never changes but you'd miss it, all the same, you know?"

He raised his head to see whether she'd agree.

"I don't miss it much, I have to admit." Flora refused to be dragged into the usual conversation. She was not a nostalgic woman and largely despised the reminiscent grumbling of her countrymen. They propped up the bar counters with endless stories of good old Poland, a place where people still had values, not like the greedy Irish who used the Poles to rebuild their precious cities. As far as she could see, everyone benefited from this little arrangement and, if pushed, she was having none of it.

"Becoming as Irish as the Irish, are you?" The man turned on her with an accusing gaze.

"No, I'm Polish, but I'm also European, and I wouldn't be here, you wouldn't be here, and he wouldn't be here" – she nodded at the young man beside them who seemed to be looking for a way to get up from the table and leave without causing insult – "unless our beloved country was incapable of giving us what we needed in life, so what's the point in complaining?"

"Do you know they pay us half what they pay the Irish? Fucking cannibals. Forget the pygmies. Sucking the juices from our bones, they are. Ask Tomasz. Tomasz, tell this cousin of yours what we've been forced to do because the Irish are bleeding us dry."

Her tall, fair-haired cousin placed three glasses on the table carefully. "That's enough, Piotr. Flora isn't here to get an earful from you."

Piotr refused to give up. "Where was it you two went to college again?"

"Piotr ..." Tomasz reprimanded him with a glare.

"Just humour me for a second. I have a point to make," replied Piotr.

"Mikolaj Kopernik in Torun, are you happy now?"

"Never been there, but I know of it. The point is that here we have two college men, two educated men, up to their knees in boxes and paid shit money. Tell her Tomasz. Tell her how much you're being paid, and how much the Irish doing the same job are being paid."

Tomasz glanced at Flora to gauge her mood. "I know you don't like to talk about this stuff, but it's true. I get 360 euros a week, and the Irish get at least 200 euros more and benefits."

"That may be so, but they've taken us in, haven't they? Who are we to complain if we're not getting the same as their own when we're getting four times the amount we'd get at home?" Flora could hear her voice rise with frustration.

The four of them lapsed into silence.

Tomasz broke the silence. "How's Omar?"

"Fine. Well, you know, the same, always the same."

Her cousin gave her a knowing look. "Are you planning a trip home soon?"

"If you mean Poland, no. Once a year is enough for me and I was back at Christmas."

Tomasz nodded. "Uncle Radoslaw isn't doing too well. I was onto my mother yesterday, and she reckons there's only a couple of months in it. I was thinking of heading home next month, just to see him."

"You should. Give him my love if you go. I can't afford to."

"But you earn pots in that fancy symphony of yours. The flights are dirt cheap these days anyway."

"Listen, Tomasz. You and I are different. I just don't want to go. I always end up feeling guilty over something, and do you know what drives me mad? No one ever asks me about my life here. It's as if they think that if we don't talk about it, it doesn't exist, and I've never left. It's all about getting me back to live the same dreary life as everyone else so I can justify their decisions, their existences. I'm an inconvenience. I hate it." She could feel anger bloat her brain, like a slow, creeping migraine.

Tomasz sipped his gin and sighed. "You've got to get over this thing with your mother."

She didn't like being told what to do. "What's that got to do with anything?"

He shrugged his shoulders. "Right, Flora. Forget it."

Flora placed her hand on his arm and smiled weakly. She wanted him to understand, but it was impossible. He was Polish through and through and had never wanted to be anything else.

"Listen, I'm off. I wanted to give you these." She threw down two tickets on the table. "They're for tonight in the concert hall. It'll be music from *Ulysses* and other music from Joyce's time. I know it's probably not your thing, but I thought ..."

"Thanks, Flora. I'd love to." He hugged her closely, and she felt the anger seep away.

CHAPTER 20

~ The Wandering Rocks ~

3:00 PM

THE RIVER LOOKED EXTREMELY LOW, even for this time of the year. Bernard O'Leary stood on the steps of The Four Courts and ran his fingers over the length of his red silk tie, repeating the gesture at regular intervals as he spoke.

"Ok, John, we understand each other, right?" He fixed John Fenton with a deep-eyed stare.

"I guess ... I don't know. Are you sure, Bernard?" asked the towering lawyer. He looked like a retired rugby player, his hulking, 6-foot-7 frame took over the footpath; passers-by had to step off it to pass.

"As I said, John, you can have your life back, once and for all. I'll get you more work than you can handle, but I need you on my side. You owe my daughter nothing."

John Fenton looked at the steel-blue eyes of the man he'd known for twenty years and could barely remember why he'd liked him in the first place.

"Do you feel nothing, Bernard, not even for your own daughter?" he asked, desperate for some flicker of humanity in the man he'd once called a friend.

"I love my daughter, John. She just doesn't always know what's good for her, that's all. She's willing to destroy her family for some high-ground ideal, and I can't let her." Bernard O'Leary's voice broke slightly as he spoke, almost as though to script.

John Fenton realised he'd never be able to break through the actor's disguise the minister had perfected for the eyes of the public. John stared at the ground and wondered how he'd let himself sink so low.

"Just call that Kinch lad and arrange a meeting. You know what to do after that."

John Fenton felt a wave of nausea grab his stomach. "Understood."

* * *

The cacophony of traffic greeted Monsignor Reidy as he descended the steps of Dr. Mc Sweeney's office. He felt like he was standing bang in the middle of a Wagner symphony with the percussion drowning out all other sound. His brain began to throb. It was only a ten-minute walk to the Pro Cathedral, where he wanted to chat about participating in the weekly Italian Mass. The native congregation had dwindled to the size of a pea; however, he was most impressed with the faith of the immigrant community. The Irish could learn a lot from them about enduring hardship and maintaining loyalty when times were hard. He felt slightly faint as he clutched the railings of the office on Bachelor's Walk.

"Are you all right, father?" An older black man gently took the Monsignor by the arm.

"Fine, sir, thank you." The man had a kind face, but the Monsignor didn't like to accept help unless it was necessary.

"Ok, then. If you're sure?"

"I'm sure."

The stranger let go of Reidy's arm and continued walking down the riverside.

The Monsignor nodded a thank you, raised his head and walked as upright as he could manage towards O'Connell Street.

Could do with a drink. Wynn's Hotel on the way for a quick one. Just one.

He felt tired, very tired. Perhaps it was for the best that he wasn't long for this life. He'd seen too much change in his sixty-five years on God's earth.

Too much change indeed.

A Romanian beggar, with a child strapped to her back, raised her cap towards the man of the cloth. He smiled at her warmly. "Bless you, my child. May God be with you." He passed by her, fingering the bunch of euro coins in his pocket.

Encouraging begging is no solution. Bring her to my church if I see her again, poor soul.

He glanced at the splinters of sunlight that bounced off the Spire like visible radio beams enveloping all of Dublin in an ever-evolving broadcast.

Stupid-looking thing. You'd miss Nelson all the same.

A group of muscular Slavs laboured in a lather of sweat as they laid tracks for the new Luas line.

Will be nice to see the trams again. A wave of nausea pulsed through his system. *In God's name, who can I tell? Who is there to tell of my misfortune?*

He turned into Lower Abbey Street, heading for Wynn's Hotel.

A group of young girls with skin-tight jeans, pierced eyebrows, and bellies the size of Brendan Behan stood at the news stall on the corner, flicking through magazines.

"Would you look at the state of your man?" said a redhead whose face resembled a palette that had been left out overnight and was now crusted with dry paint.

"Oy, pervert with your dog collar," she continued, the other three bursting their sides laughing.

Monsignor Reidy had never got used to the lack of respect that riddled the modern community like a medieval plague.

"There's one full of pretty little boys for you here, Father. You'd love that, eh?"

The girl was clearly drunk out of her mind in the middle of the afternoon. *Disgusting behaviour.* He glared at her and continued walking. He couldn't grace such vile behaviour with a response. It was hard to maintain one's composure in the face of such slurs. A collar meant something different to people now. He knew they'd done wrong, the Church, to hide the truth, to hide such people, but he wasn't one of them, and two thousand years of a glorious tradition should not be wiped out because of a small minority of evildoers.

His thoughts drifted back to his own predicament as he entered the bar of Wynn's Hotel.

I need to contact the boy. I need to let him know. It's time.

Luckily, the place was empty except for a group of older men sitting in the corner playing cards.

"Monsignor ..." One of them signalled with a tip of his cap.

"Pat, enjoying the game?" The men were old parishioners of his from way back.

"Paddy here is cleaning me out, Monsignor, but I'm going to get him back when Magnier's daughter's horse, Damson, romps home in the Queen Mary this afternoon."

"Ulysses, man, not that jumped-up Billy's mare. Ulysses is the boy for the day that's in it," replied the red-faced man, tugging on his beard.

"Sentimental shite, Monsignor. Sure, no one would put a penny on that good-for-nothing nag only for all the commotion today. Jimmy Joyce is belly-laughin in his grave at the amount of money that's going to go down the drain on that carthorse today. What do you think, Monsignor?" asked Pat, sipping on his whiskey.

"Not much in the mood for betting today, lads, I'm afraid." Reidy signalled to the barman to pour him his usual double-brandy.

"Well, if you change your mind and fancy a flutter, Damson is your only man," said the bald-headed man, returning to the cards.

"Grand, Pat, grand. I'll remember." He sat down at the solid oak counter and stared at himself in the mirror. A sallow-eyed stranger with a neat crown of grey hair and host- pale skin looked back at him. He'd never grown accustomed to this strange face, a shadow of the man he had once known.

"Monsignor," said Des O'Shea, "you're looking a little worse for wear. Everything all right?" The heavy-set barman slid the brandy towards Reidy.

"Not the best, Des, I'm afraid." He swigged back a slug of the brandy.

"Nothing serious, I hope." Des wiped a glass in his hand.

"I'm in God's departure lounge, Des, but thankfully I've managed to miss a few flights. Not for much longer though."

The barman bent into a low whisper: "You don't mean ...?"

"Just came from Dr. Mc Sweeney's. Have about six months to live. Puts the fear of God into you. Cancer of the liver actually." Reidy raised his glass and took another swig.

"Well. I'm very sorry to hear that, sir. Very sorry indeed."

"Sure, at least I'll get to meet the Man Himself, finally. Should be glad of it, I suppose."

"Are you sure you should?" The barman eyed the Monsignor's nearly empty glass.

"One more for the road, Des. Too late to stop now." The Monsignor winked. "Just hope I'm not in for any nasty surprises when I get to the Pearly Gates." He raised his glass.

"Well, if Mohammed greets you at the gates, say you were only messin."

They laughed together.

"Des, can I confess something to you?"

The barman leant over to listen.

"There's someone, a family member, that I haven't spoken to for a very long time – practically never – but he's my closest living relative. Do you think ... should I ... contact him?" The Monsignor turned his grey eyes to the bespectacled barman.

"If you feel that's the right thing to do Monsignor, of course. Is there bad blood between you?" asked Des Kiely in a whisper.

"Yes, I'm afraid, bad blood. He may not want to talk to me after I ..." His voice trailed off. The soft-voiced barman leant in further.

"God loves a trier. Remember that Monsignor."

"Indeed, he does."

"No harm in it and if it ends uncomfortably, you're no worse off. Consider the effort a penance of a kind ... if that's what you feel you need, of course." The barman touched Reidy softly on his sleeve. "Three Hail Marys, an Our Father, and ask God for forgiveness, my son." Des O'Shea made the sign of the cross and broke into a barrel of laughter.

A smile spread across the Monsignor's tired face. *What will be will be.*

* * *

Khaled Hussein watched The Traveller men get into formation in front of the Bank of Ireland. V waved to him as he crossed to the other side of Dame

Street.

"As-salamu alaykum," shouted the wiry-haired man. Khaled waved back, walking away from Trinity with the instructions that V had given him. He watched people move past him, feeling himself drift through the streets in slow motion. Their blurred faces seemed to blend into one long mass of colour streaking across his eyelid like a slow-moving comet. He began to chant silently to himself.

"In the Name of God, the Compassionate, the Merciful. By the light of day, and by the dark of night, your Lord has not forsaken you, nor does He abhor you. The life to come holds a richer prize for you than this present life. You shall be gratified with what your Lord will give you."

Khaled Hussein repeated this chant to himself in a barely discernible mumble of sound. He spotted the lady from the art gallery crossing from the Temple Bar. A wave of fear washed over him. He turned left into George's Street and continued his chant, fighting the inner voice that sought to push the divine words out of his mind.

"In the Name of God, the Compassionate, the Merciful."

Who is the woman? Coincidence. No.

"In the Name of God,"

Concentrate.

"The Compassionate."

A group of loud teenagers passed by. Probably Americans. A small girl with braces blew a kiss in Khaled's direction.

Whores. Everywhere, whores.

"The Merciful."

Mother. I need you.

"In the Name of God, the Compassionate, the Merciful."

The phone inside his pocket buzzed. He glanced at the flashing name: *Father*.

"Hello, Khaled, where are you?" asked Mohammed Hussein.

"Just picking up a book I ordered, Father. What's wrong?"

"Have you seen the time? I need to go for my angina check-up at 4:00 PM. You promised me you'd mind the shop, boy. Where are you?" said his agitated father.

"Sorry, Father, but it will take me at least 30 minutes to get back."

Khaled glanced at his watch.

"Well, get back here as quickly as possible. That should be all right." His father hung up just as Khaled arrived at the door of his Camden Street destination.

Thirty minutes, that should be enough.

He banged the brass door knocker loudly. A tall, bearded man, dressed in heavy, white robes, answered the door.

"Khaled. We've been expecting you," said the man in a gentle voice.

He led Khaled down a long corridor and into a dark, spacious room. A large group of young men knelt in rows on mats on the wooden floor. They didn't notice his entering and continued to chant loudly in response to an older man who sat on the floor in front of them. The man nodded in Khaled's direction. He finished the chant and signalled to the group to continue with their prayers.

He took Khaled into a small room at the back. Another man sat by a window. He had an oval face with strongly marked features, dark eyes, and short black hair. He was immediately recognisable. He was Abdullah Al-Khasi, a man who'd featured in a prime- time TV programme study of Islam in Ireland and in the speculative columns of the Irish newspapers. Khaled nodded to him.

"As-salamu alaykum," said the man warmly.

"Alaykum as-salam." Khaled felt excited to be in the presence of such a prominent Sunni in his community. He'd often seen him talking to his father's friends at the Clonskeagh Mosque. Since speculation on what exactly he was up to had grown, his father had warned him not to engage with this man. Khaled did not like his father's lack of commitment. They said that Abdullah Al-Khasi knew Osama Bin Laden personally, and now here he was, Khaled Hussein, one step away from this man. Bin Laden was a true Muslim. A man who knew the true meaning of the Holy Qur"an. None of the wishy-washy bullshit that the majority of his community applied to their daily lives. A La Carte Islam. Khaled knew better, and he would protect the *ummah* no matter what it meant.

"Hello ... Khaled, is it?" The pleasant-faced man gestured for Khaled to sit.

"Ahmed tells me you have been studying hard and are ready for the assignment we have for you."

"Yes, sir, I hope so." His body swayed between a mixture of elation and fear.

"Well, it's time." The man placed a firm hand on Khaled's arm. Khaled passed the package V had given to him.

"Ta"widh," said the man.

"Yes," said Khaled.

* * *

"Cómo estás, coño?" Juanma Gonzales threw his arm around Kinch's shoulders.

"Muy bien, hombre, muy bien. Y tu?" Kinch hugged his guitar teacher warmly. He and Gerry had been taking flamenco guitar lessons from Juanma for six months.

"Que día, hombre. La ostia, no?" Juanma Gonzales had the face of a man who'd spent his fifty years under the burning heat of an Andalusian sun. Dark and wrinkled, he also had the hallmarks of a man who'd lived well, who knew the joys of vino tinto and croquetas on a lazy Spanish afternoon.

Kinch looked over the shoulder of the tall, muscular Spaniard. "La Puta Madre, hombre."

Cameras snapped madly as an open-topped, Dublin sight-seeing bus drifted past Trinity's gates. Oliver Goldsmith and Edmund Burke stared stonily into the distance of Dame Street.

"Kinch, you doin anything tonight? I have two free tickets to go to de American band, Low, in Christ Church Cathedral this evening. You hear of dat?" The Spaniard pulled the tickets from his back pocket.

"You're joking, man. I would die for those."

Juanma pushed the tickets into Kinch's side pocket. "They're yours. I cannot go. Enjoy, hombre."

"Muchas gracias. Estás seguro?" Kinch drifted back into the language he had learned in the Sacromonte caves of Granada.

Juanma Gonzales eyed the 46A bus. "Seguro, seguro." It turned the corner towards them.

"Mi bus. Hasta luego, hombre. Llámame," said the Spaniard, moving towards Grafton Street at speed. Juanma waved his guitar case at the bus as it flew past. Kinch clutched the bunch of carnations he'd just bought and turned to look at the ambassadorial procession heading down Dame St. and towards him. He looked at his watch: 3:20 PM. The sound of horse hooves and buckled music drifted past. *Right, that's me off the book for a while. Time for a bit of pleasure.*

***

Paul Mullens concentrated while he ran his brush carefully along the string of Lady Lavery's harp. A couple of Japanese tourists snapped photos of the would-be artist, marvelling at the exactitude of the imitation. The dappled concrete of a Dublin footpath provided the unlikely canvas. He could feel his mobile buzzing in his pocket, set his brush aside and glanced at the flashing name. "The Boss". *Will he ever leave me a bit of peace?*

"Boss." He knew his real name – he had so many aliases: Franko, Scorpion, Scumbag, depending on who was talking about him – but Boss was all Paul needed to know about the man who ran the biggest drug-dealing gang in the city. A mesh of such gangs had encircled the city in a web of crime. It could have given New York's South Bronx a run for its money – the thick, rich pelt of the Celtic Tiger providing opportunities aplenty to those willing to make the most of them.

"Mullens, get your bony arse over here right fuckin now. Need to unload the gear pronto." The razor-sharp tones of the Boss shot through his ear like a sharp needle.

"Right, Boss. I just need to grab a quick bite to eat. I'm starvin."

"I'll fuckin chew your dick off and serve it in a sandwich with ketchup if you don't get over here now. Do you hear me, Mullens?"

"Right, sure, but what's goin on?" Paul collected the money from his baseball cap and piled the chalks into his satchel.

"There's been a monumental fuckup. The lads were nabbed by the cops this morning robbing a post-office. Some Cork lad got caught up in the middle of it all, and the lads, being the thick shits they are, thought it would be a laugh to pretend he was one of us. Fuckin dickwads!"

"Jaysus, where are they being held?"

"Pearse Street."

"Shit, was Tommo there?"

"Yeah, but they released him cos he's underage."

"Thank God."

"The rest of them are still locked up. I swear if that brother of yours had half a workin brain, I wouldn't be lookin at another botched fuckin job. You better sort him out Mullens, or you'll be scrapin him up off the street."

Paul's body lurched with fear. His Ma was going to lose it.

"Jaysus, Boss, he's not the sharpest, but he's as loyal as a cocker spaniel. He worships the ground you walk on."

"If it's worshippin I needed I'd become one of those fuckin arsehole TV evangelists. I wouldn't wipe my hole with an ounce of worship. It's fuckin results, Mullens. Results are all that matters. Do you understand me?"

"Yeah, Boss, results right."

"Right, good lad, jump in a taxi. I need you here now."

From the road in front of him, he could hear the sound of horse hooves clipping their way past. He looked up. The Taoiseach waved enthusiastically from the gold gilded carriage.

"Fuckin plonker!" yelled Paul. "It's far from fuckin regal carriages you were raised, dickhead." Paul could feel bile rising in his throat and hocked a loogie towards the passing carriage.

A Japanese couple shuffled away nervously.

He packed everything into his satchel and waited for the commotion to pass. A taxi whizzed towards him, and he flagged it down.

"Where you off to son?" asked the grey-haired driver.

Better not let them know the address. Blacklisted amongst the cabbies who're in the know.

"Crumlin, I'll show you when we get there."

He grabbed his beeping mobile and looked at the message.

Shit! The girl. She's on her way to my place.

He pushed Bláithín's number. It went straight to her answering machine. "Hi sorry, it's Paul. Will be a bit late. Something urgent came up. Sorry. Call me if it's a problem."

He'd liked the look of that girl. Snobby Southsider but nice enough – a fine thing. *Could tell she was a cokehead straight away. It's in the eyes. Wonder if she'd go for me. Stranger things.*

* * *

The woman behind the desk at the camera shop was busy gossiping on the phone. She barely registered Omar's presence as she nattered on about some guy called Terry and how he had a bloody cheek to think she'd take him back after he'd shagged her friend.

Omar sighed. "Excuse me."

She stuck her hand in the air and continued.

Omar raised his voice, "Excuse me, but I'm in a rush."

"Just a minute," she replied.

That was it. Omar could take no more. "No, NOW!"

She threw him a wicked look, excused herself, and hung up. "Jaysus, who got out on the wrong side of bed today!"

Omar pushed the photo slip towards her. "Can I just have my prints, please?"

"Yeah, yeah, don't get your knickers in a twist, luv." She took a box from under the counter and pulled out a package that matched his ticket. Her thin lips twisted into an unpleasant sneer. "Twenty-two euro, mister."

Omar sighed deeply and pushed the money her direction. He took the package, opened it, and reached inside, eager to look at the photos he'd taken. Jameson's shots of the funeral were striking, especially the one of the poor young woman following the child's coffin. He flicked through some more, spotting the sandwich men at the bottom of the pile. There were a couple of close-ups and then – bingo! – a prize-winner of a photo, taken from the island in the centre of O'Connell Bridge. The road was empty of traffic, and six of the sandwich men stood beside each other, obviously unaware that their random positioning spelled out the word REVEAL.

Although Omar didn't exactly know why, he sensed there was something special about this photo.

Definitely a front-page contender. Must talk to Will. At last, a break.

* * *

Breda Keane gazed out over the green, leafy splendour of Merrion Square. She clutched a bunch of yellow-bright sunflowers.

That should cheer her up no end, she thought, as a group of students descended the steps of the American College.

A frog croaked in her pocket.

Message, quick! She tore her pocket trying to get at the phone. *Mam, it's coming. Quick come*!

"Holy Mary, Mother of God." Her thick ankles wobbled as she took off towards Holles Street.

* * *

James C. Kenny, American Ambassador to Ireland, and his wife Margaret, accompanied by An Taoiseach, Bertie Ahern, exited the Phoenix Park gates after a substantial luncheon of kidney and red wine. The cavalcade made its way jauntily toward the Quays. The dignitaries acknowledged the warm greetings of the hard-working people of Dublin, who stepped out of their establishments for a proper gawk. The horses, perfectly groomed and attired in crimson plumage, followed the police escort with care as it moved along the Wolfe Tone Quay towards Rory O'Moore Bridge.

At the Smithfield entrance off Arran Quay, the cavalcade passed an unconcerned Ms. Portia Staunton, walking her Barbone poodle, Snow. She picked up Snow's scatological "leavings" in a cardboard box before returning to her fifth-floor apartment in Smithfield Market. Ambassador Kenny greatly enjoyed the warmth of the sun as his carriage passed Bernard O'Leary and John Fenton, who spoke gravely on the steps of The Four Courts. O'Leary raised a weary hand to his fellow party-man.

Mr. Ahern acknowledged with a gentle nod of his white head.

Two young African girls jumped with enthusiasm in front of The Ormonde Hotel, much to the delight of Mrs. Kenny, who commented on their pretty plaited hair. The river was sucked to within a trickle of its life in the heat of the mid-summer day.

The stately, plump figure of Monsignor Reidy was easy to spot as he made his way into the offices of Dr. Donal Mc Sweeney.

From their vantage point at the head of Grattan Bridge, Dick Cowen and Mark Jameson watched the passing parade with a jaundiced eye: Jameson jumped to professional attention with the click-clack of his camera shutter.

An Taoiseach noted the journalists and smiled deliberately in their direction.

The clip-clop parade jangled its way along Parliament Street to the considerable delight of a screaming group of American students. They waved their tiny American flags with unbounded enthusiasm.

Ambassador Kenny waved back with equal joy, delighted to see his fellow countrymen proudly displaying their colours in the streets of Dublin.

A Garda car passed ahead of the parade in front of City Hall; Gerry Deasy thumbed his finger with disdain.

An Taoiseach commented to Ambassador Kenny on the considerable strides that had been made by Minister O'Leary in fighting crime in Dublin.

The horses tripped around the corner, heads cocked high, and turned into the wide sweep of Dame Street. It unfurled like a giant stone carpet, Trinity's carved façade proudly standing to attention in the distance.

Mrs. Kenny noticed the cold stare of a young man who mumbled to himself as he turned into George's Street. She felt a cool breeze pass over her like a premonition.

The jaunty step of Flora Wilde caught the eye of An Taoiseach.

Flora smiled broadly at the ambassador's wife, taking note of the singular violet of Mrs. Kenny's couture jacket.

In Westmoreland Street, Bláithín O'Leary strained to see the passing parade, while the taxi driver struggled with his map. She didn't notice Omar Wilde's loping stride as he made his way to the camera shop on Bachelor's Walk.

In front of Goldsmith's stony perch, Kieran Lynch doffed his Dedalus hat appropriately to the delight of all members of the gilded carriage.

Cursing loudly as the bus flew past, Juanma Gonzales paid no heed to the passing cavalcade.

Ambassador Kenny in his turn didn't notice the discontented guitar master but gazed over his head to point out the provost's house to his wife.

The horses bristled with fright as Paul Mullens hurled unwelcome abuse at the head of the Irish government.

Bertie Ahern responded by broadening his smile, much to the disgust of the artist.

Hanan Hussein chased after Will Philips, who watched the proceedings with mild amusement.

A yellow sunflower flew across the mouth of the carriage, landing in Mrs. Kenny's lap. She acknowledged the sender as being one Mr. Matt Phelan, of Celtic Waters fame. Mr. Phelan was a sight to behold, bedecked in azure from top to toe.

At Trinity's side entrance, a group of students shouted slurs at the unfazed ambassador while clutching placards and chanting in unison, "Stop Bush Visit!" Sarah Purser stood in the centre, taking the time to protest as she'd just finished her exam.

Ambassador Kenny read The Traveller sandwich men as he passed by, unable to register the coldness in their dark eyes.

The gateman at the back of Trinity Gates doffed his cap politely.

The carriage rolled elegantly past, and an assembled group outside Sweny's Chemists delighted at the sight. The Bloomian assemblage waved their caps and canes with great aplomb, and the ambassador was most delighted.

An agitated Breda Keane sped past, bumping into Mr. Philip Lacey. His Bloomian feathers ruffled, he regained his composure and waved his cane amicably at the ambassador.

At McKenny's Bridge a group of playful children jumped into the thick waters of the canal, splashing the edge of the coach with the impact. Faces peered out of windows along the leafy avenues around Haddington Road and were acknowledged by An Taoiseach.

The entourage proceeded on its last piece of the journey to the RDS. Ambassador Kenny and Mrs. Kenny waved proudly at the sentry guards, who hopped to attention in front of the American Embassy. An Taoiseach promised that it would be a most entertaining show as the carriage reached its destination in the grounds of the RDS.

Chapter 21

KINCH

3:45 PM

KINCH PASSED THE THUNDER ROAD CAFÉ, deafened by the noise of screaming children. They hurled food at each other with great enthusiasm. A little woman caught his eye and leapt from her chair.

"Mr. Dedalus!" she shouted in an American drawl.

Kinch contemplated running, but it was too late now. He groaned and plastered on a smile.

"We saw you this morning at the tower. Fabulous, just fabulous," said the little woman.

"Why thank you. Most kind," Kinch replied while continuing to walk.

She grabbed him by the arm. "You absolutely must come into our party for a second. My friends over there have been dying to have a drink with Stephen Dedalus." She nodded to a group of weary-looking adults.

They raised their glasses enthusiastically.

"I'm terribly sorry, Mam, but something urgent has come up, and I'm afraid I can't stay."

Her face creased with displeasure.

Kinch attempted to move away from the door.

"But everyone will be so disappointed," she said. "Come on, just for ten minutes so we can get some photos for the folks at home." She grabbed his arm and yanked him into the screaming mess of children.

"Well, ten minutes then." There wasn't much point in protesting. The determined little woman gripped his arm like a crab in heat.

"Everyone, this is our very own Stephen Dedalus. Didn't I tell you he was so cute?"

Kinch attempted a weak smile and doffed his hat at the excited group. "Ladies and gentlemen."

"Ooooohhh! Mr. Dedalus, can I get a photo with you and Mike to take back to the kids? My daughter is an English professor at Yale. She'll go wild!" The woman prodded her husband. A large, rotund man smiled weakly at Kinch and moved into photo-taking position. His unnaturally tanned wife put her hand around Kinch's waists and offered a white-toothed grin.

"Great guys, now cheeeeese!" shouted the little American woman. She clutched the camera like a weapon. The group of adults joined in the cheesing and drowned out the sound of the children for a split second.

Kinch made the necessary photo rounds and contemplated as quick an exit as he could politely manage. Just as he was about to make his excuses, a plump, young boy flung a glob of green jelly into the crevice of Kinch's Trilby hat. The children erupted into laughter, high-fiving the boy, who grinned like a loon in Kinch's direction.

Cheeky little fecker. I'd love to kick that fat arse of yours from here to Sunday.

"I'm so sorry. Kyle, get over here and apologise. The rotund man grabbed his carbon-copy son by the scruff of the neck and dragged him to the adult table.

"Kyle, apologise to Mr. Dedalus right now."

The grinning child giggled as he responded. "Sorry."

Kinch wanted to belt the little fecker, who clearly was loving every minute of it. "That's all right." Kinch nodded to the father and wiped the jelly off the top of his hat.

"So sorry," replied his mother. "These boys get so carried away with all the excitement. I'm sure he didn't mean it."

Kinch was quite sure the devious little shite meant it – and a lot more. He exchanged a look with the boy as if to say, "You might be able to fool them, but I've got your number mate."

The man let go of the boy who raced back to the giggling group of youngsters. They were busily assembling other food objects for a fresh assault. *Need to get the hell out of here.*

"Sorry, Madam, but I have to go." He finished wiping off his hat and moved to leave.

She slipped a fifty-euro note and a card into his pocket. "Awww. Well, if you must. That's my friend Mike's card. He's a big businessman. Owns half of Dublin. He's looking for young actors to perform at children's parties – a new business venture of his. You'd make a bomb. Should give him a call."

Kinch smiled weakly. *I'd rather sleep in an ocean of shite than put up with a load of brats again.* "Yeah, sounds great. Thanks all the same."

He stepped into Fleet Street and turned towards Temple Bar.

Christ, I've earned my money today! He squinted in the sunlight as he put his jellified hat on his head. *No puedo ver nada.* He felt a sweat bead travel the length of his goatee and drop to the ground. Peeling off the black suit jacket, he pondered the joys of global warming. *A good ten years of solid sunshine might be better than an eternity of rain after all. Sorry, Mother Earth, but after a couple of billion years of drowning half to death, us Irish could do with a break.*

He took out a cigarette, lit it, took a long, slow drag, and blew the smoke into the air. His phone buzzed in his pocket.

"Yes, John ... What? Meet you *now*? ... But I'm supposed to be meeting someone ... Yes, yes, ok. I know. We need to sort out Gerry ... I'm sure. Ok. Five minutes, the IFI. Right. See you."

Better text her. He tapped a message into his phone and pressed *send.*

He ran through Temple Bar, bouncing his way through the crowds like a pinball. "Black is the Colour" drifted from the Quays Pub, the traditional music mecca of Temple Bar.

A group of English girls passed by dressed in identical French maids" attire. Their bellies oozed out of the outfits. The girl at the centre, who clutched a large, black dildo, compared its dimensions to the imagined girth of unsuspecting males as they passed. The girls fell about laughing, barely able to navigate the cobblestones in their towering high heels.

Pissed at 4:00 PM, Kinch thought. *Attractive that.*

Much to his relief, Kinch navigated around the screaming group without having his member virtually assessed.

He passed into the long corridor of the Irish Film Institute. A group of Bloomites exited, having just attended the Volta film screening. They acknowledged Kinch, who smiled graciously and continued into the bar.

The café buzzed with the usual mix of film devotees and wannabe bohemians. Glen Hansard's energetic voice jumped out of the PA system. John Fenton sat in the corner, abstractedly gazing at the poster of *The Quiet Man* on the wall behind him.

"Maureen O'Hara was a fine thing all the same," said Kinch, interrupting John's dreaming.

"Hey, Kinch. Yes. Don't make many like her anymore." John gestured to Kinch to sit down.

"Speaking of gorgeous women, I hear you broke up with Bláithín this morning. I guess the younger woman isn't to your taste." John's voice was tinged with disdain.

"Relationships are complicated, John. I know you like Bláthín. She's a fab girl. But it just wasn't right, that's all." Kinch felt irritated that he couldn't seem to get away from this subject. Boy, did news travel fast in this city.

Fenton shuffled the papers in front of him and sucked on a whiskey. "Right, let's get down to it. I'm afraid Gerry's in deep trouble."

"But he didn't do it. What evidence is there?" said Kinch.

"The other cons are fingering him as the contact man. His uncle is a well-known Cork drug dealer. Also an established fence who works for Tommy Fleming claims he's sold a ton of coke to your friend. Enough." Fenton didn't drop his gaze for a second.

"The word of two extremely dodgy groups of individuals. Surely that's just circumstantial," said Kinch.

"Circumstantial it may be, but damn well good enough to get your friend stuck away in the clanger."

Kinch didn't know what to think. His instinct told him that Gerry was innocent, or at least his heart told him he wanted to believe it. "That's hardly justice in action."

"Maybe not, but the country is flooded with drug dealers. A petty Cork drug dealer wouldn't exactly make top of the 'let's be nice' pile." Fenton bent closer to Kinch. "There may be another way, however."

Kinch eyed him suspiciously. "I'm listening."

"Are you aware of the trouble between Bláithín and her father?"

"Are you talking generally or specifically?" Kinch knew a lot about the way her father had stuck his big fat nose into their relationship – how he deemed Kinch an unsuitable match for his daughter, how he'd pushed her beyond breaking, until Kinch had to face Minister O'Leary and tell him to get the fuck out of their lives.

"She's not prepared to back her father up about the night he was accused of handing a bribe over to Power. It could be the end of him if his own daughter turns against him publicly." Fenton shifted as though his pants were too tight for him.

"And not a minute too soon. That man is a snake."

"Whether he is or he isn't, the thing is her dad's the Minister for Justice, and you know what that means for your friend if he steps in to support his case."

Kinch could see where this was going and wanted to hit Fenton there and then. "What are you suggesting, Fenton?"

"I'm suggesting that you persuade Bláithín to be kind to her father, and he'll return the favour."

"Jesus Christ. Is this your idea or his?" asked Kinch.

"Does it really matter? It works for everyone." Fenton drained his glass and brought it down to the table with a bang. "I'll never understand what she sees in you Kinch, but the bare fact of it is you're about the only one she listens to these days. Talk some reason to her, will you?" said Fenton. "And one more thing – I know you're strapped for cash. There might be a small reward in it for yourself if you can get her to see sense."

Kinch could feel his body shake. He jumped to his feet, shouting. "You tell O'Leary to stick his money up his fat-cat arse! Not everyone can be bought."

"Then kiss goodbye to your Corkonian friend, I'm afraid."

"Fenton, you're some shit." Kinch picked up his satchel and pushed the door open with fury.

CHAPTER 22

OMAR

~ Sirens ~

4:00 PM

GOLDEN-HAIRED BEAUTIES, eyes opal and limbs lithe and long, drifted by the doorway of the Ormonde Hotel. Omar hesitated about going in – he hated crowds, but Eileen had told him this was where the editor would be.

Miss Ireland regionals. Mmmm. Beauties abound.

A warm hush fell over the large room.

The flaxen-haired girl on the stage – mesmerising tones, like hot lavender oil drifting into the lobby. Voice of an angel. Too far away to make out. Could send me to sleep. Ignore it. Bar a safer option.

Omar crossed the lobby. He could see Jameson and Cowen chatting to two of the contestants at the far end.

Boys on the job again. Cowen's eyes engorged, leering. Watch out girls. He'd eat you whole.

The function room shook with applause. A voice Omar recognised came over the PA system.

Fecking Phelan. Strutting peacock is everywhere. Thought he'd be with her by now.

Sadness washed through him like sour milk. He looked through an open door into the function room. It was packed with an odd mixture of tourists, Joyceans, and beauty pageant devotees.

Funny how I never catch sight of the man of the hour. Blooming Leopold. Shadow walking. Too preoccupied to care about all that malarkey anymore.

He spotted Willy Farrell at a table just inside the door near the back bar. Deep in thought, he clutched a double Jameson.

Ah, the bauld Editor.

Omar stepped through the door and tripped on the frayed edge of a piece of carpet.

Farrell looked up from his meal. "Wilde. Should have dived. Sued them for a pretty penny."

"Hi, Boss. Listen, could I have a quick word?"

"Jaysus, can't a man get a second to himself?" said Farrell to an invisible God.

"Just five minutes, Willy. It's important. I was going to talk to you tomorrow, when all this shite is over with, but now that you're here ..." A group of Joyceans were gathered around a man in a black bowler hat. "Is that him? Bloom?"

"Looks like it. His back's to us." Farrell looked at his watch. "Ten past four. That's about right. Did you get those interviews for me yet?"

Omar tried to ignore the glob of mustard that dripped from the edge of Farrell's coarse red beard, but his stomach lurched. "I've been chasing that bastard all day. He's always one step ahead. I'll go over to him as soon as I've had a word, but I have to talk to you."

Farrell drained his glass and shook his head. "Never seen you so fired up, Wilde. Suppose I should be glad. There's a spark in the Arab after all. Go on then."

Omar moved the papers from the stool beside Farrell and sat down. "Willy, I have a photo I took. Just want you to look at it. Front page stuff, I'm sure."

Farrell raised his eyebrows. "That would surprise me, Wilde."

Omar pulled out the photo of the sandwich men and pushed it towards Farrell. "I have an idea for a story that could go with it too."

Farrell put on his glasses and had a good look. "These are the guys on the bridge, right? Good shot."

"Thanks, Boss. You know that piece you were asking me for this morning? I know you gave it to Cowen, but what if I interviewed these guys? Clearly, they're immigrants. Thought it would be interesting if I got their stories, you know, to *reveal* who they are, and why they're here. The photo's perfect to back that up."

"Not bad, Wilde, but Kate has the 'Focus on Immigrants' brief, and she'd murder me if I let you step on her toes."

"But you know it's a good idea." Omar tried to control his frustration.

"Buy me a drink and I'll think about it." Farrell took a bite of his kidney sandwich.

Omar gestured to Pat, who was engrossed in a conversation with two Miss Ireland contestants who held up one end of the bar.

Lynnia Mohan pulled the mauve, satin skirt around her round rump and placed herself delicately on a tall stool. The skirt slit reached to the top of her thigh, revealing a pale leg.

Silky skin, soft, young. Wish I could touch, glide over the silk of it.

She turned towards Omar and smiled. He shifted uncomfortably and smiled back. *Eyes of a minx. Suck you in.*

She pawed her ample bosom, looking down to make sure it hadn't removed itself from the strapless shift. "Pat, I'm killed trying to keep these boobs from popping out," Lynnia said, her eyes fixed on Omar. She elbowed Mona Kelly.

The tall brunette turned towards Omar, running her pearl fingertips the length of her pale-blue dress. "I know what you mean, Lynnia. Sure I'm poured into it." She placed her hands under her protruding bosoms, pushing them upwards until the nipples showed through the delicate silk.

Omar could feel a shift in his groin and stifled a groan. The girls erupted into a fit of giggles.

"Wilde, are you going to order that drink or what?" Farrell interrupted.

"Yeah, sorry ... Pat, a pint and a coke, please." *Dirty minxes. So young, lovely. Temptresses.*

The distracted barman nodded assent.

"Getting a little excited there, are we?" Farrell asked with a narrow smile. "Could be arrested for that. Barely legal."

"I don't know what you mean. I was just ..."

"How is that fine wife of yours, by the way?"

"Flora's ... good," Omar replied.

"I'm sure she is."

"What do you mean by that?" said Omar irritated.

"Nothing, Wilde. Jesus, relax."

"About the photo, Boss ...?"

"Listen, can you hang on a minute? I'm dying for a fucking slash. Don't move." The small man scampered towards the back of the room.

Omar looked towards the lobby. Monsignor Reidy had snuck in and sat with his cronies, Cowen, and Jameson. Omar could hear Phelan's voice bellowing towards them from the other side of the room.

Never far from the action, that man.

The music started up and a familiar voice crooned from the back of the room.

The room exploded in applause.

Bald Pat arrived at the table with a pint of the black stuff. "A fine pair of tarts, aren't they?" He nodded towards Lynnia and Mona. "Wouldn't mind a bit of that." He winked at Omar, who smiled weakly.

"Who's that singing? Sounds familiar." Omar strained to see over the crush of bodies.

"Ronan bloody Keating," Pat replied. "God preserve us. You think they could do better. The young ones love him, I suppose. Girls go mad for him. God knows what they see in the ginger bastard."

Omar laughed. "Sure, they always go for the musicians, don't they? He's a nice lad all the same. Good voice too."

"Maybe so but calling that guy a musician is like calling the pope an atheist. Yusuf Islam must have lost his mind to let that fella strangulate his song."

Omar looked at Pat with a puzzled expression.

"Cat Stevens. He converted you know. Has the beard down to the floor, the whole shebang. Creepy if you ask me," Pat said.

"No creepier than men in long gowns." Omar nodded in the direction of the Monsignor.

"What the hell is a man of the cloth doing hanging out in a sea of women anyway?" Pat wiped the table with a rag.

Omar watched as the two girls at the bar slipped off their stools and strode confidently past him, their stilettoed limbs moving with the satin of their dresses. Lynnia Mohan winked at Omar as she passed, raising the slit of her skirt. Mona Kelly wet her full lips with the tip of her tongue and smiled.

"See ye later, girls. Good luck with the competition. Ballybrack's sure to be a winner." Pat kicked Omar under the table. "The accents would crack your eardrums, but who cares once you have them on their backs. Sure, they're all the same then, Ballybrack or Foxrock, eh?" He laughed with a croak, picked up Farrell's empty glass, and headed towards the bar.

Mind like a sewer. Who cares how they sound? Move with grace. Lovely soft skin.

He watched Lynnia Mohan as she sat on Cowen's lap. She laughed deeply, a gloved arm around his left shoulder. Holding her phone to her ear, she pulled Cowen to her. His head against hers, they listened to a mystery sound, a hidden voice.

To breathe her in, pass through me, out and through her angel's ear, the sun-kissed edges of her lobe. To share that sound, the mystery of it, the tingle of a violin's breath on the warm summer air.

Omar watched as Phelan approached a table nearby, picked up his straw hat, said goodbye to his companions, and headed out the door.

Jaunty bastard. You're off to play her song.

Ronan Keating's light voice drifted over the crowd.

Omar felt a dull sadness seep through him.

"You look like someone died, Wilde." Farrell sat down and glanced at his watch. "Half past four. I need to get back soon."

"But my photo, Boss?" Omar could feel his chance slipping away from him.

"Give the photo to Kate. Talk to her about working on the piece with her. We'll credit you with the photo and list you as an assistant."

Omar's voice rose above the music drifting from the back of the room. "But Willy, it's *my* idea."

Farrell fixed Omar with a burning stare. "Conversation *over*. And get an interview with that bastard Bloom, will you, for God's sake!" He picked up his paper and headed for the door, tripping over the carpet on the way. "Shite!"

Omar leant forward, clutching his face in his hands. *Might as well give up now. Give it all up.*

A piece of ice in the empty glass in front of him slid to the bottom. *Tinkletickling the edge of her spine. She loves that. When the water runs down the crevices of her warm back into the crevice of her buttocks. He'll be at that now. Fucking bastard, fucking her, fucking life.*

He felt like crying but didn't want to make a scene.

A deep tenor voice filled the bar of the Ormonde. Omar turned to see the Monsignor on stage with Ronan Keating. He'd read that Reidy had been an accomplished tenor in his youth, before he became a man of the cloth. His voice was warm, like a deep, rich burgundy wine. It floated through the air to the soft accompaniment of a trickling piano.

"Tis the last rose of summer, left blooming all alone."

The room sat silently watching.

"All her lovely companions are faded and gone."

Lovely Lynnia gazed wistfully into the distance, deep in thought. Cowen looked at her longingly, stroking the nape of her neck with his index finger.

"Tho' the heart be weary, sad the day and long, still to us at twilight comes love's old song … comes love's old sweet song."

Omar sighed and took a swig from the half-drunk pint Farrell had left behind. He grimaced. *That didn't help. No time for this moping. Sucks the joy out of life. Where's Bloom? Might as well get something out of this.*

He scanned the room, but the man in black was nowhere to be seen. *For Jaysus sake. Gone again.*

His bladder started into the edge of pain. He headed to the toilet at the back of the bar. A tickle at the back of his neck stopped him before he went in.

"Mr. Wilde. You look like you could do with some comfort." Mona Kelly placed her hand gently against the seat of his trousers, moving her glossy, full lips close to his head. "Mr. Cowen told me you would be very grateful if I was nice to you." She purred, her breath pouring warmth into his ear.

"Sorry, I don't know ..."

"He told me you have great influence over the judging panel, not that I'm suggesting anything, but I can be very nice, very nice, if you know what I mean." She linked her arm with his and pulled him towards the ladies" toilets, her free hand brushing against his groin.

Omar had an erection the size of a missile and his head swam with panic and desire. For a split second he thought about lying, about taking this little pleasure that so seldom came his way.

She pulled him into the vacant toilet and towards an empty cubicle. He watched her breasts, the rise and flow of them as her breath deepened. He hesitated. "I'm sorry, Miss, but I don't know what you mean. He's lying. I'm just a journalist. I've nothing to do with the judging."

She let go of his arm. "That fucking little shite. I'm going to kill him. You're not lying to me, are you?" Her face contorted with confused anger.

"No. Honestly, he's always at me, Cowen. We work together. He's a messer, that's all."

She pushed Omar aside. "Don't touch me. I'm going to kill that bastard!"

Mona Kelly exited the toilet, her brunette curls trailing down her bronzed back, fire oozing from her nostrils. His desire exited the door with her.

Reidy's voice passed over her head. "*And from love's shining circle, the gems drop away!*"

Allowing himself time to recover, he released himself and leant against the wall with his free hand. The urine splashed against the white enamel, passed into the channel beneath him, and out into the sewers of Dublin.

"*Oh! who would inhabit this bleak world alone?*" he sang to himself, his voice cracking with relief.

CHAPTER 23

BLÁITHÍN

4:00 PM

THE TAXI PULLED INTO a concreted space in front of the towers, Snow Patrol blaring on the radio. Bláithín looked out nervously. A crowd of kids were shooting rocks off the top of a rubbish bin with what looked like a pellet gun.

"Twenty euro fifty, please," said the taxi driver.

"What? Jesus, no wonder I'm stuck with my bike." Bláithín rummaged in her bag. She passed the money to the driver. His eyes darted from side to side, the kids circling the car like vultures. Bláithín stepped out, and the taxi sped off.

A young boy with scruffy hair poked at her with his bb gun.

"Oy, Missus, got a fag?"

"No, I don't smoke. Is this building F?"

A group of ragged looking youngsters moved in behind her.

"What's it to you?" the boy replied.

"I'm looking for Paul Mullens's flat."

"The Fiddler's flat, is it?" The boy turned towards a wiry teenager with a hare lip. "She's lookin for your brother, Mullens. Jaysus he's hangin out wi some posh bitches these days."

The youngsters laughed and pushed the teenager towards Bláithín.

"Go on, Mullens. Show her what you got."

"Get off me, youse bastards." He eyed Bláithín with suspicion.

"She's after the white stuff, boys. Wants to get herself a bit of Ballymun blow, isn't that right, Ms. Southside?" Even though this boy only reached to her shoulders, Bláithín was afraid of the cold stare that lay behind his wiry frame.

"Come wi me," said the shy teenager. He nodded his head towards the doorway, and she followed him into the front of the gargantuan blocks. They had punctuated Dublin's skyline for decades but remained a world as far removed from Bláithín's as the African Delta.

"It's on the tenth floor." The boy pressed the button for the lift and stood watching the light flicker through the numbers above his head.

Something beeped in her pocket. She pulled out her phone. *Out of battery. Never mind.* Bláithín could feel sweat drip down the back of her neck. She knew it was too late to turn back. This was unfamiliar territory, and no matter how un-PC it was to admit it, she was terrified. The closest she ever got to this part of Dublin was curled up in her Dalkey bed reading Roddy Doyle novels, and she preferred it that way. She suspected she could get the shit kicked out her for just opening her Dalkeyised mouth.

"They've started to knock down one of the towers, I see." She attempted to normalise what felt like a very abnormal situation.

The teenager continued to stare at the numbers, shuffling his feet in silence.

"I hear the new houses will be modern, really nice. Suppose it will take some getting used to all the same."

The boy didn't respond.

Nonetheless, just hearing her own voice helped calm her down.

The door opened, and a tall boy with red hair and a bicycle got out. He eyed her carefully.

The young man beside her spoke to the redhead. "Any luck this morning?"

"Not bad at all." Red eyed Bláithín's wicker bag. She clutched it to her, cursing herself for being so stupid as to have brought it with her.

"Roigh, in here," grunted Tommo, not allowing his eyes to meet hers.

She followed him into the tiny lift.

Red hopped on his bike and cycled out of the building.

She breathed a sigh of relief. Tommo pressed ten, and the lift began to rise slowly. A smell of piss assaulted her nostrils, and she struggled not to gag. The space between her and the scowling teenager seemed to grow as she hummed Snow Patrol's "Run," the last song that had been playing in the taxi before she'd stepped outside.

"He's not here, you know," Tommo grumbled.

"You mean Paul? He told me he would be," Bláithín replied.

"Well, he's not. Conor will take care of you."

"Who?"

"Me udder brudder. He helps Fiddler out wit dis stuff."

Bláithín wanted to press 0 and go straight back down, but she felt trapped. The doors opened. She followed the teenager to the end of a long dark corridor. He took a key out of his jeans pocket and fiddled with the lock. The door squeaked open.

"Trew dere." He pointed towards a small living room to the left.

"Conor, dere's a lady here. Knows Fiddler. Says he said to come round to get some stuff."

A tall man with mousy hair greased back over his ears stuck his head around the corner.

"Wha? Oh, hi. Hang on. Dere in a sec."

"See ya." Tommo looked her in the eye, "Just watch yourself, roigh, he can get a bit, well ... you know." He headed out the door.

"Sorry, what do you mean?" asked Bláithín, but he'd already disappeared down the corridor.

The small room was cluttered with porcelain figurines and photographs. A framed Man United t-shirt sat proudly beside a large print of Roy Keane with his arm around a young man. The green corduroy couch had a hole at one end and the stuffing had spilled onto the edge of the pink carpet. She pushed away a mound of magazines and perched herself on the edge of the couch. She heard water gushing then a door opened.

A tall, skinny man came into the room. His blue eyes sank into his skeletal features. He looked like he hadn't eaten in weeks.

"Sorry bout that. Needed a slash. So, what can I do you for? Fiddler sent youse, did he? Always has an eye for the women, dat boy." His eyes travelled from the top of her head, around the edge of her bosoms, to the bit of naked flesh that was just showing at the top of her black boots.

"Yeah. He told me he'd be here." She clutched her bag close to her stomach.

His eyes narrowed and the dry, thin lips shaped a dubious smile. "Got a bit side-lined, I'm afraid, but I can take care of you just as good."

"I don't know. Maybe I'll just contact Paul again," Bláithín stuttered.

"Don't be so stupid, girl. I have it all – blow, speed, ecstasy pills, the hard stuff even." He rolled up his arm to feign an injection. "I'm guessing you're a blow girl. Helps you to cope with those knobhead rugby boys and Daddy's disapproving looks. Am I right?" He sat beside her on the couch so that his bony leg rubbed against the edge of her skirt.

She sucked in her breath, determined to leave with something. "Do you have some? I was thinking about fifty euros worth?"

He reached inside the hole in the couch and dug deep inside the lining. "Anything for such a pretty lady." He pulled out a white plastic bag and laid the contents on the coffee table in front of her. His thin fingers moved through the collection of pills, bottles, and needles until they fell on a bag of white powder. He dipped his finger inside the bag. "Here, try a little," he said, his finger touching the edge of her lips.

She flinched. He pushed his finger through her lips. Afraid to anger him she licked the powder.

"That's a good girl."

Out of the corner of her eye, she saw him place his other hand over his groin. She stood up suddenly and moved towards the door.

He leapt off the couch and blocked her way. "Going somewhere?"

"Get out of my way. I just want to get the fuck out of here." Bláithín could feel the tears begin to rise at the back of her eyeballs.

"You're not going anywhere, Missy." He grabbed her by the hair, dragged her to the couch, pressed her face into the cushion until she couldn't breathe, and pinned her down with the weight of his bony torso. He began to unzip his pants.

Bláithín managed to stick a finger into the corner of his eye socket. He wailed, his free hand punching her in the side of the face with all the force he could muster. A sharp pain darted through the left side of her skull, and she screamed.

"Stupid bitch. I'm going to show you who's boss."

At that moment, she heard a sound she couldn't identify, and he reeled back. Paul stood behind his brother, hair fair as corn, eyes dark and fierce, the butt of a handgun aimed at his brother's head. There was something about his strong physique that frightened and excited her at the same time, but right now she needed to get the hell out of here.

"Conor, you fuckin bastard. Get the fuck off her before I shoot you." His whole body was tensed, ready for a fight.

"I was just having some fun, Fiddler, Jesus. The fuckin bitch nearly took the eye out of me!" Conor yelled.

"Wasn't it enough you stole Karen from me? You're a right bollox. Get the fuck out of here!" Paul shouted at his brother as he stumbled towards the door. "Before I fuckin kill you. Haven't you caused enough bleedin trouble to this family? Jesus, I've been cleaning up my brothers' shite all day, with Tommo's fuck-up this morning and now you. Get out of my sight!"

Conor looked at Bláithín, blew her a kiss and left.

"Are you ok?" Paul asked.

The left side of Bláithín's head was throbbing. She pulled down her skirt and sat upright, a web of curls mashed into the side of her cheek.

"I just need to go. I need to go," she repeated, unsure whether the man who sat in front of her was any better than the one who'd just left.

"Jesus, I'm sorry about him. He's a fuckin bastard. I sent you a text to say I'd be late. Didn't you get it?" He looked genuinely concerned.

"No, I got nothing." She glanced at the phone in her pocket. "My phone's dead. Shit."

Paul sat down beside her. She moved away.

"I'm not going to hurt you, promise. Let me look at that." He lightly touched the bruise that was developing around her left temple. "It's not bad. Hang on a sec. I've some Arnica." He hopped up and ran towards the kitchen.

All Bláithín's instincts told her to leave, but she felt paralysed, numb.

He came back and gently applied the contents of the green tube to the side of her face. "I'm so sorry about that wanker. I wish I could suck the genes we share out of me. Listen, are you all right otherwise?" His brown eyes were full of worry.

She gathered herself. "Yeah, I just want to head. Can you get me a taxi?"

"Yeah sure. There's a lad in the next building who has a taxi. He's a lovely fella, no worries." He punched the numbers into his phone.

"Hi, Frank. Listen I've someone here who needs a lift to ... sorry, where are you goin?"

Bláithín thought for a second. "Long Lane. It's near Blackpitts."

He told the taxi driver to be outside the building in five minutes and helped Bláithín to get her stuff together. She eyed the white bag that was sitting on the table in front of her.

"Do you want to take some wit ye? It's why you were here, I suppose." Paul picked up the bag and poured a small amount into a piece of foil. "It's on me, considerin." He put the foil package into her hand and looked at her warmly. "I really am sorry. I'm going to fuckin kill him over this, I promise."

Bláithín smiled weakly. "Thanks." She moved towards the door. "Can you walk me down? I'm just afraid he might be ..."

"No prob."

They walked down the dark corridor together.

They stood in silence waiting for the lift. When it arrived and they got inside, Paul turned towards her. "You seem like a nice girl. It's a nasty business, this fuckin drugs stuff. Maybe you should get yourself a good ol ordinary drinking habit or hop on a plane out of here or sometin. You don't need this shit." His voice was soft, and there was a kindness in his face that made her relax.

"Maybe," Bláithín replied. She was delirious, a concoction of fear, pain and desperation gripping her head in a vice. Confusing though it was, this moment of tenderness made her want to cry with relief. He touched her shoulder gently as they walked out of the building and towards the taxi.

"I know you won't, but if you ever want to meet up, well, it'd be nice."

"Thanks again, but probably not." She got in the taxi.

Paul stood and watched as the car moved towards the main road. She watched him through the back window and felt a sadness grip her insides. She began to cry uncontrollably.

"Are you all right, luv? Did something happen?" asked the taxi driver.

"Nothing. It doesn't matter. Don't mind me."

"Where to?" he asked.

"Long Lane." She needed to talk to someone before she spun out of control, and Flora had a way of calming her like no one else. The conversation earlier hadn't been enough. She'd come clean this time, ask her for help before she sank back into the habit she'd fought so hard to beat.

Chapter 24

FLORA

4:30 PM

FLORA LOOKED AT HERSELF in the mirror. *A little bit more eyeliner.* The dark brown pencil sat beside her on the dresser. She picked it up, drew a fine line around her bottom lid. *There. Not bad.* She adjusted her dress, looked around the room, and moved to the corner to place a CD in the portable stereo.

Jeff Buckley's "Hallelujah" drifted through the room.

The doorbell rang. She looked at herself once more and smiled, danced across the room, her body tingling with anticipation. The door jammed as she opened it, and she tugged with all her might. He stood there clutching a bunch of carnations, eyes wide and smiling.

"Baby, I thought I would go mad. I haven't seen you in so long." Kinch pulled her out towards him, kissed the nape of her neck.

Her eyes darted around. "Quick, come in. Someone might see." She shut the door and fell back into his arms. The carnations went flying.

They kissed frantically and fell on the couch, his large hands cupping her buttocks.

"I thought I was going to die with frustration," Flora whispered between kisses.

He smiled, pulling her dress above her head. "Don't worry, I'll soon take care of that."

They threw themselves into it, legs elastic and groping. Flora felt him enter her, and her body seeped out its tension, his slow movement filling her need.

His fingers feathered over the small of her back, sending tingles the length of her spine. His mouth sought out her tongue, her neck, her nipple. He played on her edges like an overeager child. There was something shameful in that thought. She liked that most of all —the youthful eyes bright with lust and learning. She, the teacher, he the student, entwined in the oldest dance of all. A dance that jazzed and pivoted around the room, displacing objects, and stretching time. He switched her on in a way that no other had. The boy-man, this unexpected gift. It was like he was moulding the heat and shape of her out of dullness. It was all so easy.

He came in a slow groan of release and fell upon her, his heart beating through her skin. Her legs were wrapped around his nakedness, her body devouring its prey like a hungry cobra.

"Flora, I ..." He hesitated. "I love you. I'm driven demented." He sounded stressed.

"Do you?"

"Yeah."

She fell silent, knowing he expected a similar response. He waited.

"You?"

"I don't know, Kinch, I ... I like you, I love this." She fell silent.

"And ...?"

"I need you, but ... I don't know. Love and I, we don't get on."

He moved away, perched on the couch, unsmiling and stiff.

"Is it him? You don't love Omar. If you did, you wouldn't do this." His voice was deflated, tinged with anger.

"You don't know how it is. That's between him and me." She turned and poked at his crotch with a toe. "Oh, silly boy, don't be so serious. We're having lots of fun, aren't we? Who needs more than that?"

"I do," he replied. "I'm not just your plaything, you know."

She moved towards him, put her arms around his torso and nuzzled her head against his chest. "Of course you're not. You've brought me back to life. You've sucked out the poison. I needed that – need you. I promise you that is as close to love as I have to offer now." She began to nibble at the cleft of his neck, a hand touching his penis softly. Her lips traced the edge of his shoulder blades, down the rim of his right nipple, along the line of his hairless chest. She traced along the inside of his groin with her tongue. He moaned, the stiffness in his body leaving, his penis growing at the edge of her cheekbone.

"Flora, I ..."

"Shhhhhhhhhh." She took his penis into her mouth gently, allowed him to feel her desire, to move with her movements. He grew hard, pulled her back up towards him, entered her in one swift movement. Their bodies moved against each other, a hard energy pulsing through them like hot oil, their limbs grasping, clawing, as they exorcised their passion and pain.

A woman's voice erupted in a wail.

Flora turned suddenly.

Bláithín stood inside the front door, her face contorted with shock.

Deep inside the turmoil of the moment, Flora hadn't heard the door open.

"Feck, Bláith. What are you doing here?" Kinch grabbed a blanket from the couch and attempted to cover himself.

"Not half as much as you, you fecking bastard!" Bláithín's tears fell uncontrollably, and she pulled open the door.

Flora grabbed her skirt and dressed hurriedly. "Bláithín! Let us explain ..."

"Fuck off. I thought you were my friend and behind my back the whole time ... I'm some idiot, a complete eejit." Bláithín ran out the door.

"I'll go after her. You wait here. I'll come back." Kinch ran out the door, shirt in hand.

Flora fell back into the couch, half-dressed. She felt numb, unable to move. Guilt fell over her like an unwelcome shadow. She pushed it aside because it didn't help.

Shite, she'll tell Omar. It's all over now, everything.

Time and again she was close to finishing with him, but something stopped her. Grabbing a cushion from the couch, she hugged it close and began to cry. Jeff Buckley's sublime voice cried in unison with her misery. Her stomach grumbled out its nausea for what seemed like hours. Then she remembered Sandra. She glanced at her watch: 4:45 PM. Sandra was due with the kids any minute.

Leaving her bra on the couch, she pulled her top on, moved to the mirror over the fireplace, and fixed her hair. The music was bringing her down, so she switched it off.

The doorbell rang. She took a deep breath and opened the door.

Sandra stood with the two kids at the doorstep. The little girls smiled at Flora and raced past her into the living room.

"Mummy says you have a pond, Mrs. Wilde. Can we see it? Can we?"

Sandra smiled. "Are you sure you're ready to put up with us?"

"Of course, come in, come in." Flora glanced up and down the road but Kinch and Bláithín were nowhere to be seen.

"Why is this here?" Orisa held up Flora's bra, inspecting it closely.

Flora grabbed her undergarment and stuffed it in a drawer. "Was taking a nap. Feel more comfortable without all that. You know?" She cringed but Sandra didn't seem to take any notice.

"They're so excited to see your lovely house, Flora. I'm afraid we've been stuck in a concrete jungle so long that they get very excited when they see a garden. Do you mind if they go out the back to have a look?"

"No problem. You two, come on, let me show you." Flora ushered them through the living room and into the small but perfectly decorated kitchen. The back door was painted red and, in the old style, either the top or the bottom half could be opened. Unable to contain themselves, the girls raced past them and out into the sunlight. They ran to the pond and began to poke at the goldfish like a couple of excited kittens.

"It's so pretty. Do you do it yourself?" Sandra asked.

"Yes, I love flowers." Flora tried to suppress the fear that Kinch might arrive back at any moment. She smiled at Sandra weakly.

"Are you all right? You seem a little tired. We could come back later." Sandra was a perceptive woman.

Flora knew she'd be able to tell that something was up, but she wasn't in the habit of divulging her secrets to anyone. She preferred to keep them locked up, under control. "I'm fine. Just a little tired. It's all this practicing for the concert this evening."

The girls ran up to them, Efe dangling a fish by the tail. "He's so beautiful. Can I put him in a bowl for inside?"

Sandra grabbed her by the arm and pulled her back to the pond. "Put that poor fish back this instant. He's gasping for breath."

Flora was beginning to wonder if her nerves could take it.

Orisa, the quieter of the two, gazed into the pond, her braids trailing across the water. "What kind of fish are they Mrs. Wilde?"

"They're Japanese koi fish. They grow very big. I only got them last year. It takes years."

Sandra was attempting to quieten her younger daughter. "Efe, stop poking at the fish. You could give them a fright. They might die."

The little girl had taken the fishnet at the side of the pond and prodded underneath the pond moss, causing the fish to scatter wildly. She squealed with delight.

"Mommy, look at the big gold one," Efe said.

"Yes baby, it's beautiful, but just sit here on the bench, you two, and watch them." Sandra ushered the girls onto the wooden bench beside the pond. They sat unwillingly, twitching like trapped birds.

Sandra turned and smiled at Flora. "Sorry about that. I promise I'll keep an eye on them."

"They're just excited, I understand." Flora brought Sandra into the kitchen and showed her where everything was. She walked her around the house, and brought her to the spare bedroom, where a fold out bed had been put together beside the double bed.

"I hope that's ok for you guys?"

"It's perfect, just perfect! Thank you so much for going to so much trouble. I don't know what else ..."

Flora placed her hand on Sandra's shoulder. "Any time, Sandra. I just pray it'll all work out. Do you know where you're going tomorrow?"

"Father Ogunbosola is going to call here later to let me know. I gave him your number. Is that ok?"

"Of course. You just relax, make yourself a cup of tea. There're biscuits in the cupboard and Fanta in the fridge for the girls."

At that moment, Efe began to scream at the top of her lungs. "Mommy! Mommy! Orisa pushed me in the pond!"

Sandra raced out the back, Flora in hot pursuit. The little girl was waist deep in mucky water, crying her heart out. Orisa stood over her with a sheepish look on her face.

"Oh my God, Efe, quick." Sandra leant over the pond and pulled the drenched little girl onto the wooden deck. She was covered in pondweed.

"Did you do this?" Sandra bellowed at the nine-year-old.

Orisa moved away from her mother and towards Flora. "She was trying to scoop up a fish, Mommy. I was just trying to stop her. I didn't mean to ..." Orisa's voice began to break.

"I'm sick and tired of your messing. She could have drowned. Do you understand that? Do you?" Sandra screamed.

Orisa looked at Flora and ran towards the house. "It's not fair. I was just ..." The tears flowed as she raced inside.

"Come back here!" Sandra shouted, attempting to clean the pondweed off Efe.

"It's ok, Sandra. I'll get her." Flora followed the child, who was scrunched into the side of the couch. She clutched a cushion to her face to stifle her crying.

"Sweetheart, don't worry. I know things are tough for you and your mom. She's doing her best." Flora attempted to put her arm around Orisa, who flinched.

"Have you ever heard of a film called *The Wizard of Oz*? I have it here. It's about a little girl and her dog who go to a magic land called Oz and meet all sorts of amazing people. Wouldn't you like to see that?"

"That sounds stupid. Don't you have *Batman* or *Mars Attacks*?"

Flora sighed. "Sorry it's this or nothing." She pulled the film out from the small collection under the television and switched on the DVD player.

Orisa moaned, one eye appearing from behind the cushion.

"Somewhere Over the Rainbow" drifted through the room.

She sat up and wiped her eyes. "What's her name?" Orisa asked.

"You mean the little girl?" Flora replied.

Orisa nodded.

"Dorothy. And her dog is Toto. Do you want to watch it?" Flora could see the light of curiosity return to the child's eyes.

"I suppose."

"I'll even get you some Fanta and biscuits. Would you like that?"

The little girl nodded again, her eyes fixed on the screen.

Sandra came through the door with Efe in her arms. Flora nodded and smiled to confirm that everything was fine.

Sandra mouthed a thank-you. "She's soaked, I'm afraid. Do you mind if I take her upstairs and clean her up?"

"Pretend like it's your own home. I'm just going to go have a lie-down now, if everything's ok?"

"Go, Flora, before some other drama takes place. I'm sorry. It's a mother's life. Someday you'll know."

Flora nodded weakly. She knew full well that the time for knowing a mother's life was passing her by. She followed Sandra up the stairs, walked into her bedroom, and shut the door. She collapsed on her bed, numb with exhaustion. Her phone flashed a message beside her on the bed. *Can't find her. Will be in touch when I can. Love you. K.* She put the phone beside her on the dresser, curled up in a ball, and cried herself to sleep.

CHAPTER 25

KINCH

5:00 PM

KINCH RAN FRANTICALLY PAST St. Pat's Cathedral and on towards the Camden Street junction. He stopped to catch his breath. He spotted Hanan's halal shop out of the corner of his eye.

Maybe, just maybe.

Traffic was as brutal as ever, and he weaved his way between a double decker bus and a taxi. The lights turned red, and the bus disappeared into the distance. A taxi driver screamed, "Suicidal wanker!"

Take a chill-pill mate.

Kinch could see Hanan's father behind the counter. He'd been a little nervous of Kinch at first, but Kinch had disarmed him with his usual blend of humour and charm, and now they got on grand.

"Hi, Mr. Hussein. How are things? Just wondering, have you seen Bláithín?"

"Ah, the pretty girlfriend. She was here this morning, talking to Hanan. How are you, my friend?" The old man had soft brown eyes that peered through a mass of facial hair.

"I'm fine, thanks. Hanan around?"

"He's in the back with Khaled. That boy has me driven crazy. He was supposed to be here to take me to the doctor, and he turns up one hour late. What kind of respect is that for a sick old man?"

"That's teenagers for you," replied Kinch.

Mohammed shook his head. "He's in a world of his own these days." He continued unpacking a box of cigarettes and placed them on a shelf. "I don't know which is worse – the hippy son who doesn't give a care about his heritage or the devout loner who spends his life on some other dreamy planet."

"It's a tough call. You know what they say: children are sent to try you."

"You're very right, my boy! How do you get on with your father?"

"I'm afraid I never knew him. My mother brought me up alone." Kinch could feel this conversation going places he'd rather not visit at this moment.

Mohammed smiled warmly. "Is that right? Well, she did a good job from what I can see."

"Don't know about that, Mr. Hussein. Sorry, but could I just pop round the back to see Hanan?" Kinch moved towards the back door.

"Of course. Nice talking to you. Drop in anytime you're passing by, even if Hanan isn't here. It gets a bit boring stuck behind this counter all day long."

Kinch nodded. "You bet." He passed into the back of the shop. He walked down the small corridor and into the living room on the left. Hanan sat juggling the phone in his hand.

"Are you going to use it or abuse it mate?" Kinch said, smiling.

Hanan did not look happy. "You're not going to believe it. Sarah dumped me. For God's sake, what the feck is it? National dump your partner day?"

"You're joking. Jesus, sorry. Didn't see that coming." Kinch sat down beside Hanan.

"Bet you Bláithín didn't see it coming either," replied Hanan in a slightly caustic tone.

"Don't take it out on me. Everyone has their own ball of shite to deal with."

Hanan sighed. "Sorry, it just sucks."

"Yeah, what's her story then?" Kinch asked.

"Don't ask me. Some crap about not feeling the magic or something."

"*Cosmo*-response 101."

"Yeah, we blokes are no better, I suppose."

"Don't even ask me what I said this morning. It came out arseways anyway, and I'm in a right mess now." Kinch pulled out a cigarette. "Do you mind? I desperately need it."

"Fire ahead. I'll just light some incense or something. Dad'll never notice. So, what are you on about?"

Kinch lit the cigarette and took a long drag. "It's Bláithín. I've done something bad Hanan. You're going to hate me, but I must tell you."

Hanan's eyes narrowed. "Yeah?"

"Do you remember I told you about that gorgeous woman I worked with on the production of Brian Friel's *Performances*?"

"Yeah, yeah, you said she was hot stuff. All the lads were creamin themselves for her," Hanan replied.

"Her name's Flora. She's Polish. Her husband works with me in the *Indo*." Kinch hesitated, took a drag, and smiled weakly. "Well mate, I've been having an affair with her for two months now."

"You're joking me." Hanan stood up, and stared at Kinch, his eyes narrowing. "And Bláithín? You'll bloody destroy her. She's my friend too."

Kinch felt the guilt seep into his gullet. "I know. I just didn't know how to tell her, and the thing is she just walked in and caught us both ... well ... at it. It was God awful."

"No fucking way!"

"Fraid so. She absolutely freaked out and disappeared. I was hoping maybe you'd seen her."

"Think I'd be a bit more clued in if I had. Where were you? At your place?" Hanan asked.

Kinch took another drag. "No, at Flora's. They know each other – Flora's her violin teacher."

"Jaysus, man, you know how to fuck a girl right up." Hanan could barely look Kinch in the eye.

"I know. I feel so shite, but I just couldn't help myself. Flora's so ..." His voice trailed away. "Maybe you could call Bláith for me? Find out where she is? If she's ok? I'm afraid she'll take something, you know."

"Dear God, I hope not. You're a right bollox. Do you have her number there? I don't have it."

"Yeah, here you go."

Hanan punched in the numbers and waited for a response. The phone hit the answering machine directly. Hanan spoke urgently. "Bláith, it's Hanan. I know what happened with Kinch and that woman. Listen, please just call to tell me you're ok. You can come over here. I know you must feel like shit. Just come over here." He hung up and sat down staring at the phone. "What now?"

"I'm going to ring round to everyone she knows. Can you let me know if you hear from her?"

The door opened and Khaled walked in. "Hey," he said to Kinch and crossed the room to pick up a jacket that was lying on the back of the couch.

"Where are you going?" asked Hanan.

"None of your business!" Khaled's eyes were stony and determined.

The teenager put on his green flak jacket and moved towards the door.

"Hey, Khaled, Kinch was saying that he'd love to come over and look at your music collection, weren't you?" Hanan gave Kinch the eyes.

Loath though Kinch was to get himself involved in anything else at this moment, he reckoned it was a way to salvage his reputation with Hanan. "Yeah right. What do you think?"

Khaled looked at Kinch suspiciously. "I don't know. I ..."

"Whenever it suits, you know," replied Kinch.

"As you wish," Khaled replied and closed the door behind him.

"Fuck man, do you see what I mean? What's this "as you wish" shite? He's even beginning to *sound* like one of those fanatics. My own brother is scaring me," Hanan said.

Kinch stubbed out his cigarette. "Don't worry about it, man. I'll suss him out. Bit of a private dick in my own way. Listen, I'm off and ... thanks for not hitting me. I know I've been a prick."

Hanan smiled. "Nobody's perfect, but I can't promise I won't fuck you up if you mess with Bláithín again. I've a bit of a soft spot for her, you know."

Kinch noticed an awkwardness in his friend's tone. *He fancies her. Interesting.* "We can't all be good guys like you," Kinch replied. "It would be a fuckin boring world if we were."

They laughed, and Kinch left the shop saying a quick goodbye to Mr. Hussein.

He texted Flora to let her know what was happening. His stomach grumbled a reminder that he hadn't eaten since the morning. *Starvin. Soup and sandwich in George's Street Arcade would go down a treat.*

He took the mini-iPod from his pocket, stuck on his headphones, and pressed shuffle. Glen Hansard's voice filled his head.

Kinch chuckled. *'Seven Day Mile' is right Glen boy. Feels like this day will never end.*

Rush-hour traffic was gathering momentum. He crossed the road and hurried down Wexford Street. Cars inched their way along the long street. Their passengers chatted on phones, caught up on current issues with *The Last Word*, sang along to the latest tune. One woman curled her hair and adjusted her makeup. All attempted to ignore the building tensions from traffic hell. Kinch thanked his lucky stars that he couldn't afford a car to tempt him into this sea of frustration.

He tripped along the footpath, thinking about Flora. Her ability to switch from hot to cold in a split second was perplexing. He desperately wanted to possess this independent creature, to feed off her confidence. Could such carnal desire be considered love? Maybe not, but it was all he wanted.

Hansard wailed mournfully in his ear.

On cue Kinch began to run. He ran as fast as his body would take him – past startled schoolchildren and a group of gossiping old women. He ran straight across the Stephen Street intersection without even looking at the lights.

A bus driver screamed out the window, "You fuckin muppet! Do you want to get yourself killed!"

The music screamed in his ear and he continued to run, run his confusion out of his body, sweat out his frustrations and guilt. He gritted his teeth, the sweat pouring down his forehead. He ran past the Long Haul Pub, cut across the road towards the George's Street Arcade. The music faded and he slowed down just in front of Simon's Place. He tore off his headphones and bent over, struggling to breath.

Nope, don't feel any better, and I'm fuckin well out of shape too. Bloody great!

Passing through the door of the busy café, he grabbed a copy of the latest *Events Guide*. The ad for the Low concert was on the back page. The support band started at eight thirty. He ordered a ham-and-coleslaw sandwich and a cup of tea. It was hard to manoeuvre with the tray through the crowds of people, but he found a space at the window looking into the arcade.

He'd always loved the eclectic atmosphere of this old Victorian arcade. Vendors sat chatting at their stalls, students mulled over the latest second-hand CDs, young girls in vintage clothing shops created outfits to die for.

His phone rang as he chewed on his sandwich. *No number. Odd.* He picked it up, swallowing a bite quickly. "Hello."

"Kieran?"

And there it was. THAT voice. The sandwich got caught in his throat and he began to choke.

"Kieran? Are you there?"

The familiar voice shot like a hot arrow through his brain. He was stunned. They'd never actually spoken, but Kinch had listened to him often enough from the back of pews to recognise his voice, should the time arise, and here it was. What the fuck did he want with him now? "How did YOU get my number?"

"*The Independent.*"

Kinch fell silent.

"Kieran, I know it's unexpected, but I really need to see you."

He could hear something in this man's voice that he had never noticed before. A fragility, a need. He felt a cold anger rise within him. "I can't imagine why. We've gone a lifetime without giving in to such civilities. Why start now?"

"It's important. I know I haven't been there ... I know, but now I want to set that right."

"I suppose this is where I'm supposed to say, "Better late than never, Dad." Well, sorry to disappoint, but actually, Monsignor, you can fuck right off." He realised that he was speaking very loudly, and the girl beside him was listening in with considerable interest.

"Oh God, I knew this was going to be hard."

Reidy sounded tired, sad even. Kinch felt panicked, unable to deal with this sudden display of emotion after twenty-two years. "No kidding. That's what happens when you dump your family, reject and shame the woman who loves you, generally act the complete fucking arsehole! And for what, Daddy dearest?"

"Listen to me Kieran. Just listen for a second. I'm dying. Cancer of the liver ..."

Kinch laughed out loud. "Well, there you have it. Death, the great motivator."

"Please son, I'm so sorry, so very, very sorry! I need to tell you to your face. I need to explain. Please, just allow me that. One last thing."

It sounded like he was about to cry, which was more than Kinch could take.

"Just come over to the presbytery this evening sometime," Reidy continued. "Hear me out. Please."

Kinch couldn't believe what he was hearing. *The Devil has a heart after all, but only when he's shitless about facing the Big Man upstairs. Typical.*

"I'm sorry I can't help you to assuage your guilty conscience. Goodbye." Kinch hung up the phone and switched it to silent. A short-haired girl beside him was practically sitting on his lap.

"Would you like to hear my whole bloody life story now, maybe?" he shouted at the startled girl.

"Sorry, I only ..." she stammered, moving her chair backwards.

"Fuckin earwiggers." He grabbed his sandwich, hat, and jacket and headed into the arcade.

When his phone rang again, he ignored it. He stuck on his headphones and turned the volume to maximum. Rory Gallagher's "What's going on?" screamed into his ear.

Jesus, the music oracle continues.

Kinch started to sing at the top his voice.

Take that you bloody bastard.

He punched the air in front of him with venom.

"What's going on?"

A group of teenagers scattered wildly, looking at him like he was a madman.

He moved at speed through the stalls of the arcade and out into the sunshine, his brain about to explode.

He started to run again. This time he wasn't going to stop. He was just going to keep running until he got run over or collapsed from lack of oxygen or reached somewhere, someone ...

Flora, he was going to run to Flora.

CHAPTER 26

OMAR

~ Cyclops ~

5:00 PM

SLATTERY'S ON CAPEL STREET was normally a lively spot, but today it was half-empty. Omar had cornered Jameson on his way out of the Ormond and asked him if he'd have twenty minutes to spare for a chat. His colleague, being the obliging sort, agreed once Omar shouted him a pint.

Sure, it would get them away from the bloomin festivities for a while, Jameson suggested, and God knows he was a bit sick of it all. Omar knew that Jameson was a favourite of Farrell's and hoped he'd put in a good word for him about the article.

Omar played to Jameson's ego, praising him for his work. They chatted easily until Jameson recognised a man sitting nearby.

"Damn! It's Caoch O'Sullivan," Jameson whispered to Omar.

"Who?"

"The brother of that bollox Martin O'Sullivan, the Sinn Féin TD for South Kerry."

Omar took a good look. "Looks like a tough character. What's up with his eye?"

"It's glass – motorbike accident in his late teens. One of his favourite tricks is to pop the bloody thing out and roll it his hand, usually when he's beating the shit out of some unsuspecting fucker."

"Feck." Omar glanced over to make sure the Kerryman wasn't listening.

"I had dealings with him on a couple of articles I wrote. I wouldn't be his favourite person. Maybe we should get out of here.

Caoch turned their way. "Mark Jameson, is it? Taking a break from stitching up this country's patriots, are we?" O'Sullivan turned his stool towards Jameson.

A young man stood beside the Kerryman – piercings the length of his left ear and a mullet like a weasel's tail falling between his shoulder blades. He jumped from foot to foot like a boxer, his wiry body ready for action. There was a skinny pit bull sitting at his feet, a low growl building ominously behind his black lips.

Jameson laughed. "Doing my job, Mr. O'Sullivan. That's all. Someone has to."

"You did a nice job of trying to stitch up my brother with that pack of lies you printed last year. Tough luck, it didn't stick, Jameson." Caoch inched closer. "Got yourself kicked out of *The Sun* on your bony arse, I heard. There's justice in the world after all." He tapped whiskey glasses with the mullet-headed man, and they laughed.

Omar could see the colour rise in Jameson's face.

"Up for the match then, are you, Caoch? Got a special pass?" Jameson replied. "Didn't think they let scum like you out of the kingdom except on special dispensation."

The situation was building towards something Omar didn't want to be involved in, so he jumped between the two men and placed his empty coke glass on the bar. "My father's side of the family hailed from the great county a few generations back," Omar interrupted

Caoch replied. "Is that right? What's your name?"

"Wilde, Omar Wilde. I think it was my grandfather who was from around Killarney somewhere."

Caoch moved his gaze, his static eye cold, black, and staring. "Not exactly a Paddy with a name like that, are you? And certainly not a Kerryman!"

"I was born here," said Omar. "Hesitant though I am to admit it to a Kerryman, I'm definitely a Jackeen."

"Never seen a Dublinman with such swarthy skin. Bit of the nigger in you, is there?"

Omar shuddered. He knew this sort of man. He would have to keep his cool above all else. "My mother was Egyptian, Arab actually, but I grew up here."

Caoch shrugged. "Doesn't make you an Irishman. True Celtic blood can be traced through both sides. None of this diluting business. Watered down genes. A dangerous business." He allowed his free eye to wander.

Omar felt the black pupil of the glass eye change shape with his movements like a trick painting.

"Take Echeverria here. He's a Basque man through and through. Now I've got nothing against other nationalities, once they know who they are, once they stick to their own, you know what I mean." He moved closer to Omar ominously. "Pride in one's origins – Celt, Basque, or nigger for that matter – that's what counts." His voice was stretched thin, like the low whistle of a dynamite fuse on its way to detonation.

The young Basqueman nodded vigorously. "In my country we know what it is to be proud of our origins. *Euskal Herria!*"

His Kerry friend saluted his enthusiasm.

"Good man yourself, Itor. *Eire Abú!*" They clinked glasses once more.

Jameson caught Omar's eye and gave him a "told you so" look.

The door swung open behind them, and Kate O'Reilly bounded over with a smile. "There you are, Wilde. You won't believe it! Your horse ran away with it. Twenty to fecking one, you lucky bastard!"

Omar looked at her in disbelief. "You're kidding."

"No messing. As soon as I found out I had to find you. Cowen told me you and Jameson had disappeared here. Jesus, man, you've won a fortune. Here." She pushed a piece of paper his direction. "Your bet. And I expect at a four-course champagne meal in Chapter One for bringing you the good news."

Omar stared at the little piece of paper that was now worth four thousand euro. He could feel the presence of the two men bearing down on him from behind.

"How much did you pull in there, Arabman?" asked the Kerryman, his blue eye narrowing. Omar signalled to Jameson and Kate with his eyes to keep quiet.

"Not much. Might get me a nice suit, right Kate?"

His co-worker looked at the two men and no doubt understood. "Yeah, a nice cheap Hugo Boss if you're lucky in the sales or else a night out with me – whichever's cheaper." She smiled at Omar.

"I'm afraid you're out of my price-range, Kate, so Hugo will have to do."

"Well, if you change your mind, you know where I am," said Kate, "chained to my desk."

The Kerryman looked Omar in the eye. "Tell me Arab. Can you translate our national anthem then? Let's see what kind of a Dubliner you are."

The pit bull pawed his owner, who threw him a piece of leftover sandwich.

Omar shifted nervously and looked at Jameson who shrugged his shoulders.

"Leave him alone, O'Sullivan. Half of Ireland can't even say it in any language, and sure who gives a fuck at the end of the day?"

The one-eyed man began to sing. *"In valley green, on towering crag, Our father's fought before us, and conquered 'neath that same old flag that's proudly floating o'er us."* Now tell me what you Arabs, niggers, and wops have done for this country apart from clean our toilets and shag our women."

Omar could take no more. "What do you know of the Arab world? You've probably never stepped outside this country except to go vomit your guts up on your once-a-year holiday in Santa Ponsa."

The Caoch's voice rose an octave. "What the hell do I care about other cultures or any of that shite? It's this world I'm living in, Arab. In Ireland ... 2004." His fat cheeks were raw red and glowing.

"For a man who's living in 2004, you spend a hell of a lot of time talking about the past."

"Come on, Omar. Let's get out of here," said Jameson.

Caoch rose above Omar, his towering frame casting an ominous shadow over him. "Let's see what you're made of son of Saddam. Let's see how you Arabs can fight. I hear that's what ye do best."

The dog jumped up, held back by a tight rope wrapped around the wiry Basqueman's bare knuckles.

Omar could feel the hairs stand up on the back of his neck but remained calm. He spoke softly. "Fighting and hatred are of no value to me, Kerryman. There's only one value which I respect on this godforsaken mess of a planet, and I'm afraid it's something that you are clearly lacking."

Jameson tugged at Omar's jacket sleeve nervously. "Just leave it, Omar."

The Kerryman moved closer to Omar. "What would that be, Mr. Wise Man?"

Omar raised his eyes to meet Caoch's cold stare. "Love."

The Kerryman chuckled. "Me heart is bleeding, Arabman. Hand me a tissue there, Itor," he said to the sneering Basque.

Omar wasn't finished with Caoch yet. "Bet it's a long time since you felt love, Kerryman. Wouldn't be too many women out there looking for a one-eyed brute to bed them now, would there?"

Caoch roared.

Jameson ran out the door, while Omar, a few steps behind, slipped under a giant armpit.

The muscular hairy hand of the Kerryman grabbed a bottle that was sitting beside him on the counter. "I'm going to cut you up, you fuckin Arab!" He banged the bottle against the counter, the one good eye, bulging out of his head.

Omar flung the door open and turned back. "Not with a plastic Miwadi bottle, you're not!"

The Kerryman flung the bottle. It soared above Omar's head, bouncing on the street outside.

Growling ferociously, the dog reared in the hands of the Basqueman. "Will I let Pinch go?" he snapped.

"Let him savage the little bastard! Go, Pinch, go!" screamed Caoch, his black eye popping out of his head.

Omar stumbled out the door. He'd fallen victim to this door once, its heavy swing unexpected but deadly. Now it would save him.

The wild pit bull, mouth foaming, careered his direction. Omar listened with relief as the spring-loaded door whipped into the head of the unsuspecting creature. From the other side of the door, Omar heard a loud whine and the mad shuffling of feet. He sighed – sure, the mutt would only be dazed.

Omar picked up his satchel and raced after Jameson, who was pegging it towards the river like a madman. As Omar sped through the street, he thought he could hear a voice above him, singing in the distance. He looked up and a black cloud, winged and demonic, descended on him. In its layers he could hear his mother's voice, twisted and writhing. He couldn't make out what she was singing, and before too long the sound multiplied, a cacophony of voices exploding in his head.

Stop, Mother, make it stop!

Omar collapsed in a heap as he caught up with Jameson on the boardwalk.

"Omar, are you ok? Omar?"

His colleague's face snapped into focus.

"Think I might be going mad, Mark."

"Join the club. Come on." Mark Jameson picked Omar up, put an arm around his shoulder, and walked him down the boardwalk. The two men continued in silence.

Omar looked back to see the last trace of the hawk-like shadow disappear over The Ivy Chambers. *Christ, I need to see a doctor.*

CHAPTER 27

BLÁITHÍN

5:30 PM

THE CORRIDOR OF BLÁITHÍN'S Christchurch apartment had been newly painted. The stench hit her nostrils like airplane-model glue. She stumbled up three flights of stairs, her eyes raw from crying. No. 39 was the usual Dublin shoebox affair. She shared it with Niamh, a mousy but sweet girl who worked for the Bank of Ireland and was always at her boyfriend's or home in Galway for the weekends. It was almost like having the place to herself, so Bláithín didn't mind that there wasn't room to swing a cat although she did wonder why anyone would ever want to do that in the first place.

She locked the door behind her, threw her bag on the green couch, and began to wail like a banshee. The contents of her bag went flying onto the floor.

Her eye fell on the small bag of powder. *I fucking deserve it.*

She sat down on the couch and spread the powder on the table in front of her in several long lines. She pressed her nose to the table and ran it the length of the first line, inhaling deeply. When she got to the end, she sniffed loudly, shook her head, and stared out the window. Like hard rain in a gutter, the powder coursed through her veins, shot straight through her system, and sang to her sadness. She could feel her lips form a soft smile, the pain sinking into the background like a bad dream in daylight. The bells of Christchurch rang out across the city, their deep, clamorous joy at odds with her pain.

Fucking Bells, I'll drown you out.

She grabbed a PJ Harvey CD from the shelf beside her and stuck it in the stereo, turning up the volume to near maximum. At last the dark, growling voice drowned out her sobs. She sang along, the words of "Sheila na Gig" encircling her like screaming ghosts. Spinning, dervish-like, her body twisted like a tree on the edge of a violent storm.

Bláithín wailed, "No more!" She punched the air frantically and sat back down on the couch to snort up the second line. Thoughts of Flora, Kinch, her father, and mother ran around her head like a 3D film reel. PJ's words twisted with her own thoughts.

She stared at the coke. *Fuck you all, I'll worship at whatever altar I choose,* and she bent to inhale another line. Everything speeded up. The cars on the street below blurred into lines of pure white light; seagulls swooped and dived through the traffic like military jets; the words from the stereo sounded like an old vinyl record speeded up.

Bláithín laughed shrilly. "Indeed, PJ take these dirty pills away from me, but not yet. All helps me to forget you, YOU BASTARD!" She could feel her body heating up, like someone had switched her on.

Beginning to sweat she got up and stuck her mouth under the tap in the kitchenette.

There was another sound in the background, a banging. It got louder.

Someone at the door. Fuck!

A voice screamed through the door, "Bláithín! Bláith! Are you ok?"

It was John bloody Fenton. She couldn't believe it. What was he doing here? She ran around the room and scooped up the gear, the laundry basket in her bathroom providing the perfect hiding place.

"Bláithín, I'm going to have to call the police if you don't answer. I'm worried."

Her nose was raw and dripping. *Fuck. Fuck!*

She grabbed foundation from her dresser and wiped her nose, attempted to cover the redness.

"That's it, Bláithín. I'm going to kick this bloody door down."

When she opened the door, Fenton was up to high doh, but his face quickly resolved itself into a picture of relief. He looked at her with concern. "Jesus, Bláith. What the hell is with the music? I can't hear myself think!" he screamed.

"What?" she shouted, unsure of what he'd said. Her brain jumped around like a demented flea.

"Turn down the fecking music!"

"Right."

She left the door open, and he followed her in as she switched off the music.

He closed the door, his expression forming a question across his brow.

"Your neighbours will call the police if you keep that up, girl. Are you all right? You don't look the best."

"I'm fine," she replied. Her eyes darted around her head like doll's eyes.

"Have you been taking something?" He stared at her intently.

"No, no, of course not! I'm just not feeling great. Monthly stuff you know." She sat down on the couch – no sign of powder on the table. Nerves propelled her knee towards the top of the coffee table. "Ow! ... What do you want?"

"I just wanted a word about your friend, Gerry," Fenton replied. "Do you mind?" He pointed to the space on the couch beside her.

She nodded. "And?"

"Did Kinch have a word with you yet?"

"Hah, if that bastard comes near me, I'll cut his balls off. Why? Didn't know you and he were getting friendly." It took all her power to concentrate on the conversation.

"Had a word with him earlier, that's all. It's about your friend. Just want to let you know, it looks like he doesn't have a prayer, and they're talking jail time. Not sure how much."

"Oh feck. No more. John, I ... I don't think I can deal with this ..."

"There is a chance, Bláith, but only you can help him."

Bláithín's head was pounding. "What are you talking about?"

Fenton got up and walked to the window, stared out at Christchurch spires. "It's your Dad. I know you don't want to hear it. He needs your help ..."

"I've been through this with him already, John. No can do." She walked to the kitchen and sucked down a glass of water.

John lowered his voice. "The thing is, he'll put in a special word for Gerry, get him off the jail time if you help him out." His large frame shifted in the seat beside her.

Bláithín fixed her gaze on him. "Nice work, John. Finally taken the position as Dad's axeman. I thought you were better than that."

"It's not like that, Bláith. It's just ... I need him. I'm screwed without him. You know what it's like for me now."

There was a sadness in his voice, but all she could feel was burning hate for this pathetic man she'd once counted as a friend.

"Get out. Get the fuck out!" she screamed.

"But ..."

"Out!"

He moved to the door. "Just consider it. It's your friend's life. You don't want to mess with that. You'd never forgive yourself."

She sped past him, grabbed the handle of the door and opened it wide. "Now!"

"Ok, ok, I'm leaving." He hesitated. "I'm sorry," he added.

Bláithín pushed him into the corridor.

"Get away from me! You're just the same as everyone else. You're all fucking bastards!" She slammed the door in his face.

The coke ripped through her system, tiny explosions of raw confidence bursting through her brain. She, Bláithín O'Leary, was better than that shower of dickheads. She'd show them. In the mirror, her pupils shone like newly mined coal. Her skin was pale, translucent. She liked this woman.

"Molly."

Grabbing a scarlet-red lipstick from the bag beside her, she traced the line of her lips. Slowly, she moved towards the face in the mirror, and kissed the cold hard surface, delicately, intently.

PJ Harvey chanted in the background, *"No more ..."*

Bláithín joined in, "No more ..." Her voice gathered volume. "No more!" She began to shout, "NO MORE!" She spun her body around and around chanting and singing. Her leg hit off the side of the coffee table, and she fell with all the force of her weight against the thin glass. It shattered like a Saturday-night beer bottle.

Motionless, she lay waiting for tiny points of pain to etch themselves into her. A large, jagged piece of glass lay about an inch from the side of her head. She moved slightly and stood up, shaking the shards off her clothes like dust.

Wow, that was close. Not a scratch.

Exhaustion washed over her. Now she could feel nothing, absolutely nothing.

CHAPTER 28

FLORA

6:30 PM

VOICES TRAVELLED UP THE STAIRS from the living room below. Flora lay on her bed, half awake, clutching a pillow like a lost child returned. She could hear Sandra, then a man's voice – Kinch, yes – then footsteps. He entered the room quietly, moved towards her. She kept her eyes shut and waited. She could feel his breath approach, the soft familiar warmth of it against the nape of her neck. He kissed her softly.

"Are you awake?" His voice a delicate whisper.

She turned. "Mmmm."

He smiled and sat beside her on the bed. His hand caressed the inside of her thigh. "Are you ok, my love?"

She hesitated, a feeling growing inside her that she knew she could not prevent, a slow, grinding refusal, a negative pulse that had come to her in her sleep, to push this love away from her, back into the shadows where it belonged, the twilight zone of unacceptable things. She pulled herself up, her back resting on the headboard. "Did you find her?"

"No. I left messages everywhere. I'm really worried, Flora."

He looked like a sad child, a penitent boy whose actions had brought misery that he couldn't possibly have foreseen.

"She'll be ok." She could hear the deep-blue cold of her words.

He looked at her, his eyes pleading for comfort.

She surprised herself with her ability to move away from his space of need. Like a soldier hardened by the decisions of war, she could feel herself withdraw. She moved off the bed and looked at the clock on her mobile phone.

"It's 6:30. I need to get ready for the concert. Omar could be back any second. I need you to leave." There was no affection in her voice.

Kinch looked at her carefully. "What do you mean? You sound so ..."

"I need you to leave, Kinch – for good." She'd made a decision in an instant, and she was sure.

"You can't be serious. What the hell have I done?" Kinch asked in disbelief.

"I just can't do this anymore."

"You can't love me. Is that it?"

"Listen, Kinch. I'm too tired for this and I don't have time. Can we just talk about this another day?"

"No, we can bloody talk about it now. I just messed up someone I care about – and someone you're supposed to care about, by the way – because I believe in us no matter how crazy it might seem to other people."

"I'm sorry, I can't. While it was just us, it was fine. Fun. But now ..." Flora looked at him and felt sorry she had to hurt him, but it had gone too far.

"Fun, Flora? Fucking fun?" He moved towards her, reaching out to touch her. "Please, Flora, just think about it."

She recoiled. "It's over Kinch. Please leave." She felt terrible for him, but there was no other way. She knew that if she gave him a sliver of hope, he'd cling onto it like a dying breath.

"Jesus, I'm some eejit. I thought you felt something for me, but you're as cold as ice, aren't you? The fucking Polish Ice Queen." He grabbed the pillow on the bed beside him and beat the bed frantically until the feathers flew around the room. "Aaaggghhhh!" he screamed.

Flora heard a flurry of footsteps on the staircase.

Sandra flew through the door. "Flora! Is everything all right?"

Flora raised her hand and nodded her head. "It's ok. Kinch is just leaving."

He put down what was left of the pillow, looked at her, his blue eyes loaded with anger, grabbed his hat and jacket, and ran down the stairs and out the door.

Chapter 29

KINCH

7:00 PM

THE SWANS WERE OUT IN FORCE, their white feathers brilliant in the sunlight. A clutch sat by the edge of the water, their long wings stretched wide to catch the heat of the sun. The local celebrity, a lone grey goose, lived as one of them, clearly unaware that he was any different. He'd been adopted by the group and moved proudly amongst them, providing much amusement for passers-by.

Kinch walked carefully along the edge of the canal. *Different in the animal kingdom. None of this ego-driven vanity. The little bugger doesn't have a clue, or else he does a damn good job of pretending.*

Clannad's "I Will Find You" sang through his headphones.

His thoughts ranged among Flora, Bláithín, his mother, that man ... *that man! God, what does he want with me now? Why is it always too late?*

He watched two ducks and two swans drift along beside him, content in their little space of the world.

Hope I come back as a swan. Mate for life. Content. Not like us lot.

He walked past the little, red-brick artisan cottages that lined the edge of the canal, spilling their inhabitants onto the path. Young mothers pushed their curly-haired youngsters in the latest jog-friendly stroller; old women chatted about the heat at the gates of the houses where they'd spent their whole lives; and Spanish students soaked up the bit of sun Ireland had to offer, desperate to be transported for just a few moments to the dry heat of their homeland.

The willow trees dripped over his head, their long tendrils casting shadows, rustling like whispering ghosts. He imagined the people who'd once walked this path, how they too had danced and dreamed, and how once, just once, they'd died, disappeared, only to be traced back into existence in the memories of those who had known them. Kinch wondered who would remember him and for how long he would cast a shadow on the memory of others.

He looked at his phone to see whether anyone had got back to him about Bláithín.

Not a damn thing.

He sat down on the bench by Paddy Kavanagh, the poet's bronze gaze ever transfixed upon the canal bank walk he'd so loved. Kinch laid his bag on the statue's lap.

"There you go, Paddy, make yourself useful."

Kavanagh kept staring stonily ahead.

"Suppose it gets a bit boring sitting around here, looking at the same ol' spot every day. Still, it's a relief from all this bloody messing we call life, eh, mate?"

He dragged his brain for the words of this great poet. "*Leafy-with-love banks and the green waters of the canal pouring redemption for me, that I do the will of God.*"

"The Leaving Cert English comes in handy all the same. The will of God, eh? Not a believer, I'm afraid. Probably do better if I was. So, what do you reckon – should I move over to the dark side of the Force? Shag a man? Get myself away from all the tortuous complexity of the female mind?" He looked sideways and moved closer to the statue's head. "You're looking cute yourself there, Paddy." He stroked the cold bronze knee and split his sides laughing.

A middle-aged woman walked past at speed, her eye fixed on Kinch as though he were a recent escapee from St Pat's mental institution.

"Howya, Missus? Lovely day." Kinch doffed his hat and chuckled to himself as she practically took off running. "That one could do with a bit of a rooting, Paddy, but no, that's it, I'm off women, do you hear me? The celibate life for me ... at least for a while."

Kinch tapped a cigarette on the poet's knee, pulled out his matches, and lit it. He took a long satisfying drag.

"Fancy a fag, Paddy? No? Sound man. Tear the lungs out of you it would, not that you care about that anymore."

"Can I try?"

The little voice, the size of a ladybird, had come from behind him. He turned around. It was the little girl from Flora's house. He'd noticed her on the couch while he'd been talking to that lady – her mother he supposed.

"You're the girl from Flora's. What's your name?" Kinch asked softly.

"Orisa, but don't tell my mum I'm here. I don't want to go back." She stood, half-hidden by the tree, her little mouth pursed and determined. "Can I try? The cigarette ... please?"

"That would be a bad idea. Your mum wouldn't be happy with me."

Her dark eyes looked sad, tired from crying. "I don't care about her."

"Are you ok? Did something happen?" Kinch was unsure how to deal with this child. He wasn't comfortable around children at the best of times.

"I've run away," she replied. "My mum's angry with me all the time, and she lies to us. I just want to talk to my dad, and she won't let me. We're always moving. I hate her." She began to cry.

Kinch moved awkwardly towards the little girl. "I'm sure she has her reasons. Sometimes it's hard for adults, and they don't do a good job of explaining why. I'm sure that's all it is." He knew that he had to take this little girl back, but the last thing he wanted was to go back there.

"No ... she hates me." She sat down under the tree and continued to sob.

"I guarantee you, Orisa, your mum loves you. It's just hard for her. Flora told me a little about you guys. It's hard for your mum to have to look after you both alone in a strange country." Kinch sat down beside her. "Just let me take you back. She'll be frantic looking for you."

"No, I won't go back. She'll be even madder now." She pulled away, clearly unsure of her newfound confidant.

"I'll make a deal with you. If you go back with me, I'll stay with you to make sure she's not mad, which I promise she won't be, and if she is, I'll explain everything to her and make sure she understands." Kinch had no idea what he was saying really, but he didn't want to be responsible for anything happening to this emotionally fragile little girl. She was such a tiny thing, all bones and beauty, her dark brown eyes like those of a frightened doe. He guessed that she didn't share the goose's blissful ignorance of difference; her skin must have invited comment from other children, not always kind. "And I'll buy you a Cornetto on the way. What do you reckon?"

She looked at him carefully, her crying reduced to a sniffle. "You promise you won't let her get mad at me?"

"I promise."

She picked up the little plastic bag at her side and took his hand.

They started to walk, her little hand feeling out of place in his large man's hand. He felt awkward but simultaneously overwhelmed by the need that this little person had of him, the innocent trust she had placed in a stranger.

They walked back towards the Blackpitts. Kinch asked her many questions – about her school, her teachers. He avoided mentioning her country. Flora had filled him in, but this was not a subject to discuss with a nine-year-old.

"Do you like your mother?" she asked him, her face an open book of curiosity.

"I'm afraid my mum died," he replied, wondering whether he should have used one of those more listener-friendly phrases like "passed on" or "has gone to heaven," but they just bugged him, even in the presence of a child. After all, children were no fools. They knew exactly what it meant.

"Oh." Her hand squeezed his for just a second. "You must be very sad about that."

"Yes, I was – am sad about that, but there was nothing I could do. That is why you must love your mum no matter what, Orisa, because one day, she may no longer be there, and then you will be very sad."

She looked at him and nodded.

Kinch nipped into a newsagent on Clanbrassil Street and bought them both Cornettos. They walked in silence, Orisa chomping on her Cornetto contentedly.

As they approached number seven, the door of the house flung open, and Sandra came running out, her face cracked with worry. She scooped Orisa into her arms. "Baby, where on earth did you go? I was so worried! Orisa, I would die if anything happened to you." She clutched the little girl to her.

"Mum, please don't be cross anymore. Please."

"Of course, baby. I just ... I'm just tired sometimes, Orisa. I worry so much about you and Efe. You know that, don't you? It's just because I love you so much."

Kinch looked at this mother's anguish and remembered his own mother's face as she lay on her deathbed, the life sucked out of her by the ravages of cancer. That last day, all she could think of was him, her boy left behind without her to fend for him. He could tell that hurt her more than any cancerous growth. How cruel life was sometimes. But he was over all that now. He'd got on with it, pulled himself together. He missed her of course, but what was the point in wallowing in all that misery? She was gone and that was that.

Flora walked out behind Sandra. She saw Kinch, her face one big question.

"Thank you," Sandra said, "She must have followed you. We were too busy chatting ... didn't notice."

Kinch knew only too well what they were chatting about. "No problem." He looked at Flora, who was shuffling awkwardly behind Sandra. She couldn't look him in the eye.

"Right, I'm off." He turned to leave, and Orisa ran after him. She wrapped her arms around his waist and looked up at him smiling.

"You look after your mum now."

She nodded and ran back to her mother. Kinch turned in the direction of the city centre. He wanted more than anything to turn around and beg Flora, plead with her to let him love her, but he kept walking.

CHAPTER 30

OMAR

~ Nausicaa ~

8:00 PM

JUNE SUNLIGHT DRIFTED TOWARDS the earth, slim fingers of yellow spread around the bowl of the world as it moved towards the slumber of night.

A sharp rock irritated the edge of Omar's right buttock. No matter how often he shifted position, it seemed to find a new place to poke into his flesh.

My bloody arse! Still the smoothest stone around. Grin and bear it.

He had picked up the money from the bookies earlier and given it to Jameson to put in the office safe. Maybe he could surprise Flora with a piece of jewellery, and then whisk her away to some exotic location. They hadn't had a proper holiday in years, and it was exactly what they needed to fire things up again.

On the edge of the black-blue bay of Sandymount Strand, he caught sight of the first star, its delicate light struggling to be seen against the dying embers of the day. The tall cylinders of Poolbeg Station sat on the horizon, steam billowing from the cement stalks into the darkening sky.

Looks filthy it does. Belching stale air into the world. Supposed to be harmless – still, surely in this day and age they can come up with something a bit easier on the eye.

To his left, a small group of people played on the damp sand. Two children raced along the edges of the water. The young girl turned to splash the tiny boy, who cried a storm in response.

Children can be cruel, little beggars. Love to torture each other. Don't need to hide it behind the lies and deceit of age, just let rip right in your face. She's the brat of the bunch all right.

He watched the skinny little girl, a smile spread across her freckled face, as she tripped innocently along the water's edge. A harried woman folded the small boy into her arms.

Little torturess! They all start the same. Never leaves them. The sharp edge of beauty's tongue. Cut you open like the jagged edge of a shell. We're a dumb lot, men. Plain feckin stupid how we keep running back for more.

The little boy ran to a young woman who sat on a rock, her tanned skin like dark glass in the shadow of the day. She handed him a bucket and spade, and he raced back to the other woman – the child's mother perhaps – who was busy piling sand for the children. The woman stretched her long, supple legs and lay back along the edge of the rock. She was close enough to Omar so that he could make out the edge of her breast as it fell out of her bikini top, the dark pink of her large nipple like the inverted navel of an exotic fruit. For the second time today, he could feel desire build in his groin, but this time it was different – not the pure physical reflex of lust, but a rounded intrigue, a sensual urge, a mystical desire of the unknown.

The girl looked in his direction. Her dark-red lips formed a pretty smile, shy and unhurried, trusting yet nervous. She looked away, the smile lingering on the edge of her lips.

Knows what she's at, all the same. Beautiful! Wonder what it's like? Close the eyes, it all smells the same. The salty egg of sex. Funny how we can't smell ourselves. Just as well, might explain too much.

He watched as she shifted her body towards him, the edges of her full breasts barely clinging to the ocean-blue bikini. She was not one of these skinny women who pushed and shoved their bodies into a shape it was never naturally supposed to hold. The skin and bones of the women who graced the front of *Hello* and *OK* did nothing for Omar. Their gaunt faces and haunted smiles like diaphanous shadows of the real person underneath.

This one knows who she is, like Flora. Women in the know, a rare thing. To dream of possessing a woman like that. In the end they possess you, that's the danger, I suppose.

He glanced at his watch.

Stuck at 4:30. Odd that. He shook it, but the hands didn't move.

Thought he'd be here – Mr. Bloom. Might as well accept I'll never catch the bugger. Who cares anyway? Needed a break. Long bloody day.

The little girl ran up to the woman, a dead crab in her clutches. Omar could just make out the conversation.

"Gretta, look, look. He's pink underneath." She pushed the dead creature into the lap of the surprised woman.

"Shauna! I hate dead things. Here, take it, love." She handed it back, her thin fingers holding the leg of the crab, her face the picture of disgust.

"But he's so pretty. Look, his shell is all pink and orange and red, like the sun." The girl's blond ringlets dripped wet around her pinched little face. Her mother approached with the little boy, who dragged his bucket behind him. She was a small, thin brunette. Omar guessed her to be about forty years old.

"Girl, I'm going to lose it if I ever have to build another sandcastle again," said the mother.

Gretta laughed. "Do you want me to take the kids for a walk?"

"Nah, it's ok. It's good for me to spend a bit of time with them. You take a break and relax. Sure, you have them all day long." The mother walked back to the water's edge.

Gretta looked in his direction and smiled.

He smiled carefully. He didn't want to be seen as a dirty old man. After all, there was probably at least twenty-year age difference between them. But love could be found in the strangest and most unexpected forms. Not that this was love but maybe ... under different circumstances.

She sat back down and turned to give him a small smile. A perfectly plaited braid crept down her muscular back. She undid it slowly ... the black hair fell in slow waves around her long neck, like the flowing surface of an underground river.

Jesus.

Omar was sitting behind the rock; they could only see his upper body from the beach. He found his hand reaching into his trousers as on those nights when Flora lay beside him, dead asleep and unaware of his desire. He watched her as she rubbed cream along the inside of her slim legs.

Damn, the snake is rising from his den. No harm, it's nearly night. No one can see.

A fountain of silent lights – blue, green, gold – shot through the sky in the distance. They looked like fireflies playing on the edge of the dying day. The little girl screamed with joy and pointed at the display.

"Look! Look, Gretta, the fireworks at the docks!"

Gretta stood up and stared out to the sea. Her face looked like a mixture of wonderment and fear, like a lost child in a strange but beautiful place. Her rounded figure reminded him of one of those paintings he'd seen by that French fella, Gauguin.

He could feel the desire rise beyond the point of control. A warm tingle rose from his toes, his breath heavy and deep. He reddened and turned away afraid she would notice.

She turned.

He was sure she couldn't have seen – her face remained open, shy but approachable.

Much to his surprise, she was walking towards him.

He panicked, throwing his jacket over his excitement. *Oh God.*

"Excuse me, I was just wondering if you might have the time?" She had a deep, pure voice, like a thick, warm syrup.

He glanced at his watch; it had stopped at exactly 4:30 PM. "I'm afraid my watch is on the blink, Miss. But it must be eight-something with the height of the sun and all." Excitement and panic washed through him as his mind scrambled for something original to say, but not a word formed on his lips, and he looked at her blankly.

Eejit. Right there, right in front of you, and all you can do is gape at her, mute.

"Thanks anyway." She turned slowly, revealing a pink stump at the end of her right arm. It had been hidden behind her back as she'd approached. She walked back towards the children, a slow grace belying her deformity.

Nasty looking thing that. Wonder how it happened? Poor girl. Would put a lad off all the same.

The family were gathering their things to go. Omar watched as Gretta pulled on her clothes, her movements awkward yet determined. She picked up her bag and looked back towards him with the hint of a smile. He nodded his head, and she followed the family back towards Sandymount.

Flawed Beauty. Makes them want you more. If Flora weren't so … oh blast

... the time, concert. Completely forgot.

He glanced at his watch, forgetting it was broken. Frustrated, he picked up his things and ran towards the Dart station.

On the platform the digital clock counted down the minutes to the next train.

Too late now. Give it a miss. She won't even notice. Pick up the money from the bet and go home.

Omar got on the train as it slowed to a stop, grabbing the last available seat in the carriage. It was packed with people heading in for the festivities and the fireworks. A heavily pregnant lady stood beside him. Omar watched the group of youngsters in the seats surrounding him; no one moved to let her sit down.

Ignorant scuts.

He stood up, signalling to the heavily made-up girl beside him to shift over. "Excuse me, Ma'am, would you like to sit down?"

"Thanks so much," replied the pregnant woman, her smile relieved and grateful.

"Looks like you're about to pop any minute there."

"Have about four weeks to go still. Feels like four years at this point though." She patted her stomach. "They say the first one's always early though, please God."

"You're a brave woman heading out on the town in that condition," Omar continued.

"Jesus, no bloody fear. I'm just going into Holles Street for a check-up. The car's on the blink, but it's as easy on the train."

"Hope you don't pop on the way because I'd probably faint at the sight of it. This lot don't strike me as medically inclined." Omar nodded towards a group of twenty-somethings done up to the nines for a night on the town.

The woman laughed. "I think you're safe enough, but you'd definitely be my best bet, so you better start praying."

Omar liked the look of this confident young woman. He noticed no ring on her left hand, not that that meant anything anymore, but he strongly suspected she was alone in this predicament. He didn't feel he should ask and embarrass her in front of a train full of strangers.

"You don't have the time there, do you?"

The woman glanced at her watch. "Ten past nine."

Omar thought for a second. "You don't mind if I walk with you, up to the hospital? I could check in and see how my friend Annie is doing."

"Of course. That would be grand."

CHAPTER 31

BLÁITHÍN

8:30 PM

THE LOBBY OF THE SHELBOURNE HOTEL was packed with people milling around in post-election-party mode. The local elections had gone well for Bernard O'Leary's party, not that Bláithín gave a shit. They were all a crowd of money-grabbing, corrupt bastards in her book. She was properly buzzed now – on the kind of invincible high that meant she was capable of anything. She'd show him. He wasn't going to wrap her around his fattened little finger like everyone else.

The doorman, dressed in his usual high-hatted regalia, eyed her suspiciously, her white lace skirts blowing up as she spun through the revolving door. She was past him before he had a chance to intercept her.

She began to speak from the moment she set foot in the lobby. "*Yes because he never did a thing like that before as ask her to get his breakfast in bed with a couple of eggs since the City Arms Hotel he used to be pretending to be laid up with a sick voice doing his highness to make himself interesting to that old faggot Mrs. Riordan ...*"

Her voice was soft, barely audible. She moved easily through the flow of words that had obsessed her for over a year. It had taken her six months to memorise the soliloquy, section by section, and now the words had become part of her thought process, a separate language as familiar to her as the English language.

She walked through the lobby, and up the stairs towards the front function room.

"*... she had too much chat in her about politics and earthquakes and the end of the world let us have a bit of fun first God help the world ...*"

People on the stairway looked at her with curiosity.

Her voice built momentum as she moved towards the high-ceilinged room at the front of the hotel.

"I think that's Molly Bloom. Must be part of it all," said an older woman to a young lady beside her.

The words flew from Bláithín's lips like jets of poison: "*... and her dog smelling my fur and always edging to get up my petticoats ...*"

She entered the long room and spotted her father at the far end, engrossed in conversation. A small group of confused men sped out of her way. The centre of the long table looked like the perfect stage, and she jumped up, her high boots pushing the plates and cutlery onto the floor. She decided to move ahead, treat them to the juicy bits.

"*... yes because he must have come three or four times with that tremendous big brute of a thing he has I thought the vein or whatever the dickens they call it was going to burst ...*"

God, Bláithín loved this bit. It made her want to strip naked and writhe like a banshee, but she reckoned she was making enough of a show of herself as it was.

Her father's horrified face gave her all the inspiration she needed to continue. He screamed at her, the blood vessels on his forehead popping out.

"Bláithín, have you lost your mind? Get down for God's sake." He reached out and grabbed her arm.

"But Daddy dearest," she sneered, "remember you asked me to come and perform the soliloquy? So here I am!"

"Get down!" He pulled her with force, and she fell against his chest, knocking them both over.

Nigel Murray appeared out of nowhere. He grabbed her right arm firmly and helped Bernard O'Leary up with his left hand. "That's enough, Bláithín. Come with me now and we'll sort this out."

Nigel's voice was firm and commanding. There was a reason her father used him to sort out his messes. He was the kind of man who never had to raise his voice; he could terrify or influence by lifting an eyebrow.

"Nigel, get your hands off me. I'm just giving Dad what he wanted. Oh yeah, and what else is it that you want from me?"

Bernard O" Leary eyed his daughter, the glint of fear resting in the corner of his eye. "Bláithín, I'm warning you."

Bláithín turned towards the room. A small group of photographers and journalists had converged on the commotion. On the brink of nailing her father before the press of Ireland, she stopped short, realising that she was now the one in the position of power. She had one more thing to ask of him. At that moment, as the press gathered for a lynching, she reckoned he would give her anything she wanted.

Murray attempted to pull her away from the room. A microphone was shoved in her face.

"Ms. O'Leary. Are you hinting that your father asked you to lie?" Charlie Bird's familiar face stood in front of the RTE camera.

She stared straight at her father. He looked shocked, defeated, maybe even a little heartbroken, but she had to ignore that. She had to come out from under his shadow and be her own woman. She had her own vision of the world, which was sharply at odds with the man who'd brought her into it. It was a crushing realisation but one they would both have to accept.

"No comment."

Her father let out a long, slow breath. There was a cold light in his eyes that had extinguished all affection between them. They were at war, and he was used to winning, but this time it was she who would gain the upper hand.

Bernard O'Leary spoke to the room. "If you don't mind, I'm going to take my daughter home so that she can be looked after. I ask you all to show me some respect with this difficult situation and to give us both some space. I will answer any questions you have after she is properly looked after." He nodded to Nigel to continue.

The journalists stepped aside.

Bláithín let Murray guide her mutely down the corridor and upstairs to a guest bedroom her father had reserved.

Bernard O'Leary followed her into the room. They stared at each other until her father broke the ice.

"I'm calling your mother. Nigel will take you back to Dalkey." He hesitated, a shadow of pain visible behind his cold eyes. "You've gone too far this time, Bláithín. You're out on your own after this." He turned to leave.

"I've been out on my own a long time, Dad. You've just been too busy to notice."

He looked back and shook his head.

"Dad?" She summoned her sweetest voice for what she was about to ask.

"What?"

"I could have said what I really think out there, but I didn't." She hesitated. "I have just one thing to ask, and then I promise, really promise, that I won't be any more trouble. I won't open my mouth again."

He narrowed his eyes. "Yes?"

"Please get Gerry released? There's no real proof against him. Just the word of some scumbags. At least bail him out until the situation is a bit clearer. Ask John to represent him. He has no one. I know he's innocent, Dad. I promise." She held her breath and waited for the response.

O'Leary looked tired. He sat on the edge of the bed, deep in thought. He looked at Nigel Murray, who nodded to him silently. "All right. I'll have him bailed out, and I'll get John to look into his case, but that's all I can do. If the facts are against him, that's not my fault."

"Thanks, Daddy. Thank you." She meant it if only for that moment.

"Nigel, look after it. I must get back and sort out this mess."

She watched her father compose himself, arrange his features into the face of the public man, confident and competent. He left the room, and she sat on the edge of the bed, her head in her hands.

"Bláithín, let's go. The sooner you're home, the better you'll feel," said Nigel Murray.

She knew that facing her mother was the last thing she wanted. Whatever last bit of energy she had was summoned to figure out how to get out of this.

"I just need to use the bathroom, Nigel."

He eyed her suspiciously. "Let me see your purse."

"Fuck off. None of your business."

"It is if you're about to snort more of that shit. Let me see." He grabbed her bag and emptied the contents onto the bed.

"See, I'm not that fecking stupid to bring the stuff out with me. Now, I need to use the toilet!"

"Go on then."

She locked the door behind her, turned on the tap and pulled her phone from the pocket inside her petticoats. Hanan's number popped up as she shuffled through the numbers. She rang the number.

"Bláithín?" The voice on the other end sounded anxious.

She whispered. "Hi, Hanan, I can't talk now, but I need your help desperately. It's a long story but I'm in the Shelbourne Hotel. My dad has me locked up with his ape of a minder. He's going to ship me back to Dalkey, and I just can't face it. He'll probably get me locked up again. Please, please, can you do me a favour and call the Shelbourne desk? Say I've locked myself into room 327 and can't find the key?"

"Wha? But won't the guy be there with you?"

"Not if you call him after – I'll text you the business card after I hang up. Are you at your father's?"

"Yeah. Why?"

"Go to the public phone on the street outside your shop. Change your voice a little. Say that Nigel's wife's been in an accident, is unconscious, and in the emergency ward of St. Vincent's."

"Jesus, Bláith, that's a bit harsh. What if he asks me questions I can't answer?"

"Anyone who's just been told something like that isn't going to look for the fine detail. Just say that's all you know, and I guarantee you he'll rush out of here like the arse of his pants is on fire. That way, if he locks me in, the bellhop should get here in time to open the door. It's all I can think of."

Hanan sounded worried. "Christ, I don't know, but if it's all you can think of, ok. I'll hop on my bike and meet you at the main Stephen's Green entrance, ok?"

"Grand. If anything goes wrong, I'll call you."

"Ok. Soon." Hanan hung up the phone.

"Bláithín, are you ok in there?" asked Nigel Murray.

"Yeah, grand. Out in a sec." She looked at herself in the mirror. Dark circles ringed her blue eyes. She splashed her face with water and opened the door.

Nigel looked at her suspiciously. "I hope you didn't have anything hidden in your knickers or somewhere?"

"Give me a break, Nigel. I just needed to freshen up. I feel like I've been run over by a double-decker."

"Come on, let's go," said Nigel.

Bláithín eyed Nigel's mobile phone by the bed in the corner. She willed it to ring. "Just one sec. I just need to make a phone call to the concert hall. I'm supposed to be performing the soliloquy there in a half an hour. If I can't go, I'd better let them know. It's a big deal."

He sighed deeply. "Go on."

She rang her own number knowing it would hit her message machine and spoke into the phone. "Yeah, hi, can I speak to Mr. Phelan please?" Nigel's mobile began to ring in the corner. Nigel moved to pick it up. Bláithín continued to talk.

"Sorry, my wife ... what? What happened?" He looked like a vein was about to pop in his head.

She felt sorry she had to cause him such stress, even temporarily. He wasn't a bad sort, really, but this was no time for guilt.

"Oh my God. Where is she? ... Ok, I'll be there in thirty minutes." He put down the phone and turned to Bláithín who hung up her mobile.

"That was St. Vincent's Hospital. My wife's been in a car accident. Oh my God! I have to get there now." He looked distressed.

"Shite. Is she all right, Nigel?" She could feel the actress in her kicking into action.

"She's unconscious but stable. They couldn't tell me more. Listen, Bláithín, hang on here, and I'll call your father on the way ... and no messing, right."

"Yeah, of course. Go find out what's happening. I'll be good as gold." She could feel the smile build behind her eyes.

"I have to lock you in. Sorry, but your Dad would never forgive me if you scarpered."

She broke out her best saddened and weary look. "I know, I know. Go on."

Nigel left the room and locked the door behind him.

She sat on the edge of the bed and chewed on her nails while she waited. Five minutes later a bunch of keys rattled on the other side of the door. It opened and a small, thin man smiled at her. "Ok now, Miss?"

"Great, thanks. Don't know what I did with it."

He handed her a spare key, and she waited until he'd turned a corner in the corridor. Then she bolted the other way, down the stairs, keeping an eye on the function room. Inching her way along the edge of the wall, she slipped into the bar, and out the side door of the hotel that opened onto Kildare Street. She turned left and raced across the road. The usual line of taxi drivers were parked the length of Stephen's Green.

Hanan was standing underneath the arch and spotted her as she turned the corner.

She felt a warmth in the pit of her stomach.

His smile was wide and embracing.

"Thanks a million, Hanan. That was stressful."

They hugged.

He took her head in his hands. "Bláith, I've been so worried about you. Kinch told me everything, and even though he's my pal, I gave him a kick up the arse for being a right shit to you, I promise."

She smiled and kissed him on the forehead. "You're a real friend, Hanan."

He blushed slightly, letting go of her head. "The least I could do. I'm not having the best of days myself. Sarah broke up with me."

Bláithín decided to crush her joy and feign sympathy. "You're kidding!" She slipped her arm through his. "We're a right pair of losers." They laughed. "Let's head for a coffee and a chat. I could do with a break from all this drama."

"Sounds good to me."

CHAPTER 32

FLORA

8:30 PM

WHEN SHE GOT TO THE National Concert Hall, the crowds were out the door. She felt fairly drained after that business with Kinch, but she'd been looking forward to this, so she wasn't going to let it bother her too much.

The mayor was in the corner of the wide lobby, surrounded by Dublin's glitterati. As usual, they looked like they'd just stepped out of a Brown Thomas window display.

Flora wasn't in a very sociable mood, so she kept her head down and headed for the dressing room. Matt Phelan intercepted her as she was about to slip through the door. He clutched a bunch of worse-for-wear flowers.

"Flora, my dear. These are for you. A little inspiration for the event at hand." The sweep of white hair perched under his straw boater made his recently acquired tan all the more noticeable. It looked suspiciously fake.

"Matt. You shouldn't have, really." She had been fighting off the advances of this silly man for months now. He was far too old to hold any attraction for her, but he was good to her, she had to admit, always hooking her up with top-class gigs. She knew she encouraged his interest in her – it worked to her benefit – but she never brought it so far that anything happened. Rumours were flying around about them, and she did nothing to dispel them, knowing it would help to deflect attention from what she was up to. A dangerous game, but she knew how to work it.

"Flora, there's a little party after the gig at my apartment in Hanover Quay. Champagne, the works. You should come. Promise me you'll come." He grabbed her hand and cupped it in his.

"I'm very tired, Matt. Had a rough day, but if I can summon up the energy I will, I promise." She smiled sweetly, removing her hand carefully. "I have to get ready but thanks."

"See you later." He bounded across the room, happy with his progress.

Flora threw her eyes to heaven and went into the dressing room.

The musicians milled around, putting the last touches to their makeup. Flora wasn't in the mood to chat, so, apart from a few polite interchanges, she put her head down, deposited her belongings in her locker, and made her way to the orchestra pit. Placing the sheet music in front of her, she began to tune her violin.

The audience – predominantly white-haired, well-dressed, and middle class – made their way to the seats. Nothing about the beautifully proportioned, bright, modern edifice of the concert hall aroused her senses. Maybe she was too used to the gold-leafed splendour of European opera houses. It struck her as odd that a people so well-known for their passion and creative soul allowed the most sublime music to be played to them in what had once been a university examination hall. But the Irish were like that. Architecture was never their strong point.

She liked them all the same, their boundless enthusiasm and drive, their ability to shape even the worst of circumstances into something to be laughed at with an excessive consumption of life and all it had to offer. She hoped this wouldn't be their undoing. They reminded her of a child who, fed bread and water for many years, brings himself to the vomiting point when presented with a box of rich chocolates. There was certainly a childlike quality about the way this nation enjoyed its new-found wealth, almost as if they expected it to be taken away from them any second.

Still, she was comfortable here. She'd always been outside the norm in Poland, an oddity that people didn't quite know what to do with. Here, the same difference meant that she was exotic, desirable, an unknown quantity. Perhaps she was lucky. The colour of her skin and her Catholic background provided enough of a connection to this people so that, instead of inspiring fear and suspicion, she aroused desire. She wondered how different it might be for Sandra, her beauty an incalculable mystery to all around her. The average person liked to see a bit of themselves in "the other", after all.

She continued to exercise small musical phrases, her fellow musicians joining in as they slowly took their places. Her phone beeped beside her, and she cursed herself for having forgotten to switch it off. Curiosity got the better of her. It was her parents' number in Poland. It was very unusual for them to contact her first, so she stepped outside the pit and pressed 171 to listen to the voice message. Her father's voice sounded immediately distressed, broken.

"Flora, call home immediately. Something has happened to your mother." Her stomach lurched violently. The concert was about to start – the conductor waved an irritated hand at her to signal that she should take her place. Confused by the demands of the moment and a wave of panic, she decided she had no choice but take up her instrument and wait for the end of the concert.

"Are you all right?" asked her fellow violinist, Maura O'Shea.

Flora hesitated but decided it wasn't the moment. "Fine, thanks."

The musicians readied their instruments. The conductor raised his baton, nodded his head, and moments later his arm swept through the air. The opening chords of "Blumenlied" by Gustav Lange filled the air.

Flora allowed her violin to guide her into the ocean of gentle sound. She poured her anxiety into the music, her face the picture of concentration, while never losing consciousness of the great ensemble of which she played a small but significant part. Even in such a moment of doubt and fear, the grand sweep of it all gave her a reason to be, an understanding of the possibilities beyond her immediate existence.

Her mind darted through the music. She thought of her mother – the woman she'd known as a child, the pride she had felt in Flora's accomplishments, the love she didn't know how to shape into understanding. Their last conversation laden with anger. Flora's violin absorbed her desperate prayer: that this woman, who had so deeply affected her life for the good and the bad of it, hadn't gone to a place where they couldn't have that last conversation. A conversation where understanding is found. A soft resolution.

Chapter 33

KINCH

8:30 PM

HE FELT LIKE SHIT, but he wasn't going to wallow in misery. There were a couple of hours to kill before the Low concert. Kinch walked around the city aimlessly, listening to Van Morrison. The slow rhythms of "TB sheets" drifted through his brain. The lights of the white colonnades of the Dáil were beginning to show against the shadow of dusk.

He crossed over to Merrion Square and climbed over the high fence into the gardens. The years he had spent rock-climbing in Dalkey Quarry came in handy after all. An abundance of rhododendrons flourished around the edge of the newly cut lawns. Lying down in the middle of the square, he watched the day's light disappear behind the black slates of the Georgian rooftops. The earth had tilted into shadow, and he felt relieved that this day was drawing to a close. He thought about the previous inhabitants of this fine square, Wilde and Yeats inking their pens in the candlelight of the high-roofed mansions.

So much for the penniless writer.

Sarah and Will would be off their shifts soon. The roof of Holles Street Hospital was visible above the line of beech trees in the Northeast corner of the square. A flap of seagulls led the way to the gates near the hospital. He had a quick look to make sure there were no guards in the vicinity and he climbed back over the fence.

A 45 bus passed as he crossed the road towards the National Maternity Hospital.

His phone rang, and he dug it out of a pocket. Gerry's name flashed on the screen. He stopped the music.

"Gerry?"

"Hi boy, I'm out. Where are you?"

"That's great, man. I'm heading into Holles Street to meet up with Will and Sarah. We're heading to the Low concert. Did they tell you why they let you go?"

"Not sure. Think it has something to do with Bláithín. They just let me go and said something about a guy called John Fenton getting in touch with me tomorrow. Think he's a pal of Bláith's Dad."

Kinch stopped at the top of the steps. "That bollox. You might be better off inside. Yeah, he's a crony of Bernard's. Wonder what he's up to now?"

"What do you mean?"

"Nothing, man. I was worried shitless about you. You're out. That's the main thing." Kinch suspected that all was not as it seemed, but he didn't want to distress his friend with his fears. "Anyway, jump in a taxi and get your arse over here. I have a spare ticket so come with us. After the day you had, you deserve it."

"Bloody right. Be there soon."

"Great! Ask for the Intern's Canteen." One more problem temporarily stalled at least.

He pressed play. Van Morrison growled into his ear.

A tired-looking man descended the steps of the hospital with a bewildered smile on his face.

First-timer. No clue what's ahead of him, poor bugger.

Kinch found maternity hospitals vaguely disturbing. It was a world he was incapable of accessing – happy family life. Secretly he suspected that the happiness surrounding the "great event" was one large conspiracy concocted to trap a man within the wheels of procreation, thereby ensuring the continuation of the human race. Jumping on that wheel, had the appeal of a medieval torture instrument.

The entrance smelt of newness, not just cleanliness. The air was laden with the screaming breath of new life. How appropriate that the first instinct of a baby on the way out of its mother's womb was to scream blue bloody murder. Even in the first moment, these tiny beings could sense what was ahead of them.

The corridors were brimming with proud and panicked fathers clutching newly purchased bunches of flowers, their confused toddlers being dragged a foot behind.

A skinny young girl, no more than seventeen, passed in a dressing gown. Her enormous bump looked like it would topple over her tiny frame.

The surgical smell of hospitals had always made him queasy, and he smiled as Van the Man sang about the smell of TB sickbeds. *Thank God we don't live in the past where a deadly virus can wipe out half the population. The Big C is enough to contend with.*

Kinch climbed the stairs to the second floor. The staff canteen was at the end of the corridor. His pals had been interning in this hospital for two months now, so he knew the drill. Strictly speaking, outsiders weren't allowed in, but the students could slip a few friends into the canteen without much comment. He spotted Will sitting at a table with Sarah. They were laying into a plate of dodgy-looking pasta.

Kinch switched off the music and licked his lips. "That doesn't look half bad."

"How it looks and how it tastes are two completely different stories. Want some?" Sarah stuck a fork full of pasta in his face, and he swallowed.

He grimaced. "They don't call it 'hospital food' for nothing."

"We do have a little something to wash it down. Will signalled to the hipflask that he had hidden under his seat. "Neat Paddy. Can't beat it."

Sarah scrunched up her face. "Yuck."

Will passed the flask to Kinch under the table. He turned to the wall and swigged several mouthfuls. "Whoah. That hits the spot."

"Any crack?" asked Sarah.

Kinch leant in to talk closer to them. "Yeah, never got a chance to tell ye, but Gerry got into a spot of bother today. Ended up getting arrested. Anyway, he's out and on his way over here."

Sarah's voice rose an octave. "Arrested? But why?"

"It's a long bloody story. I'll let him tell you. Listen, I have to go to the jacks. Can you throw me the flask, so I can have a proper swig while I'm in there?"

Will leant into his bag and pulled out another silver flask. "Here, I have a spare. Just keep it."

"Ace." Kinch made his way to the men's. He took a slash and moved to the mirror to wash his hands. Large rings were forming around his eyes.

Sorry, Stephen, not looking the best today.

Barely stopping for air, he took out the flagon and gulped down half of the contents. The hot liquid flew through his system, raising his pulse and his mood instantly.

That's more bloody like it.

When he returned to the canteen, Gerry was sitting beside Will, stuffing his face with a plate of pasta. Sarah tapped on her phone distractedly.

"Prison food didn't suit, eh mate?" said Kinch.

Gerry jumped up and hugged his friend fiercely. "This shit tastes worse to be honest. Disappointed you won't have to engineer a jailbreak?"

"Fuck yeah. Was all geared up to do a Pacino-like, blast-you-out-of-prison move."

Gerry leant in and sniffed Kinch. "What's that I smell off your breath, boy?"

Kinch looked around the canteen. When no one was watching, he passed the flask to Gerry. "Neat whiskey. Now that will cheer you up." Gerry gulped it down.

Sarah sighed. "You lot are desperate – getting wasted in a maternity ward. If we're caught, we're in big trouble."

"Chill out, Sarah. It's grand. There's no one here who can bust our balls. They've all gone home."

She threw her eyes to heaven. "I'm pleading innocence if anyone smells a thing. You had better back me up."

"Your honour, the fair damsel was a mere victim of unfortunate locational circumstance," said Kinch.

"That's contagious," said Gerry, bursting into laughter.

"Feck yeah."

They all laughed.

Sarah picked up her handbag. "I'm off to the loo. A girl has to look her best when newly single." She looked at Kinch and lowered her voice. "Do you think Hanan will go after ...?"

"Ah yes, I heard you broke his heart. Join the club."

Sarah arched her eyebrows, "What, you too? Bláithín ok?"

"I guess not. Feel like a right shit, but worse to stay when it's not right, I suppose. I doubt either of them will be in the mood, but they'd have to get rid of the tickets, so who knows if they'll be there. We'd better watch out for the incoming missiles." Kinch laughed nervously.

"You're a right pair of heartbreakers," Gerry interrupted.

"Somebody has to be." Sarah grabbed her bag and moved towards the door. "Right, time to slap on the face."

"How'd the day go anyway, Kinch? The performances and all that?" asked Gerry.

"Lots of drama, and I'm not talking about the Joycean crap. Flora dumped me. Guess it's celestial karma." Kinch had confided in Gerry about Flora. His moral radar was pen to the grey of life.

"Ah no. That's mank. I blame the gods," said Gerry.

"Bloody right. I reckon they all sit around up there, laughing their godly asses off at the sad little human eejits they created. One giant celestial Subbuteo game."

They laughed, attracting the attention of a young, blond nurse.

"Keep it down, boys. It's not a brothel in here." The green-eyed Westerner attempted a sharp look of disapproval with the hint of a smile sitting on the edge of her thin lips and disappeared out the door.

"Wouldn't mind a bit of that," whispered Gerry under his breath.

"Watch out, I know the women from the West. They'd chop you up and serve you for dinner as quick as let you into their knickers," Will said.

"I can guarantee you, my friend, that I would have that woman in a lather of sweat in quicker time than your morning playtime." Gerry cocked a dark eyebrow at his two friends, who threw their heads in the air in mock dismissal.

"You Cork blokes might strut around with GAA muscles and cheeky smiles, but as soon as ye open your mouths, the shite that comes out of them would confuse a feckin saint. We can actually be understood, which means that we can nail women for the rest of our sorry lives!" Will gave Kinch a high five — Gerry grinned and took a long slug from his cup.

Kinch investigated the corridor. His heart skipped a beat when he saw who was coming his direction. "No feckin way, lads! It's the Arab."

"Who?" said Will.

Kinch looked at Gerry, who arched his eyebrows in response. Before either had a chance to come up with a fumbled lie, Omar walked through the door of the canteen and spotted Kinch.

"The actorman. How are things going today? What a coincidence. I was hoping to get a hold of you just to ask a few quick questions for the piece on the Bloomsday performances. Making a right arse of it, to be honest. Too much other stuff going on. Do you mind?" Omar signalled to the chair beside the lads.

They all looked at each other, unsure how to react.

Kinch took the lead. "Sure, Omar, take a seat, but we have to warn you, we're oiling ourselves up slightly for the night ahead, so don't be shocked if you get a whiff of "uisce beatha" from under the table. You know what I mean?" Kinch gave Omar a conspiratorial wink.

"Is that right? Well as long as I don't have to partake, I can smell nothing." Omar winked back.

"Take a seat." Kinch found himself sitting beside the one man who could make him feel guiltier than he already did about what had happened that day.

CHAPTER 34

OMAR

~ Oxen of the Sun ~

9:00 PM

OMAR COULD SEE BREDA KEANE talking to the nurse outside the door of the canteen. The puffy wool of her pink mohair jumper reminded him of the tired candy floss of the carnival that his father used to bring him to every year. Breda looked exhausted but happy. Her transparent, pale face was delicate and tired, like an overused doll. He took a gulp of his coffee and tapped Kinch on the shoulder.

"Will ye be around for a while yet?"

Kinch nodded at Omar and took another swig from the bottle under the table. "We're leaving in about fifteen."

"Right, just spotted the person I came to see. Be back in a sec."

Breda Keane's bloodshot eyes fell on Omar as he walked into the corridor. She clutched a vase of wilted flowers. The pungent odour of the yellow water seeped into his nostrils.

"Omar. So brilliant you could drop in. Just trying to find a bin for these."

"They look a little worse for wear all right," he replied.

She chucked the flowers into a nearby bin and handed the vase to a hassled-looking orderly who passed by pushing a trolley of empty bottles.

"She's had it at bloody last. Thank Christ. It's a little boy. He's so cute."

"That's great, Breda."

"Well, he looks like a little scrunched-up ball, but he has big, brown eyes. Suppose they're yer man's, but sure, what can you do?" Mrs. Keane linked her arm through his and pulled him down the corridor with considerable force. "It happened this afternoon around 3:30. Poor thing is completely wrecked. I told her I'd met you."

"I suppose she's too tired for visitors, but I was just passing, and I thought ..."

"Absolutely right to drop in, Omar. Just right. However, between you and me, a woman's vanity kicks in even at a moment like this, and she told me, she said, "Mum, if you let Omar Wilde near me and me looking a complete state, after not seeing the man for ten years, I'll never forgive you."

He found it hard to focus on Breda as she jumped from foot to foot, like a child running across hot burning sand.

"That's what she said, Omar, but she'd love you to drop in the day after tomorrow, when she's had some rest. Would that be ok? She really wants to see you."

Her voice tripped through his eardrums like a record at double speed.

"That's grand, Breda. No bother." He felt relieved, no longer sure he wanted to see this woman from his past, this ghost of a memory. What was the point in bringing it back to life? Better left alone.

Breda's tired eyes stared at him for a second. "God, Omar, you've become so like your mother, it's amazing." She hesitated, looking at him as if she wanted to take back the words, pull them from the living, breathing world of which his parents were no longer a part.

Omar fell silent, not sure how to respond.

Breda shook her head. "Come on now and I'll show you the baby quickly. Sure, he's a gorgeous little thing."

Before Omar had a chance to respond, he was dragged down the corridor and into the post-natal ward. The wet, soft breathing of the newborns hung in the air like a cool morning. Something about the way they were lined up in long rows of identical glass receptacles reminded him of his second-year science class. A deep, growling dread had grabbed him by the balls when greasy-haired Mr. Leary had wheeled in a row of live frogs in identical glass jars. His enthusiastic classmates, eager to sample the taste of a sanctioned kill, had readied their blades. Omar shrank to the back of the room, fighting the instinct to flee the execution. For a second, he'd imagined himself the hero of a grand epic, sent to save these helpless creatures by smashing the jars to the ground in one grand anarchic gesture. Instead, he'd watched in silence as pungent gas filled the jars. Frantic, the frogs had slid down the glass surface, their sinewy limbs waving in the air in a final act of desperation.

The new-borns were laid out before him like a mini assembly line of humanity.

"There he is." Breda pointed to receptacle number five in row three. "She hasn't given him a name yet. Wants to take a good look at him before she decides how to label the poor child for the rest of his life. I'm terrified to ask or suggest. You know what Annie's like. Would eat the head off you if you gave a sideways opinion about somethin, so I'm keepin my mouth shut."

The child wriggled noiselessly. His bright brown eyes stood out amongst a row of pallid babies. *Doesn't stand a chance, poor thing.*

"He's lovely."

"Any ideas?" asked Breda, nudging him in the side.

"Sorry?"

"For names?"

He could feel it forming on the tip of his tongue, *Ruairi,* as though it were the only name available in a universe of possibility – *Ruairi.*

"No, sorry. No good at that sort of thing." He suddenly felt sick and wanted desperately to get away from the humidity of this confined space. "Sorry, Breda, but I just need to have a word with the lad I was talking to earlier before he disappears." He moved towards the door and pointed back towards the canteen.

"That's fine, luv. You'll drop in another day, won't you? To see Annie?"

"I will, yes. I will." Omar hugged the woman, his body as stiff as a shop-room dummy, and walked in short, hurried steps, towards the canteen. He opened the top two buttons of his shirt, his breath heavy and laboured.

As Omar approached, Gerry was on his feet, gesturing wildly to the small group around the table. The pretty blonde looked disgusted.

"Still at it, lads?" Omar was aware that he was entering the conversation at none too comfortable a point.

Laughter trailed into a wave of uncomfortable giggling. "Yeah. Hi. Sit down." Kinch gestured to Omar to retake the seat beside him. "I apologise for my Cork friend. He has a mouth like a beggar's arse." The boy's eyes were watery and bulging, his breath the scent of a vat of Paddys.

"I've heard worse." Omar sat down. *It could have been him. This open-faced boy.*

"Did you see your friend?"

"No. She's sleeping but I saw the baby. Gorgeous little boy. No name as of yet."

Kinch nodded. "Hard to know what suits, on first glance."

"So how did the day go?" Omar asked Kinch, who played with the hat on his lap.

"Yeah, grand. Didn't have much to do really. Just wandered around looking like a thespian. Not that difficult." Kinch continued to fumble with his hat.

"Didn't you dump your girlfriend and ... oh yeah, get dumped by your mistress a few hours later?" Gerry smiled wickedly.

Kinch glared at him, a hot blush covering his face. "My friend has an active imagination."

"What's he talking about?" Sarah looked at Kinch carefully.

Gerry, three sheets to the wind, wasn't letting go. "This is a man of mystery, lads, you don't know the half of it."

Omar didn't like the Corkman's tone. "We all have our secrets, and better kept that way sometimes."

Kinch dropped his hat.

Omar bent to pick it up and placed it on the young man's head. "It suits you."

Kinch looked at Omar with a shy smile of acknowledgement.

The blond-haired boy interrupted. "Listen lads, the concert's starting in fifteen. Better get a move on."

Kinch turned to Omar. "Sorry man, we're heading to a concert in Christchurch." He took a pen and wrote his number on a piece of paper. "Give me a buzz if you want to chat about today ... well, you know." His voice tapered away, a shadow building in the corner of his eye.

"Actually, I have to head over to Christchurch myself. Picking up something. Do you mind if I tag along?" He didn't feel like going home yet. He knew Jameson would be heading home soon and could nip over the bridge to give him his money.

Kinch looked surprised. "Yeah, sure. Are you going to the concert?"

"No, no. I'm just meeting someone nearby. Rock concerts aren't really my thing. A bit beyond that." He could tell they all look relieved, but he couldn't blame them for not wanting a man of nearly 40 hanging out with them. "Thanks."

They all gathered their things and scrambled out the door.

Omar looked at Kinch as they exited the building. *Something about that boy. Fragile. Needs protecting.*

CHAPTER 35

BLÁITHÍN

9:30 PM

THE COFFEE POT GURGLED in a corner of Bláithín's apartment.

Hanan rummaged through the pile of CDs by the stereo. Bláithín watched him from behind, her eye following the curve of his taut body. Funny, she'd never noticed how attractive Hanan was. His white Talking Heads t-shirt clung to the dark, fine muscle of his upper arms. He bent over the CDs, body coiled tight, tattered jeans just loose enough to allow the imagination to enter. She felt a warm gush of blood through her body.

Radiohead's "Where I End and You Begin" seeped into the room, a dark, juicy infusion of sound.

She cracked open a bottle of wine.

"Are you sure that's a good idea?" asked Hanan.

"Absolutely. I need to chill out a little."

She poured them both a glass and sat close beside him on the couch. The full-bodied wine slid down her throat easily.

"Are you very cut up about Sarah?" She stifled a smile.

He filled his glass. "You're bloody delighted no doubt." He turned to face her, his hazel eyes taking her in.

"Plenty more flies in the dung heap."

"Optimistic."

"I'm speaking from experience." The remains of the coke jangled at the edge of her senses.

"And you? What about Kinch?" He looked at her carefully.

She lowered her voice. "Speaking of dung."

He smiled. A nervous air hovered between them. Hanan leant forward and began to roll a cigarette.

Thom Yorke sang about a gap in between where one ended, and another began. Now she could see how to get the other side.

"Feeling any better?" he asked, his eyes fixed on the line of the rolling paper.

"Mmmmm."

He licked the paper carefully, her eyes following his movements.

"I could run down to the video shop around the corner and grab us a film if you like. It would be a good way to get your mind off things."

"Guess so." She continued to watch as he tapped the cigarette on the table and searched through his pockets for a light.

She reached out silently and flicked her thumb on the silver lighter Kinch had bought her in the bazaar in Paris the year before. The flame flickered delicately. She waited for Hanan to notice, watched as he turned towards her.

He smiled and sat back beside her, one leg tight against her body. "Ah." He bent towards the light, eyes lifted towards hers, the hard pull of soft lips on the slim cigarette. He moved the cigarette, and the space between them fell away.

Their eyes locked.

Pure instinct took over. The magnetic pull towards him surprised her. Their lips met, hard and fast. Music drifted through the air behind them, wrapped them into each other. She slipped her hand underneath his t-shirt, dug her nails into his skin. Air played between their bodies like the fingers of a master guitarist – two tautly wound strings. She ripped open the belt of his jeans, pulled the t-shirt over his head.

She felt like a hungry cat as she licked the edge of his nipple.

He shuddered. Grasping the threads of her bodice, he loosened it until her small, pert breasts fell under his fingertips.

There was the power of the hunter about her – the watcher in the darkness. This excited her as she felt his cock become hard as a baseball bat, forced him into her body. *Fuck me*, she thought to herself, *fuck me, fuck me, FUCK ME!*

She wanted him to abuse her, to hurt her, to suck the poison out of her.

He grabbed her head, forced her to look into his eyes. She tried to look away, but he held her there, his voice a calm whisper, "Bláith, slow, Bláith, slower."

She kissed him hard, moving her head away and down to his left nipple. It rose to greet her, and she bit down hard drawing blood.

She felt him loosen inside her, pull away from the space of her anger.

"BLÁITHÍN, THAT HURTS!" He grabbed her arms, silencing her rabid movements. "Stop!"

She froze.

"What the fuck?" he continued.

She looked away and fell backwards, shrouded in shame. He pointed the remote control at the player and pressed "Stop."

"I didn't mean ..." She began to cry.

He looked at her silently.

The cathedral bells sang into the air in the distance. Pulling her to him he held her while she sobbed into his warm skin.

"It's ok." He stroked the back of her head.

A white calm quietened her tears. His smell was the deep wet of pine after the rain has cleansed the earth. Holding her tightly he stroked her head until they both fell asleep stretched across her green velvet couch like elfin lovers in the dark womb of a forest.

CHAPTER 36

FLORA

10:00 PM

THE MOMENT SHE STRUCK the last chord of the performance, Flora raced to the changing room and grabbed her bag. She'd spotted Tomasz in the audience with Kate, the girl he'd been dating, but she was in no mood for unnecessary chat, so she walked straight out the back door and into the Iveagh Gardens. She knew the caretaker, Joe, a shy, balding man with a crooked eye. It was hard to get used to that eye at first, but he had such a sweet nature that this small defect almost became a point of attraction, a failing that brought out the mothering instinct in women. He always let her in, after hours, if she needed a moment to herself after a long concert.

A dark cloud hovered over the pristine gardens. She could see the golden strands of the day's dying light skirt the park's high walls. A deep shadow followed her through the park and sucked the warmth out of her body. It reminded her of a dream she'd had the night before – she'd been alone on a dark country road, the sky bright and full of stars. Out of nowhere a giant craft hovered above her, its creeping shadow enveloping her in dread. She grabbed her bicycle and pedalled frantically through the dark boreens but couldn't escape the crawling, silent shadow. Exhausted, she hit a pothole, crashed to the ground, and scraped the inside of her leg. Frozen by fear, she watched a door slide open in the belly of the giant craft. A shaft of light descended upon her, blinding her. She woke in a lather of sweat and pounding heartbeats.

That same fear engulfed her now as she put on her black woollen shawl and sat on a bench near an ornate stone fountain. It spat water into the cool evening air dancing in unison with two other fountains nearby. A man-made waterfall sang proudly in the distance reminding her of a gushing glacial stream. She'd seen a documentary about the underground rivers that were growing in the Arctic. The water flow caused large pieces of glacial ice to break off and move into the Northern seas like massive ghost-ships.

No good can come of it. Her thoughts lingered on the edge of a space she was desperately trying to push away from her.

No one was to be seen except a pair of squirrels playing around the base of a large oak tree. They remained oblivious to her, scampering up and down the wide trunk like happy children in a playground. Flora stared at her father's number on the screen of her phone. She hesitated, aware that a moment without such dark knowledge is lighter, freer, unburdened. She willed a sign that would show her all was ok, that all would continue its steady path towards the future.

Out of nowhere, a man sat down beside her on the bench. As the day descended into darkness, she knew the parks of Dublin became dangerous seedy places, but this old man didn't look like the type who would harm her. He had a large, red satchel full of newspapers, which he laid down beside him. He turned and smiled. His face showed the story of his life, the gritty brown of Dublin streets, a face like the city itself, the crevices and alleyways etched into his tawny skin. His moist blue eyes smiled at her above a neat, greying moustache.

"Bit chilly." Voice deep and gravelled.

"Mmmmm." She didn't want to be rude, but this was not a moment for meaningless chit-chat.

They sat in silence, the old man staring at the fountain.

Flora watched the squirrels as they began to wrestle over what looked like a chestnut. "You know Joe then?"

"Yes."

"Old pal of mine. Always lets me in here in the evenings. I love it. Gets you away from the madness out there." He smiled at her.

She nodded.

The old man continued to stare at the water. "Reminds me of music."

"Sorry?"

"The way the water moves, falls in great crying streams it does – like an Irish ballad."

She turned and looked at the man who continued to stare at the fountain. He looked sad, his eyes filmy and wet, although in the dark it was hard to tell. Maybe he always looked like that. Maybe he was always sad.

"I used to come here with my wife when we were courtin, a long time ago. She was a singer. Used to sing to me here, just the two of us. Had a beautiful voice. Do you sing?"

"No, I play ... the violin."

"You play the fiddle. Sure, that's fantastic. I knew you had a creative air about you. Play anything I know?"

"Mostly classical. Some Polish folksongs. You wouldn't know them."

"Polish, eh?" He eyed the violin case sitting on the ground beside her. "You wouldn't play a quick tune. Anything you like. I'd love to hear one."

The mobile phone with her father's number displayed on the screen sat beside her ready to be rung. "I don't know. I was about to make a call."

"Well, if you're too busy ..." His voice trailed away, and a sad light covered his eyes like a film.

She looked at her violin case. "If you really would like me to ...?"

"Yes, I would ... please?"

There was something about this sad little man that she couldn't refuse, so she took out her violin and began to tune it. He sat by, his face eager with anticipation.

She began to play "The Flower Duet," from Delibe's Opera, *Lakme*, a favourite of hers. The music drifted over the gardens like a soft mist.

He smiled and stood up, his small feet stepping out a familiar dance, his arms outstretched to the air. A cloud moved away from the face of the moon, and a light fell on the little man as he circled the fountain, his ruddy face beaming with happiness. They stayed wrapped in that moment for what seemed ages, until Flora noticed her phone ringing on the bench beside her and stopped playing.

She grabbed the phone but too late.

The man stopped dancing.

"I'm sorry. I need to ring this person back. It's very important."

"No bother, luv, that was beautiful." He sputtered a cracked, warm laugh, picked up his satchel, and stuck out his hand. "Mick Kelly."

"Flora Wilde," she responded.

"Pleased to meet you, beautiful Flora. Well, I'll leave you to it."

She nodded and smiled.

He began to walk away but turned at the edge of the fountain. "Just remember, Flora, they never really leave us – the ones we love. Thank God for that." He turned and disappeared in the direction of the back entrance.

She picked up her things and walked towards the entrance.

It was time.

She pressed her father's number and waited for him to pick up.

"Flora?" His voice sounded anxious.

"Dad. What's happening?" She almost had to think to speak Polish now although chatting to Tomasz had helped.

"Your mother had a heart attack this afternoon. The doctor only told me an hour ago that she's going to be all right. I'm sorry if I frightened you, but I just didn't know."

She felt her body shed its worry. "Thank God. I thought ..."

"I know. Thank God. Do you want to talk to her? I'm sitting beside her."

Flora hesitated. Conversations with her mother were never easy at the best of times.

"Flora?" Her voice sounded weak.

"Mum. Are you ok?"

"Yes. I'm fine. Your father is fussing over me like I have one foot in the grave, but I'm just fine. A small fright that's all."

This had to be the first time since Flora was a young girl that she welcomed the sound of her mother's voice. Sucked it up like hot milk.

"Thank God. I got an awful fright."

"You can't get rid of me that easily. I'm going to be a thorn in your side for a little while longer, I'm afraid."

"Don't talk like that, Mum." Flora fought the usual irritation that came with her mother's baiting her into an endless cycle of arguments.

"How's Omar?"

"He's fine – just fine." She could hear the shadow of doubt penetrating her words and braced herself for the usual stream of criticism that flowed out of her mother when she asked that question – how she should be a more dutiful attentive wife, how she should try for more children, how Flora's wilful independence didn't allow her husband to be a real man – the head of the household – as it should be. That made Flora laugh, considering that this small, feisty woman had dominated her father for four decades and still managed to convince herself that she was a deferring, dutiful wife.

"That's good."

Not the usual response. Flora waited.

"How are you?"

"Ok. I guess."

"I'm glad."

Flora was surprised by how good those two simple words made her feel. The lack of questions floated to her like a peace offering, a rare moment of tender silence.

"Mum, mind yourself, will you?" She meant it. Though this woman had caused her years of pain and guilt, not to have her in her life was impossible. So much of who Flora was had come from her mother, for the good and the bad of it.

"Yes, love, I will." Flora could feel something enter between them, like a quiet breath. It might be better now – just maybe.

"I'd better go. I have a few people staying in my place. Need to get back to them."

"Ok, Flo." She hadn't called her that since she was a little girl.

"Bye."

"Goodbye." There was something so definite about the way her mother said that single word that it scared her. In the speaking of it, she was saying, "I love you, and I may not get another chance to say it."

CHAPTER 37

KINCH

10:00 PM

THE SKY ABOVE CHRISTCHURCH hung heavy, devoid of light, except for the stagnant glow that hovered over the city like a shroud. Kinch followed his friends through the iron gates, Omar at his side. He felt light-headed; the whiskey had done its job, sucked the day out of his brain and replaced it with a numbing warmth. Gerry was babbling at Sarah about some gorgeous girl who'd just walked past him.

Who would believe he'd spent the day in a cell?

The black woman from Flora's apartment passed by. She didn't spot him. He couldn't help noticing her succulent curves, the way the purple t-shirt clung to the outline of her perfect breasts.

Like a sumptuous maenad. God, I'm just as bad. Flora might be here.

His stomach churned audibly.

A group of students chattering in Italian jumped into the excavated ruins outside the main cathedral. They climbed onto each other's shoulders, a plump girl with a camera encouraging their gurning antics. He imagined the Viking lord, Sitric, bearded and broad, sitting in the corner of this crumbled ruin, the remnants of his great construction, an homage to the Christianity to which he had converted. Kinch wondered what he would have made of this scene.

History repackaged for the masses.

Crowds flowed around him towards the main entrance to the cathedral. Suddenly there was a mad rush as he could hear Dave Fanning take the mike and announce the arrival of Low, the feature act, to the stage. From inside the cathedral, the crowd erupted in raucous enthusiasm as the Mormon

American rock band took the stage. A long, slow, wailing note erupted into the air, a blade of sound introducing the layered voices.

Kinch shrugged, and decided to take his time, desperate for a last fag. Omar walked beside him, observing the buzz and flow of it all. Kinch spotted Hanan's brother, Khaled, shuffling towards the entrance. He was bundled up in a hoody, his eyes cast to the ground.

"Strange that. My friend's brother, Khaled, is here. He's a weird one. All caught up with his Arabness now. Doesn't seem his style to be at a rock concert." He spoke more to himself than anyone in particular.

Omar tuned in. "I recognise him. Interviewed him with his father this morning. The old man's a moderate, but the boy made some odd comments that made me wonder about him."

"Easy for the young ones to get caught up in the fanaticism of it all, I suppose." Kinch felt uncomfortable talking about this subject with Omar.

"I suppose." Omar gazed at Khaled, who was clearly deep in thought. "I'll leave you guys to it. Meeting someone at the gates here. Enjoy."

"Sure. See you round." Kinch nodded at Omar and headed into the concert.

"Hurry up, girl. It's started." Gerry grabbed Sarah and ran through the great arched entrance. Will trailed after them, turning to see where Kinch was.

"I'll follow you in." Kinch didn't feel up to idle chit-chat. Everything blurred around him like a lucid dream, the kind where you know you're dreaming, but it feels so real, and you can't wake yourself up no matter how hard you try.

He glanced up towards the hulking stone edifice of the cathedral. It split the dark sky like a great golden eagle, its beak pointed towards the heavens, wings spread wide around the sprawling city far below. The austere, cold eye of history looking down on the chaos of the Irish capital.

A cold shaft of air passed over Kinch like the shadow of the giant bird, and he shivered. He grabbed the silver hipflask from his pocket and took a swig. The bulky bouncer at the entrance to the cathedral hadn't spotted him, thank God. He'd had more than his fair share of run-ins with these characters – failed rugby players and wannabe thugs whose idea of fun was to chuck some randomer out on the street because their runners had happened to fall into a vat of white dye. *For Jaysus sake.*

Anyway, Mr. Pecs-as-big-as-an-elephant's arse was concentrating on his next victims: a traveller couple whom Kinch recognised from the streets. They'd wandered into the melee – perhaps, for once, out for a night on the town.

No fear. So much for the Church's open arms.

The hollow sound of horse hooves on asphalt drifted into the courtyard behind Kinch. The stragglers turned towards the gleaming carriage of the Lord Mayor as it made its way through the bulky gates. Kinch could see Ambassador Kenny, his wife, Taoiseach Bertie Ahern, and Councillor Royston Brady, Lord Mayor of Dublin, readying themselves to descend. They were there because part of the concert proceeds were being donated to the *Save the Children Northern Ireland* fund, which the USA supported. The ambassador was to say a few words at the interval and make a quick exit before his eardrums imploded.

Campaigners were out in force, banners waving, voices blaring, "No to Bush visit!"

Kenny and Ahern stuck on their best "we can't hear a thing" smiles, ushered by the dean of Christchurch into a quiet area at the back of the cathedral where their eardrums would not be blown away by the dense music, which had already begun.

The crowd was clearly unimpressed. They knew that it was extremely unlikely that Ambassador Kenny would declare from the altar that George W. Bush was a misguided, Bible-thumping eejit whose invasion of Iraq was as morally intact as a whore's fanny.

Ah well, one can dream.

Mrs. Kenny looked a little worse for wear after her long day but soldiered on like the dutiful politician's wife that she no doubt was.

I'm sure the Ambassador's Residence in the Park makes up for the bunions and the sore face, Mrs.

Royston hopped out gamely. He grinned at the crowd and showed no sign of spotting the indifferent shrugs. The blinding gold chain around his neck provoked comment from a thirty-something Dublin girl beside Kinch: "Hasn't anyone told the fool that bling jewellery is out?" Her well-made-up friends laughed raucously.

Poor Royston … old politicians failing … starting to believe his own publicity. The aul ones turn on him and his career's in the shitter.

A group of young Americans waved flags at the ambassador and his wife as they passed Kinch. Bertie trailed behind, nodding like a marionette. He had a way about him, it had to be said, no matter what he was up to behind closed doors, and who really wanted to know.

Sure, life was good, all that mattered really.

The Teflon Taoiseach was all smiles, readying to show off his latest pal to the assembled masses. The last stragglers followed the dignitaries through the arched door. Kinch took a last swig of whiskey. Even he, lapsed Catholic and hardened agnostic, couldn't take a chance that the God who might exist would spot him drinking the Devil's juice on his doorstep.

Better safe than sorry.

He turned to enter the cathedral. Khaled was shuffling his way like a medieval penitent behind the last of the crowd, hoody wrapped around his head despite the warmth of the evening. He didn't spot Kinch, who stood a foot behind. A girl, standing between them both, tapped Khaled on the shoulder.

"Khaled, is that you?" She had a pretty smile, unhurried but a little shy.

Khaled jerked his head around. His normally languid stare was shot through with what looked to Kinch like fear.

"Hi." There was no hint of a smile in the boy's tired face.

"I thought that was you. All bundled up in that hoody, it's hard to tell. Aren't you boiling in that?" She moved to touch the fabric, and he jumped backwards bumping off the woman in the queue behind him.

"Hey! Watch it!" she shouted in a lilting accent.

"Sorry." Khaled looked impatient, hopping around like a featherweight before a fight.

He's not into you, girly. Dying to get away.

A silence fell between them. Khaled continued to look anxiously from the girl to the crowd in front as it moved forward.

Low continued to play, oblivious to the latecomers.

The girl looked embarrassed but continued to smile at him, her light-blue eyes and elfin features delicate and vulnerable. "I … I'm sorry. I was thinking of dropping into your shop to ask you … well," she continued.

Khaled looked irritated.

"I was just wondering if you were free next weekend? It's my Debs and Cathal, who was supposed to be coming with me, can't cos his granny's sick, something about her stomach – cancer I think. Poor thing. Anyway, I was just wondering if you'd like to come?" She let out a long slow breath and waited.

Khaled was next in line to pass through the ticket booth. He stared at her, the lines in his forehead starched and pronounced.

Odd boy. You'd think he'd be delighted. Gorgeous little thing. He should be so lucky.

"No."

It was so definite. *Bastard!* Kinch looked at this normally shy boy and saw a strength in him he'd never spotted before, a surety, a hard, cold anger that ripped through the young girl like the edge of a sharp blade.

She stared at him, unable to speak, clearly fighting to control a well of tears.

Kinch wanted to grab the little fecker and beat him to a pulp. He decided then and there that he was going to have a sharp word with him as soon as they got through the door, sort out the rude little tosser.

Kinch watched Khaled hand over his ticket, his eye trailing after him as he walked through the nave and into Musician's Corner at the back of the cathedral. Kinch tapped the shoulder of the distressed girl, who was handing the ticket to the woman at the entrance.

"Don't mind him. I know him. He's a sullen little prick. You can do a lot better. He should be so lucky to get a pretty girl like you."

She smiled weakly, her eyes moist and grateful. "Thanks. I just feel like a fool."

"He's the only fool around here." He put his hand on her shoulder and handed his ticket to the teller. "In five years, you won't even remember his name, I promise you."

"Maybe ... thanks again."

Kinch nodded.

She moved quickly up the right side of the great arched nave, past Strongbow's granite tomb, and disappeared into the crowd.

Kinch's eye fell on the great invader's tomb, covered in a mass of wires that protruded from the sound engineer's desk beside it. "The Ra would love that," he chuckled.

His eye followed the line of the line of limestone columns as they soared upwards like giant birches, a gentle glow seeping from one of the chandeliers. It lit the elegant curves of the great vaulted ceiling, the graceful arches dressed in their dying light. He glanced at the crowd, who gazed with rapt awe as Mimi Parker's and Alan Sparhawk's voices wrapped around each other like lovers.

The crowd were an odd mixture of scruffy, twenty-something would-be rock critics, trendy, middle-aged liberals – some sporting the Joycean attire of the day – and a clutch of heavily made-up, high-heeled beauties, rail-thin and waiting impatiently for the IT magazine photographer to snap them into the back pages of the *Who's Who* of Dublin's best. Not to forget the gaggles of tourists – American, Asian, European, Antipodean but certainly not African (the black face of Flora's friend an anomaly). Her compatriots, firmly stationed outside the gates on the other side of the Liffey, were working hard to afford a ticket to the good life.

Kinch glanced towards Musician's Corner. He saw Khaled staring up at the second-level balcony. Its discreet space sat like a royal box above the bustle of proceedings far below. There was something in the way Khaled moved that reminded him of a hunter plotting the hushed precision of his next kill. The boy disappeared inside a narrow wooden doorway. Kinch followed, wondering what Khaled was up to.

CHAPTER 38

OMAR

10:00 PM

OMAR STOOD AT THE GATES in front of Christchurch Cathedral. The ambassadorial cavalcade had just passed by on its way to the concert.

Jameson approached, clutching a brown leather satchel. "I'll expect a tip."

Omar winked. "Don't worry, Mark. There'll be an ocean of free pints coming your direction after this. I just didn't feel like going all the way across the river. I knew your shift was off around now. Thanks a million."

Jameson handed him the bag. "For God's sake, don't get yourself mugged with this."

"I reckon I'm safe enough, having been involved in one robbery today already. Luck has to turn my way."

Jameson shook his head. "Only the unlucky believe in luck. Watch your back."

"Don't worry. I'm going to jump in a taxi and head straight home." Omar eyed the yellow plastic bag. Looked harmless enough, but he knew that this might be a ticket to getting himself and Flora back on track. Although he'd been back to Poland with her many times, they'd never really had a chance to relax together in a beautiful place far away from the daily routine. He was sure that would help, jolt them out of their stupor. He wasn't taking any chances. He'd get home with this as soon as possible. Omar put the plastic bag in his satchel.

"Right then. I'm off. See you in the office tomorrow." Jameson nodded and walked towards Dame Street.

A girl walked past with a bag of chips, and the smell assaulted Omar's nostrils. He suddenly realised he was famished. A clutch of people across the road were demolishing big bags of deliciously greasy Burdoch's chips. He glanced at his satchel.

Just take five minutes. What can happen?

Packed double-decker buses whizzed past as he crossed the road. A small queue reached out the door. His stomach groaned its approval, and he took his place. The day's copy of *The Irish Times* stuck out of the side pocket of his satchel, and he had a quick look.

There was an article in the crime section about an Al Qaeda strike expected within the British Isles, possibly in the next couple of weeks. It discussed the possibility of an Al Qaeda cell operating in Dublin, and speculated that, although unlikely, Dublin could be considered a target because of the landing of American military planes in Shannon. Extra tight security was to surround Bush's visit to Ireland. There were several suspects listed with their photographs. His eye fell on one of the faces. He froze.

The man was immediately recognisable.

He scrambled to take out the photo he'd taken earlier and held it up against the photograph in the paper. Sure enough, it was V, the billboard man from the bridge. The cutline read *Abdullah al-Ashraf, Commanding Officer, Egyptian al-Jihad. Known ally of Al Queda and Osama Bin Laden.*

His heart racing, Omar felt sick. He didn't know what to think. He glanced across to the cathedral. The empty ambassador's carriage stood outside, waiting. He stared back at the article. The word "target" jumped off the page. He ran to the corner, crossed the road, and spotted Kinch disappearing through the door just ahead of Khaled.

Jesus ... maybe.

CHAPTER 39

KINCH

10:30 PM

KINCH HAD SPOTTED THE DIGNITARIES' platform, from which the ambassador was due to speak, raised high above the audience. The dark spiral staircase Kinch was climbing seemed to lead to the tiny balcony directly above the platform. He ascended into the darkness. Kinch felt lifted by the wave of music, but his head spun in circles. It reminded him of that scene in *Vertigo* where Jimmy Stewart climbed the stairs, the walls tumbling around him. Kinch grabbed the railings and pushed himself forward.

He emerged into the soft shadow at the edge of the empty balcony. Tremulous harmonies floated through the air like voices from the underworld, the crowd below transfixed. Khaled stood underneath the third arch, his body stiff and upright, staring at the people below. He unzipped his jacket, revealing a khaki vest bulging with explosives. A wire ran from the explosives to a simple red button on a black plastic trigger mount. Khaled held it in his hand. Kinch's stomach lurched. Below him, Alan Sparhawk sang in a grinding rasp about a monkey dying. A wave of adrenaline passed through Kinch like a shot of crystal meth. *Not the only one dying tonight by the looks of it.*

"Not sure I like your taste in fashion these days, Khaled. Looks a little restricting, don't you think?" The boy turned abruptly, pulling his hoody around the pack of explosives. "And in this heat. Are you mad?" Kinch could feel his heartbeat through his chest. His instinct told him to keep his voice a calm measure of restraint.

"How did you find me?"

"Spotted you in the queue. You weren't very nice to that poor girl. Now

I can see why."

"She's just a whore like all the others."

"She likes you, man, that's all."

"No one likes me."

Kinch felt an opening. "She does. Practically ate you with those beautiful blue eyes of hers."

"Whore."

"Looked more like an angel to me, but what do I know? Always fucking up with the women. Did you hear I broke up with Bláithín today?" His instinct told him to keep it light, until some part of his panicked brain knew what the hell he should do.

"I've no time for this."

"All the time in the world. The concert lasts an hour and a half. Why rush? Make the most of it." Kinch was struck by how vulnerable this young boy looked, weariness forming dark shadows under his eyes, his frail body like a child in fancy dress swamped in the clothes of some grown-up he was trying to imitate. Kinch knew he was walking a tightrope in hiking boots, but this was the time, the only time in his long, empty life, that mattered. He sucked in a breath and calmed the thoughts that bashed against his brain like bats in daylight.

"You don't understand," Khaled said. "That's your misfortune."

"Enlighten me if I'm about to die. Might as well give me a chance in the next life as I pretty much sucked at this one." Kinch took out his silver hip flask and offered it to Khaled. "Want a swig?"

"Don't drink that foul poison."

"Sorry, forgot." He took a drink and swallowed hard into the beating chasm of his body. "Anyway, what's this all about? Because I'm not much up on the religious stuff. Got the shite beaten out of me by the Christian Brothers in Belvedere. Leaves a bad taste in your mouth."

"Why should I waste my breath on you?"

"Because I'm the last face you'll see on this glorious earth of ours."

Khaled stared at the band, who continued to scream, "*Tonight the Monkey dies.*"

"Little do they know how right they are," said Kinch laughing. *How the fuck can I find this funny? Keep it together, man.*

Khaled's finger hovered over the little red detonator. "A glorious victory for Islam."

"How so?"

"That man." His voice was thin and cracked, venomous. Khaled pointed underneath him, through the stone balcony to where the American ambassador was being ushered to the podium. "He's the Devil's representative on this earth."

"I never liked George W., but don't you think that's a bit harsh?"

"The Americans declared holy war on Islam the day they unjustly invaded Iraq. There'll be no peace in this world until they've been wiped off this planet."

The crowd erupted in applause as Low finished just in time for the interval.

"And the rest of us?" Kinch was determined to keep this going, knowing that every second the boy was talking there was a chance they might be spotted.

Dear Lord, I'll never say a bad word about skinhead security again if they just do their job and spot us up here. Mother put in a good word, will ya? I'll say a Novena every day for the rest of my life, I swear.

"*Kuffars*. There's no one innocent in this war. Everyone here is guilty."

"Heavy stuff. I hate to burst your bubble, Khaled, but I never had a choice. Was told what to think as soon as I was born into this Catholic-ridden culture. Copped on eventually. Now that I can choose, what if I choose Islam?"

"You wouldn't. You're brainwashed."

"So are you."

"I know what I'm doing?"

"You sure?"

The boy stared into the crowd. The ambassador was introduced by Dave Fanning and a ripple of polite applause drifted through the cathedral. Ambassador Kenny began to talk about the strength of Irish-American relations, "our great tradition of friendship," and Ireland serving as a bridge between the United States and the European Union.

Kinch felt sick, desperate to find a connection between himself and this boy who was about to blow them all to kingdom come.

A voice emerged from the darkness behind them: *"Those who defame honourable women and cannot produce four witnesses shall be given eighty lashes. Do not accept their testimony ever after, for they are great transgressors – except those among them who afterwards repent and mend their ways. God is forgiving and merciful."*

Omar stepped into the light.

"Who the hell are you?" Khaled stared at Omar in disbelief, Kinch with surprise but relief.

"A fellow Muslim – Omar Wilde." Omar quickly nodded his head at Kinch and turned back towards the confused teenager. "You don't want to do this, son."

Where the hell did he come from? Kinch sat down. *Thank God.*

The boy shifted nervously, his finger hovering over the button. "Sunni or Shia?"

"Does it matter? We're all one in the eyes of Allah," Omar replied.

"*Permission to take up arms is hereby given to those who are attacked, because they have been wronged,"* the boy responded, his voice strong and clear.

"Bravo, you know your Qur'an, but you sound Irish to me."

"I am a Muslim and a part of the ummah."

"And Irish too. That means you're about to blow up your own. Mind you, we are good at that."

The boy narrowed his eyes. "Every Muslim has a duty to fight for the preservation of the ummah."

"Then why did you ask me if I was Sunni or Shia? Are we really all so pally in the Muslim world?" Omar replied.

Kinch watched beads of sweat build on the end of Omar's nose, and hoped he knew what he was doing.

"We've been attacked by the evil *kuffars* of the West – they are the worst." The boy nodded towards Ambassador Kenny, who was still speaking.

"In a 150-year relationship, there are going to be bumps in the road. Going to war in Iraq was just one of those bumps. We'll get over that. We'll have a great relationship. I'm here to do that. The president wants that."

Khaled laughed and looked at Omar. "I'm going to do this."

"Go right ahead. Do you mind if I have a swig of that?" Omar pointed at the hipflask in Kinch's right hand.

Khaled looked at him with disgust. "I thought you said you were Muslim?"

"Yes, but I'm also an Irishman. Even Allah wouldn't begrudge an Irishman a drop of uisce beatha on his way out of this life and into the next."

Khaled shrugged. *"But whoever of you recants and dies an unbeliever, his works shall come to nothing in this world and in the world to come. Such men shall be in the tenants of the Fire, wherein they shall abide for ever."*

"I'll drink to that," said Omar.

Kinch eyed the security at the front door. A spotlight sat on the wall to the right of the guard's head. It was aimed at the wall directly below the balcony where they were standing. Kinch moved the metal flask and slipped his hand through the railing hoping to deflect the light towards the security guard.

"Have you ever been to the Dome of the Rock?" Omar asked the increasingly agitated teenager.

"No. Why?"

"Do you know that the oldest existing Qur'anic text is carved into the walls?"

"Yes, I learned that from my imam, and?"

"I saw it, you know. It's very beautiful. I went there with my mother in 1977. She was a singer."

"Was she a Muslim?"

"Yes, Egyptian. Her voice sounded like it had descended straight from the breath of a ūrīyyāt."

Khaled looked at Omar, a sliver of emotion penetrating his stony expression. "My mother is dead."

"So is mine."

Something shifted in the boy's face: a beat of hesitation. Kinch stared at the explosive device. He imagined the ignition spark travelling at warp speed through the device, plunged into the nitrate packet like a flaming diver into a pool of gasoline, the blinding flash of light. *We won't feel a thing. I hope.*

"Do you know what it says on the ceiling of the south side of the Dome?" Omar asked.

Kinch stretched his arm desperately, the flask half an inch from the light. He hoped Omar had a strong point to make.

Khaled shook his head.

"People of the Book, do not transgress the bounds of your religion. Speak nothing but the truth about God."

The boy fell silent.

Omar moved slowly towards him. "It's not your fault."

Khaled turned slowly and stared at Omar. The boy looked tired, defeated. His hand moved slowly down to his side.

"You don't want to do this."

A beam of light fell on the hipflask. Kinch glanced quickly at Khaled to make sure he didn't spot what he was up to. He began to trail the light slowly across the white-stone wall towards the entrance.

The ambassador sounded as though he was wrapping up his speech. "Ireland does have a role to play, and they've offered to play that role, and we are very cognisant of that and very appreciative of that."

Omar moved closer, placed his hand on the boy's shoulder.

"These men you know. They've forgotten how to live in the here and now. Paradise can exist in this world too, trust me. Mohammed lived a full life. He loved this world as well as the next. There's no harm in that."

Kinch strained to hear. He thought he saw something change in Khaled's demeanour. A creeping doubt, a palpable relief.

Omar continued. "You've committed no crime yet. No one need ever know. I know someone who can help us to get that off you." He took a long slow breath and whispered.

"Trust me."

The beam of light hit the face of the carved monkey at the entrance pier. Kinch hesitated, turned to listen.

Khaled nodded silently and slumped to the floor. Omar slid down the wall beside him, his hand gently resting on Khaled's right shoulder. "You've chosen well. I'm proud of you."

Kinch stared at the beam of light as it lit up the monkey's grimacing features and began to trail it down the wall towards the security guard's head.

He glanced back at Khaled and Omar. They looked exhausted, sitting there in silence, their breaths deep and heavy. He could almost imagine them painted onto canvas, the perfect study of a father and son at the moment of reconciliation, relief and fear etched across their tired features.

The security guard began to move away. Kinch sighed heavily, carefully drew the flask away from the spotlight, and placed it on the ground beside him.

The crowd rippled with faint applause as the ambassador left the nave.

"Everything ok, lads?" Kinch was eager to get the hell out of there.

Omar looked at Khaled.

"Let's go."

The boy stared anxiously at the security guards grouped around the entrance.

"Don't worry about them. We're not going to say a word, are we, Kinch?" Omar urged a positive response with his eyes.

"Yeah, no worries. I was never here."

"But what about this?" Khaled pointed to the explosives wrapped around his body like a cobra.

"I know a guy, ex-IRA, expert with stuff like that. Did him a favour last year, kept his name out of an article I was working on. He owes me one. I'm sure he won't say a word. Needs to stay out of the papers, you know." Omar stood up.

"Are you sure?"

Omar reached out his hand. "Sure."

The boy placed his hand in Omar's. Like a pregnant woman burdened by the weight of her body, he stood up slowly.

Kinch was unsure whether he should be a part of what was to follow. "What about me?"

He knew how these things played out, at least on TV. They take the boy to the IRA guy, he shops them to the police, and they all become implicated in the plot, even though they were the bloody saviours of the day. Nice end that would be.

"Come with us. It's better that way. I need you to help me anyway. Let's see this out together."

Kinch had to admit that he'd underestimated Omar. There was a strength in this quiet man although he still didn't understand how he'd found them here. *Strange one, the Arab. Suppose I have no choice.*

"Ok."

They descended the dark, winding staircase – Kinch first, then Khaled, Omar last, the two men forming a protective shield around the boy. He could barely look Khaled in the eye and wished to God he'd paid more attention to Hanan's worries earlier that day.

Little did he know.

They emerged into the glowing light of the nave. Low had retaken the stage, Mimi Parker's silk voice undulating through the arches of the holy space.

A soft whisper of sadness washed over Kinch like the death of a loved one.

They crossed the back of the cathedral. Kinch glanced nervously at Omar; the security guard stood in front of them, large as a house.

They passed straight by him. Not a word was said.

Kinch fell into the courtyard, smiled at Omar, and grabbed the cigarette packet from his pocket. "God, I need a fag."

CHAPTER 40

OMAR

~ Circe ~

11:30 PM

PACKED WITH RESTAURANTS, BARS, and clubs, the narrow cobblestone streets of Nighttown oozed life in all its bawdy glory. The door of Ruby's on Dame Street, slender and unassuming, gave little clue as to the activities it led to off this bustling city-centre street, south of the Liffey. A well-known strip club, Ruby's sat on the edge of Dublin's notorious Temple Bar. Cleaned up to present a white-toothed smile to the newly arrived tourist, what went on behind its carved wooden doors and wrought-iron gateposts was a truer reflection of the excesses that the overfed Celtic Tiger had to offer. Pretty, architect-designed apartments became rented-out brothels, funding a 100-million-euro business that continued to elude the establishment's efforts to "do something about it."

Girls flooded in from Estonia, Lithuania, South America and anywhere survival had become too difficult. The perennial argument, whether they were there by choice or by force, filled many pages of crime correspondence in *The Irish Times*.

Omar was not a fan of the former premise and had become only too familiar with the pimps and hustlers who made a fortune on the backs of these women. He'd worked around the edges of this story with Cowen the year before, providing research for a controversial article for which he was, of course, never credited. Still, he'd learned a lot about the underbelly of the Irish sex industry and had been sure that someday such knowledge might be of use to him.

Someday had arrived.

He'd met Bernie Farrell three times while working with Cowen. An ex-IRA gunman, he spent five years in the Maze prison for blowing up a Belfast barbershop and killing eight innocent bystanders. While Cowen banged down the door of every big-name gangster happily residing in the leafy Dublin suburbs, Omar traipsed through the scumbag- and drug-dealer-infested neighbourhoods of Crumlin and Coolock. This led him straight to Farrell, a man who preferred to reside out of the limelight that the Scorpion and the General had courted with Hollywood-like enthusiasm.

"Are you sure about this, man?" Kinch asked Omar, swallowing another gulp of whiskey.

"You should take it easy with that stuff," Omar replied. *Hope this lad can hold it together. More than he bargained for.*

"It's something a lot harder I'll be looking for after this bloody day."

Khaled stood between them, silent, his eyes cast downward.

Omar touched his arm. "It'll be all right, son, don't worry." He had no choice but to trust Kinch with the lad. It made him nervous, but he couldn't bring a boy wrapped in explosives into a strip club. "Can you look after him for ten minutes or so?"

Kinch looked very far from sure but stuck on a nervous smile "No problem. Just don't be too long."

"Right, like I said, go to the park in front of St. Pat's Cathedral. Shouldn't be a sinner around there at this time of night. I'll come and get you as soon as I'm finished here." Omar looked straight at Khaled. "I'll be right behind you, son. Just relax, ok?"

Khaled nodded.

Omar knocked loudly. The door opened. A dark-skinned bouncer looked at him suspiciously. "Regular?"

"I know Bernie. Can you tell him Omar Wilde is looking for him? It's urgent. Just say I need that favour – right now." Omar tried to throw the right amount of punch into his voice, aware that his normal disposition never got him through the door of anywhere more illustrious or indeed debauched than Annabelle's nightclub.

The bouncer, a bug-eyed man, stared at him with a "not too sure" look on his face. "Hang on a second." He tapped a number into his phone, turned his back to Omar, and waited for a reply.

Omar strained to hear above the noise of the traffic.

"Yeah boss, Omar Wilde ... yeah, says he needs a favour ... yeah ... right." He hung up the phone and turned around. "Right, in you come." He gestured for him to descend the narrow staircase. "Zara will show ye where to go."

Omar nodded his thanks and descended the stairs into a dimly lit room. It was lined with tall mirrors, comfortable seating, and a well-stocked bar. It had the feel of a modern city-centre pub, except for the scantily clad girls who wandered around the room with trays and wrapped themselves around a succession of poles like snakes in heat.

A perfectly toned young redhead, in a bright-gold bikini and matching high heels, greeted him in broken English. "You Omar?"

"Yes."

Zara touched Omar on the shoulder and smiled, her lips full and glossy. "Come with me a second. The boss will see you through here."

He followed the buxom girl to a door at the back of the room. Her buttocks, bronzed and smooth, jangled in front of him like two succulent nectarines.

"Through there." She smiled and a gold tooth shone from the back of her moist mouth.

What I wouldn't give to mine that gold.

A voice like a tenor's – deceptive, visceral, narcotic – greeted him as he entered the small, plush room: "Omar, so good to see you again. How the hell are you?" A casual bystander would have guessed it the greeting of lifelong friends.

Omar smiled. "Grand, Bernie." He thought better of that casual sentiment. "Actually, I'm in a spot of bother. Could do with a hand. Remember the favour ...?"

"Don't say another word, my man. Sit down there and have a drink – tell me what's up. Is it the missus again? Up to her old tricks? If you don't mind me saying, I've heard through the grapevine that fidelity isn't her strongpoint. Saw her playing in that Celtic show of hers last year. Talented, gorgeous thing you have there, Wilde. How the fuck did you do it?" He poured green liquid into a glass and handed it to Omar.

"I don't drink, Bernie, sorry."

"You do now. It's the best absinthe money has to offer. Straight out of the depths of Pigalle. Drink up and don't be insulting me with this "I don't drink" nonsense. Are you an Irishman or what?"

The tone of voice that accompanied Farrell's broad smile didn't allow room for protest. "Ok then, just this once." He gulped down the hot, green liquid. It hit the pit of his stomach and smouldered like a long-lit fire.

"Good stuff, eh?"

Omar struggled for breath. "Yeah, lovely."

Farrell filled the glass again, and Omar smiled weakly.

"So, this little problem of yours?

I hope I'm not making a big mistake. Omar struggled to regain his composure. "Do you remember we talked about your expertise with bomb-making equipment the last time I was here?"

Farrell raised his bushy eyebrows. "Planning to blow up the *Independent* offices, are you, Omar? Heard they pay shite these days but perhaps that's a little excessive." He laughed.

Omar smiled and took a deep breath. "Not quite. You're a well-connected man. You must have heard all about the undercover Al Qaeda cell that's "supposedly" operating out of a house on Camden Street."

Farrell widened his eyes. "I've heard rumours. Please tell me you didn't bring one of those crazy motherfuckers into my club?"

"No, no, I left him outside."

"Far outside, I hope. Here, boyo, down the hatch." Farrell raised his glass and gestured for Omar to do the same.

"I don't really want ..." Omar protested.

"Don't take no for an answer, Wilde, you know that. Now, down it."

With no choice in the matter, Omar swallowed the large glass of absinthe. It shot through his system like molten lava.

"Good man, that's what I like to see." Farrell refilled the glass. "A bit of fuckin balls. Now what do you have to do with those flamin skirt-wearers?"

"It's a long bloody story. Don't ask for the details now. Let's just say Christchurch Cathedral would have been looking like Baghdad Central tonight if I hadn't talked a kid called Khaled down from blowing himself to kingdom come with ten kilos of dynamite. These bastards are experts at twisting their minds."

Farrell spit out his drink. "What? You're fuckin kidding me, right?"

Omar shook his head. "Afraid not."

"What in God's name ...?"

"I have him waiting with a friend in the park beside St. Pat's Cathedral. Sorry, Bernie, but I had no choice, honest. You were the only one I could think of who could get the bloody thing off him."

"Jesus, Omar, when I said I owed you a favour ..."

"I know, it's a lot to ask."

"These guys are another level of fucking crazy." Farrell moved towards Omar, his bulky frame tense and threatening. "It's not my problem and I want you out of my club right now." He ran to pick up the phone.

Omar grabbed his arm to stop him, "Just wait a second, Bernie."

Bernie clutched the phone like a semi-automatic. "You have ten seconds."

"We have nowhere else to go, and those fuckers will rip that boy apart for changing his mind. Just consider it an act of humanity, your civic duty, saving the republic from another invader of a kind. That is your expertise, isn't it?" Omar knew he was teetering on the edge of a very high building with that one.

"You're one cheeky bastard, Wilde. Never saw this side of you before." Farrell hesitated, put down the phone, and pulled up a chair beside Omar. His eyes were cold as ice. "If I do this, we're even, and don't you ever darken my doorstep again. Understood?" His voice was pulled as thin and taut as a tightrope wire.

"Understood." A bead of sweat travel down the back of Omar's neck.

"Ok. Take the boy to Diana's place on Bachelor's Walk. You remember where it is?"

Omar remembered only too well. Ms. Diana Flaunt, Madam Sin to her friends. She operated a notorious brothel out of a swanky apartment on the banks of the Liffey. A stone's throw from the heart of Dublin's Financial District, it housed sixteen prostitutes charging anything up to 220 euros an hour. Sounded like a lot but amounted to a mere two nights" drinking bout for the affluent clientele who frequented the place at all hours.

Omar had met Farrell and Diana there several times while working on Cowen's piece. During those short visits, he'd seen all sorts – thirty-something stockbrokers out for a quick lunchtime thrill; ageing civil servants, the white mark of their wedding rings clearly visible on their shaking left hands; well-known politicians; prominent members of the media; priests, rabbis, pastors, you name it. They'd shuffled through the door, ogling the line of juicy girls presented to them with the eyes of hungry beasts.

Ah yes, sex, the great equalizer.

The feisty twenty-eight-year-old Madame, herself a hooker of no small repute, watched over proceedings with an eagle eye. The 50,000 euro she earned annually was a paltry sum compared to the millions earned by her silent bosses. Still, she seemed happy enough, although Omar suspected the Englishwoman might one day find herself the attractive face of an industry under tighter and tighter surveillance from the Gardaí special operative forces.

"Yes, I remember." Omar's head buzzed; the absinthe had kicked in.

"There's a guy called McCaffrey, does the security nightshift there. An expert with explosives. Used to work closely with me. You don't need to know any more. I'll fill him in. I can trust him to keep his mouth shut. I'll get Goldy to walk you guys there, make sure you don't come to any harm. Now, get out of here."

Omar nodded and moved at speed towards the door. "Thanks, Bernie."

"I won't say 'anytime'," replied the irritated looking ex-IRA man.

The absinthe was starting to take serious effect. Omar stumbled through the glittering room clutching his stomach.

The bulky bouncer descended the staircase and walked up beside them. "I hear I'm your escort for the night."

"If you don't mind, I'm not feeling the best. Would you just go and get the two lads? They're in the park of St. Pat's Cathedral. Khaled looks like ET all bundled up in a hoody and Kinch, Stephen Dedalus."

"Stephen who?"

"Never mind. Here's my phone number if there are any problems." Omar's stomach lurched violently, and he grabbed the barstool beside him. "Just take them straight to Diana's." I'll follow on as soon as ..." His head felt like it was twisting on its axis.

Goldy smiled. His teeth shone like a jeweller's window. The letters L-O-V-E were etched into the front four. "See you in hell." He turned and walked out the door.

Omar suddenly felt very faint and sat against the mirrored wall. He could see his own reflection undulate in the mirror, morph, and twirl until he could no longer recognise himself. Bubbles of music twisted his senses into an unfamiliar, grotesque space.

* * *

The room spins like a merry-go-round. Bikini-clad girls, like graceful circus performers, stand on the backs of their gilded horses, sliding their tanned bodies along the poles of the carousel. Their voices, lush and syrupy, gush through the room like supernatural djinn.

Zara: Fancy a ride, mister?

The Djinns: (*They sing.*)

Out on the road from west Marin,
In a cloud of dust, I met two djinns.
One bright as pride and thin,
The other was fat and black as sin
Isn't this how all good tales begin?

Omar: (*Rubs his eyes.*) Definitely going mad.

Sila: (*In red velvet bodice and black suspenders, a feather boa wrapped around her slim shoulders. She writhes and weaves atop a shiny black carousel horse.*) Do you recognise me? (*She wraps the boa around her crotchless bodice, bends forward, places her fingers against the lobes of her vagina and stretches it until the space between her lips opens to the size of a head.*) Do you know me yet? (*Her voice morphs and twists, deepens to the sound of a dull, speeded-down forty-five.*)

Omar: I don't know you. Leave me be.

(*He moves towards the staircase. The seven ghouls laugh raucously in the background.*)

Sila: (*Her shape begins to twist into another form, her voice modulating to a sound that Omar recognises.*) Omi?

Omar: Flora?

(*He looks up. His wife looks handsome, her neck draped with scarlet pearls. The gold-tinged embroidery of her bodice catches the light from the ceiling, hugs her curves. Her white blouse is open to her breastbone, the billowing white skirt blowing as though a soft breeze had entered the room. Like a mountain in the morning light of the spring sun, a garland of flowers sits on her long dark curls.*)

Flora: Miss Florentyna Molka from here out, my sweet little man.

(*She walks with a heavily pregnant cow on a lead, a red silk bow around its thick neck. The cow's eyelashes are unnaturally long and black, its eyes like hazel-coloured diamonds.*)

Flora: Would you like to milk her? She'd like that.

(*The cow bats its eyelids, smiles, and Omar feels an erection grow to the size of the Manhattan skyline. Omar covers himself with shame, his eyes bashful and pleading.*)

Omar: I can give you ... well, you know ... Flora.

Flora: Oh, Omi.

Omar: Yes, my dear.

Flora: (*Her voice cracking.*) Ca tremble un peu la coeur?

Omar: ل أنت دائما (*For you, always*)

Zara: Ms. Florentyna. You've got a customer.

(*She points to a fat, bald man, eyes bulging, lips like overdone sausages. His tie hangs around his neck like a redundant noose. He waves a one-hundred-euro note in his right hand.*)

Flora: Gotta run.

(*She sashays across the room, loosens her bodice so that her breasts ooze over the top.*)

Omar: Suppose so.

(*Omar grabs his hat, stumbles up the stairs and out onto Dame Street. Cars, taxis, and buses screech by. His eyes are blinded by the brightly painted pubs, their gilded window frames glistening in the streetlights. A cacophony of chat and loud, searing music oozes from within the vast chambers. Clusters of mini-skirted girls and drunken lads gather around the entrance sucking on their fags.*)

Omar: Bloody hell, who is that?

(*A dark shadow follows his steps like a ghost. Turns into the Temple Bar, trips along the cobblestones. Gretta, dressed in a tight, denim mini-skirt and gold, sparkly high heels, crosses the street towards him. Her dark nipples push like iron bullets through a purple, strapless top – the stump of her long arm is bright pink in the light of the streetlamp. She glides along the pavement, spots Omar and leers.*)

Gretta: You took me for a whore – dirty bastard.

Omar: Me ...? I never.

(*He walks quickly. A group of black-clad youths emerge from the arch of Meeting House Square, cross in front of him as they head towards the lengthening queue for the Temple Bar Music Centre.*)

Gretta: I like you for it – dirty, sexy man.

(*She caresses her right breast with her good arm, a cluster of brightly coloured bangles jingle, tingle against her skin.*)

Omar: I must be dreaming.

(*He rubs his eyes, opens them slowly. Breda Keane's pleasant, round face emerges from the shadows under the arch.*)

Mrs. Keane: Omar Wilde. (*She stares at Gretta dubiously.*) Out and about with "other" women, I see. Bold boy.

(*She waves a wrinkled finger, her voice full of amiable chastisement. Her eyes follow Gretta from the top of her raven hair to the edge of her delicate ankles. The younger woman backs away, crosses the street, and disappears into the crowd in front of the music centre.*)

Mrs. Keane: Have an eye for the dark woman, do ya?

Omar: (*Hassled.*) Don't know the girl at all. She just asked me the time once, honest. Imagine, three times in one day to see you. Mad. Out for a bite? Me, I'm just meeting some friends over the river. Lovely evening. No light but who needs it? City lights and all. Gotta go ...

(*She follows him the length of Eustace Street, smiles out of the corner of her mouth.*)

Mrs. Keane: What a load of horseshite. Wait till I speak to that wife of yours.

Omar: Flora knows all about it. Everything. No use ...

(*They turn right, past the red-painted façade of the Temple Bar. Sir William Temple and Lady Martha Temple step down from the wall gracefully. Omar shakes his head and sighs. Sir William, dressed in a red velvet doublet, green satin knee breeches, silk stockings, white lace trimming around his strong neck, takes his Lady wife delicately by the hand. She wears a matching green silk gown similarly trimmed with white lace, her golden hair neatly bundled in a silk kerchief.*)

Sir William: If you don't mind me saying, Mister Wilde, she doesn't look your type at all.

Lady Martha: Not at all. (*Shakes her head like a disapproving schoolteacher.*) Tut tut.

Sir William: That's right dear. Not at all. (*They look at each other disapprovingly.*) We hear you are a man of the world, a Renaissance man, so to speak. Would love to hear your impressions on Lord Chichester's "Articles of Plantation". Immediate removal of the Irish to specially designated areas, replacement with "loyal subjects". Hear, hear. What does the Moor think of that?

Omar: (*Moans audibly.*) I don't know any Lord Chichester, sir. Just need to get to Bachelor's Walk.

Sir William: All in good time, my boy. Why not follow us into our lovely home? I can offer a fine malt whiskey, shipped in straight from the depths of Scotland.

(*Omar brushes them aside, Mrs. Keane racing behind him, her stout heels clacking loudly on the cobblestones.*)

Omar: I have no time for this, I'm afraid. Oh dear. Oh dear. I shall be too late.

Lady Martha: Well really. How rude.

(*Omar and Mrs. Keane run past a pair of black buskers. Oversized jeans hang around the cracks of their muscular behinds. Mandela's t-shirted image clings to the well-defined chest of the singer — the other has his dreadlocks piled into a woollen Rasta cap.*)

Busker: Yo, we at war.
We at war with terrorism.

(*The Rasta man sounds like the percussion section of an orchestra. Drum and bass ooze from his lips acapella style. He ducks and dives like a cat on hot coals.*)

Omar: Wish he was walking with me right now. I need all the help I can get.

Mrs. Keane: You have me ... and Annie, of course. (*She blushes.*) Always had a soft spot for you meself, Omar. Who says a woman's ever past it? (*She winks a bright blue eye and laughs suggestively. He smiles nervously, turning left into Merchant's Lane.*) You'll be heading across the Liffey then. Gotta stay on this side, case Annie needs me.

Omar: (*Looks relieved.*) Grand then.

Mrs. Keane: You just remember there's always a place for you at my table, Omar Wilde.

(*She squeezes his left buttock with her hand, winks and walks away.*)

Omar: (*He smiles.*) Not a bad ol crone.

(*He turns and climbs the stone steps towards Merchant's Arch. A Romanian gypsy argues with two policemen.)*

Garda Fox: There's no place for you here.

Romanian: I'm doing no harm.

Garda Coffey: (*Sternly.*) Don't force us to make you.

Romanian: My baby is tired.

(*A small baby sleeps in her arms, a crust of snot under its tiny nose.*)

Garda Fox: So are we – of this shite, night after night. Now you know the law, Maria ... I don't have to repeat it to you for the thousandth time. Go home!

(*She picks up her baby, and Omar slips a euro into her hand as he passes.*)

Romanian: Bless you.

(*She crosses herself. Omar continues, drops down the steps to the bustling Wellington Quay.)*

Garda Coffey: (*Shouts.*) Sure, you're only encouraging her.

Omar: (*Mutters under his breath.*) Go arrest a real criminal for a change. I can show you one or two.

(*The traffic flows past like rapids. Omar watches the little man turn to green and crosses to the Halfpenny Bridge. He climbs the back of the bridge. Its pale wrought-iron railings and Victorian lanterns glow against the black of the water. He walks upward until the floor beneath him starts to move.*)

Omar: What the hell now?

(*He grabs the railings and looks into the water. A large eye emerges from a shiny body underneath. The great beast's marble-white skin swims slowly from out of the dark of the Liffey, his forehead wrinkled and serious.*)

The Whale: Going to the north side, sir?

(*Omar continues to cling to the railings as the giant body of the whale glides forward.*)

Omar: If you don't mind.

The Whale: Hang on.

(*The eye disappears beneath the water; the floor shifts forward slowly, like a moving walkway. Omar clings to the railing, allows himself to be moved slowly towards the north side of the river. The walkway comes to a stop at Lower Ormond Quay. A gush of water sprinkles the centre of the bridge like a single sparkling firework. Omar glances back into the waters and the eye opens, the corner of a smile glinting through the dark pupils.*)

The Whale: Happy hunting.

(*The eye winks, closes, and submerges beneath the murky Liffey waters.*)

Omar: Well, that beats Banagher.

(*A group of gulls hover overhead.*)

Gulls: (*Squawking loudly.*) Duck!

Omar: (*Jumps aside suddenly.*) What the hell?

(*A large, wet turd splatters white over the footpath one inch from his shiny black shoes.*)

Gulls: Sorry bout that. George is having a bit of bother with the bowels.

Omar: Thanks for that.

(*He doffs his hat and turns to cross at the lights. The harsh grating sound of the crossing signal cuts through his brain like a blunt saw. He feels faint and sits down by the statue of the chatting women on Liffey Street Lower. A young man in a green tracksuit, red New York Yankees baseball cap, and white runners sits beside him, his eyes glazed and shot through the colour of his cap.*)

Junky: (*Eyes darting around him. Speaks out of the corner of his mouth.*) Need some gear, mister? I can look after you.

Omar: (*Warily.*) No, that's ok. I just need to sit down a sec. Seeing funny things. Don't know what's up.

(*The junky looks at him and laughs.*)

Junky: Bad trip, mister, that's all. I can sort that out for you, no fuckin bother. (*He puts his left hand into his pocket and pulls out a bag of pills.*) See this little beauty here?

Omar: No really, it's ok.

Junky: (*Holds a blue pill in his hand. His eyes continue to circle around them.*) Now, this little baby is the latest in brain-reversal technology, a veritable genius she is. (*Omar stares at the blue pill.*) It's called "Oz". You know why? (*Omar shakes his head.*) Because, my friend, all you have to do is pop this little baby, tap your feet together three times, say the words "There's no place like home," and you're right back where you started, sober as a judge. Fuckin amazin.

Omar: (*Interested.*) Really?

Junky: Does my granny fart in bed? Fuckin A. Now, you look like a man whose hard drive could do with a wipe? I can throw you this minor miracle for a mere fifty euro.

Omar: (*Loudly.*) Fifty bloody euro? Are you mad?

Junky: (*Puts his hand over Omar's mouth.*) Sssshhh. Keep it fuckin down, mister. Do you think fuckin miracles come cheap? Even Jesus would pay for this boy. Forty-five is the best I can do.

Omar: (*Hesitates. Rummages in his pocket and pulls out a fifty-euro note.*) You're not messin with me? It's not ecstasy or acid or something? I never heard of this Oz thing. Just fecking promise me.

Junky: (*Eyes the money.*) You can go and look it up on the Web if you don't believe me. Trust me, this is as fuckin real as it gets, man. Only a poxbottle with an appetite for grief would mess with his clients. This is my business and you're my client and that's as real as it gets for me, mister, get it?

Omar: (*Takes the pill from him and hands him the money.*) Anything I should know about this? Any aftereffects?

Junky: A head as clear the pope's conscience, that's all.

(*Omar looks down at the pill. It begins to move in his hand, two little eyes opening. It smiles at him like a cartoon M&M, and speaks in a tiny squeaky voice, "Eat Me!" He looks at the junky, who smiles.*)

Omar: Right then.

(*He pops it in his mouth. A blinding light flashes through his skull. He feels his body drop, his head bangs off the bench, and all is black. He wakes up at the feet of the statue on Liffey Street. The chatting women have come to life)*

Betty: I don't know what that lad handed you, but it rightly messed with you, my dear. (*The old lady looks at him kindly, a bag of shopping by her side.*)

Mary: Been out cold for a good half hour, you have. Isn't that right, Betty?

Betty: No word of a lie. You've been droolin all over my Sunday-best shoes. Not a pretty sight. Shouldn't be hanging out with such wasters. Shame on you.

Mary: Give the poor lad a break, Betty. He doesn't look the best.

Betty: No wonder. You young ones are always at the drugs these days. You should get out there and get yourself a good job and stop all that messin, do you hear?

(*Omar struggles to his feet, rubs his head.*)

Omar: Sorry. I don't know what happened. But you're not ...

Betty: We're not what?

Omar: (*Moans.*) Oh never mind. Sorry to bother you. I'd better get going.

Mary: That's right, young fella, and mind yourself. If you ever want a chat, we're right here. Going nowhere.

Omar: No kidding.

(*Smiles, doffs his hat, and walks along Bachelor's Walk towards O'Connell Bridge. His head continues to spin, the absinthe still rolling through his system. He turns left into the Bachelor's Walk apartments and rings the red buzzer.*)

Intercom: Now state your business.

Omar: (*Looks at the piece of paper in his pocket.*) I want to see the Wizard.

(*The door clicks open. He climbs three flights of steps and knocks twice on the red door. A good-looking brunette – eyes heavy with mascara, lips a lurid red – opens the door. She is dressed in red patent leather high heels, a tight, red velvet bodice and black leather trousers. A whip in her right hand, she holds a black folder in the other.*)

Diana: (*Stares at him from top to toe and smiles seductively.*) Omar Wilde, how the hell are you?

Omar: Hi, Diana. Are my friends here?

Diana: We've been taking right good care of them, ducky, don't you worry. Come on in. Just doing the accounts. Can't be too careful these days. Light fingers everywhere.

(*She winks. Omar smiles and follows her into the small living room. Two girls, scantily clad in silk negligees and suspenders, sit at a small, round table, painting their nails. Kinch is at the other side of the table, a squeezebox in his hands, a young Asian girl draped around his shoulders. He looks up and acknowledges Omar, his eyes rolling around his head.*)

Kinch: The Maestro. At last.

(*The room spins. Kinch's face changes shape: his nose grows and then retracts; his eyes are on the ends of wires, like joke-shop balls. Omar tries to continue the conversation.*)

Omar: Sorry, not feeling the best. Still out of it. Where's the boy?

Kinch: They're sorting him out. Took him to a warehouse in the street behind ... in case the whole thing goes (*throws his hands into the air*) ... BOOM. We wouldn't want that. These lovely ladies splattered from here to the Phoenix Park ... God, no.

(*He smiles at the Asian girl who is stroking the inside of his leg.*)

Omar: (*Anxiously.*) You should have gone with him.

Kinch: No choice. The guy – Malone, I think – said I had to stay but not to worry, and they'd be back as soon as it was sorted. And Mimi here's been keeping me company.

(*His eyes red and moist, he slurs his words.*)

Diana: Come on, luv. Relax yourself there. (*Pushes Omar onto the red velvet couch and sits beside him, stroking his hair.*) Now you look like a man who could do with a little fun. I'll take care of you myself if you like. Sixty euro a pop and worth every penny let me tell you.

(*She whispers into Omar's ear, her breath like a mistral wind. He shuffles uncomfortably, his eye falling on his wedding ring.*)

Diana: Don't mind that. If I was you, I'd take that hunk of lead off your finger and let me remind you what a real woman feels like.

(*She rubs the edge of her whip across his crotch. Omar glances at Kinch.*)

Kinch: (*Stares at the Asian girl's breasts as she straddles him in the chair.*) I never saw a thing, Omar, if you're worried about that.

Omar: (*Diana unbuttons the top buttons of his shirt.*) I don't know if I ...

Diana: Oh yes you do.

(*She cuffs him to her, places her hand on his crotch, and pulls him slowly off the couch. Guides him to the bedroom off the main living room. He follows her, unable to control his lengthening hard-on. She shuts the door behind them, rips open his belt, and his overlarge trousers fall to the floor around his ankle.*)

Diana: Well, that saved me a little extra work.

(*She unclicks two fasteners on both sides of her leather trousers, and they fall to the floor. She is wearing suspenders and a tiny, red velvet G-string.*)

Omar: (*Omar moans.*) Just don't hurt me too much, please.

Diana: (*Softly.*) What was that you said, dear boy?

Omar: (*Nervously.*) I never did this ...

Diana: No, but you wanted to, I can tell. (*She pushes him to the floor.*) Get on your knees.

(*Her voice is hard and direct. He falls to his knees, and she straddles him from behind.*)

Diana: I could tell you needed a good hiding, from the minute I saw you, you bold boy.

(*She runs the whip the length of his spine. He watches in the mirrored wall as she raises the whip and brings it crashing onto his right buttock.*)

Omar: (*Screaming.*) Mother of Jaysus!

Diana: You like that, don't you? You very naughty fella, so naughty I'll have to teach you a proper lesson, you dirty pig.

(He feels the whip flame his skin once more and is surprised by the dart of pleasure that runs the length of his hard prick.)

Omar: Please.

(*His voice is soft and pleading.*)

Diana: I'm going to show you who's boss around here, you filthy boy.

(*She turns him over and straddles him. She begins to take on another form. He rubs his eyes. She waves the whip in her hand, and it changes into a black rosary, the same that his grandmother had wrapped around her hands on her deathbed.*)

Omar: Holy Mary, Mother of God.

(*He looks up and Diana is in a long black dress and starched nun's habit. She turns him over once again, swirls the beads around her head and brings them crashing once more onto his behind.*)

Diana: A right thrashing is what you deserve, Omar Wilde, for all that interfering with yourself, those dirty thoughts. I've seen the way you look at me, you dirty boy.

Omar: Please, Sister, I didn't mean. I just needed to be touched, to touch someone, and she won't let me.

Diana: No wonder with those filthy hands – you never wash. What you need is a good ride, and I'm going to ride you like a prize mare at Cheltenham.

(*He is on all fours. She sits on his back and whips his backside.*)

Diana: Go on, boy. Show me what you're made of.

(*Omar begins to shuffle around the room on his knees. She continues to beat his hind quarters.*)

Diana: That's it, boy, move.

Omar: No more, Flora ... no more.

(He shuffles towards the end of the bed, collapses, and begins to cry.)

Diana: Ah now, no need for that.

(She places her arm around him, and he nestles his head into her breast.)

Diana: It's all just a bit of fun.

(She caresses the top of his head. He closes his eyes and continues to sob. Her voice changes pitch and modulates to the familiar Middle Eastern tones of his mother's voice.)

Diana: I'll take care of you love. Don't be afraid.

(He keeps his eyes shut. His mother's sallow face, hazel eyes, and raven hair appear before him. She smiles, reaches out to touch him.)

His Mother: Feeling better, luv?

(He stretches himself across her lap. She cradles his head in her arms as he slips into sublime darkness.)

* * *

"Omar, wake up."

A hand struck the numbness out of his face.

"Omar."

Diana's voice was shrill and harsh. Pain gripped his skull. Her features filled his eyes – a pretty, overdone face with a hard, cold stare.

"For God's sake. I have a client due in fifteen minutes. You've been out cold for ages. Snap out of it." She shook his shoulders and pulled him to his feet.

The room snapped into focus. "Where am I?"

"At Diana's, remember? Now come on. We've gotta get a move on."

Omar struggled to his feet. The right side of his brain felt like it had been crushed by a hammer.

"Anytime you fancy another "clearing" of your emotions, you know where I am. Now cough up, mate." Diana stuck out her hand, her long sharp nails like tiny, beautiful weapons. Omar picked up his trousers and rummaged for some money. He handed her sixty euro and she smiled.

"Right, let's go see what those young ones of yours are up to."

Pulling on his trousers and shirt, he followed Diana back to the living room. Kinch was in the corner with the Asian girl perched beside him. He clutched an accordion, his fingers tripping over the keys while Mimi poked at his ribs.

"Please, play that one again. It is so vely fun. I like."

Kinch's eyes rolled around his head like stray marbles. "Pour toi le monde, mon poupée."

He began to play the squeeze box. Music filled the room, and the girl clapped with delight. Kinch sang, "The Port of Amsterdam" with his eyes shut.

The two girls at the table jumped to their feet, laughed, and waltzed around the room. Their feather boas swung around their ample bosoms like dragons in a Chinese parade.

Diana smiled, put her things on the couch, and grabbed Omar.

"Come on, luv, let's give it a lash." She spun Omar around the room.

Kinch continued to sing about dancing sailors and grinding women.

He snarled at the top of his voice and squeezed the accordion with determination. The others circled the room, spun, wheeled, and swirled around each other.

"I'm killed laughin." Diana let go of Omar, who spun empty-handed onto the couch.

The girls continued to twirl and twist, the music building to a crescendo.

Kinch howled into the room like a man possessed.

He stopped playing, stared straight ahead of him, and started to scream. "Mother, no! MOTHER!"

The Asian girl tried to calm him. "There's no one there, sweetie, no one."

"It's not her. It's a demon." Kinch's eyes were wide and wild. He stared and pointed at a blank wall.

Omar moved towards Kinch, but Diana jumped in front of him.

"Oh for God's sake. Is everyone off their heads around here today? Sit down. There's nothing there." She attempted to guide Kinch towards the table.

Now feeling almost a hundred percent sober, Omar decided to take things under his control.

"It's this absinthe stuff. God knows what else they put in it, bloody bastards. Kinch, you're all right, lad." Omar turned to Mimi. "Can you get some water please?"

She ran into the kitchenette.

Kinch grabbed a whip by the wall, jumped onto a chair, and swiped at the air. "You cursed creature. I don't know you. My mother died. She's gone. That's all. Leave me be."

Diana screamed, "The fucking chandelier! Jaysus."

Kinch's whip sliced the air and landed full force on the faux chandelier. Splinters of glass shattered and spun through the air like tiny fireflies. "Leave me alone!"

The girls ducked.

"Get out of here, you feckin looper, before I get Malone to come back and sort you out." Diana grabbed Kinch by the scruff of the neck and turfed him out the door. He ran down the corridor and disappeared.

Omar grabbed his jacket. "Shite. I'd better go after him. Give me Malone's number so I can find out what's happening with the other one."

"I knew you were trouble as soon as I laid eyes on you." Diana waved her scissor-sharp nails at Omar. "Give me your phone." She grabbed Omar's phone and tapped the numbers into it. "Now get out of here and don't come back." She slammed the door behind him.

Omar descended into the street.

Kinch had fallen on the kerb and vomited into a flowerpot. Garda Fox bent over him with a disapproving look. Omar stood to the side and watched while deciding how best to approach the Guard. It was the same fella he had pissed off not long ago, so he would have to go easy.

Garda Fox held his nose. "Young man, I suggest you move yourself home and sober up before you spew onto half of Dublin."

Kinch breathed with difficulty. He turned his face towards the unimpressed Garda. "Things fall apart; the centre cannot hold; mere anarchy is loosed upon the world." He fell about, the whip still in his hand, and slashed the air like a drunken swordsman.

"What kind of shite are you talking? Anarchy, is it? Are you one of those troublemakers that likes to cause havoc in the stands, beating on poor innocent soccer supporters?" The Garda attempted to grab the tumbling man. "Give me that whip."

Kinch danced around the garda like a marionette talking about a Seargeant Pluck and people atomically mixing up their personalities with those of their bicycles making them half people and half bicycle. He laughed madly and knocked off the Garda's hat with the whip.

"Right, that's it. I'll sort you out, you drunken scut. A good lockup will sober you up." Garda Fox grabbed Kinch by the scruff of his jacket and pulled him towards the Garda car parked opposite.

Omar raced over to intercede. "Sorry, Guard. It's all right. He's my ... son. A little under the weather, but I'll take it from here. Don't you worry." Omar grabbed Kinch by the arm.

The Garda looked unimpressed. "Your son, is it? What's your name ... and his?"

"Omar Wilde, Guard and ... Owen."

Kinch laughed out loud.

"Owen, come on lad. I'll get you home."

"All right then, but you better have a strong word with this son of yours, Mr. Wilde. Attacking a police officer with a whip, pissed out of his mind, will get him in a lot of trouble. I'll be keeping an eye out for him, so you better sort him out, d'you hear?"

A tourist horse and trap pulled up beside them. The driver saluted Omar.

"Omar, in a spot of trouble there?"

"Howya, Matty? No, no bother. Just looking after my son, Owen here." Omar winked noticeably (the Garda stood behind him).

"You know this man?" asked Garda Fox.

"Course I do. One of our finest journalists, Guard. If you're lucky, he might do a piece on the strength and bravery of our fine police force, isn't that right, Omar?" The cabman spoke with a smile two millimetres shy of a laugh.

"Less of the cheek, but all right then. Will you give this man a hand to take his son home?"

The cabman winked. "Leave it to me, sarge. I'll sort them out."

Garda Fox helped Omar to pile Kinch into the back of the horse cab. "Right, I've had enough of this. I'm off." He crossed the road, got into the Garda car, and sped across O'Connell Bridge.

"No fear he'd ever be stopped for a ticket." The cabman finished chewing on a piece of gum and shot it through the air in the direction of the river. It landed on the boater of a passing Joycean. "Bullseye. That lot have been giving me a pain up my hole all day."

"Thanks, Matty, but now that he's buggered off, I need to take this lad and head to sort something out." Omar hopped out of the cab and took Kinch by the arm.

"No bother, man. How do you know this fella?"

"Long story. He's a nice lad really. Was a bit worse for wear myself earlier. Bloody absinthe stuff some fecker gave us to drink. Deadly." Omar wrapped himself around Kinch. "Anyway, have to head. Thanks again."

"Anytime, Omar. Going to drop the horse home and head over to Mulligan's later. Do a night-time shift with the horseless carriages. Good spot to hang out and wait for a call." The cabman glanced at the time on his phone. "Better get a move on. Drop over later if you've nothing better to do. Not much happening around town tonight, so I'll probably be sitting on my arse half the night."

"I'm a little occupied, but you never know."

The cabby flcked the grey mare's flank gently and began to ease her into the flow of night-time traffic. The large bells around the mare's neck jingled, the clop of her iron-shod hooves like hollow music against the tarred streets.

Kinch raised his head. "Cast a cold eye on life, on death. Horseman, pass by!"

"Right, enough of the poetry. We're going to get you sobered up.

They turned right into Litton Lane.

A young boy passed by on a bicycle. He was dressed in a red velvet confirmation suit complemented by a black tie and held a copy of the Qur'an in one hand.

Omar blinked.

As the boy passed, he smiled. He had Flora's green eyes, as recognisable to Omar as his own. "Ruairí."

Ruairí stared straight through Omar and cycled past, singing in Arabic.

Mama zamanha gaya
Gaya baedeh shiwaya,
Gayba al'ab wa hagat
Gayba maha shanta

Omar recognised it immediately as the song his mother used to sing to him when she put him to bed as a child. Omar watched silently as the boy disappeared around the corner.

CHAPTER 41

BLÁITHÍN

12:30 AM

THE SOUND OF A PHONE penetrated Bláithín's dreams. She jerked awake. Hanan lay beside her, naked and in the depths of sleep. She glanced at the clock on the stereo. Half past midnight. *Damn! Missed the concert.*

The phone rang again.

Who the hell is ringing at this time? She extricated herself from Hanan's arms and raced to the couch. *Not my phone just same ringtone. Funny.* Kinch's name flashed on the screen. She hesitated, struck by a wave of panic and guilt, and picked up the phone.

"Hi, it's Bláithín."

"Bláith, what are you doing with Hanan?" Kinch's voice was odd, slurred and distant. "Oh, never mind. Shite, I feel sick ..."

She heard vomiting and then another voice.

"Hello."

It was an older man's voice. She thought she recognised it. "Hi. This is Bláithín, Kinch's ... friend. Who's this?"

"Omar Wilde. You know, Flora's husband."

What the hell are they doing together?

"Kinch isn't feeling great. Is Hanan there? We need to have a word."

She looked in Hanan's direction. A gentle snore hummed through the room. "He's asleep."

"Can you wake him? It's urgent."

Omar sounded anxious, determined, unlike his normally hesitant self.

"Yeah ... hang on." She walked over to Hanan, shook his shoulders, and pushed the phone in his face.

"Wha?" His eyes opened slowly.

"Sorry, babe, but it's Omar Wilde for you. He's with Kinch. Says it's urgent."

He looked at her, his face forming a question.

She whispered. "Don't ask me. I don't have a clue."

Hanan shook his head and took the phone.

Bláithín signalled to him to put it up to her ear, so she could listen too.

"Hi."

"Hello, Hanan. I'm a friend of Kinch's and I have your brother with me here. There's been a bit of drama here tonight. I need you to meet us straight away so I can explain."

"Khaled? With you? What time ...?" He glanced at the clock. "What's happened? Is he ok?"

"Yeah, fine now. Can you meet us on the James Joyce Bridge in fifteen minutes? Are you far away?"

Hanan raised his eyebrows at Bláithín. "No, really close ... but I don't understand?"

"Just trust me," said Omar

"Ok, fifteen on the bridge."

"Right."

The phone went dead.

Bláithín threw her hands in the air. "What the hell is going on?"

"I don't have a fecking clue. This guy, Omar ... isn't that your music teacher's husband?" He looked confused.

"Yep. What the feck's Kinch doing with him – under the circumstances? And your brother? Jesus."

Hanan pulled on his clothes quickly. "Are you coming?"

Bláithín grabbed a large glass of water. "I suppose. Think I'll beat Kinch to a pulp ... but what the feck?" She pulled on a crimson skirt, a t-shirt, and knee-high flat boots. "No more of this bodice shit for me. Bye-bye, Molly!"

They walked down Winetavern Street towards the Liffey. The grey, bunker-like Civic Offices loomed over the river, casting a dark shadow across the moon-lit night. Late-time traffic drifted past as they turned onto Merchants

Quay. Two homeless people slept on cardboard boxes on the edge of the road. This was a part of Dublin largely deserted at this time of the night.

Bláithín felt a little nervous as they passed along Ushers Quay. It was not unknown, at the foot of the Liberties, to cross paths with strung-out junkies looking for a fix. She thanked God she'd never tried heroin. It led to a kind of desperation that even she couldn't touch. The hijacking of an unsuspecting passerby with a potentially HIV-infected syringe was the latest way of feeding the habit, and this was not something she wanted to experience. She kept a sharp eye on her surroundings.

"Are we going to tell Kinch ... about us?" Hanan asked.

"Is there an us?"

He looked at her carefully, took her hand in his. "I hope so."

She hesitated and stared at the river. "Ok then."

He smiled and pulled her under his arm. They walked in silence towards the bridge.

Kinch was leaning over the bridge and staring into the water. The other two stood beside him.

Kinch stood up to look at them as they approached. "You two look very cosy. Something I should know?" His voice was sharp and cold.

"It's none of your fucking business, is it?" Bláithín could feel a slow, necessary anger seep through her system.

"So much for the understanding best friend." Kinch propped himself up against the bridge edge precariously. His face was pale as a death mask, his words slurred and angry. "Didn't take you long to bone my woman."

"You might remember, Mister Holier-Than-Thou, that the last time I saw you, you were starkers and banging like a mad thing with ..." Bláithín stopped and looked at Omar. He looked wrecked and was clearly embarrassed at being a part of this domestic dispute.

Kinch glared at Bláithín. His eyes pleaded silently.

Hanan interrupted swiftly. "Never mind all that. What the hell are you doing here?" He walked towards his brother, who stood silently by Omar's side, his eyes cast to the ground.

"I'm sorry, I ..." Khaled's voice trailed away. He began to cry gently and took a step towards his brother.

Hanan looked at Omar and waited for an explanation. Khaled rested the top of his head against his brother's chest as he cried.

"He's had a very rough day. I think you should just get him home. He'll tell you about it on the way. Ok?" Omar touched the boy on the shoulder.

"Yes, Mr. Wilde ... but what about the imam?" His face was creased with worry.

"I'll sort that out for you. You just look after yourself."

Bláithín had no idea what they were talking about, but Khaled seemed comforted by Omar's words.

Hanan looked concerned. "I don't understand."

"You will." Omar signalled to Hanan not to push Khaled too hard.

"Can you take me home, Hanan?" Khaled asked, his face grey and fragile.

Bláithín could see Hanan's surprise. His normally truculent brother needed him – wanted his help.

Hanan turned to Bláithín. "I'm going. I'll give you a buzz tomorrow. Ok?" He kissed her gently on the forehead and whispered in her ear, "No more reason to be afraid. I'm here. Promise." She nodded silently. Hanan put his arm around his brother and guided him in the direction of City Hall.

Bláithín suddenly felt very awkward. On one side stood the man who'd smashed her heart to pieces by banging her friend and mentor right in front of her. On the other side, innocent and unaware, the cuckolded husband. She didn't know Omar as such, but the few times she'd met him he'd struck her as friendly and kind although a bit of an eejit to be blunt about it. The kind of man who drifted through life thinking the best of people, even when they thought the worst of him. She could imagine how his passivity had driven a woman like Flora crazy. How she'd ever married him in the first place was a complete mystery. But all the same that was no justification for the traitorous bitch to seduce Bláithín's man. There were rules about that sort of thing, even in bloody Poland.

She looked at Kinch. He was clearly terrified that she was about to reveal him for the cheating bastard that he was.

A wave of powerful calm washed over her like winter sleep. For the first time in 24 hours, she could see clearly. She knew what she had to do to suck the stress out of the day, to bring some resolution to her rampant anger.

"Do you mind, Omar? I just need a quick word with Kinch."

"No bother. I'll just stand over here. Could do with a small break from all this madness." Omar walked to the far side of the bridge and stared towards the grandeur of The Four Courts, its Grecian-pillared façade and domed roof floodlit and bright against the night sky.

Bláithín walked to within breathing distance of Kinch and spoke clearly and calmly.

"It's a miracle I made it through this day, thanks to you, but all things considered, I'm willing to forget it all if you promise me one thing?"

Kinch raised his eyebrows. "Yeah? Of course. Anything. What?"

"Tell him." She pointed towards Omar. He had his back to them.

"What? About Flora?" Kinch looked dumbfounded. "Are you mad? It'll kill him. He adores her. It's over between us anyway. We finished it ... after you ..." Kinch looked embarrassed and started to play with a box of cigarettes in his hand.

She fixed him with her eyes, spoke clearly and definitely: "Do it. It's the decent thing. He deserves to know." She looked at her watch. "It's one o'clock. I'm giving you until 2:30. If I don't get a text telling me you've done it, I'm phoning him. I have his home number, remember."

She felt proud of the strength she'd summoned from within herself. She could see him look at her with different eyes, and she liked it.

He shuffled from one foot to the other. "Jesus, is that it? Would you like me to jump off this bridge as well, with a lead weight tied to me of course? *Heav'n has no Rage, like Love to Hatred turn'd, Nor Hell a Fury, like a Woman scorn'd.*"

She laughed. "That feckin poetry of yours drives me mad, but it has its uses sometimes. Oh, and chucking yourself off the bridge, that would be a nice dramatic extra ... if you feel like it."

He scrunched up his features in a twisted smile. "Well, O'Leary, you're a tough bitch after all. Who'd have known?"

She felt satisfied with herself and knew that she had one more thing to do to feel fully rid of this shite day. "I've got to go. I'll be awake a while more and watching the phone, so don't forget."

"Head like an elephant. Not a chance." Kinch doffed his cap and walked across the bridge towards Omar.

Bláithín waved goodbye to them both and walked back towards Parliament Street.

One more thing.

CHAPTER 42

FLORA

1:00 AM

A DANCING LIGHT FLICKERED from the television through the otherwise dark room. The sound was muted. Flora lay on the couch, drifting in and out of sleep. She'd offered to babysit the children after the concert so that Sandra could get out for an evening. It had been a long day and she was glad to give her ticket to Sandra for the Low concert in Christchurch. Although exhausted, she felt somehow unable to return to her bed.

She opened her eyes. *The Wizard of Oz* was playing on TCM.

At one in the morning? How odd. The world seemed out of kilter, skewed, like an amusement-park mirror maze.

Flora glanced at the TV again. Dorothy was locked in the Wicked Witch's castle. She could see Aunty Em in a crystal ball but couldn't call to her. Flora loved this scene. No matter how many times she'd seen it, she was always afraid Dorothy wouldn't escape. She sat watching Judy Garland speak silently into the darkness.

The doorknocker banged loudly, and she jumped off the couch with fright.

Maybe Sandra? Lost the key?

She opened the door. Bláithín stood on the doorstep, her face composed and unyielding.

"Can I come in?"

She spoke softly but definitely. There was only one response.

"Yes. Of course." Unsure of what was to come, Flora felt slightly sick. She shut the door and they turned to face each other. "I, ehm ..."

"Let me speak first. Can I ...?" Bláithín gestured to the couch.

"Naturally." Flora sat in the armchair opposite. Unable to relax, she teetered on the edge, her back as straight as the spine of a hardback.

"I came to tell you that I don't hate you." Bláithín spoke softly.

Flora let out a long breath of air.

"But I do think what you did was despicable."

Flora sucked it back in. She decided silence was her best option for now.

"I know it's not easy for you and Omar. You're as different as the Virgin Mary and Heidi Fleiss."

Flora looked at her blankly.

"Listen," Bláithín continued, "I just want you to know that I don't hold anything against you, but I don't ever want to see you again. It's just better that way." There was no hint of a smile on her face but no anger either. Instead, her expression evinced a kind of cold wisdom, the maturity gathered from pain.

Flora recognised this quality. "I understand … I'm sorry." She knew that a weeping apology was not what Bláithín was looking for.

"Ok then." Bláithín stood up to leave. "Oh, by the way, I met Kinch. He's going to tell Omar. I thought you should know."

Flora thought she saw the hint of a smile on the edge of Bláithín's lips.

Dorothy threw a bucket of water over the witch on the screen behind Bláithín's shoulder.

Flora smiled. "Touché."

Bláithín nodded. "Bye then." She turned the door handle but hesitated. "Maybe you should leave him – Omar. It might be better for everyone."

Flora nodded silently. *So much you have to learn.*

She closed the door, walked to the couch slowly, and sat down. She waited for the emotion to hit her like a wave, but instead she felt oddly calm, satisfied even. She'd never felt good about her deception, but some small part of her almost felt that people like Omar and Bláithín brought it on themselves. It was too easy to fool them. They needed toughening up to survive in the world, the same world in which Flora had carved her own space, out of isolation and loneliness. She was glad to see Bláithín standing up to her.

The television continued to flicker in the darkness. Flora stared into space for what seemed ages. She snapped out of it when The Good Witch,

Glenda, was granting Dorothy her three wishes. Flora clicked her heels and mouthed silently to herself, “There’s no place like home, there’s no place like home, there’s no place like home.”

CHAPTER 43

THE TRAVELLER

~ Eumaeus ~

1:00 AM

AFTER THE NIGHT THAT WAS in it and the still ropey state of his young friend, Omar decided he'd take the cabby's advice and leg it to Mulligan's. Everywhere else was jammed with young ones puking their rings and screaming their heads off. At least they could get a quiet coffee and sober up a little.

Kinch tripped along after him listlessly.

Much to Omar's astonishment, The Traveller men were still perched on the wall of the bridge. A wave of nausea passed through him. He stood back and took a close look at them before he passed. They looked different now, African.

Must be the second shift.

As always, they were out of position: the T and the two Rs threw scraps to the birds over the bridge; one of the Ls talked frantically on a phone; the other five, EVAEL, leant listlessly against the bridge.

Kinch glanced at them and laughed like a madman. "A message from Dog," he mumbled and laughed.

"Are you ok?" Omar asked.

"Yeah, no worries."

Kinch looked distracted. He stared at the Docklands, deep in thought. Omar suddenly realised that he had a major scoop on his hands. He had spoken to Khaled about going to the Gardaí, convinced him that because he'd backed down and was a minor the police would protect him in turn for what he knew. This was Omar's big chance to break through with a front-page story, and no one could take it away from him. He'd taken the photo and he was the only one involved. He decided he should have a quick word with the men.

He walked up to A and tapped him on the shoulder. "Excuse me. Do you mind me asking if you know the men who were on the shift before you?"

"No, man. We always do the second shift, and the others are gone by the time we get here." The young man had a Nigerian accent and a kind face. His right ear, seriously deformed, looked like it had been burnt away from the side of his head. Omar couldn't help wondering what had brought this man, minus an ear, so far across the world.

"Anyone else know them?" Omar pointed to the others, who were scattered across the bridge.

The young man shouted to his colleagues, none of whom knew the earlier shift. "Call into the office. Maybe they can help you." He scribbled a number on a piece of paper and handed it to Omar.

"Thanks." Omar took a brown envelope out of his satchel, slipped the paper into it, and placed it back in the satchel. *Deal with that first thing in the morning.*

Kinch was hanging over the bridge, looking like he was about to vomit again.

"Come on, Kinch. Let's get you something to settle that stomach of yours." Omar took Kinch by the arm and led him across the bridge. He was no longer sure about this young man. "You'll keep it to yourself. Everything that happened tonight, right?" Kinch had displayed a certain instability, a lack of control, a liking for the edge of life.

"Yeah, of course. I'm not an eejit," Kinch replied.

They continued past Messrs Maguires in silence and turned into Hawkins Street. A young girl squatted behind a parked car. Clearly plastered, she pissed a stream into the street. Mascara dripped down her right cheek, and she smiled at them as they passed.

"Charming," said Omar.

Kinch laughed. "*Les Desmoiselles de Dublin.* A classy lot. Think I prefer the foreign floozies. At least they're not pretending." He hesitated. "Might pay a visit back there. Mimi was a hot wee thing."

Omar didn't like the sound of that. "Keep far away from there or anywhere like it. That's no place for a smart lad like you. Just get you in trouble."

"Thanks, Dad, but I think I'm a big enough boy to look after myself now." There was a note of dismissal in Kinch's voice that Omar didn't really like. He suddenly felt older than his thirty-eight years.

They crossed the road towards Poolbeg Street. A figure approached from Trinity College direction and shouted to get Kinch's attention.

"Lynch, is that you, you bollox?" The light fell on him as he approached. He was a man in his twenties, his blond hair in dreads, an assortment of metal rings protruding from various parts of his anatomy. There was blood around the edge of his right eyebrow.

"I thought that was you."

"Jimmy, what the feck happened to you man?" Kinch pointed at the blood.

"Ah, just some wanker in the Brazen Head. You know one of those Polo-shirted, up-your-fuckin-arse Southsider types. Decided I was lookin at his fuckin bird sideways and popped me one. Caught the edge of my brow ring. I wouldn't even touch the posh slut with yours, for fuck's sake." He rubbed his forehead with the sleeve of his overlarge jumper. The blood stuck to the wool like jelly.

"Tough luck."

Kinch looked uncomfortable around this fella. Omar tried to signal that they should move on.

Jimmy wasn't moving. "Listen, man, you wouldn't have a few bob? I just need to catch the Nightlink? That fucker and his friends thought it was bloody hilarious to grab my wallet on the sly."

Kinch fumbled in his pockets. "Yeah, sure, hang on."

Jimmy picked at his wound. "I was meaning to ask you, I've been a bit down on my luck with the actin and all. You wouldn't know of an openin, any old thing?"

Kinch thought for a second, handed him four euros, and a card. "Well, actually, an American lady handed me this card this afternoon. Something about kids" parties, performing. Anyway, not my thing, but if you fancy it."

"Fuckin A man. Great. You're a pal."

Omar stood watching the two talking on the corner of Poolbeg and Hawkins. Out of nowhere a bicycle sped past him and ripped his satchel off his arm. He recognised him immediately as the same tracksuit wearer who had grabbed the woman's red bag earlier in the day, but he moved too fast to get a look at his face.

"Come back here you fuckin knacker!" Omar raced down Hawkins Street.

The tracksuit disappeared around the corner.

"FUCK!"

Kinch and Jimmy caught up with him as he caught his breath on the corner, the boy flying over Butt Bridge in the distance.

"He's well gone, mate," said Jimmy, panting.

"No bloody kidding." Omar sat on the edge of the path and screamed into the night air, "Nooooooooo."

Kinch and Jimmy glanced at each other concerned. Although increasingly sober, Omar suddenly felt very sick as he watched his money, and his chance with Flora disappear over the bridge with bicycle boy. Not alone that, but the photo that was to give him the scoop of his life went with it. He cursed the Gods of Fortune that were well and truly operating against him today.

"Anything important in that?" asked Kinch.

Omar took a deep breath, fought back tears, and sighed. "No, not really." What was the point in explaining? It was gone, and that was that. At least he knew he could tip off the police, but without the photo it was their word against his.

Jimmy glanced at his watch. "Five to one. Better leg it to the bus. Sorry about that, man. Have to have eyes in the back of your head around here." He clapped Kinch on the back. "Bye, Kinch, and thanks for that."

Jimmy took off at a run towards the Nightlink.

Omar tapped Kinch on the shoulder. "Come on if we're to get into the pub."

Kinch nodded.

When they arrived at the big wooden door of No. 8, Poolbeg Street, the blinds were pulled down. Omar knocked the way the cabby had told him. The door opened slightly. A deep-voiced, balding, burly man, with a beer belly the size of a sack of cement, squinted to take a look at them.

"Do I know ye?" He had a thick country accent.

"Is Matt Maher there Christie? It's Omar Wilde, from the *Independent*. He told us we could drop round. We're only lookin for a cup of coffee or a Coke or something."

The barman laughed. "A coffee, is it? What the hell's that?" He opened the door carefully. "Come on in then, Omar." He was a man of the girth appropriate to an ageing Dublin barman, with a deep infectious laugh. "A pair of pioneers we have here, lads." The assortment of late-night drinkers laughed raucously.

Omar recognised Matty's voice coming from a corner.

"It's not the Catholicism that taught him not to drink, Christie." Matty winked at Omar. "Good man for dropping in. That young fella's looking a little more with it at this stage." Matty nodded at Kinch.

Kinch scratched his head and looked at the bearded cabman with a look of confusion. "Do I know you?"

Matty let out a deep wail of laughter. "Never mind, lad. You sit down here, and we'll give you a good tonic for that head of yours. Christie, rack up the young man a rock shandy. Just the trick when the thirst of the damned grabs you by the throat. Omar ... yourself?"

"Just a coffee, thanks. Milk, no sugar."

Omar sometimes found himself in this famous Dublin establishment where his work cronies hung out. One of the few places left in Dublin that hadn't stripped away its Victorian splendour. All over the city, the mahogany counter tops and confessional screens of Dublin's cosy corners and crevices had been replaced by brightly coloured, trendy, and totally vapid alternatives. Mulligan's down-and-dirty atmosphere was the stuff of legend and a small comfort in the swirl of chaos and change that enveloped the city at its doorstep.

You could find all sorts hidden away in its dark corners: writers, politicians, journalists, actors. A president of the United States had even walked its boards. But only the chosen few got to cosy up late into the night – the traditional pub lock-in was fast becoming a thing of the past. Such illegal pleasures had been driven away by a Garda force that actually believed in doing their job, more's the shame.

"Sorry, Omar, the call of nature. Might be a while. The bowels are not cooperating right now." Matty winced to emphasise his digestive difficulties.

"Know all about it myself, Matty. The feckin piles, that's the real killer."

Kinch winced. A man sat beside them. Omar could see he wasn't far from his own age although his face was lined and leathery. He had the look of a man who'd spent half his life under a distant sun. He wore his ginger hair in a ponytail and cultivated a beard that gave him a wild, artistic edge. The lines around his sharp blue eyes were pronounced and smiling. He seemed to be observing Kinch, sussing him out as a potential conversationalist. Omar wasn't sure this man's company was what they needed at this moment.

He spoke to Kinch, his voice deep and growling, like a great vat of salt and tar boiling in the heat of the day. "You a writer?"

Kinch had been staring at the names carved into the oak table. He looked up. "Not exactly ... an actor."

"Ahhhh. I knew there was a bit of an artist in you. Would I have seen you ...?"

"Nah. Well, I did a few ads on TV but no ... probably not."

"It's just ... you look familiar. Remind me of a lad I once met when I was sailing in the Caribbean. Nice fella, a writer. That's why I thought maybe ...?"

Kinch smiled. "I'm afraid I haven't made it out of Europe, so sorry ... not that I wouldn't mind." His voice trailed away.

"Never left Europe? That's feckin mad. You gotta get out there, lad. There's a fuckin amazing world out there. I've been at it twenty years now and don't regret a day of it, let me tell ya." He took a slug from his pint. "This is the only thing I miss – a decent pint of porter. Tastes like shite everywhere else. They brew it in Barbados and Nigeria, so it's not so bad there. Still, not the same. You need the wet and the misery to give it that little bit extra. Never ceases to amaze me when I see a gang of Rasta lads, sweating like pigs in the heat of the Caribbean, downing the black stuff to quench their thirst. Mad feckers, fair fucks to them."

The barman arrived to the table with a pot of extremely watery-looking coffee. "There you go now. Would you like a snack bar or something with that?"

"No thanks, that's grand."

"The Guinness tastes like shite over there and the coffee tastes like shite over here. Don't know how you drink it. Like pisswater." The red-bearded man was determined to drag Omar into the conversation.

"I wouldn't know, but I'm not that fussy," Omar replied.

The bearded man grabbed his opportunity. "They're fucking bastards, those coffee ranchers. Spent a year in Guatemala – a feckin glorious place. Volcanoes spitting lava into the night sky, lakes like oceans, gorgeous!"

Kinch looked interested. Omar not so much.

"They're violent mother fuckers, the Ladinos. Treat the poor Mayan Indians like fuckin slaves. Don't pay them enough to shite and ship this stuff out in barrel loads for Gavin the bloody stockbroker and Portia the feckin model to suck down skinny lattes like they've gone out of style. Make you want to weep." The edge of his long beard twitched, his eyes popping out of his head.

"So, you're a bit of a traveller then?" asked Omar, more to have something to say than out of interest.

"Yeah. I've been working on the yachts for a good twenty years now. Done a bit of fishing here and there too, but mostly skippering. Worked on a divers' boat in Livingstone, in the north of Guatemala. Been a little bit of everywhere, I suppose."

Kinch sat up straight, his chair turned towards the traveller. "That must be great. To just wake up and not be sure where you're off to next. Christ, I'd love that."

"It's the best, man. It's in the blood I suppose. Come from Rathkeale originally, from a good travelling family, the Paavy kind. Pat, Pat Casey, and you?"

"Kieran Lynch. Everyone calls me Kinch."

"Why's that?"

"It's a character in *Ulysses* ... you know, Joyce and all that, and a knife blade too apparently. I've been playing him for the last few years on Bloomsday, hence the garb." He pointed to his worse-for-wear Latin Quarter hat. "So, my actor friends kind of stuck me with it."

"Right. Get it." The traveller stuck out a calloused hand. "Well, Kieran Lynch, my friends like to call me Paavy. I should be insulted but it gives them a laugh, so I don't mind. That's the ones on the boats – can get away with it when you're far from Irish shores but sounds a bit weird here. Like calling a black man a nigger in New York. You'd last about five fuckin seconds." He let go of Kinch's hand apparently without noticing the grimace etched across his forehead. "There's a lad on the boats, black as the ace, from Tobago, and we're always messin with the N word and he laughs himself stupid every time. The ocean's a great place for not giving a shite about all that nonsense. No borders, no barriers ... the only place for me."

Omar decided that this guy was hogging the conversation and interrupted. "I fancied myself as a travel journalist once. Imagined myself flitting around the world interviewing all and sundry, but then I met herself, and it just didn't happen. Have been to Poland a couple of times but that's about it."

The traveller looked at him aghast. "I hope she's worth it."

Kinch dropped his glass and spilled his shandy all over the floor. "Jesus, sorry." He ran to the bar and grabbed a cloth to clean it up.

Omar continued. "Flora ... yes ... she's worth it."

Pat looked him straight in the eye. "Are you happy?"

Omar thought for a second. "It's overrated, happiness. I know what life is ... at least I think I do. It's as easy to grasp that here as out there once you walk around with your eyes open."

Kinch put the cloth on the table between them. "Not in my book. I'm out of here as soon I can scrape a few bob together. Any advice for me, travelling man?"

The bearded man sat back and thought for a second. "Do you have a woman?"

Kinch looked surprised. "No ... definitely not."

"Then you're grand. But if you have, that might come back to haunt you one day." He suddenly looked unhappy, his eyes sad and heavy.

"There's a story there," said Omar. "I can smell it."

"There's always a story, for the good and the bad of it. Let's just say I'm back for a funeral, and I wish I wasn't." He fell silent.

Omar nodded. Kinch drank what was left of his shandy. They waited for him to continue, but he chose not to.

"Are you a believer then?" Omar asked sympathetically. "Can help."

"Ah no." he replied emphatically. "They're useful for blaming though."

"Who?" Omar looked confused.

The traveller winked, "The gods. What else are they good for?" He laughed into his pint.

"So, are you happy then? Omar asked.

The man laughed. "What do you think? Guess you're right, it's overrated."

Omar raised his cup to the sailor.

He nodded in return.

Kinch fiddled with his glass.

Matty returned and sat down beside them. "Jaysus, that was a long one."

They all laughed.

"Ye"re all looking a little sorry for yerselves. Has someone feckin died or somethin?"

Omar kicked Matty under the table.

"Wha? That feckin hurt."

Kinch smiled and hoisted his empty glass. "I raise a glass, gentlemen, empty and all, to our traveller here – Mr. Casey – a resourceful man who was driven to wander far and wide ... by curiosity, the Mother of Creation ... an inspiration to us all to get off our fat arses and get out there into the world and start living it."

"Too fuckin right." Matty clinked his pint of Guinness off Kinch's glass.

Matty's phone beeped a message. "Right, better get a move on. See you round, Omar. If you fancy a spot of poker some night, give us a buzz."

"No bother." Omar glanced at the clock on the wall. He wanted to make it home before 2:00. He was going to have to wake Flora up because he'd forgotten his key. He knew that Kinch lived miles away in Sandycove, so he decided to offer him a place to sleep on the couch downstairs. Flora wouldn't mind. She'd like the fact that he was an actor and an artist of a kind.

He looked at Kinch and the traveller. They were rabbiting on about

World Heritage Sights and remote places to visit. Omar interrupted. "Sorry, lads, but, Kinch, I'm going to head home. I know you live far away. If you like, you can kip on my couch. I'm sure my wife won't mind. It costs a fortune to get a taxi. The night buses are slow and full of dodgy people. What do you think?"

Kinch hesitated and looked at his watch. "Right ... I think I'll take my chances with the night bus thanks."

Omar felt somewhat dismissed by his young friend. He wanted to think it was just his own insecurity that drove him to these conclusions, but Kinch barely seemed to notice him in the presence of the traveller.

"So, where you off to next?" Kinch asked the traveller.

"Not that exciting. I'm taking the Ulysses ferry at 8:00 this morning. Have a job as a skipper for some posh Welsh bloke who wants me to take his family down the west coast of Portugal for a couple of weeks. Sure it's a few bob in the pocket." He stopped and looked at Kinch. "Actually, they're looking for someone to cater and do the scrub work, help keep the boat clean and all that. It pays well. Just for three weeks. Interested?"

Kinch opened his eyes wide. "Wow. Are you serious?"

"Nothing like acting on impulse is what I say. Brings you places you can't even imagine."

Omar, being the non-impulsive type, thought that this sounded way too sudden an invitation.

"Eight this morning. Jesus, that's impulse." Kinch sucked back the last of his shandy. "You know what? Yeah! Why the hell not?" Kinch stuck out his hand. "It's a deal."

Omar spoke up. "Are you mad? Sure, you're just coming down from one of the worst highs of your life. You don't know this fellow from Adam." He could hear his voice had risen several octaves.

Kinch glared at Omar.

"Well, I suppose if it's what you want." Omar realised his interest in this young man had gone one step too far. He wasn't Ruairí and he never would be. He stepped back and let them make their arrangements. *Could have been me, under different circumstances, I suppose.*

The barman picked up the empty glasses and cleaned off the tabletop. "Right, lads, time to get a move on. Need to get back to the wife before she divorces me."

Kinch was writing down the traveller's details.

"Sorry to interrupt, but under the circumstances, I suppose you'll be wanting to get home quicker?" Omar asked.

"Oh yeah, I guess so. I need to get back to Sandycove to get my stuff. The bus takes forever, and the taxi rank is always a mile bloody long. Shit." Kinch looked perplexed.

"Well, if you like, come back to my place anyway, and I'll call one from there. Know loads of taximen personally. Sure, Matty might even be free by then." Omar wanted to have one last chat with the young man to make he'd be ok after the evening's events

Kinch played with his hat for a second. He looked a little worried. "That makes some kind of sense, if you don't mind."

"Of course not."

The sailor picked up the ragged backpack beside him. It was stitched from top to bottom with stickers from all over the world.

"Well, I'll see you at the Ulysses, around a quarter past seven. Great stuff. Nice to meet you." He shook Omar's hand, picked up his bag and left.

Chapter 44

OMAR / KINCH

~ Ithaca ~

1:45 AM

WHAT DID THEY DISCUSS as they passed the grand stone edifice of Trinity College and proceeded onwards towards Long Lane?

The events of the day, the madness of religion, the politics of love, taxi queues and their curse upon the nation, loose women, looser men, a traveller's soul, the late-night pint and the lack of options, the way the Guinness ripped through the gut like a tornado after a hard night's drinking, yuppie wankers, the branding of a nation, strangers among us and us among them, absent fathers.

How did Kinch react to the aforementioned subjects?

Evasively, awkwardly.

How did Omar proceed following this reaction?

Cautiously, determinedly, with delicate precision. Sensing the aforementioned subject to be a vital influence on the boy's personal journey, he probed, commented on his own lost son, suggested that to delve deeper, to find a resolution, might bring some peace to a troubled mind. He spoke of his own father's death, the series of rumoured lovers that had filled his beautiful mother's life, of the last man, Roberto, her Italian co-star, with whom she'd run away, his father's desperation and self-imposed expiration. He counselled him to find the man in question and have it out with him because unanswered questions inject little darts of poison into a life until over time it withers away.

Did the young man agree with his suggestions?

He acknowledged his advice and suggested that he might well do something about it sooner rather than later. He hinted that his situation was not the norm but acknowledged that if he was to embark on a new departure, certain elements of the past needed cleaning up. He commented that he saw life as a giant labyrinth, with an entry and an exit point, and innumerable twists and turns, each of which required a solution simply to advance. It was the motion that mattered. It gave one the impression of progress when, in fact, the walls remained tall, dark, and identical, no matter which turn was taken.

Better to keep moving, to blur the images with the passage of time, as close to control as man could muster. And to Love — a moveable feast — as easily attached to one as another, a question of timing and convenience. Movement, therefore, within that sphere of experience, was also highly desirable.

Did Omar vary from his young acquaintance on such issues?

He agreed wholeheartedly with the labyrinthine surmise but differed in his ultimate belief that it was all in the way one looked at a thing. It wasn't the motion that gave the illusion of control, but the way in which a man chose to perceive his surroundings. He thought it not a bad idea at all to take a very long rest, and watch the world move around oneself. It reminded him of that building in Rome, the Pantheon. He once saw a documentary in which the two millennia that surrounded this august building were speeded up so that the giant pillared structure stood like a God — silent, majestic, masterful. The markets and cafés of Rome swirled around its feet. Faces, clothing, styles, transport, changed at warp speed, but the giant stone façade remained unchanged, calm, serene. It absorbed time through its granite skin and held it in its belly like an unborn child. Omar strived to be that solid, that silent within himself. As to love ... while he indeed concurred that there were any number of possibilities wherein love could rest its weary head, his preferences did not even lie completely towards one sex or the other. Love should be treated as a newly born infant, nurtured and fed. This showed a greater depth of purpose than to simply chuck the baby out with the bathwater and start again.

What direction did the two walkers take to arrive at Long Lane?

Walking at a similar pace, the younger of the two tread the footpath with a heavier, more determined step. Turning right from Dame Street into Great George's Street South, they passed several late-night bars, still heaving with determined revellers. Omar, a naturally cautious man, hesitated at each crossing light, while his younger friend launched straight ahead, glancing momentarily to make sure he was not to be unexpectedly transported to the next world by an overlarge vehicle. Slowing his pace somewhat for his hesitant acquaintance, Kinch was first to arrive at the corner of Kevin Street Lower. He turned right, forgetting that the knowledge of his eventual destination was something that should at least *appear* uncertain.

Passing the literary ark of the people, the Dublin Public Library, they continued towards New Bride Street, where the spires of St. Patrick's Cathedral rose like great metal spears into the night sky.

The older man hurried his pace, caught up with his acquaintance, and declared surprise at the young man's accurate knowledge of the lesser-known lanes and byways of Dublin. Kinch assured his companion that he and his actor colleagues frequently used Long Lane as a short and direct route between the legendary music establishment of Whelan's Bar and the primary residences of many of the aforementioned actors in the Blackpitts. Omar affirmed that, indeed, he was aware that it was an area frequented by those of an artistic nature, owing to its low rents and old-world character.

How did Omar enter his abode at 7 Long Lane?

He remembered that his house keys had probably resided on his kitchen table for the length of the day. Thus flummoxed, he turned to Kinch, who suggested that perhaps his wife might be in the habit of leaving a spare key — women being far more practical creatures — in a secret hiding place. Omar, certain it could not be so, indulged his young friend by raising the mounds of flowerpots that adorned the garden edge and looking underneath them. Lo and behold, there it was, shining like a golden star in the moonlight, a small key he knew immediately to be the key to his front door. He professed much surprise at the event but thanked his wife in her absence for her presence of mind.

What did Kinch perceive on entering the house?

That the spacious living room was largely unchanged since his prompt exit yesterday afternoon. The man in front of him made a signal, finger to lips, and closed the door gently behind them. Omar noticed a lit candle over the fireplace and moved towards the marble surround. He bent low to blow softly against the light. It flickered for a second and died. He then beckoned silently for Kinch to follow him down the corridor and moved left into the kitchen. He flicked a switch. A dim light filled the small room.

Kinch felt sick, claustrophobic, wished that he could reach over and open a window so that the sharp light of the moon would clear the space of his guilt. He glanced nervously at the stairs. She was a heavy sleeper, thank God. Needed to get out of there. Enough drama. But he did not. Instead, he sat at the glass table, and watched as the older man poked at the wood burner, threw some splinters into the dying embers to bring them to life.

What did the host do immediately upon entering the kitchen?

He rummaged through a selection of CD's that Flora had placed beside the hand-held stereo in the kitchen. Aware that the younger generation needed constant music accompaniment, he struggled to select something that he hoped would cast him in a favourable light with his younger companion. The choice at hand ran as follows: Victoria de Los Angeles "Sur les ailes du chant," Debussy "Clair de Lune", Chopin "Cello Sonata in G Minor", Bob Dylan "Blood on the Tracks", Christy Moore "Ride On", Damien Rice "O", This Mortal Coil "Song to the Siren", and, much to Omar's extreme mortification, Westlife "Greatest Hits", which he promptly dropped behind the stereo lest he be accused of having purchased such an item. Although inclined towards Dylan and This Mortal Coil, he reckoned that Damien Rice would strike a more youthful and trendier note. Not sure how long Kinch would be keeping him company, he forwarded the disc to his favourite song, "I remember", to strike the best possible opening note.

How did Kinch react to the choice of music?

Not at all, which Omar took as passive encouragement, aware that a young man of Kinch's musical interest would be incapable of refraining from derisive comment if the offending accompaniment was not to his taste.

What beverage did the host propose his guest?

A Moroccan tea known locally as the du Hammam, a relaxing blend of green tea, rose petals, green date, and red fruits — something his mother had been in the habit of drinking before going to bed. The young man accepted, provided he could be given the number of the taxi to arrange transport to his house in Sandycove. The host gladly obliged, accessed the drawer of the wooden dresser, and searched for approximately twenty seconds before he spotted two cards belonging to taximen with whom he was well acquainted. He passed the cards to his guest, who called them posthaste, and spoke in a most hurried manner, urging the taximan, Bernard Carr — an old schoolfriend of Omar's — to arrive as quickly as possible.

What did the host discuss with his guest while they waited for the taxi to arrive?

He proposed a theory that he had been working on privately for quite a while. The fluxes of history being as they were, it was his observance that two strong waves of change were converging towards each other, the first being the advent of climate change and the second, the growing strength of Islam and its influence on the world, whether extremist or pacifist. It suited Planet Earth better if human society was, by its very nature, conformist, conservationist, minimalist, and based on the benefit of the ummah or the group at large, and not the individual. Unfortunately, it was when the individual was allowed to break free, apply his free will, and behave largely as he chose, that greed became the driving force and consumption its offspring, thus leading to the cannibalism of the host organism.

So, in brief, Omar believed — much to his dismay — that the restoration of the order of nature and the natural conditions by which humans could optimally live on this earth, required, at this point in time, the conformist mentality of Islam (although preferably not the radical nature of some of its advocates). His biggest fear was that while conformism would save the planet, the forced application of it by dogma or dictator – not simply Islamic — would herd humanity into a slaughterhouse of its own making. This was the inevitability that this century would lay out before us for the good or the bad of it unless we were all wiped out by a deadly virus, in which case Mother Nature would have her revenge and who would blame her? Not, he stressed, that his theory was based on any inherent loyalty to the Islamic belief system; it was simply the pragmatic conclusion of a scientifically minded man who had read enough to know what was what.

How did Kinch react to such a dramatic suggestion?

He respectfully declined to agree. Kinch was a believer in the chaos theory. As he saw it, although certain cycles of activity seemed to emerge over a long period of time, the random nature of events meant that each of these cycles differed in key ways, thus making accurate predictions of future events impossible. He did acknowledge that systems that exhibit mathematical chaos are deterministic and thus orderly in some sense. It was not a question of complete disorder — there was definitely an unexplainable element to the Universe, whether referred to as God or, for the more psychologically minded, the collective unconscious (Kinch's personal favourite) — but once the chaotic nature of existence was acknowledged, predictability was a futile exercise. Thus, carpe diem, because the day is all there is.

Did the host acknowledge the difference of opinion gracefully?

Most definitely.

What fragmented thoughts crossed Omar's mind as Kinch continued to elaborate on his premise?

The unbridled enthusiasm of youth. The vast and impossible conundrum of the Universe. His wife's lack of interest in all things scientific and questioning. By contrast, her unfettered need for sensual pleasure, which she seemed to find everywhere except in her own home. The overemphasis placed on the decline of the body, as opposed to the growth of wisdom and intellect — a most troubling tendency.

Had he given in to the quest for eternal youth?

Only so far as travelling by foot whenever possible to avoid using the car and attending a weekly soccer session with his journalistic colleagues on the grounds of UCD.

What caused Omar to leave the room posthaste?

A sudden explosive wave through his digestive system, indicating an immediate need to relieve himself.

How did Kinch react?

He assured him that he was perfectly comfortable and picked up the February edition of *National Geographic*, which ran as follows: "Han Dynasty", "Polar Bears", "Phoenix Islands", "Lost Inca Outpost", "Fastest Monkeys", "Carbon Cycle". Omar hoped that would keep him happy and occupied. Damien Rice's "Eskimo" played a melodious accompaniment to his literary explorations.

Did Omar peruse the pile of reading accompaniment while in the lavatory?

No, he concentrated on passing the Guinness-fuelled movement. It stuck to his guts like glue. Although not wanting to reawaken the blinding pain of the bleeding pile he had suffered the week before, he strained with caution, aware that his guest awaited him. He eyed the shelf beside him for the tube of Scheriproct that he, no doubt, would have to make use of in the morning. Instead, his eye fell on a blue plastic wrapper, the brand DUREX clearly marked near the torn edge. He knew what that meant, and although he was well aware that Flora was known to "entertain" while he was out at work, he couldn't bear to have the hard evidence laid out before him. He searched for the paper roll — to no avail. Instead, he reached for the May edition of *Time* and tore off the front page. George Bush's big head stared out at Omar. He glanced at the title, "MOMENT OF TRUTH: Does the president who led us into Iraq know how to lead us out?" For once he decided that an intellectual response was not appropriate and ran the page the length of his arse. This brought him considerable satisfaction.

What sight greeted Omar on the return to his kitchen?

A vacant seat, the pages of the article on speedy monkeys open on the table, and a handwritten note propped against the still-full mug of tea. The Cd had been changed to "The Song to the Siren," a personal favourite. Disappointed that the taxi had clearly arrived in his absence, he picked up the note, expecting a brief thanks for his hospitality.

"Sorry Omar, I had to run. I know I'm a bloody coward, but I have something I have to tell you. I was too chicken to tell you to your face. I slept with your wife — several times. I know this will come as a complete shock. Honestly, I'm sorry! Please don't take it out on her. With all the talk of clearing out the messes from the past and starting again, I just felt it was only right you should know. If you want to beat the shite out of me, I will be at the Ulysses ferry on the Dublin Docks at 7:15 AM. Probably not coming back. Sorry again!! Kinch."

The respondent felt like he'd been hit in the guts with a hammer. Parallel waves of sadness and anger crashed within Omar like orchestral symbols. This Mortal Coil sang mournfully in the background. He stabbed the stop button. His life was absurd enough without such an accompaniment.

What reactions did he immediately consider against both parties?

Murder — messy and resulting in more harm to his person than satisfaction achieved; a proper beating inflicted on both parties — same as above; divorce — upheaval on a scale that he was not prepared to accept; emotional retribution, chuck her out on her ear temporarily and threaten divorce even though his intentions lay elsewhere — oddly appealing; immediate destruction of her favourite thing, her violin — also very appealing but not in his nature to destroy beautiful things.

What did he find himself doing immediately after these reflections?

Climbing the stairs towards the offending party. He observed her as she slept, the curves of her body wrapped around a white cotton sheet, her long hair a fluid wave sweeping across the sheets like a river flowing through sunlight. Accepting the inevitability of forgiveness, he removed his trousers and placed them on the chair to the left side of the bed. His posterior perched on the side of the bed, he removed his right sock, then his left, unbuttoned his shirt, and as always, climbed into bed, Dunnes white jocks forming the ever-appropriate barrier between him and behaviour no longer deemed acceptable by the woman he'd married. Despite such limitations, he bent to observe her in slumber. Her skin was pale, translucent. Her lashes long and dark. He kissed the soft skin of her haunches. He lay with his left side against her rump, the weight of the day dragging him slowly into sleep. Barely conscious of his surroundings, he felt her hand move towards him. She laid it cautiously on his bare skin, her fingers moving as gently as the wings of a moth.

Did such unexpected intimacy surprise him?

Yes.

How did he respond?

He allowed her hand to rest itself against him and followed his subconscious into the dark forgetfulness of sleep.

CHAPTER 45

KINCH

2:30 AM

THE SEVEN-POINTED SHAPE of the Plough hung low in the shimmering night sky. Although he found himself looking up far less these days, Kinch always looked for it when he thought to. He asked the taxi driver to wait outside Monsignor Reidy's presbytery. It was going to cost him a fortune, but he couldn't get on the boat in the morning without putting a shape to the anger that had festered within him throughout his childhood. He planned to get away and stay away. He didn't want any dormant grievances dragging him back.

He climbed the steps in front of the red-brick building and hesitated under the stone arch of the front door. A series of images flashed through his brain: his mother alone and crying when they were evicted from their home in Dun Laoghaire; Paddy Maloney, the red-haired boy in primary school who referred to Kinch as "the bastard"; receiving his first communion from the man his mother had just revealed to be his father and hoping to be noticed, to no avail; numerous visits to the back of the Monsignor's Sunday mass; many letters sent to this very house with no response. He thought he had learned how to accept it – the rejections, the hypocrisy, the lack of love – but hearing the man's voice earlier in the day was enough to remind him that certain things can never be forgotten.

He pushed the large doorbell and waited.

Silence. Then the scurrying of feet. The door opened slowly. A middle-aged, honey-haired woman stuck her head around the door and squinted at him suspiciously.

"Yes? What on earth?"

"Hello, sorry to bother you so late, but ... I need to see the Monsignor. Tell him it's Kieran."

She looked more than a little surprised. "Excuse me, but who? I'm afraid it would be impossible to wake the Monsignor at this time. He has a very busy schedule tomorrow."

"I can assure you, Miss, he would want you to wake him. If I'm wrong, you can call the Guards directly and have me dragged off and incarcerated. Please, it really is urgent."

She stared at him carefully. "Well, all right, but God help you, son, if this is some kind of messing you're up to. Just wait there." She put the door on the latch and shuffled up the stairs.

Kinch chewed on his fingernails. The taximan had put his seat back and was grabbing the chance for a quick nap.

The door opened. The housekeeper stood wrapped in a pink dressing gown. She smiled warmly although clearly puzzled by this unexpected development in the middle of the night. "Follow me, dear." They walked down a long corridor and into a room on the right. "Just wait right here and the Monsignor will be down to you in a second. Would you like a cup of tea and a biscuit?"

"Thanks a lot, but I'd hate to keep you up any longer. I'm grand, thanks."

"Don't worry about that. I'm making one for himself, so I'll throw in an extra bag for you." She winked and disappeared through a door at the end of the corridor.

Kinch sat down in the corner of the large, red velvet couch and poked at the copies of *Reality* and *The Messenger* that sat on the table in front of him. His right foot beat a fast rhythm on the oak floorboards. He could hear shuffling on the stairs. He looked up and saw a pair of legs slowly descending the staircase. He wished more than anything in the world that he could suck the life out of a fag to give him strength, but, sure, the whole country was a smoke-free zone now—worse, this was one of God's own gaffs.

A haggard face appeared in the doorway. Kinch had seen the man many times, mostly from a distance, but tonight in his dressing gown he looked frail, aged.

"So, Kieran. I'm glad you came." The Monsignor spoke softly. "Do you normally pay visits in the middle of the night?" It was not an accusation, merely a gentle attempt to break the ice.

"Not usually. I'm leaving the country a bit later this morning, and I've a funny feeling I might not be back for a while, so I thought, maybe ..."

"You were right – to come. I'm glad."

Kinch stood up, to be on the same level as the large man standing in the doorway. The space between them felt like an unbridgeable valley, a dense and undiscovered jungle.

A silver tray full of goodies appeared, carried by the lady in pink. "There ye are now. A pot of tea and a plate of biccies. Just the trick to keep ye awake." She set it on the table.

"That's great, Maggie, thanks. You head off to bed now. We're grand."

"No bother then. Enjoy yer chat. Goodnight." She tottered up the stairs.

The Monsignor moved towards Kinch and sat on the couch at the other side of the table. "Sit down now, lad. Grab a cup of tea."

"I don't know what the hell I'm doing here really." Kinch suddenly felt very awkward. He sat a couple of feet away from the man whose absence had been a looming anger throughout his life. He was no longer sure it would make him feel better to try to understand.

"I suppose you'd like me to answer some questions ... about your mother and me." Reidy's grey eyes looked straight at Kinch.

He felt bolted to the chair even though every instinct in his body screamed at him to get the fuck out of there.

"That'd be a start." Kinch picked up the mug of tea, sat back and waited.

The older man sat on the edge of the couch and stirred a teaspoon of sugar into his tea. "I know it'll be hard for someone of your age to understand, but it was such a different country in the early eighties, when you were born."

"Ah yes, the good ol Celtic Tiger and how it's changed us all for the better. One thing that'll never change is human nature, so you won't get away that easily," replied Kinch.

The older man raised his eyebrows. "I loved her you know, your mother."

"Really?" Kinch could feel the anger build inside him.

"We're all products of our time," continued the Monsignor.

"Then I should be preening around the Financial Centre in a pinstripe with a Beamer stuck to my arse. Not everyone falls prey to the inevitable."

Reidy sighed. "Then you're a better man than I am."

"She trusted you and you used her, chucked her out like a dirty dishcloth when you were finished with her."

"It wasn't like that. Your mother and I, we spent all our time around each other. Who can explain these things really? It grew into something it shouldn't have. I take full responsibility. I was weak, young and, to be honest, we just needed each other then."

"And she didn't need you after?" Kinch struggled to retain a veneer of control, his voice stretched wire-thin.

"Of course, of course she did, but I was, still am, a man in an important position. Back then it was just after the pope's visit. What a priest had to say still mattered somehow. It's all changed now. If it was now, maybe ...?"

"Maybe you'd have left your comfortably protected life and lived like an ordinary man raising your family?" Kinch wanted to hit him. "Give me a break."

"It's not something you'll ever understand. It's a calling and you don't just walk away."

That was it. Kinch could no longer hold it in. "But it's ok to walk away from the woman you supposedly love and your son, and leave them in the shits, excuse my French. Do you fucking know we were evicted from two houses? My mother worked her arse off, but she suffered from depression – I wonder why? I was only a boy. I used to have to cook and clean and look after her. She was out of it, sometimes months at a time. Don't get me wrong. I don't blame her. She loved the hell out of me. I blame the person who put her in that state. Fucking you. I fucking blame you with your holier-than-thou, I'm-God's-representative-on-earth crap. Jesus never said you guys had to be celibate, he never said a bad word against a gay person, and for that matter I can't remember a single bloody passage from the Bible where bloody condoms are an issue. It's some Roman Emperor who came up with all that shite. Not that ye're all bad, but, man, if you're going to fuck up your family, your bloody family, not the holy family or the royal bloody family but your own family, at least check out the veracity behind the shite you spout daily." Kinch was standing, bent over the table, his whole body arched towards the older man, who sat silently, his eyes wide and staring.

"I'm sorry, son."

"Don't fucking call me *son*. You have no bloody right. I touched you ... on my Communion Day. I wanted you to smile, to see me, whisper something, touch me back, any little gesture to show you gave a damn. You shook my hand away, shook it away and moved onto the next boy, without even a smile." Kinch could feel the tears begin to pour down his face. "You fucking shook me off, like I was a beggar, or a leper. FOR FUCK's SAKE!" His whole body shook.

The Monsignor stood, moved to embrace him. Kinch pulled away, ran to the fireplace, and leant on the marble surround. He caught a glimpse of himself in the mirror above the fireplace. His face was red and puffed up, his eyes burning. The Monsignor stood behind him, ashen and tired looking.

"I don't blame you being so angry after all this time. I just hoped that maybe ... maybe it's not too late. It's hard to break away from all that you know. I entered the seminary when I was fifteen. It was impossible for me to understand that there might have been other options. There always was only one option for me."

Kinch narrowed his eyes. "Ah, how shameless – the way these mortals blame the gods. From us alone they say come all their miseries, yes, but they themselves with their own reckless ways compound their pains beyond their proper share."

"Sorry?"

"Homer, *The Odyssey*. Your precious Bible isn't the only book out there, you know."

"How learned of you." The Monsignor took a deep breath. "I don't know, Kieran. It's a bloody mess, but all I can offer now is to make it up to you, with what little time is left."

Kinch laughed. "Well, we have about three hours and then I'm on a boat."

"I meant my time. I don't have much time."

"Oh yeah, the cancer." Kinch felt bad for sounding so casual, but he wanted to hurt this man as much as he had hurt him.

"I won't be in this life much longer. They've given me about six months."

"I suppose we should hug now and declare how happy we are that we've finally found each other. Well, tough shit. That's not my style. If you need me to forgive you so St. Peter doesn't stop you at the pearly gates, you're on a loser."

Reidy smiled weakly. "To be honest, I'd just like to know you a little before I'm gone."

"Well, I wouldn't call this the best timing in the world," replied Kinch.

The Monsignor moved closer to him. "It's never a good time for something this complicated."

"You got that right." He hesitated. "Listen – I'll think about it."

"Ok." The Monsignor sounded disappointed.

Kinch took a pen from his inside pocket and tore off a corner of *The Messenger* magazine. He scribbled on the paper and handed it to Reidy. "My email."

He smiled briefly. "Right."

Kinch picked up his hat. "I'd better go. The bloody taxi's going to cost me a fortune." They both stood awkwardly, three feet of space between them, a muscular barrier that Kinch was far from ready to surmount. "Ok. I'll see you ... maybe."

The Monsignor nodded.

They walked in silence to the front door.

The older man undid a complicated series of locks. "It's like Fort Knox in here." The edge of a smile remained on the corner of his mouth, and Kinch smiled back, inside himself, where it couldn't be seen.

Chapter 46

BLÁITHÍN

2:30 AM

A LONE FOX RAN ACROSS the grass in front of Bláithín. *So beautiful. Hidden away out of the waking world.*

The stars were unusually clear tonight. Despite the glow from the city, Bláithín could make out the luminous cloud of the Milky Way.

Falling stars fascinated her. She often lay on her back counting the August Perseids. Her record was twenty-six in a thirty-minute period. *No Tears of San Lorenzo in June but you never know.*

She lay in the middle of the perfectly manicured lawns of Kenmare Heights. Her parent's garden, with its angular privet hedges, trimmed flowerbeds, and lawns like putting greens, was never a place a child could run wild. When she was about ten years old and desperate to mark it with her own brand of creativity, she mapped out a small nature trail, created paths through the rockery, the flower beds, and the wooded area at the back of her house. She dug holes and planted bamboo sticks with the numbers of the trail. When she presented her work of inventive genius to her mother, the woman had a conniption fit, accused her of destroying hundreds of pounds worth of shrubbery, and locked her away in her bedroom for a week.

Sure, was it any wonder she was so fucked up?

The ground beneath her was hard as a slab of cement. Unusually dry weather for Ireland at any time of the year. She glanced up at her parents' bedroom window. The light was out. Feeling less brave now than on her long journey out on the night bus, she thought about turning around, but she was sure there was no bus back, and taxis cost a bloody fortune. Anyway, for some reason, this day had brought her to a place where resolutions were being sought and found. She rang the doorbell even though the front door key nestled cosily in her jeans pocket. It would give her an excuse to wake them. The lights went on in the room upstairs. She glanced at her reflection in the side window. Her blue eyes were tired, her jaw clenched and tense. She spoke to herself out loud (a habit of years): "Don't let him fuck with you. Sort it out. Now!"

The alarm was switched off, and the door opened. Her mother stood in the doorway, dressed in a nightgown of red silk, her hair in rollers. "Oh my God, Bláithín. Your father has been looking for you everywhere. Where the hell were you?"

Bláithín stepped through the door. "Where's Dad? I need to speak to him."

Her mother shut the door. "He's fast asleep. He has a press conference first thing in the morning. I think there's been enough drama for one day. Just go to bed, and you can talk to him tomorrow evening."

"Too late, I'm afraid. It's now or never."

Her mother threw her eyebrows to the sky. "Ever with the dramatic ultimatums. I don't think so, young lady. You have us run ragged."

Two pairs of slippered feet appeared at the top of the stairs. Her sisters sat on the top steps, eager for a bit of family theatrics.

"She's been snorting again, Mum. Look at her nose. It's raw red." Rachel spoke with a slight sneer. Gráinne laughed.

"Have you?" asked her mother.

"It doesn't matter. I'm finished with that, but I need to see Dad. DAD. DAD!" She shouted at the top of her voice. Her mother tried to put her hand over her daughter's mouth, her two sisters purring with laughter like preening cats.

"She's high as a kite, Mum. Time to lock her up again, I reckon." Gráinne dug Rachel in the ribs. They stood to the back as their sleepy father walked past them and down the stairs.

"Dad, Bláith's high again," said Gráinne with a big smile on her face.

Bernard O'Leary pushed back the shock of white hair from his eyes. "Jesus, Bláithín, I've had it with your drama. Where the hell did you run off to? Nigel ran the length and breadth of Dublin looking for you."

"It doesn't matter where I went to. It's where I'm going that matters."

She looked him straight in the eye, determined not to be talked down to.

"What? Where?" Fionnúla O'Leary looked at her husband with the look of indignant confusion that she had mastered over the years of fighting with her daughter.

"Out of this family if it's the only bloody way I can survive. I can't do this anymore."

"Daddy, she's an ungrateful tart. Kick her out for once and for all." Gráinne's voice was shrill and clear.

Her father's milky blue eyes were unmoving. "There's no need for that, is there Bláithín?"

"Go on Daddy," Gráinne goaded. "Stand up to her, for God's sake. She's always causing hell in this family. You don't deserve that."

Bláithín couldn't bear the sound of her sister's jealousy. It had surrounded her whole life like a cloud of poisonous gas. She couldn't help it if her father had loved her the most. Despite their disagreements, she knew deep down that he saw himself in her strength. That same strength had taken her places he refused to recognise.

"Dad, I just want to tell you that I love you, not in the snivelling, lick-arsy way those two go on with, but I do."

"Oh, boo hoo. Get out the bloody hankies." Rachel rubbed her eyes mockingly.

"Shut up, Rachel!" Bernard O'Leary's voice was loud and clear.

Bláithín smiled at her sister. "But it doesn't matter anymore because I don't respect you. There's no reason to go into the reasons why. We all know those."

Her father spoke slowly. "I'd be very careful what you say next, Bláithín."

She could feel the fear creep up her spine like a tarantula, but she kept going. "I will guarantee you, Dad, one of these days your lies will catch up with you, and it won't be those two standing by your side when you realise your mistakes." She pointed at her sisters. "That day, call me and I'll be there, but not before."

"You ungrateful little bitch." Fionnúla O'Leary slapped her daughter across the face.

Bláithín winced, fought back the well of tears, and looked at her mother with a look of composed defiance.

"Fionnúla, for God's sake." Her father silenced her mother with a withering glance. He turned to fix a hard stare on Bláithín. "Are you sure this is how you feel?" His voice was cold, unyielding.

"Yes."

"So young and so cruel. It's impressive," replied Bernard O'Leary.

"Young and honest," replied Bláithín.

"Well, Ms. Holier-Than-Thou. This is the last time you darken this doorstep. I have two daughters now, and God knows that's enough. Your mother is right. You are an ungrateful little bitch and I rue the day I brought you into this world to cause me and your mother such heartache. Well, you have it your way in the end, and don't think you'll get a penny out of us either. You're on your own, Bláithín. I hope you like it." He walked to the door and opened it.

Her mother stood silently watching, her hand to her mouth.

Gráinne and Rachel stood smiling at the top of the stairs.

Bláithín glanced at her family a last time before walking out the door. It shook with violence behind her.

As she descended the steps, a small star ripped across the sky.

Bláithín spoke quietly into the warm night air, "One."

CHAPTER 47

FLORA

~ Penelope ~

∞

ONCE I BREATHED I WAS and now I knew I had to keep going despite the odds wrapped around me like a marauding snake squeezing my life into a tube of space travel towards something anything movement keep up the pace once I listened to the blur of speed that could engulf me in a cloud of forgetfulness a slow seeping green haze of dull contentment a teardrop of hope an icicle of air kissing my bottom like that as though everything were normal between us he didn't know how to fill me up so I could swim through it all he just pushed and panted until his big red roundness lost itself in the folds of my need seeped within me like a crawling disease ridden by his lust lost to me he was in a sea of men who claimed my body like a citadel breached birth it was purest horror to see my baby empty of life giving me nothing to show for the pain of expectation once I was full with anger at a God who could give me hope only to take it away so cruelly I never gave birth again and never would allow him to touch me because he had injected me with this pain although I knew it was not his fault I could no longer feel like a woman in his hands I became a failed mother how I wished he could hold me in this moment of failed womanhood meant other things to me now like wet burning lips embracing moments of hard male skin moving within me the sweet-smelling softness of his young hands on my breasts devouring me with his touch moving with his long limbs wrapped around me until I open like a flower petal sucking up the air to stay alive is all that matters at the end of the day once I left Poland and felt free to reinvent myself in the world I had known I was a problem to my family my strength of will had broken rules spoken and unspoken like that Russian who came to stay with my father who had no idea his guest would sneak into my room late at night with his breath a reek of vodka and his prick as large as a cactus and twice as sharp it cut into my cunt like blunt glass a dull pain like monthly pressures and pints of blood waiting to explode out of me like a slaughtered cow women might as well be to half those brutes who stick it inside you without a word of thanks the effort of touching me became too much for Omar eventually he forgot how in hell is a woman supposed to last a life with a want in her the size of an ocean tell me that there is a solution to a lustless marriage and I'll call you a liar is what he is with his skulking around the brothels of Dublin in the name of journalism he touches them his skin smells unfamiliar after a woman always knows though she may choose to deny it not that I'm a saint wouldn't put up with his lack of warmth drove me into other arms where I could feel myself explode again into a life I can't deny that he was handsome when I met him with his shock of black hair and olive skin like Karim in The Dark Seed of Damascus strikes only fear in the hearts of people now after them flinging themselves out of those tower windows like dying birds in the burning heat of hell is where they'll end up good riddance to the evil bastards everywhere nowadays taking advantage of the weaknesses of people to fight and for what but their own greed and power is all that matters to them is nothing in the end there will be nothing it frightens them to think of that they kill to stop the fear once is all there's no point in worrying about all this politics he goes on about in that paper of his they all treat him like he's an eejit to care what they think with their shovelling blow up their nostrils like it's the giver of everlasting life is something I would never not want to feel the danger in the nowness of it all the pens of man have tried to tie our hot passions into a pretty pink bow is a thing I hate the way some of them expect you to lie down and take it without a word yes I want to scream fuck me FUCK ME until they come in rivers inside me or on top of me or behind me I don't care they can hold me after curled up behind me like the words of a love song an old sweet song is something I never tire of Nat King Cole's velvet voice when I fall in love it will be forever if forever is a day then there's some truth in it that love is a fickle but necessary friend is all that Omar is to me now friendship may be the best kind of love after all the hump and grind is nothing but the sweat on the skin deep beneath the outer layers lies the ugliness that only a friend can love his heavy breath and peculiar ways but he looks after me with a soft hand and a blind eye to my darker side can't be easy for a man to handle after the want has been exorcised out of him once there's a need for more all the same why doesn't he leave me and be done with it would at least be an end if an end were what I wanted to keep going is the truth of it is to battle on makes more sense is not what we are made for sucking in air without a thought as to why we do we just do within the silence around me lie too many questions unanswered they should stay like music in the air with no need of an answer like a singing orchestra in the forest of the night lips touch air and shape it into the colour of the waves the crashing bliss of water upon the skin like blue silence broken by the delicate whistle of the wind against the molten earth blown into the sky like a dancing nymph swirling upwards gushing sliding through the air like rubbish blowing through the city streets late in the vacant hollow of the night when the lights flicker and glow like fireflies in a lost jungle of wet green light and the night and the light of the radio as it asks me to fill the silence once I'll flick the switch and click soft now not to wake him and bend close to him softly just to stop the questions dissolve into the sound like a soft drum beating once *badum*.

RESOURCES

INCLUDING
CAST OF CHARACTERS
AND
SOUNDTRACK

Cast of Characters

(As they appear)

In order to make your reading of my well-populated novel clearer, I have decided to list all 73 of the characters in the order in which they appear. My excuse for taxing your character limitations is that in order to shadow Joyce's *Ulysses,* which contained 84 characters, I need a world just as complete.

1. *Omar Wilde:* 40-year-old half Irish, half Egyptian. Journalist.
2. *Flora Wilde:* 38-year-old Polish violin player. Wife of Omar. Lover of Kinch.
3. *Ruairí Wilde* – Omar and Flora's child who died at birth.
4. *Willy Farrell:* Editor of the *Irish Independent.*
5. *Hanan Hussein:* An Irish born Trinity student of Lebanese origin, and Kinch's best-friend.
6. *Khaled Hussein:* Hanan's fanatical Islamic extremist teenage brother.
7. *Mohammed Hussein:* Hanan and Khaled's Lebanese-born father.
8. *Kiaran James Lynch* (Kinch): 22-year-old actor playing *Stephen Dedalus*
9. *Bláithín O'Leary:* 24-year-old actress playing *Molly Bloom*
10. *Gerry Deasy:* Musician and friend of Kinch's from Cork.
11. *John:* Joyce Museum caretaker
12. *Philip Lacey:* Art Empresario
13. *Julian Guinness*: Events Manager
14. *Paul Mullens* (Fiddler): Street Artist

15. *Sarah:* Hanan's girlfriend
16. *Will, Portia, Naria, Indira:* Trinity students
17. *Matt Phelan:* Creator of 'Celtic Waters'. Worked with Flora in the past. Suspected by all to be her lover.
18. *Mick:* Newspaper seller
19. *Kitty:* Pregnant girl in post office.
20. *Monsignor Reidy:* Mary Nolan, Kinch's Mother was his housekeeper.
21. *Dick Cowen:* Unscrupulous journalist in the *Irish Independent.*
22. *Mark Jameson:* Nice guy journalist in the *Irish Independent.*
23. *Bertie Macken:* Deputy Editor, *Irish Independent.*
24. *Eileen: Irish Independent* Accountant.
25. *Kate:* Female Journalist in the *Irish Independent.*
26. *Bernard O'Leary:* Bláithín's Father, the Fiana Fáil Minister for Justice.
27. *Nigel Murray:* Bernard O'Leary's Assistant.
28. *Fionnúla O'Leary:* Bláithín's Mother.
29. *Gráinne & Rachel O'Leary:* Bláithín's sisters.
30. *Sandra Michael Sampson:* A Nigerian asylum seeker.
31. *Father Ogunbosola:* A Nigerian Catholic Priest
32. *Efie (9) & Orisa (6) Michael Sampson:* Sandra's daughters.
33. *Guarda Sheila Kelly:* A female guarda in Pearse Street Guarda Station.
34. *Breda Keane:* Old friend of Omar's Mother. Mother of Annie, Omar's old girlfriend.
35. *Zaria Sha'rawi:* Omar's Mother, a professional Opera singer from Egypt known as *the Egyptian Songbird*. She ran away to Ireland in 1962 and was discovered by Omar's father, John Wilde, singing in a bar. He promoted her and turned her into an operatic success. She ran away with a co-star and abandoned him and Omar.

36. *John Wilde:* Arts Promoter who promoted Omar's mother to success. He adored her but controlled her, so she ran away with her co-star. John committed suicide when Omar was 20 years old.
37. *John Cronin:* An actor playing the part of a blind man in the streets of Dublin.
38. *John Fenton:* Bernard O'Leary's Lawyer.
39. *Maria Vleski:* Romanian woman who begs in the street with her child.
40. *Margaret Kenny:* The real wife of the American Ambassador.
41. *John McCluskey:* Caretaker of Dunsink Observatory.
42. *Des O'Shea:* The Barman in Wynn's Hotel.
43. *Garda Seán Boylan:* The young country Garda who drives Quixote to Mountjoy.
44. *Abdullah Al-Khasi:* The man Khaled meets at the Camden Street Mosque.
45. *Juanma Gonzales:* Kinch's Spanish guitar teacher.
46. *The Taoiseach, Bertie Ahern:* The then prime minister of Ireland.
47. *Brian Ward:* Teenager in Ballymun who robs people from his bicycle to get money for his sick Mother's operation.
48. *Ambassador James C. Kenny:* The real American Ambassador at the time.
49. *Lynnia Mohan & Mona Kelly:* Two contestants in the Miss Ireland Dublin Regionals competition.
50. *Pat:* Barman in the Ormonde Hotel.
51. *Red:* boy in lift who robs the handbags.
52. *Tommo:* other boy in lift in Ballymun flats.
53. *Conor Mullens:* Paul's drug dealer brother.
54. *Eddie O'Sullivan* (Caoch): Notorious brother of the South Kerry Sinn Féin TD, Martin O'Sullivan. He owns a dog called Pinch.

55. *Itor Echeverria:* The basque friend of O'Sullivan.
56. *Gretta:* Black *au pair* girl on the beach.
57. Flora's Mother and Father
58. *Royston Brady:* The then Lord Mayor of Dublin.
59. V: *Abu bin al-Shibh,* Commanding Officer, Egyptian al-Jihad. One of the sandwichmen from the bridge.
60. *Bernie Farrell:* Ex – Ira man, gangster, and owner of Bordello's strip club.
61. *Diana Flaunt, Madam Sin:* the manager of a brothel on Dublin's Quays and an ex-hooker (based on a real woman called Marie Bridgeman)
62. *Goldy:* Security man on the door of Bordello's strip club
63. *Sila:* Stripper in Bordello's.
64. *Garda Coffey*
65. *Garda Fox*
66. The Junky
67. *Betty*
68. *Mary*
69. *Mimi*
70. *Jimmy:* Dreadhaired friend of Kinch's
71. *Matty Maher:* The Cabman.
72. *Christie:* The Barman, Mulligans.
73. *Pat Casey:* THE TRAVELLER, Kinch and Omar meet in Mulligan's.

Soundtrack

How We Mortals BLAME THE GODS

DUBLIN IS A CITY OF MUSIC, and just like Joyce, I felt it could only come properly alive by framing the story in the sounds of the city. I myself cannot imagine life without a permanent soundtrack. Music is everywhere in the streets, cafés, pubs, homes, ears and imaginations of Irish people. Therefore, I decided to embed a soundtrack into my novel. I have tried both to reflect the music I was hearing all over Dublin at that time, as well as music I consider appropriate to the theme. I hope more than anything that some of these works will be a reflection of the incredible wealth of musical talent that our poetic island has to offer. The non-Irish pieces are personal favourites and appropriate to the scene at hand. I invite anyone who wants the full experience to download the tracks on their music providers and play them while reading the appropriate scene. If you have Spotify, the songlist has already been put together for you and is at this location online.

https://open.spotify.com/playlist/5p0qFxaP66bn6uC77NP3cM?si=94a1c318a8ff47d9

On the next page is a printed soundtrack list.

CHAPTER 4: Christy Moore - *The Rocky Road to Dublin*

CHAPTER 5: Afro Celt Sound System (With Sinéad 'O Connor) - *Release*

CHAPTER 10: Victoria de Los Angeles - *The Irish Lullaby*

CHAPTER 11: U2 - *11 O Clock Tick Tock*

CHAPTER 12: Vaughan Williams - *The Lark Ascending*

CHAPTER 15: Edward Elgar - *Salut d'Amour*

CHAPTER 18: Bell X One - *Beautiful Madness*

CHAPTER 21: The Corrs - *Black is the Colour*

CHAPTER 21: The Frames - *Fake*

CHAPTER 22: Ronan Keating – *Father and Son*

CHAPTER 23: Snow Patrol - *Run*

CHAPTER 24: Jeff Buckley - *Halelujah*

CHAPTER 25: Rory Gallagher - *What's Going On?*

CHAPTER 25: The Frames – *Seven Day Mile*

CHAPTER 27: PJ Harvey – *Sheila Na Gig*

CHAPTER 29: Clannad – *I Will Find You*

CHAPTER 32: Blumenlied – *Gustav Lange*

CHAPTER 33: Van Morrison – *TB Sheets*

CHAPTER 35: Radiohead – *Where I End and You Begin*

CHAPTER 36: Léo Delibes - *The Flower Duet (Lakme)*

CHAPTER 37: LOW - *Cue the Strings*

CHAPTER 37: LOW - *Silver Rider*

CHAPTER 39: LOW – *Monkey*

CHAPTER 40: Jaques Brel – *Port of Amsterdam*

CHAPTER 44: Damien Rice - *I Remember*

CHAPTER 44: Damien Rice – *Eskimo*

CHAPTER 44: This Mortal Coil – *Song to the Siren*

Map

I have put together a custom-made Map of the routes the characters take throughout the book. It is colour-coded according to character, and the original 'Ulysses' route which corresponds with *How We Mortals Blame The Gods* is highlighted. Please feel free to download it if you would like to visualize where the characters are walking. Download Here

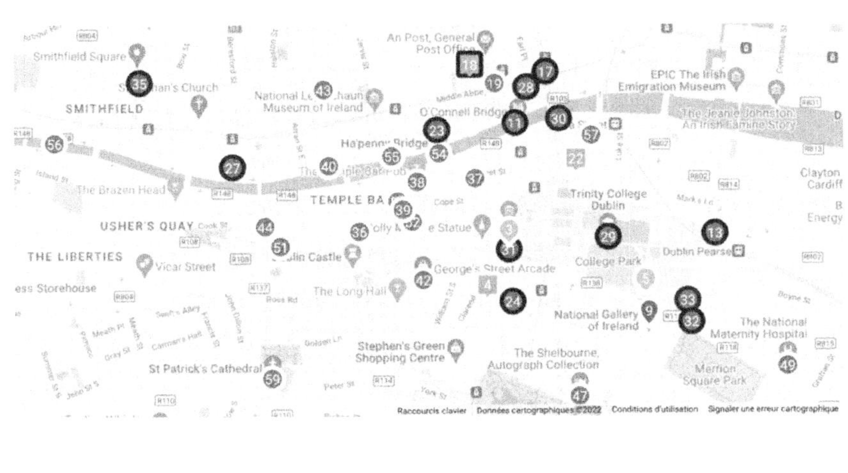

KEY:

Omar Kinch Flora Bláithín Ulysses

About the Author

Máirín Mc Sweeney grew up in beautiful County Kerry, Ireland. With her family she moved to Dublin at age 14 and fell in love with the city which would become the subject of her debut novel *How We Mortals Blame The Gods*. She has had many varied careers from running her own interior architecture business, working on humanitarian projects in Gautemala and South Africa, to more recently becoming a teacher of English Literature in Geneva, Switzerland. She earned an MA in Creative Writing in the University of Cape Town, South Africa. An avid traveller, she currently lives on Lake Annecy in France.

How We Mortals Blame The Gods is Máirín's first novel, which follows the intricate twists and turns of two couples living on one day in Dublin, June 16th 2004. Inspired by her favourite book *Ulysses* by James Joyce, her prose is punchy, and modern with a nod to the great man himself.

Contact: arabypublishing@gmail.com
Social media links:
Website: mairinmcsweeney.com
Facebook: Máirín Mc Sweeney Author
Instagram: máirín_mc_sweeney_author
Twitter: Máirín Mc Sweeney

Acknowledgments

The realisation of this book has been a long Odyssey, sometimes joyful, sometimes painful, but most of all a dream come true. I have many people to thank for that. I would like to start with my parents, Maura and Ted Mc Sweeney. They have been a shoulder to cry on every step of the way in the realisation of this book and a lot more. My father, Ted, painstakingly copy edited the first draft of this book many years ago. Although it has gone through considerable tranformations since then, his hard work and moral support helped to lay the strong foundations which I could build upon. My mother, Maura, is always at the end of a phone line to pick me up when the world gets too much, which it often does. Her eternal optimism and boundless love is both contagious and the foundation to my sanity.

The other people who light up my life and have always been there for me through all the ups and downs, are my one and only brother, Donal, my wonderful sister in law, Rachel, and my gorgeous nieces, Isobel and Rebecca. Donal is my best friend and without his support I would be lost. He is an optimistic and eternally positive supporting force, and we have shared so much together. Rachel is the sister I never had who has served me up more delicious gourmet meals to nourish my body and soul than any Michelin star restaurant. Isobel and Rebecca are like two little hearts beating inside me inspiring me with their laughter, crazy energies, and of course, gentle mocking, to keep their errant Aunt in line. Outside my immediate family I want to give a special mention to my godmother, Eileen O Sullivan, whose generous heart, eternal youth and endless support and love has been a constant inspiration to me. On the Mc Sweeney side I want to thank my Aunty Ann who has also been a supportive empathetic ear in times gone by.

I have so many wonderful and supportive friends from my many travels and adventures throughout my life, that I could fill another book. Therefore, I thank everyone who knows that they are a true friend to me and have remained in my heart. You know who you are! Special mention goes to those who have supported me during the process of this book: Liz Burland, Helen Irwin and Clement Rohmer whose couches have become a temporary home to my gypsy soul on many an occasion. They are special humans whose big hearts are open wide for partying, crying and laughing when I need it most. I also have to mention Amalia and Pierre Le Marchand whose back door is always open for me to walk through. This has been a gift to combat the frequent loneliness of being far away from my own family.

Writing a book is harder than I thought and more rewarding than I could have ever imagined. None of this would have been possible without my book editors: Henrietta, Rose-Innes, Susan Cahill and Vincent Czyz. Their incredible professsionalism, over and above personal support was invaluable. I also want to thank the artist John Nolan, for kindly offering me the wonderful image of Joyce and Nora to go on my cover for free, and Donna Cunningham of Beaux Arts for designing such a great cover and interior. I also must thank my lovely friend, Dani Harmsen for the professional photos for my bio and social media.

I cannot forget all those wonderful friends and family who have been a part of supporting me on the way to realising my dream: Cecilia Speranta, Fiona Zuccani-Heard, Ellie Forbay-Johnson, Lasaríona Power, Julian Hills, Siobhán Savage, Colleen Cooper Mc Fadyen,

Printed in Great Britain
by Amazon

Eileen Taylor, Deirdre Michel, Rebekah Pothaar, Sura Alrawi, Tanya Andrew, Cesca Bourne, Claire Bell, Clare Briscoe, Mien Krooglik, Nicolas de Szentjob, Kristen Peterson, John Foxe, Mia Trew, Janice, Aleigh and Dillon Bracken, Stephanie Scull Aziz, Thibaut Oustry, Nathalie Cauvi, Katinka Lund-Waagsaether, Serena Deegan, Clare and Ian Dewar, John Cronin, Máirín O Grady and Elaine Casey. Lastly, my friends and colleagues in Florimont make me laugh and keep me sane on a daily basis. Sorry if I have forgotten anyone. Many more are in my heart.

I would also like to thank the Curtis Browne creative writing group, especially Julia Derbyshire and Jayne Rice for their encouragement, and Wendy Goldman Rohm and Debra Moffit for their wonderful writing retreats.

As for the men in my life. Thanks for the highs and not so much for the lows (let's be honest), but some of you are still in my life for good reason. Once again, you know who you are.

I leave the final word with the man whose work has inspired me my whole adult life, and whose thoughts and words have dug me out of the deepest holes and sometimes shot me to the moon. Thank you Mr. James Joyce!

"Your battles inspired me - not the obvious material battles but those that were fought and won behind your forehead." — James Joyce